NOBLE BLOOD

NOBLE BLOOD

Charles O'Brien

This first world edition published in Great Britain 2004 by
SEVERN HOUSE PUBLISHERS LTD of
9–15 High Street, Sutton, Surrey SM1 1DF.
This first world edition published in the USA 2004 by
SEVERN HOUSE PUBLISHERS INC of
595 Madison Avenue, New York, N.Y. 10022.

British Library Cataloguing in Publication Data

O'Brien,   Charles
   Noble blood
   1.   France - History - Louis XVI, 1774-1793 - Fiction
   2.   Detective and mystery stories
   I.   Title
   813.6 [F]

   ISBN 0-7278-6104-2

Typeset by Palimpsest Book Production Ltd.,
Polmont, Stirlingshire, Scotland.
Printed and bound in Great Britain by
MPG Books Ltd., Bodmin, Cornwall.

Acknowledgements

I am grateful to Professor H. Arnold Barton of Southern Illinois University for guidance through the Marie-Antoinette–Fersen relationship. Thanks also to Professor Jennifer Nelson of Gallaudet University for help in issues of deafness, to my agent Evan Marshall for encouragement and good counsel, to Andy Sheldon for computer assistance, and to Fronia Simpson for critical readings of the text. Gudveig Baarli brought her expertise to the production of the maps. Finally, Elvy O'Brien has been an indispensable research companion at numerous libraries, museums, and historical sites, as well as a sharp-eyed, astute editor.

Cast of Main Characters

In Order of First Appearance

Anne Cartier: *teacher of the deaf, assistant to Abbé de l'Épée, wife of Colonel Paul de Saint-Martin*

Abbé Charles-Michel de l'Épée: *director of the Institute for the Deaf*

Colonel Paul de Saint-Martin: *provost of the Royal Highway Patrol, Anne Cartier's husband*

Baron Breteuil: *Minister for Paris and the Royal Household, a relative of Paul de Saint-Martin*

Lieutenant-General Thiroux DeCrosne: *chief of French police*

Denise de Villers: *a young deaf maid to the Duchesse Aimée de Saumur*

Georges Charpentier: *adjutant to Colonel Paul de Saint-Martin*

Duchesse Aimée de Saumur: *wife of Duc Henri de Saumur*

Marquis Pierre de Sully: *provost of the Palace of Versailles*

Robinette Lapire: *Duc Henri de Saumur's cook and Marthe Bourdon's half-sister*

Marthe Bourdon: *Duc Henri de Saumur's housekeeper*

Comtesse Marie de Beaumont: *Paul de Saint-Martin's aunt*

Michou de Saint-Esprit: *deaf artist, protégée of Comtesse de Beaumont*

Sylvie de Chanteclerc: *cousin of Saint-Martin*

Victor Hoche: *keeper of the Duc d'Orléans' art collection*

Hercule Gaillard: *journalist, a hack, a scandal-monger*

Chevalier Richard de Beauregard: *Aimée de Saumur's lover*

Comte Axel von Fersen: *Swedish nobleman, Queen Marie Antoinette's friend*

Historical Note

In the spring of 1787 the French nation, numbering some 26,500,000, reached the brink of the most profound revolution in modern times. The royal government fell into a deep financial crisis, unable to borrow money or to pay its creditors. Interest on huge war debts, most recently from the American War of Independence, had contributed to an annual deficit of 100,000,000 livres, a 15 per cent shortfall.

With royal credit ruined, Comptroller-General Calonne's only feasible alternative was to raise taxes. The common people could pay no more. The clergy and the nobility, barely 2 per cent of the population, owned over half of the nation's wealth but enjoyed tax exemption. Led by the Paris Parlement, France's highest court, they refused to pay unless the Estates-General approved.

This representative body, the French equivalent of the British Parliament, had not met since 1615. The King, who claimed the sole, divine right to govern, refused to yield any of his authority. As *Noble Blood* begins, public affairs in France are at an impasse.

A Pandora's box of grievances was about to burst open. Urban and rural workers felt trapped in poverty. The cost of their rents and basic commodities rose, while their income remained static or declined.

The most rapidly growing class, the bourgeoisie, resented the unmerited privileges of nobles and clergy and demanded a more rational and efficient government. The country's journalists and intellectuals argued persuasively for a free, just, humane, and secular society, and relentlessly attacked divine-right monarchy, cruel arbitrary justice, parasitical aristocracy, and hidebound religious leaders.

Noble Blood's principal actors, fictional and historical, went about their lives, concerned about conditions in their country, but with no idea of the bloody cataclysm that lay just two years ahead.

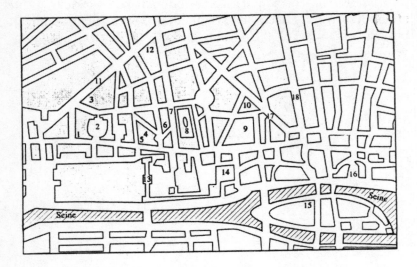

CENTRAL PARIS 1787

1. Residence/office of Paul de Saint-Martin & Anne Cartier,
   Rue Saint-Honoré
2. Place Vendôme
3. Bureau of Criminal Investigation, Rue des Capuchines
4. Abbé de l'Épée's Institute for the Deaf, Rue des Moulins
5. Church of Saint-Roch, Rue Saint-Honoré
6. Comtesse Marie de Beaumont's townhouse,
   Rue Traversine
7. Rue de Richelieu
8. Palais-Royal
9. Central Markets (Les Halles)
10. Church of Saint-Eustache
11. The Boulevard
12. Café Marcel
13. Palace of the Tuileries
14. Louvre
15. Conciergerie
16. Place de Grève
17. Rue Montmartre
18. Rue Saint-Denis

PALAIS-ROYAL 1787

A. Hoche's Office
B. Duke's Art Gallery
C. Camp of the Tatars
D. Comédie Française (under construction)
E. Circus (under construction)
F. Café Odéon
G. Café de Foy

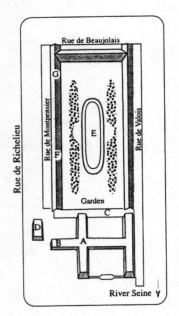

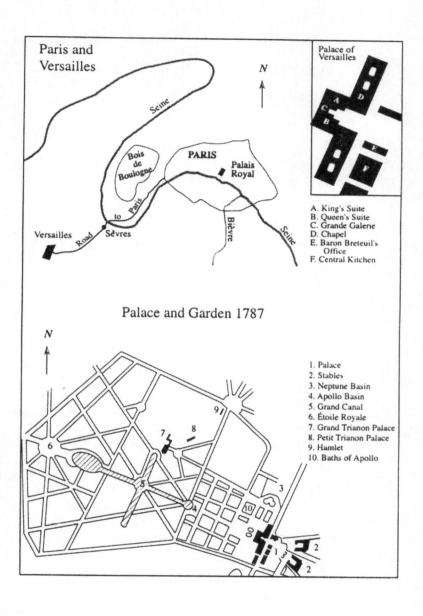

Paris and Versailles

Seine

N

Bois
de
Boulogne

PARIS

Palais
Royal

to Paris

Versailles   Road   Sèvres

Bièvre

Seine

Palace of
Versailles

A. King's Suite
B. Queen's Suite
C. Grande Galerie
D. Chapel
E. Baron Breteuil's
   Office
F. Central Kitchen

Palace and Garden 1787

N

1. Palace
2. Stables
3. Neptune Basin
4. Apollo Basin
5. Grand Canal
6. Étoile Royale
7. Grand Trianon Palace
8. Petit Trianon Palace
9. Hamlet
10. Baths of Apollo

CHAPTER ONE

Accused

Paris, Friday, June 1, 1787

The morning was still fresh and cool. Anne Cartier left her home on Rue Saint-Honoré and walked briskly toward the school for the deaf on Rue des Moulins. Several young students were waiting for her. She was about to pass by the Church of Saint-Roch, where she and her husband, Colonel Paul de Saint-Martin, had repeated their marriage vows three days ago. But a commotion on the front steps caught her eye. She stopped to look.

A robust countrywoman selling bunches of violets had gathered a crowd. Words tumbled from her mouth.

'Murder . . . at the palace. . .'

Anne drew closer.

'A duchess . . . all bloody . . . head smashed in.'

'Have they arrested anyone?' asked a man.

'Not yet.'

The crowd dispersed in small groups, passing the news on to others in the street. For a moment, Anne stood stock-still, astounded by what she had heard. Who would dare to kill such a prominent person in the King's own palace? Anne wondered if Paul would become involved in the investigation as head of the police for the region surrounding Paris. No, she remembered that another officer was responsible for the royal palace at Versailles.

The thought of her husband drew her up the steps to the door. They had married first in her own church, St John's, in Hampstead, near London, after an adventurous visit to Bath. They had agreed then to repeat their vows in Saint-Roch, Paul's parish church.

She walked through the main body of the church and into the circular Lady chapel. They had stood there side by side beneath the tall painted dome. Catholic bishops did not allow 'mixed marriages' in their churches. She was Anglican, Paul was Catholic. Nonetheless, a friendly priest led the ceremony, and a few invited friends and relatives attended.

It had been one of the happiest days of her life, except for a sudden, powerful attack of anxiety while leaving the church. Had she given away too much of herself? She had been independent since childhood. For years, she had worked as her stepfather's partner on stage, earned her own money, called no man her master.

Would Paul keep his pledge to honor her, treat her as an equal? In the law's eyes, he enjoyed the exclusive rights of a man and an aristocrat. Her property and the outward aspects of her life were subject to his control. She had no rights, only a woman's servile obligations. As a commoner, she could not even share his name. Their children could not inherit his title or his privileges. At that moment, she felt as if the law as well as the Church frowned on her.

The law notwithstanding, Paul had promised to treat her according to the mutual understanding they had reached over the year of their courtship. They would be equal partners, respecting each other's wishes, sharing each other's interests. His character was her guarantee.

Though the attack was nearly overwhelming, she reminded herself that he had been tested and had proven to be an honorable, generous, and enlightened man. Sensing her distress, he had glanced at her, pressed her hand, dispelled her fears. Her peace of mind had returned.

Church bells announcing the hour nudged her back to the present. They seemed to toll for the murdered woman. Shuddering, Anne prayed for her, then slipped out the side door, and hurried to her students.

The air in the small classroom was warm and stuffy. Beads of perspiration gathered on Anne's brow, as she surveyed the half-dozen young children seated in front of her. They had just gone through an hour of exercises in signing. Their

2

shoulders sagged with fatigue, their eyelids drooped. In another minute they would fall asleep.

It was mid-morning at the institute and time for a brief rest. She gestured the children to a puppet stage off in a corner and began a shortened familiar version of Punch and Judy with simple text. Their faces brightened immediately, as if inner lights had been lit.

This was a cherished moment for Anne, when her art brought joy to others. As the story progressed, the boys and girls eagerly entered into the illusion, spontaneously signing to the figures on the stage.

Suddenly, the door burst open. Françoise Arnaud rushed breathless into the room and beckoned Anne to follow her. Anxiety furrowed her usually calm brow. 'Abbé de l'Épée wants to see you right away,' she signed as they hurried to his office. 'Something terrible has happened.'

While Françoise hovered nearby, Anne knocked softly on the door until a feeble voice invited her in. Small, gray, and bent, the priest was seated at a table behind a pile of books and paper. He inclined his head apologetically. 'Forgive me, madame, if I do not rise to greet you. I am a tired old man, but I am nonetheless grateful that you have come.' He waved her to a chair. His hands trembled noticeably.

'How can I help you?' Anne couldn't imagine what had upset him so much. The many frustrations of his seventy-five years had made him patient and wise. Just recently, the Archbishop of Paris had blocked the government's attempt to move the school to larger, more suitable quarters in an empty convent. The prelate and the abbé disagreed on some point of theology, Anne had heard. When asked about it, the abbé had merely shrugged. 'After I'm gone, His Excellency will have no reason to object. A new director will be found, and the institute will prosper.'

The abbé glanced down at his hands clasped tightly before him, as if reluctant to ask a favor, then sighed and looked up. 'Madame, I'm sorry to trouble you. Would you kindly speak to your good husband Colonel Saint-Martin and find out what has happened to our Denise at Versailles? The police have arrested her—they say she murdered Duchesse Aimée de

3

Saumur. A deaf servant at the palace has brought the news but knew nothing more. I am most distressed. She was one of my best students and I helped place her in that household.'

Anne consoled him and promised to ask Paul if he had heard anything. 'I'll go to him now.'

Mademoiselle Arnaud was still in the hall, biting her lip, pacing nervously. Anne took her by the hand, calmed her, then signed, 'Come walk with me to my husband's office in our home on Rue Saint-Honoré. It's a short distance. I'll explain on the way.'

Out on the street Anne related the news from the palace. Her companion read Anne's signs intently, shaking her head in disbelief.

'I know Denise well—she couldn't do such a terrible thing.' Françoise signed that the young maid had a good character as well as a pretty face and a shapely figure. 'Men notice her.' Françoise smiled a little. 'But she's strong and knows her worth.'

'And her hearing?' asked Anne.

'Deaf from birth.' Her companion explained that Denise came from a respectable family. Her father was once a magistrate in the royal court at Abbeville, had lived in a fine house and owned a handsome carriage. Her mother died shortly after giving birth to her. A kindly aunt raised her and eventually placed her in the institute. Two years ago, her father also died, leaving Denise a modest sum of money.

'How long was she with you?'

'At least three years.'

For the rest of the way, Françoise appeared absorbed in thought, her brow creased by the effort. Anne wondered if Denise's character were less straightforward than appeared at first glance.

'Here we are.' Anne pointed to a portal. A small plain sign announced the residence of the provost of the Royal Highway Patrol for the Paris region. In the courtyard a coach stood ready. A team of four horses snorted with impatience and rattled their harness. A somber-looking man in buff breeches, blue coat with red cuffs and lapels, and a sword at his side, strode out of the building.

'Aha!' Anne exclaimed, waving at him. 'That's my husband about to leave. We've arrived in time.' She embraced him and introduced Françoise as Abbé de l'Épée's assistant.

Paul bowed courteously. 'Please excuse me, ladies, I must drive quickly to Versailles. There's been a murder. Baron Breteuil has involved me in the investigation.'

Anne placed her hand on his arm. 'Before you go, Paul, you need to hear what I've learned from Françoise about the suspect you're going to meet.'

He stared at the women, surprised. 'How did you—?'

Anne cut him short with a teasing smile. 'Word reached Abbé de l'Épée.'

He hesitated for a moment. 'Would the two of you ride with me to the palace? Then Mademoiselle Arnaud could inform me about the young maid. I'll share what I've been told.'

The coach rolled past the city gate and out on to the road to Versailles, 12 miles away, Anne sitting next to Paul, Françoise facing them. He spoke carefully for the deaf woman's sake, while Anne signed. 'The victim, a lady-in-waiting to the Queen, was found shortly after dawn, beaten to death. Evidence at the site implicates Mademoiselle de Villers, her personal maid.'

Paul looked sideways at Anne. 'It's odd that Baron Breteuil has called me. The palace at Versailles lies outside my jurisdiction.'

Anne wasn't surprised. Breteuil was Paul's distant relative and patron. As Minister of the Royal Household, the baron must believe that the murder of a person in the Queen's circle might raise delicate issues. Her enemies were hungry for scandal, the closer to the Queen the better. Paul's habitual discretion had earned the minister's respect. Two months ago, he had sent him to Bath, in England, to catch a rogue who had assaulted the baron's goddaughter, Sylvie de Chanteclerc. It was a difficult mission in a country traditionally hostile to France. The fugitive was well connected and wily. Paul completed his task without creating a diplomatic mess. The baron was grateful.

5

'Tell me, Mademoiselle Arnaud, what you know.' Paul spoke gently and signed, looking to Anne for help. She had begun to teach him.

Françoise swallowed nervously. Her hands were stiff, awkward. The colonel's high rank seemed to scare her. He came from one of the kingdom's oldest noble families. His father had been a general of cavalry in the royal army. Though well bred, Mademoiselle Arnaud rarely ventured outside the circle of her friends and acquaintances at the institute or in the Parisian deaf community.

With a nod of encouragement from Anne, the young woman took a deep breath, glanced shyly at the colonel, and related Denise's story.

At the end, Paul remarked, 'An unusually gifted young woman, this Mademoiselle de Villers.' His head tilted skeptically. 'But deaf nonetheless. I would have guessed that she worked in the laundry. How did she come to be Duchesse Aimée's personal maid?'

'Through talent, ambition, and good fortune,' Françoise replied. 'She once told me God had destined her for a higher place in life than the other deaf girls at the institute. They would sew in a milliner's shop from morning to night for the rest of their lives. She would one day have her own shop and cater to great ladies.'

Paul frowned. 'She appears more presumptuous than ambitious.'

Françoise waved her hands, appearing to misunderstand him.

Anne hastened to explain. 'To my husband it seems rash for the young maid to have aspired to a station in life that was well above her reach.'

Françoise nodded guardedly. 'Perhaps Denise is a little vain and may take pride in her superior intelligence and good looks. At the institute, she also cared more for her appearance than other deaf girls did. Her gowns were simple but of the finest wool and well cut.' Françoise signed emphatically. 'Still her ambition is reasonable, her goals within reach. She's energetic and resourceful—paid her own way at the institute. Deafness is an obstacle she feels sure she can overcome.'

6

'What did fellow students think of her?' asked Paul doubt-fully.

Françoise took a moment to ponder his question, then replied guardedly. 'Most of them respected her. She was expert in lip-reading and signing, as well as kind and generous. But a few others resented her superior attitude and envied her talents. Sometimes they were rude or played tricks on her. That hurt her feelings. She told me she had begun to feel it was time to leave the institute. When the opportunity at the palace came, she seized it.'

As Anne translated this report to Paul, she was strongly moved. She had not known Denise, who had left the institute before Anne arrived in Paris last year. But Françoise's description was so graphic, so sympathetic, that Anne could put herself in the deaf maid's place and share her hopes. These were now in jeopardy. To be arrested on suspicion of murdering a great lady was a very grave matter. Anne tried in vain to avoid thinking of the dire consequences.

CHAPTER TWO

Interrogation

Versailles, Friday, June 1

A nne's foreboding grew stronger as the coach rumbled into the precincts of the royal palace. Its vast, ordered, pitiless mass loomed up before her and on both sides. She had the feeling of being trapped rather than welcomed. For a moment she imagined a gigantic crowned figure living there, reducing ordinary mortals to insignificance, like insects in his garden. Wasn't this how the King ruled France? Even the country's greatest noblemen had to attend to his wishes, hand him his slippers when he got out of bed. With a stroke of his pen he could put them in prison for as long as he liked. If he or his ministers accused the deaf maid, how could she prevail? Anne felt a churning in the pit of her stomach.

Liveried grooms met their coach and drove it away. A steward led them into the palace and through a maze of rooms to an antechamber. An officer of the guard told them to wait. Baron Breteuil was in conference with Lieutenant-General DeCrosne in the adjacent office.

The Minister of the Royal Household and the head of the French police were no doubt discussing the murder of the Duchesse de Saumur, Anne reasoned. It must preoccupy the minds of the entire court. No crime had touched the royal family so closely since the madman Damiens had attacked Louis XV with a knife thirty years ago. He had barely scratched the King. Nonetheless, he was cruelly tortured, then drawn and quartered before a crowd of thousands.

Recalling this incident triggered a similar horrendous scene in Anne's memory. A year ago, recently arrived in Paris, she had witnessed the public execution of a young peasant woman in front of the Hôtel de Ville, the city hall. She now imagined the young deaf maid Denise tied to the fiery stake, her mouth open in futile screams. Anne tried to turn her mind away.

Paul noticed her struggle and drew close. 'Is anything wrong, my dear?'

'I fear for the maid.'

At that moment, the officer appeared again and waved the visitors in. Baron Breteuil, a stout, brusque man, rose from his desk and came forward to meet them. DeCrosne was a step behind. Neither man smiled.

As Anne met Breteuil's eye, she felt a stab of apprehension. The baron was one of the most powerful men in France. In charge of Paris, influential in the royal councils, an experienced diplomat, he enjoyed the confidence of the King and Queen. Several months ago, he had befriended Anne, arranging a private audience with the King so she could return a priceless collection of stolen jewels she had recovered.

With her marriage to Paul last month in Paris, however, she had lost the baron's goodwill. In his eyes, by marrying a commoner, who was English, Protestant, and a former music-hall entertainer, Paul had besmirched his family's name, lost social standing, and endangered his career in the King's service. As mentor and kin, the baron regarded the marriage as a reckless personal affront. He had chosen not to attend their wedding ceremony at Saint-Roch.

'*Bonjour, madame.*' The baron bowed politely. His gaze was cool and distant. His eyes seemed to accuse her. But that might have been a figment of her imagination. She was aware of her own worth and determined to show neither impertinence nor servility.

'*Bonjour, monsieur.*' Her greeting to him had exactly the respect due to his office, no more, no less. She knew better than to provoke him.

In the same cool manner, the baron then addressed her husband. 'The provost of Versailles, the Marquis de Sully, has jurisdiction in this case. He has already examined the scene of the crime, questioned the servants, and taken the maid into custody. Your task is to investigate the murder of Duchesse Aimée fully and fairly. Pay special attention to evidence of a conspiracy against the royal family. Lieutenant-General DeCrosne and the Paris police will lend you their support. Keep me informed. I shall report to the Queen on your progress.' He inclined his head, inviting questions as if he didn't expect any, then returned to his desk. The others left.

DeCrosne drew them together in the empty anteroom. 'Very good, Colonel,' he said, glancing at the two women. 'I was hoping Madame your wife and Mademoiselle Arnaud could help interrogate the suspect. The few deaf servants who work here have met my questions with blank faces. I suspect they're afraid to be associated with her, as if her guilt might rub off.'

To Anne's eyes, the lieutenant-general seemed reassuring. She felt a twinge of hope for Denise. His appearance, for the most part, was unremarkable. Thin lips and a rather large nose were the most striking features of his face. He appeared to be a gentleman, well bred and courteous, kindly and humane, intelligent too. But Anne wondered if his duties might require a more devious, callous character. Qualities of a man like Sartine, for whom Georges Charpentier, Paul's adjutant,

9

worked years ago and still claimed as his model. A lieutenant-general of police should not blink at the pain he might be called upon to inflict.

DeCrosne beckoned Paul toward the door. 'Since you will conduct the investigation, Colonel, you may as well begin now. I have spoken to the servants and studied the scene of the crime. I'll take you there and share what I've learned. The suspect will lead us through her movements last night and early this morning.' As an afterthought, he glanced with concern at the two women. 'Are these ladies prepared to view a scene of violence and death?'

Anne stepped forward, signing as well as speaking. 'Sir, I've witnessed violent death and its aftermath. I shall not faint. But Mademoiselle Arnaud seems distressed. She might wish to wait for us in the garden.'

Wide-eyed and drawn, the young woman did indeed appear nearly overcome. Nonetheless, with Anne translating, she protested to DeCrosne, 'I appreciate your kindness, but I think I should join you. Mademoiselle de Villers needs to see someone she knows.'

The lieutenant-general smiled sympathetically. 'Splendid. Come along.'

For a few minutes, Anne gazed silently at the duchess's large airy bedchamber, stunned by its elegance. Gold-embroidered creamy silk drapes framed three tall windows. Patterned apple-green painted paper hung on the walls. A dark-green marble fireplace occupied the center of one wall, a spacious bed another. Bookcases covered part of a third wall. The door to a dressing room stood open. Anne saw herself reflected there in a full-length mirror.

'Elsewhere in the apartment she merely entertained.' DeCrosne waved vaguely toward four comfortable upholstered chairs, a graceful chest of drawers, an oval tea table, and a splendid oak and speckled mahogany roll-top desk with chiseled gilt-bronze mounts. 'Here was where she lived.'

DeCrosne noticed Anne's interest. 'The furniture comes from Monsieur Riesener's workshop. Gifts from the Queen.'

'The desk alone is worth a small fortune,' Paul added evenly.

Anne found it hard to imagine what had happened here at dawn. A poker and a bedside table lay near a dark spot on the parquet floor. The victim was strangely present, though her body was gone.

'Colonel, I believe the maid has arrived,' observed DeCrosne. Footsteps were heard outside in the hall, then a captain of the guard entered followed by two armed officers with a young woman between them. Though her hands were manacled, she moved with unusual grace. She was still wearing her maid's apron. Tears had stained her clear complexion. Strands of dark brown hair escaped from beneath her cap.

As she approached, she looked up at the lieutenant-general. Fear filled her large brown eyes. When she recognized Françoise, she brightened. Her hands struggled against the manacles in an attempt to greet her.

'Remove them,' DeCrosne commanded.

The guards hesitated, glanced at each other and at their commander. He stepped forward. 'Sir, the provost has ordered us to—'

DeCrosne cut him off. 'She's deaf, Captain, and talks with her hands. Release her and withdraw to the hallway. The colonel and I shall manage without you.'

Her hands free and the guards gone, Denise stood still for a moment, then threw herself sobbing into Françoise's arms. The others waited silently until she seemed comforted and stepped back. Françoise introduced her companions and explained why they had come.

Denise bit her lip, shrugged nervously, and began signing her story. Anne translated for Paul and DeCrosne. The maid led them into the kitchen, one of the rooms shared by the duke and the duchess. In the center stood a long thick wooden table. Above it hung a few pots and pans. A rack of knives and several cabinets for other utensils and tableware lined the walls. The stove, like the room itself, seemed too small to prepare food for the elaborate banquets that Anne expected from a duchess.

DeCrosne anticipated her question. 'There's a central kitchen adjacent to the palace, which produces bread, roasts, and other food in large quantities. This kitchen usually serves only a small household.'

11

The maid went to the table and described her routine with signs and gestures. 'I rose at dawn to prepare a breakfast tray for the duchess. No one was here but the cook and her cat.' The maid went through the motions of getting the tray ready, then carrying it to the duchess's bedroom. The others followed her. She knocked softly on the door, waited briefly, then entered.

'Wasn't the door locked?' Anne asked.

'No,' Denise signed. 'It usually wasn't, unless the duchess was having company.' Denise crossed the room, signing rapidly. 'At first, I didn't see her, so I set the tray on a table. As I left, I noticed the bed hadn't been slept in. A bedside table lay on the floor. Curious, I walked to the far side of the bed, then saw her.'

Denise stopped abruptly, staring at the dark spot on the floor. For a moment she stood trembling, fighting back tears. Françoise put an arm over her shoulder, stroked her cheek. She recovered sufficiently to resume her narrative.

'The duchess was lying on her back in her dressing gown. Blood had trickled from her mouth and had flowed over her forehead. Her eyes were open but sightless. The iron poker was next to her body.' The maid's gaze drifted back to the spot on the floor, her arms dropped to her side. She stared transfixed, as if overcome by ghastly images crowding into her mind.

Anne waited a moment, then sought her eye. 'What did you do next?'

'I went back to the kitchen. The cook fetched the house-keeper. I wrote her a note that the duchess was dead. She went to the bedroom to check, then came back and called the guard. They took me to the basement and kept me in a room. That's all I know.'

Paul raised a hand to catch the young woman's attention. 'You found the duchess fully clothed. She hadn't slept. Was that unusual for her?'

'No, she was often up all night—suffered from insomnia, breakfasted at dawn. I would help her undress. She would sleep till noon. Last night, she left a note for me not to wait for her. A little after 9 o'clock, I said my prayers, went to bed, and fell asleep.'

DeCrosne turned to Paul. 'The cook let the duchess into the apartment at about three in the morning. She didn't see anyone else enter.'

'There's a private way to her bedroom,' offered Denise unbidden. She had read his lips and guessed his meaning. At a section of the wall near the hallway to her room, she lifted a hidden latch, and opened a wall panel. A circular stairway descended to the floor below. 'This was installed a month ago. She tried to keep it secret.'

'How did you find out?' asked Paul.

'She talked about it with the carpenter while I was dressing her. Their gestures and lips were easy to understand.'

'Did others know about the secret door?' Paul asked.

'I'd rather not say. That's personal.'

'The lady's dead. She has no more secrets.'

Denise shuddered. 'During the past month, a gentleman often spent the night with her. I served them breakfast.'

'Her husband, Duc Henri?' Paul asked doubtfully.

Denise shook her head. 'A younger man. Handsome. Charming. Richard was his name.' She paused, searching her memory. 'He had a thin scar on his chin.'

'Anyone else?'

She shrugged her ignorance. 'The housekeeper might know. Nothing escapes her eye, but she keeps it to herself.'

'We shall talk to her later,' DeCrosne remarked. 'Now, show us where you slept.'

She led them to a room too small for all of them to enter— little more than a closet with a bed, table, chair, and chest of drawers. A small, high window admitted air and light.

While the others peered in, DeCrosne pulled open a drawer and pulled out several brightly colored silk ribbons from beneath neatly folded undergarments.

'Duchesse Aimée gave them to me for my trousseau,' the maid explained, color rising on her cheeks. 'I was to keep them out of sight, lest other maids become envious.'

DeCrosne pointed to the straw mattress. 'And what did the police find there?'

She shook her head violently. 'I didn't steal it. Someone else must have hidden it when I was gone.'

DeCrosne left the room and joined the others. 'The provost's agent Jacques Bart found a ruby brooch belonging to the duchess. She was seen wearing it last night. The provost has it now. Twenty gold coins, *louis d'or*, are missing. The duchess had attached them to gold bracelets to wear as a novelty. Brought her good luck at cards. Had them on last night.'

Anne studied the young woman's wavering eyes, shaking hands. A guilty conscience? Hard to judge. She could have discovered the coins in the course of her duties. They could buy the millinery shop she dreamed of. She yielded to temptation. Surprised by the duchesse, she struck wildly with the poker. DeCrosne surely must think so.

His eyes had turned cold and dark. 'The coins, mademoiselle. Where did you hide them?'

She turned to Anne and threw up her hands. 'They won't believe me. What can I do?'

Sympathetic but uncertain, even wary, Anne searched the young woman's face. 'I'll try to discover the truth.'

CHAPTER THREE

A Difficult Person

Versailles, Friday, June 1

DeCrosne and Saint-Martin opened one of the tall windows and stood side by side, gazing out over the palace garden's south parterre. It was a clear late spring afternoon. Dozens of visitors milled about the flower beds admiring the roses in full bloom. For a moment, Saint-Martin yearned to join them, but he was recalled to his present duty by the lieutenant-general's voice.

'Well, Colonel, what do you think? Is the maid guilty?'

'That remains to be seen.' Saint-Martin walked to the secret stairway. The door had been left ajar. He opened it and peered down into the darkness. 'She might be a scapegoat. Another

14

person *could* have committed the crime and escaped undetected.'

DeCrosne joined him, studied the door thoughtfully, then closed it. 'I agree, Colonel, the private stairway greatly complicates the case. Unfortunately, the provost is of a different mind. He insists the maid is guilty beyond any doubt. If he has his way, her trial will be quick, followed by rigorous punishment. He distrusts servants and expects the worst from them.'

Saint-Martin groaned inwardly.

'I know how you must feel, Colonel. Nonetheless, you will have to work under his authority.' DeCrosne seemed genuinely sympathetic. 'Granted, it will not be easy. Sully's family has owned the provost's office for generations. He inherited it some fifty years ago. Unfortunately, time has neither improved his disposition nor made him wiser. He has woven a wide web of influence in palace circles. His spies lurk everywhere.'

'How do the King and the Queen regard him?'

'They fear him, I suspect, and keep him at arm's length. Outwardly, he defers to them, even courts their goodwill.' DeCrosne raised a warning hand. 'Be prudent, Colonel. The Queen loved Aimée de Saumur and would be less than human if she did not feel a desire for revenge. Moreover, the duchess's violent death has the appearance of *lèse-majesté*, an insult to the Crown. The King as well as the Queen will insist the killer be promptly arrested and convicted, and then punished with the full force of the law.'

'I see the need for caution, sir. Nonetheless, I must question everyone who might have had a reason to kill the duchess. That may take a while. We don't know yet who they are. But, for a start, the young man with the scarred chin.'

'Baron Breteuil and I shall assist you where we can.'

'I shall depend on you.'

A guard entered the room. 'Monsieur Charpentier to see you, Messieurs.'

The square figure of Georges hurried toward them, like a man about to take charge.

DeCrosne sniffed with annoyance.

'He's my adjutant,' Paul said. 'I left a message at the office

15

Georges leaned over the body. 'She's been hit above the right ear, probably from behind by a right-handed person. He may have struck as she reached for the bell cord on the wall. She died soon after. As she fell, her head hit a sharp corner of the bedside table.' He pointed to the gash at her hair line. 'I'd feel more sure if I'd seen the body before it was moved.'

They examined the woman's hands. Rigor was setting in. She still wore a gold ring with a large cabochon diamond inset. 'Why didn't the killer take this?' Saint-Martin asked. 'It couldn't have been overlooked.'

'And it would be no more difficult to fence than the brooch or the *louis d'or*,' Georges added. 'The killer might have acted in haste. Or . . . he had a special reason for taking what he did.'

The colonel remained noncommittal, though he noticed his adjutant assumed the killer was a man. 'We've done here what we can. It's time to visit the provost and hear his view of the case. We'll gain a better sense of what we must do next.'

The office of Provost Pierre de Sully was in the prison near the town market, a ten-minute walk from the palace. At the portal Saint-Martin announced himself and Georges to a guard, who handed them over to a liveried servant. He led them across a courtyard into a large, plain stone building, past offices with clerks at work, to a thickly varnished oak door. The servant knocked, hearkened to a low voice, then opened the door into a spacious, richly furnished room. The provost rose from behind his heavily gilded, long, brown mahogany table and greeted Saint-Martin.

'Baron Breteuil said I could expect you, Colonel.' The provost cast a skeptical glance at Saint-Martin's adjutant.

'Monsieur Charpentier, my chief investigator. He needs to hear what we say.'

The provost hesitated a fraction of a second, then waved them to chairs in front of the table. Without further formality, he leaned forward and addressed Saint-Martin. 'The baron has explained to me your role in this case. Allow me to recollect for you what has transpired thus far.'

His explanation added little that was new. Saint-Martin

feigned interest and used the opportunity to study Sully, having never met him before. He was an elderly man with a narrow, wrinkled face, tight thin lips, cold crafty eyes. In palace circles his vanity was legendary. He fancied himself irresistible to beautiful young women. When he smiled, he flashed a beautiful set of porcelain teeth, the finest money could buy. His wig was brushed high and powdered. His cheeks were lightly rouged to enliven a sallow complexion. On this occasion he wore a cavalry officer's uniform—blue coat with red cuffs and lapels.

He was said to be a fawning toady to those above him, a rigid, unfeeling tyrant to those beneath. He appeared close-minded but certainly not stupid. In all likelihood, Saint-Martin concluded, this man would be a prickly person to deal with.

'And, so, Colonel, I believe we have here a simple crime. Duchesse Aimée surprised the maid in the act of stealing. She impulsively struck her lady with a poker, killing her. We found the duchess's ruby brooch in the maid's mattress.' He handed a file of papers across the table. 'Your copy of my report. My agent Bart and I thoroughly examined the scene of the crime and the other rooms of the apartment. We also questioned the servants.' He looked down his long, thin nose at Saint-Martin. 'You hardly have much to do in this case beyond searching for the stolen items.'

This was the conclusion Saint-Martin had expected. 'Baron Breteuil has asked me to undertake a full investigation—within reason, of course. Thus far, the evidence does point to the maid. But, someone else, either alone or in the pay of others, could have committed the crime and shifted the blame on to her.'

'Highly unlikely, Colonel,' objected the provost, a frown gathering on his brow.

'But possible, sir,' rejoined Saint-Martin. 'Several other servants in the lady's household could have killed her. And, there are persons outside the household who knew of her private entrance and were familiar with the lady's routine.'

'For example?'

'Her lover—a certain Richard. For that matter, her husband.'

'Colonel! Are you insinuating that we might be dealing

with a crime of passion in a *ménage à trois*?' The provost sneered. 'This is too absurd!'

The colonel raised an eyebrow, inviting further explanation. As the chief magistrate at Versailles, the provost would receive all manner of palace gossip.

'The Duc de Saumur cared not one wit how his wife satisfied her need for love. Theirs was a marriage of social convenience and perfect decorum. The duchess had a succession of young men, all of them amiable and discreet, not a murderer among them. The latest one, Chevalier Richard de Beauregard, was like all the others.'

This revelation took Saint-Martin aback, though he was careful not to show it. When he had heard of Beauregard, the possibility of a crime of passion had in fact crossed his mind. 'He may have been indeed, but a man can conceal evil motives beneath an amiable appearance. I shall consider everyone who had an opportunity to kill Duchesse Aimée.'

The provost's expression hardened. 'The Queen demands swift justice. I shall do everything in my power to see that she gets it. The maid's guilty. If you prolong this investigation, you shall bring the royal wrath down upon your head.'

'Georges, what do you think of our provost?' Saint-Martin was eating lunch with his adjutant on a quiet shaded bench in the palace garden. At the town market, they had bought bread, fruit, cheese, and wine. Nearby, a fountain bubbled, shielding their voices. They wanted to speak without fear of being overheard. Clouds were drifting in from the west. Georges looked up apprehensively, sensing the threat of rain.

The burly adjutant had been uncharacteristically quiet since leaving the provost's office. He stared straight ahead, his jaw set firmly. The magistrate had ignored him as if he weren't in the room, rarely making eye contact.

At the colonel's question, Georges bristled. 'A pompous ass! His spies feed him cartloads of gossip, but he selects what suits his own bigoted, preconceived opinions. He has got it in his head that servants think only of stealing from their masters or killing them. No aristocrat will sleep safely until a horrid example is made of Denise de Villers.' He tore off a piece of bread and chewed on it fiercely.

'You're right, Georges, and he's stubborn into the bargain. We'll have nothing but trouble from him.'

After their meal, they walked to the Grand Canal, which stretched for more than a mile along the garden's main axis, and embarked in a small boat—the colonel rowing. 'How shall we proceed, Georges?'

The adjutant shifted in his seat to gaze at the garden façade of the great palace in the distance. 'We can interrogate the duchess's servants easily enough. But, beyond them, we'll need help. The provost's spies are of no use to us, and we don't have enough time to create our own network. Yet, we must quickly penetrate the circles of high-born people who live and work there.' He gestured grandly at the palace, then met the colonel's eye. 'The person best suited to help us is Comtesse Marie de Beaumont.'

'That's not a good idea,' said Saint-Martin, recalling the elegant lady who was his favorite aunt. True, she was also Baron Breteuil's friend and, years ago, drew many important men and women to her salon. She still had good connections in high places. But she had grown weary of sophisticated life and had retired to her country estate, Beaumont, a few miles south of Paris. Only occasionally did she venture back into the city, where she kept a town house on Rue Traversine. She had not visited the court at Versailles since her husband died almost a decade ago.

Georges pressed on, ignoring his superior's reluctance. 'She's quick-witted and skeptical, and fears no man. With the baron's help, she could make useful inquiries for us.'

'I think not. She enjoys her peace and quiet too much to step into this nest of vipers.' Saint-Martin pulled vigorously on the oars, sending the little boat lurching over the water.

'Sir, if your aunt were to understand that a young deaf woman, one of Abbé de l'Épée's students, is otherwise going to die a horrible death on Place de Grève, she might want to help us.'

'I'll give it some thought, Georges, and talk it over with Anne.' The idea had begun to show merit, the colonel realized.

Besides, he couldn't think of anything better to do. 'In the meantime, I want you to interrogate the servants. I'll try to find the two men in the duchess's life, Chevalier Richard de Beauregard and Duc Henri de Saumur.'

CHAPTER FOUR

Contrary Views

Friday, June 1

Anne sat patiently at the kitchen table waiting for Marthe Bourdon, the housekeeper, away on an errand. It was late morning. Françoise Arnaud had returned to Paris. The cook was stirring a pot of lamb ragout on the stove. A rich aroma wafted over Anne's head. To pass the time, she idly stroked the cook's cat, a long-haired orange male tabby brushing against her leg.

'What's he called?'

'Bijou.' The cook turned part way around, still stirring. Anne had learned her name, Robinette Lapire. She was about fifty years old, though she looked sixty, wiry and gray-headed, with a small wrinkled face, reticent, and perhaps sly. There was devilment in her eyes.

The cat became playful, attacked Anne's shoe when she moved. She threw a ball of string on to the floor. He gave chase, worried the ball, batted it back and forth.

Robinette watched out of the corner of her eye. A faint smile appeared on her face. 'He's a hunter. At night, we let him roam. He kept the duchess company when she couldn't sleep. Mice terrified her. She ordered a carpenter to install a small swinging panel for Bijou on every door in the apartment. I haven't seen a live mouse in weeks. He brings the dead ones to me.'

Anne learned that the woman was a widow, and her only child had died at birth. For many years she had cooked in a large hotel managed by her half-sister, Marthe. When Marthe

21

became the duchess's housekeeper, she brought Robinette with her to Versailles. Marthe was a practical person and a leader among the servants. 'They do what she says,' said the cook. She tasted a spoonful of the ragout and nodded with approval. 'Even Duchesse Aimée . . .' Robinette hurriedly crossed herself. 'Even the duchess treated Marthe with respect.'

At that moment, the cook abruptly stopped talking. Marthe had walked into the kitchen and laid down a basket of spring vegetables. She moved quickly through the room, putting things away, instructing the cook about meals. Her voice was calm, if not kindly. Her dark eyes switched to Anne at the table, studied her for a moment. 'How may I serve you?'

Anne introduced herself as an assistant instructor at the Institute for the Deaf.

Marthe lifted her hands in a welcoming gesture. 'I know the good abbé and am acquainted with his school. Come to my rooms, please, we can speak more comfortably there.'

Buxom and tall, Marthe Bourdon would be noticed in a crowd. She carried herself regally, back straight and head high. Authority seemed to come naturally to her, without affectation or presumption. Her hair was black, her complexion creamy. Her features were strong like those of a Roman matron. In her youth, she must have been a striking beauty. She was now forty-two and had become a model housekeeper.

As a senior servant, she had rooms of her own off the kitchen. She led Anne into a small, rather austere parlor. The furniture was simple and worn but of good quality. A door in the far wall apparently led to her bedroom. It occurred to Anne that, with doors closed, Marthe couldn't have heard sounds of violence from the duchess's room.

Two windows to an interior courtyard threw light upon exotic vases displayed on a high shelf on the opposite wall. 'Gift from a guest,' Marthe remarked, having noticed Anne focus on a jade vase. 'From the time I managed a hotel.' She took it carefully from the shelf. 'A Chinese merchant gave it to me in lieu of payment for his rooms.'

Anne rubbed the vase's smooth pale-green surface, fingered its delicate inlaid-silver design. A valuable object, she guessed, and a sign of good taste.

'What may I do for you, madame?' the housekeeper asked, as she replaced the vase. They moved to a small table. She poured two glasses of cider.

'I would like information about Denise de Villers to bring back to Abbé de l'Épée. He would ask this for himself, but he is too ill to travel. I understand that you hired her upon his recommendation.'

'Yes,' she replied. 'Denise was bright, cultivated, even-tempered, eager to serve, alert and attentive. Even her deafness proved to be little more than a minor inconvenience. A skillful dressmaker, she altered and repaired gowns. The duchess also employed her at copying. Her handwriting was exceptionally beautiful. I was happy to help the institute place one of its young women in such an advantageous position, truly a companion as much as a maid.'

Marthe frowned, gazed out the window, as if her mind were wrestling with what she was about to say. Her posture stiffened. Though she had spoken well of the maid thus far, she could not conceal an undertone of antipathy in her voice.

The pause lasted only for a moment, then she resumed her remarks. 'Denise seemed perfectly suited to the duchess's needs. With the duchess as her patron, Denise would have had a splendid future before her. But, she ruined it. Simply inconceivable.'

Suddenly, Marthe looked to one side, apparently overcome by emotion, but she quickly composed herself. 'You see, I feel responsible for what happened. I had been forewarned of her weakness.'

'What do you mean? What weakness?' Anne was shocked. Françoise had mentioned only the young maid's vanity, a minor blemish on her character, hardly an inclination to murder.

The housekeeper drew in a breath, as if it were painful to go on. 'Well, a few years ago, a fellow student at the institute accused Denise of stealing a lace collar. She denied it. By the time I heard of the matter, the abbé had already hushed it up. "A simple misunderstanding" was all he would say. But I knew the girl who had made the accusation and could think of no reason why she would want to lie.'

Anne was tempted to ask if it were fair to judge Denise without hearing her side of the story. Then again, better to wait, Anne thought. Marthe was now aroused and had more to say.

'Recently, a small silver plate went missing after a banquet. Denise had cleared the table, so she was the most likely suspect. I hinted to her that I knew the guilty party. A few days later the plate returned mysteriously to the kitchen.'

Anne had to interrupt. 'Did other servants have access to the plate?'

'I suppose so. . .' The question brought a frown of displeasure to Marthe's brow. 'The cook and the steward were also there. But I've known them for years and they've never stolen before.'

She paused for a moment to recover the thread of her story. 'There's more. While searching Denise's room, the provost's agent found silk ribbons belonging to the duchess hidden under the maid's clothes. If she had come by them honestly, she would have displayed them. She's that kind of girl, primps herself, acts the fine lady. And, of course, there's the ruby brooch.'

Marthe fell deeply silent, eyes downcast, as if reliving a dreadful moment in the past. A clock ticked away the minutes. Finally, she overcame whatever dark vision had seized her and looked directly at Anne. 'In hindsight I shouldn't have hired Denise. She coveted expensive things that lay beyond her reach.'

A cool calm came over the housekeeper's face. She folded her hands. 'Is there anything else I can do for you, madame?'

'Not at the moment, perhaps later.' Anne felt numb. She had passionately wished the young maid to be innocent. Now, there was reason to believe otherwise. The formidable Marthe Bourdon was convinced of her guilt.

Anne rose from the table. 'Thank you, madame, I now have much to think about.'

The afternoon sun had begun to throw long shadows over the road to Paris. As the coach rumbled on monotonously, Paul leaned back, brushed a speck of dust from his cuff, and asked for him to come here.' He introduced Charpentier. 'First-rate investigator. He must examine the scene of the crime and view the body.'

The lieutenant-general studied Georges for a moment, then forced a thin smile. 'I'm pleased to leave the matter in good hands.' He bowed and left the room.

While the guard waited outside, Saint-Martin showed Georges around the duchess's apartment. In the bedroom he pointed to her private door.

'Let's see where this goes,' Georges said. He lit a candle and led the way down a narrow, winding flight of stairs, through a concealed door into a small, empty storeroom. Another door opened to a short hallway. Saint-Martin understood they were not far from the Queen's private apartment.

Georges stroked his chin. 'The lady's lover, and anyone else who knew the secret, could have gone up those stairs, killed her, and lurked in the darkness. When the maid left her room nearby to fetch the morning coffee, the killer could have hidden the brooch in her mattress and run off with the coins.'

'That's the easy part,' the colonel remarked. 'It's of no use unless we discover someone who would want to kill the duchess and knew intimately the household routine.'

Georges grimaced. 'We may learn that the maid did it after all, perhaps for good reason.'

Saint-Martin knew that his adjutant held French aristocrats in low regard and might even excuse a person for killing one of them. He *would* give the maid the benefit of the doubt.

Upon their return to the bedroom, the guard brought them down to the basement of the palace. The victim was being kept in a cold storage room. The guard removed a heavy black cloth covering the body. She was clothed in a pale blue dressing gown.

'A handsome woman,' Georges murmured. 'Looks like she's asleep.'

Her eyes were closed, her face was tranquil and wiped clean of blood. Death's aftermath had mottled her once clear complexion. She was about forty, fine-featured, medium height, shapely. Her dark brown hair was gathered in a chignon behind her head.

levelly, 'What have you learned from the housekeeper, Marthe Bourdon?'

Sitting opposite, Anne studied his face for an instant. No trace of aristocratic hauteur or male superiority. He respected her opinion. She appreciated the effort it cost—and the love behind it. Paul's attitude was rare among men. He had agreed when they married to treat her as equal partner, as well as friend and lover. She would have it no other way. She and her stepfather Antoine had worked side by side at Sadler's Wells and other London music halls. When Antoine moved to Paris, she had worked alone. Since childhood, she had never been subservient to a man and never would be.

'She told me more than I had bargained for,' Anne replied. 'Denise, it seems, has a reputation for thievery. And it's all the more troubling since the housekeeper isn't one to gossip or to repeat unfounded rumor.'

'Give me the details. I was beginning to believe in the maid's innocence.'

'So was I. But Denise could in fact be guilty.' Anne shared the gist of her conversation with Marthe Bourdon. Already while at the institute, apparently, Denise had shown an inclination to steal. This weakness, together with her desire to shine in the world, might well have drawn her to the duchess's treasure—and to murder.

During Anne's remarks, Paul's brow creased with concentration. When she finished, he remained silent for a few moments, then began carefully. 'Marthe Bourdon's views deserve respect, but the provost's opinion may have influenced her. She also appears to dislike the maid and may judge her unfairly.'

'I agree,' Anne said. 'Denise could have hidden the ribbons for good reason. She *does* seem to attract envy. And another servant or even a guest could have taken the plate.'

'The issue of the lace collar,' Paul warned, 'is more compromising. I'd like a second opinion from someone intimately acquainted with affairs at the institute.'

'Françoise Arnaud, of course,' Anne exclaimed. She felt a twinge of hope. 'I'll speak to her immediately.'

*　　*　　*

25

Shortly after sunset, a servant led Anne to a door on the ground floor of the institute. Françoise was resting before an evening meal. She greeted Anne with a wide-eyed look of apprehension and motioned her to a chair.

Anne met the young woman's eye. 'I've discovered a problem. You must help me.' With a calm voice she reported the housekeeper's remarks about Denise de Villers. 'She seems to have stolen a lace collar last year.'

The young woman gave a start. 'That's wrong, madame. I can explain what really happened.' Françoise's signing became so agitated that Anne held her hands to stop her briefly, then let her continue. She explained that, a year ago, a girl at the institute, Cécile Fortier, reported the loss of a fancy lace collar, her most valuable possession. She had always stored it in a special place. That afternoon, Denise had visited her, apparently to reconcile after a quarrel. The girl had refused, called Denise haughty, and ordered her to leave. The collar was missed shortly afterwards.

A thorough search failed to find the collar. The girl accused Denise. She denied taking it and appealed to Abbé de l'Épée, who spoke privately to both girls. A few days later, the accuser found the collar under one of her bonnets. The abbé made her apologize to Denise and declared the matter closed. But the accuser later claimed Denise had sneaked into her room and returned the stolen collar to create the appearance that it had only been misplaced.

'Are you convinced that Denise never took the collar?'

'Yes, I'm sure she didn't.' Françoise seemed close to tears. 'You trust her, don't you?'

'I do.' Anne signed with as much confidence as she could muster without convincing evidence. 'You've relieved my mind.' She got up to leave. 'I'll relate your story to my husband. He will be pleased to hear it.'

CHAPTER FIVE

The Hunt Begins

Saturday, June 2

The next morning, the sky was clear, the streets were dry, and traffic was congested as usual. Anne and Paul were on foot nearing Comtesse Marie's town house, a ten-minute walk in fair weather. Anne looked forward to this meeting, the first in three days. Marie was chief among Anne's friends in Paris. A witness to the marriage contract, she had also organized a reception at her town house near the church. Most important, she had reassured Anne whenever anxiety threatened.

Anne's report on the lace-collar incident prompted Paul to remark, 'I'm personally inclined to trust Mademoiselle Arnaud, who was much closer to the event than Madame Bourdon, and free from the provost's influence. Yet, if I were a magistrate, I would want more proof of Mademoiselle de Villers's innocence before clearing her reputation. As matters stand now, it's Arnaud's word against Fortier's.'

This careful reasoning dampened Anne's hope for the maid. But a year's experience with Paul had taught Anne the need for patience with his cautious method of investigation. In the end he had to satisfy the rigorous demands of royal magistrates for proof.

They found the countess standing by an open window in her study, gazing contemplatively over the back garden. Her tall slender form was clothed in a flowing pink silk gown. Her silver-gray hair fell loosely to her shoulders. The faint smell of breakfast coffee still lingered in the air.

'Anne and Paul, what a pleasant surprise!' She embraced them.

'We're calling early,' Anne said. 'Hope you don't mind.'

'Not at all. I judge from the expression on your faces that you have something serious to talk about.' She led them to upholstered chairs around a mahogany tea table.

Anne went directly to the point. 'Marie, do you recall Mademoiselle de Villers, one of Abbé de l'Épée's students a few years ago?'

'Yes, I met her occasionally at the institute—a very bright young woman from a good family. Stood out among the students. Stylish and cultivated, as I recall. I've heard she's accused of theft and murder. Dreadful news—it's all over Paris. They say she has stolen things before, but this time was caught.' She stared at her visitors. 'Tell me it's not true.'

'We hope not,' Anne groaned. 'We haven't heard the latest rumors.'

Paul added, 'I fear the provost has had a hand in them. His spies must have discovered that lace collar incident at the institute. He thinks it bolsters his case against Mademoiselle de Villers.'

'What incident?'

'I can explain, Marie.' Anne repeated what Françoise had told her. 'Unfortunately, students who disliked Denise continued to accuse her. And this stain on her reputation has followed her to Versailles.'

'How dreadful! Could the abbé persuade the accuser to retract and speak up for Denise?'

'It may be too late for that,' replied Paul. 'At least as far as the provost is concerned, the damage has been done.' He gave his aunt a summary of the murder investigation thus far. 'We can't be certain the maid's innocent, though I'm inclined to think so. There are other possible suspects we must investigate—for a start, Duchesse Aimée's lover and her husband, plus the servants.'

'Is there anything I can do?' Her hands clasped with concern.

'Yes, indeed,' Paul replied. 'You could make inquiries for us at the court in Versailles. Baron Breteuil has pledged to cooperate. You would have access to certain high-placed persons who would not speak freely to Georges and me.'

She stared at her silk dressing gown for a minute, smoothed

it twice, then looked up. 'It's been several years since I set foot in the palace, the most godless place in France. If slander, spite, and malice could kill, blood would flow knee-deep through the state rooms out into the garden. No one is spared, least of all the King and Queen.' She breathed a deep sigh, as past scenes of palace life came back to her. 'But I'm still in touch with some people who could help.'

She winked at Anne, then turned to her nephew. 'This may displease you, Paul, but I would like your dear wife to come along as my personal companion. I would need her support—she's courageous and resourceful. I cannot imagine going alone into that den of deception and treachery. Baron Breteuil could arrange accommodations for us.'

Paul frowned but, before he could speak, Anne leaned forward and raised a protesting hand.

'I realize, Anne,' the countess hurried on, 'that the baron is disgruntled about your marriage, but I shall manage him.' She stared at her visitors, inviting agreement. They nodded, one after the other.

Anne consented reluctantly. The countess's request had taken her by surprise. She hadn't wished to become deeply involved in the investigation. The students at the institute had laid prior claim on her time. She also disliked the idea of living in the palace even for a short while. Its rituals and routine lacked any purpose or joy that she could see, and the courtiers' conceit would be insufferable. Still, she could hardly refuse the countess who had overcome her own antipathy to the place.

The countess caught Anne's eye. 'Do you need to think it over?'

'No, Marie. I'm ready and willing.' Anne smiled inwardly. The countess had rightly sensed that she felt annoyed—and less than willing. Marie had taken for granted she would play the mistress and Anne the servant. She immediately rebuked herself. The situation, of course, dictated the roles they would play.

Marie gave her an understanding smile. 'The matter is settled. We have no time to waste. There's work to do.'

* * *

As they left the study, Paul asked his aunt about his cousin, Sylvie de Chanteclerc. Anne knew her story. Almost five months ago, Captain Fitzroy, a renegade Irishman in French service, had assaulted the young woman. Her body healed quickly but her spirit sank into deep depression, and in March she attempted suicide. Paul and Georges had saved her at the last minute. Comtesse Marie had nursed her at Château Beaumont, and introduced her to Michelline de Saint-Esprit, a petite young deaf artist known as Michou. Sensitive and compassionate, she had become a good friend. Sylvie was now on the way to recovery, or so Anne had been told.

'May we visit her?' Paul asked.

His aunt gave his request careful consideration. 'Yes, I believe that would be good. I've hesitated because, until recently, any reminder of that horrid episode troubled her. But she seems close to normal now. A few days ago, she moved here with Michou and servants I trust.'

She led Anne and Paul through the house to a second-floor room fitted out as an artist's studio. A large window gave a diffused northern light. They entered quietly. At the far end Michou sat at an easel. In front of her stood Sylvie in a Grecian costume—a sleeveless, knee-length tunic, girded at the waist, and sandals on her feet. She had tied her hair back and crowned her head with a diadem. Her right arm was reaching for an arrow in the quiver on her back. Her left arm hung down holding a bow. At her left foot sat a patient dog. Sylvie leaned forward in a striding posture and glanced sharply to her right as if catching sight of prey.

'The huntress,' Comtesse Marie remarked, 'and my spaniel Caprice.' At first glance, Sylvie's expression seemed severe, pitiless. As Anne observed the scene more closely, she sensed this was play. The hint of a smile appeared on Sylvie's lips. Anne whispered in the countess's ear, 'What are they doing?'

'Acting out works of art. This is the ancient Greek statue of Diana in the Grande Galerie at Versailles. Sylvie knows the masters of painting and sculpture quite well. Michou learns by sketching her.'

They watched silently until Michou laid down her pencil and stretched. Sylvie dropped her pose and caught the visitors in her glance. As they approached, she smiled broadly and aimed the bow at her cousin Paul. The dog Caprice rose, shook herself, and nuzzled the countess.

'Paul! How delightful!' Sylvie laid the bow down and embraced him. 'I owe you so much.' She gazed into his eyes. 'Thank you for saving me. At the time I couldn't appreciate what you did.' She turned to greet Anne. 'I'm pleased to meet you. Michou sings your praises.' Sylvie smiled, studied Anne closely. 'They say we look alike.'

Sylvie could be considered a younger version of herself, Anne thought. Tall, blond hair, blue eyes, lively, expressive features, but a prettier face and a softer body. Her eyes still showed signs of her recent anger and depression.

Michou removed her smock and joined the group. She had grown more self-assured since Anne had last seen her almost a year ago. She could now read and write well enough for simple needs. Her sketches had attracted some attention among Comtesse Marie's acquaintances.

They all gathered at a table in the studio, Caprice reclining at the countess's feet. Anne explained what had happened to the duchess at Versailles. 'Denise de Villers is accused of the crime.'

For a moment, Michou stared at Anne with disbelief, then signed vehemently, 'Impossible. I know Denise. She showed me the garden at Versailles and Diana's statue in the palace. Who else could have done it?'

When Anne mentioned Richard de Beauregard's name, Sylvie gave a start, then frowned. 'I've met him at the Palais-Royal. A charming libertine. Flashing brown eyes, long black lashes, a little scar on his chin.'

Paul showed immediate interest. 'When was that? What was he doing?'

'Once, last year at this time. We were together at a party in the duke's palace. Aimée de Saumur was there, too, but they didn't seem intimate. Beauregard danced beautifully, flirted with pretty girls. I didn't like him. Seemed false.'

Paul was silent, brows knit, as if trying to grasp Beauregard's character.

'And I saw him again yesterday.'

31

'Where?' Paul stared at Sylvie. 'That was the day of the murder.'

His interest encouraged her. 'In the Palais-Royal just before noon. Michou and I had been sketching in the garden and were about to leave. Beauregard and another man came to a table behind us. We were dressed like commoners. They paid no attention to us. I could tell something was wrong, Beauregard looked so nervous. I was curious and tried to listen.'

Michou broke in, signing to Anne. 'I sat facing him, but it was hard to read his lips. He waved his hands in front of his face. I think he mentioned Aimée de Saumur.'

'He asked the man to say he had spent the night at Versailles,' Sylvie added.

'Did you recognize his companion?' asked Paul eagerly, like a hunting dog on a scent.

Sylvie shook her head, but Michou nodded and signed, 'He lives in the palace, works for the duke. Looks like a clerk. Don't know his name.' Michou pulled out a sketch pad, thought for a few moments, pencil in hand, then drew his likeness. A middle-aged man, short and fat, stubby nose, small pouting mouth.

'Why do you suspect Beauregard?' asked Sylvie.

'He was Aimée de Saumur's lover,' Anne replied. 'They may have quarreled and he killed her.'

'How could he have done it?'

'He often used the private entrance to her room. We would like to know where he was that night.'

'Michou and I will help you find out.' Sylvie glanced at her friend, who nodded. They would eavesdrop at the Palais-Royal and identify Beauregard's acquaintances for Georges to investigate.

Since arriving in the studio, Anne had noticed a transformation in Sylvie. Her light, playful smile vanished, the line of her jaw grew firm. In Richard de Beauregard she must have recognized her assailant Captain Fitzroy's cynical contempt for women, his cunning strategies for exploiting them.

'I can truly believe that Beauregard killed her,' said Sylvie in a low, strained voice, her eyes shifting from Anne to Michou and Marie, stopping at Paul. 'Perhaps Duchesse Aimée broke off their relationship, he threatened her. She turned to summon help. Angered, he struck her, shifted the blame to the maid, and left by the private stairway.'

'A good theory to start with,' Paul agreed, rising from the table. 'Now we must prove it.'

CHAPTER SIX

Getting Acquainted

Saturday, June 2

Later that morning Anne, Paul, and Comtesse Marie shared a coach for the dozen miles to Versailles. While the coach rattled over the paving stones, they discussed Sylvie's lively interest in the case. The countess shook her head. 'I feel concerned about leaving her. She might become too involved in the investigation and put herself in danger.'

'Trust Michou to look after her,' Anne remarked. 'There's little risk in eavesdropping and asking a few questions in public places.'

At the palace in Versailles, the coach rolled to a halt. The countess set out on foot for Baron Breteuil's office, to arrange for accommodations. Paul and Anne walked the short distance through the town to the provost's prison to visit Denise de Villers.

The officer on duty looked askance at Anne, then at Paul. 'My wife will interpret for me. The prisoner is deaf.' The officer led them into a small room with bare, dingy walls, a table, and four chairs. A square, barred opening in the door allowed a guard to observe them. A few minutes later Denise was brought in, shivering as she entered. Her maid's apron had been taken from her. She was clothed in a shapeless gray woolen gown, girded at the waist, and wore wooden shoes. Again her hands were manacled.

'Free her,' Paul ordered the guard, then turned to the officer in charge. 'Why is she kept in irons?'

The officer sniffed. 'She might take her own life. We keep her alone under constant watch. She leaves her cell once a day for exercise.'

'What makes you think she would kill herself?'

'She's certain to be convicted and would try to escape punishment. The provost wants her to pay for her crime.'

The cruelty of this constraint appalled Anne. Even a single day in prison had taken a toll on the young woman's health. She seemed numbed, her face pale and blank, as if she couldn't comprehend what had happened. Her expression hardly changed, even when she recognized Anne. Only when her hands were freed did she begin to revive. Still, she glanced anxiously at the officer and the guard until they left.

In the conversation that followed, Anne translating for Paul, Denise explained that she was being held in a tiny cell in a dirty, moldy basement. A small, high window admitted a little air and light. The guards fed her coarse brown bread and thin broth. No, they had not abused her, but she couldn't help thinking that everyone assumed her guilty of a heinous crime and deserving of a dreadful punishment. How could she defend herself before stern black-robed judges, when she couldn't speak or hear?

'Abbé de l'Épée and your friends believe in you.' Anne pointed to herself and Paul. 'And we will try to find the true villain. Do you know anyone who disliked Duchesse Aimée enough to kill her? Chevalier Richard de Beauregard, for a start. Did he ever quarrel with her?'

'From the way he looked at her when she wasn't watching, I could see he didn't love her. Sometimes he complained she didn't help him enough to get a good pension from the Queen.'

Paul turned to Anne. 'It seems unreasonable for him to blame her. For the past few months, the Queen has given out hardly any pensions due to the Crown's financial crisis.'

'He may have other hidden motives.'

'We will dig them out.'

Anne signed to Denise again. 'Duc Henri, what kind of man is he? Did he care for his wife?'

'He's cold and distant to servants, lives in a different world than ours. When he's with other nobles, he struts like a peacock, gambles. He was a stranger to his wife. They never slept together. He only wanted her money, I suppose.'

'Did either man bother you or have any reason to implicate you in Duchesse Aimée's murder?'

'No, the duke hardly noticed me.' She lowered her eyes a fraction. 'Once, in the kitchen, Beauregard tried to kiss me when the duchess was away. No harm came of it. Madame Bourdon arrived and the chevalier fled.'

'Fortunately!' Anne remarked. 'A vigilant housekeeper. How well did she get along with her mistress?'

Denise bit on her lower lip for a few moments, carefully pondering an answer. 'Madame Bourdon is a devout Christian and a strong, intelligent woman who knows her place. The duchess feared her, I think, and treated her with respect.' She hesitated, as if uncertain. 'Madame was always obedient and respectful when facing the duchess. But, when no one was looking she sometimes sneered at her.'

Anne nodded. A servant as upright as Marthe might well hold her self-indulgent mistress in contempt. 'How did Marthe treat you?'

'As she should. Always proper. Never friendly. She showed me what to do, corrected my mistakes. I could tell from her eyes that she didn't like me. Don't know why. Maybe thought I was stupid as well as deaf.'

'Did she ever hint that you stole a small silver plate?'

'No. She told me only that it was missing. Maybe I missed a hint. Anyway, it returned to the kitchen. No more was said about it.'

'And how did you get along with the duchess?' It unsettled Anne even to wonder if Denise might have killed her mistress after all. It seemed so unlikely, but it had to be considered.

'I think she liked me and tried to be kind. I was her pet—kept her company like Bijou. On the spur of the moment, she would tie a lovely ribbon around my neck, stand back, and admire it. "It's yours," she would say. Once, she hung her ruby brooch on my chest—the one they found in my bed—

to see how it would look. We were about the same size and shape, had similar brown eyes and hair.'

The maid's eyes moistened. This wasn't pretense, Anne thought, the young woman felt affection for her murdered mistress. She had *given* Denise the ribbons which the provost claimed were stolen.

'Cook was good to me,' continued Denise, unbidden. 'She let me play with Bijou and gave me treats when Marthe wasn't looking.' Suddenly, tears flowed down the maid's cheek. Her body shook with grief. Anne went to her side and put an arm over her shoulder, soothed her with gentle strokes until she grew calm again. Anne offered her a handkerchief to wipe away the tears.

While the two women spoke, Paul had sat back, brow creased in thought. Finally, he asked Denise, 'Have you ever met the provost before?' He turned to Anne and explained, 'When Georges and I spoke to him, I sensed he was too quick to condemn the maid, as if he held a grudge for some reason.'

Denise looked away, embarrassed, and nodded. 'A year ago, I had only just arrived at the palace. Marthe sent me to a linen closet for fresh sheets. This old gentleman stopped me in the hallway. Earlier in the day, I'd noticed him staring at me. I didn't know who he was, though he acted like I should. When I tried to leave, he grabbed my arm, said he was the palace police and needed to speak to me. He led me into an empty room and began to fondle me. I protested and tried to get away. He laughed and began to loosen my bodice. I slapped his face so hard that his porcelain teeth flew out of his mouth and shattered on the tile floor.

'At first, he merely stepped back and stared at me, shocked. His mouth was a gaping hole. He looked so odd. I began to laugh—I knew I shouldn't but I couldn't help myself. I was so frightened. Then, he turned red in the face. His eyes grew black and very angry. He tried hard to speak but couldn't get words out clearly. Spittle drooled from his mouth. Finally, he stooped to pick up the bits of porcelain on the floor. I ran from the room. Later, I learned who he was and became afraid. He's powerful in the palace and could hurt me. I've never mentioned the incident to anybody.

He hasn't forgotten. From time to time, I see him or his agent Bart watching me.'

'He has waited until now for his revenge,' said Anne, forced to imagine the depth of Sully's hatred for the maid. A fair trial was out of the question. Anne didn't have the heart to tell Denise that the provost was also using Mademoiselle Fortier's accusations to bolster his case against her.

'What will become of me?' pleaded the young woman, fixing Anne, then Paul, in her gaze. 'It seems so hopeless. Maybe I *should* kill myself.'

Anne felt chilled. Words failed her. Then Paul leaned across the table, gripped the maid's hands, met her eyes. 'Fear not.' He formed his words carefully. 'Your friends will save you. Trust us.'

In the meantime, Comtesse Marie had arrived at Baron Breteuil's office, brushed past a footman, and entered with a loud rustle of skirts. The baron looked up, surprised, then rose from behind his desk.

'What brings you to Versailles, my dear? I thought you had vowed never to return.' He pulled up a chair for her.

'Not until I had a very good reason,' she replied emphatically. 'I have one now. I want to see justice done.' She went on to present her understanding of the case against Denise de Villers and the need for further investigation. 'I can be of some help here in the palace. Would you please arrange accommodations for me and a companion?'

The baron leaned back in his chair, pulling on his chin. Marie smiled inwardly—the old fox is puzzled, doesn't know what to make of my request, and doesn't want me to see it on his face. She gave him a few moments to reflect. 'I'm serious, you can be sure.'

'I can see that.' He sat up, rested his arms on his desk, clasped his hands. 'How do you propose to help us? The maid appears to be guilty, but others could be involved. Do you imagine you could sift through the gossip, malingering, and outright lies that stand in our way to the truth?'

'Despite my long absence, Baron, I still have contacts here who would rather speak to me than to a policeman. With their help I might uncover evidence pointing to someone other than the maid as the killer.'

'That could prove difficult. Both her lover and her husband, the chief alternatives to the maid, have claimed alibis. Beauregard says he last saw her alive when she left Princess Lamballe's apartment. He went directly to his own room and played at cards with another gentleman until dawn.'

'And Duc Henri?'

'He spent the entire time with his mistress in her town house on Rue Royale.'

'Dubious witnesses! I've hardly begun, and I've already found reason to challenge Beauregard's story.'

'Oh?' The baron leaned forward. 'Tell me more.'

'Your goddaughter Sylvie overheard him in the garden of Palais-Royal, asking someone to lie about being together at Versailles.'

'Hmm, Paul will look into that.'

'Yes, he has been informed.' She caught his eye. 'Now, about my request . . .'

'Of course, I hadn't forgotten.' The baron tapped a pile of papers in front of him. 'There are vacancies here. The Queen has sent the Polignac clan and other favorites away. I should be able to locate an apartment large enough to accommodate Paul and his adjutant as well as you and your companion.' He lowered his voice, measured his words. 'I must warn you, Marie, the Queen demands this investigation be concluded promptly. You will have no more than a week or two for your inquiries.'

'So be it.' Marie uttered a silent prayer for help.

'Good, I shall arrange quarters for you immediately and look forward to having you nearby.' He paused. 'May I ask, who will be joining you?'

'Madame Anne Cartier, Paul's new wife.' She almost cringed as she spoke, anticipating a sour look, a head-shaking, even a thump of his fist on the desk.

Instead, he nodded thoughtfully. 'Wise choice, Marie. She's clever and courageous. I only wish she hadn't married Paul. But, what's done is done.'

* * *

Early in the afternoon, Colonel Saint-Martin sat comfortably in an upholstered chair in the duchess's bedroom, reading Voltaire's *Dictionnaire Philosophique*. He had just pulled it off her shelf of gold-embossed leather-bound books, a representative sample of the century's enlightened authors. Many of the books appeared worn.

As he read her marginal comments, he saw her in a new, surprising light. She had wrestled with Voltaire's arguments for an end to superstition, torture, and other inhumanity in the criminal law. With a cluster of exclamation points, she applauded the great skeptic's ironic thrusts against the bigoted magistrates who put the young Chevalier de La Barre to death many years ago. Saint-Martin wondered why such issues would engage her so strongly? She was said to have a shallow mind.

He rose to return Voltaire to the shelf. At that moment, Georges walked into the room.

'You look starved, sir. There's food ready in the kitchen. I'll bring it here. While we eat, I'll report on my interrogation of the servants this morning.'

A few minutes later, Georges brought in a luncheon tray and the two men ate at a breakfast table by a window. The cook had left a veal roast for them and gone for a walk in the park. The housekeeper was out on an errand to the central kitchen. Other servants were in their rooms. Anne and Marie had returned to Paris.

'Find any suspects, Georges?' The colonel cut a piece of the veal and took a helping of green beans.

'Possibly Duc Henri's valet, who also serves as the household steward.' Georges broke off a piece of bread and wiped the gravy from his plate. 'The other servants have solid alibis or appear to have had no reason to murder their mistress.'

Saint-Martin looked up from his food. 'Why is the duke's valet a suspect?'

'He badly needs money. His master could have employed him as an assassin. Or, he could have acted on his own. He knew the household routine and the private entrance and was alone in his room all night.'

'Then I should see him.' Saint-Martin quickly finished his meal.

Georges cleared the table and walked to the door. 'I'll fetch him now.'

In a few minutes he came back with a trim, athletic man in yellow livery. What impressed Saint-Martin most was his high brow and the intelligence in his uncommonly light blue eyes. 'Your name, if you please,' asked Saint-Martin, motioning him to sit at the opposite side of the table. Georges moved off to one side and began taking notes.

'Jules Blondel, sir.'

'How long have you served as the duke's valet?'

'Five years, sir.'

'And before that?'

'Five years in the Royal Army, sir, two of them with the Duc de Lauzun's legion in America.'

'Then we may have crossed paths. Your rank?'

'Sergeant, sir.'

'A remarkable achievement in so few years.'

'The duke chose me to be his servant. I owed the rank to his favor.'

Saint-Martin smiled at the man's candor. 'Tell me more about yourself.'

He learned that Blondel came from a good family in Paris. Son of a lawyer, he was well educated but had to enlist in the army when his father died, leaving the family penniless. His commanding officer recommended him to Duc Henri. Blondel looked after the duke's apartment, his wardrobe, his works of art, and ran errands for him.

'What's your ambition in life?'

'I can't do better than serve a duke and live in a palace, can I? I have a room and some time to myself, good food and drink, the duke's livery.' He pointed with a flourish to his silver-embroidered lapels.

'And money?' Saint-Martin had detected a faintly ironic undertone in the valet's remarks.

Blondel hesitated, his eyes grew cautious. Georges had said the duke owed his valet more than a year's back wages and owed others far more. Finally, the valet shrugged. 'As you apparently already know, I have none. My master is temporarily hard-pressed, but I'm confident he will pay me.'

40

'Soon enough for you to start a family?' Saint-Martin guessed at the young man's ambitions.

'True,' replied Blondel, his lips tensed. 'I would like to marry but cannot afford to. The time will come.'

'Are you more confident now that Duc Henri will inherit his wife's fortune?'

Blondel appeared to flinch resentfully at that question. 'My master will pay when he can.'

'How did the death of the duchess affect you?'

'It saddened me, as it did the other servants.' The reply seemed perfunctory, what he felt obliged to say.

'And the maid? What can you tell us?'

'I've had little to do with her. A pretty young woman . . . but deaf. Unfortunately, she gave in to her weakness. She had stolen at least once before.'

'A false rumor, contradicted by Abbé de l'Épée, director at the Institute for the Deaf.'

Blondel appeared startled. 'True or false, I can't say. But other servants told me the rumor came from the provost's office.'

Taken aback by this riposte, Saint-Martin carefully studied the young man's expression, looking for signs of insolence or duplicity. He could find only wary, guarded eyes. The valet expertly concealed his true feelings, a talent he had prudently cultivated in the service of his noble masters. 'That will be all for now,' said Saint-Martin, gesturing to the door. 'Oh, by the way, where was your master during the early-morning hours of Friday?'

Blondel stopped in his tracks, his hand reaching for the door. He turned to face Saint-Martin, obviously reluctant to reply.

The colonel's voice was low and insistent. 'This is a murder investigation. I expect the truth from you.'

'Duc Henri left the apartment a little before ten in the evening without saying where he was going.'

'According to the statement he gave the guards yesterday, he went to his mistress in the town. She confirmed his statement. We shall check it later. When did he return?'

'At about nine in the morning to identify his dead wife.'

41

'Did you hear them quarrel before he left?'

Blondel hesitated a fraction; his lips tightened. 'Yes.'

'About what?'

'Money, of course. He asked for more. She said no.'

'Did he threaten her?'

A longer pause. Blondel began to perspire. 'Yes, he said he would get the money from her one way or another.'

'And?' Saint-Martin urged Blondel on.

'She had money for her worthless lover but not for her own husband.'

'Now you may go.' Saint-Martin understood that a special clause in the duchess's marriage contract kept her inheritance from her husband's grasp and allowed her to dispose of at least some of it as she wished. At her death her husband would inherit it all.

When Blondel's steps disappeared in the hallway, Saint-Martin turned to his adjutant, who laid down his pen and blotted his notes. 'What do you think, Georges?'

'A capable but frustrated man, virtually the duke's slave. What would he need to escape to a position of comfort and respect?'

'I can guess, but please tell me.'

Georges paused, a wry grin on his face. 'What else, but money! Could the duke have persuaded him to kill the duchess in return for a handsome sum? Or, might he have done it on his own? It's hard to say. We know little about his moral character. He's a lawyer's son. I doubt if he has many scruples. Before killing the duchess, he would calculate the odds of getting caught. They would greatly decrease if he could shift suspicion for the crime on to another person, especially one who could defend herself only poorly.'

'You may be right, Georges. How shall we prove it?'

'The missing coins would do very well! I must search Monsieur Blondel's room.'

'Later, Georges.' Saint-Martin rose from the table. 'First, we shall find Duc Henri and learn what he has to say.'

The door to the duke's study was open. The colonel and Georges entered without announcing themselves. The duke was sitting at a table covered with paper and file boxes. At a glance, Saint-Martin could see no books. If the duke had any, he kept them elsewhere. The furniture was an odd lot—a few shabby tables and chairs probably from the palace attic. Despite his ducal title, he apparently lacked power and respect at Court. And his wife hadn't used her influence on his behalf.

A clerk sat facing the duke, sorting loose papers. The duke was dressed for mourning, in a black velvet suit accented by silver embroidery on the lapels. Otherwise, he gave the impression of being more absorbed in the paper in front of him than in grief for his wife. Georges bent toward Saint-Martin and whispered. 'The clerk worked for the duchess. Those should be her financial records.'

Duc Henri looked up, annoyed at first, then brightened. 'You must be Colonel Paul de Saint-Martin. Baron Breteuil said you would call.' He waved the clerk out. 'This is a good time. I'll finish this business later.' He pushed the papers aside, rose to greet his visitors, and invited them to chairs by a window overlooking a cramped interior courtyard. The colonel bowed and shook the duke's hand, then introduced his adjutant. The duke nodded in Georges's direction but otherwise took no notice of him.

The duke adopted a cordial, gracious manner toward Saint-Martin, whom he regarded, if not as an equal, at least as of the same privileged class as himself. His face had once been handsome, but a life of dissipation had left it ravaged. Bleary vacant eyes, hanging jowls, sores concealed by black patches. He opened the conversation with pleasantries, then asked, 'Your visit would have something to do with the death of my wife, I believe.'

'Yes, we must ask you some questions.'

'I will have little to add to what you already know, Colonel.'

Saint-Martin smiled respectfully. 'Then our visit will be short and pleasant.' Or, he thought, more likely a painful one. Before coming to the duke's apartment, Saint-Martin and Georges had visited the duke's mistress and had learned he had spent only an hour with her, then left at about eleven in the evening, saying he was going to Paris. He returned to her at eight the next morning to learn of his wife's murder. He demanded that his mistress offer an alibi for him. She did so later when the provost's agent questioned her. Afterwards, feeling the duke had slighted her, she confessed the lie to Saint-Martin.

'Where were you between two and eight on Friday morning?'

The duke's smile changed to a tentative frown, as if he sensed a trap. 'True, I misled the provost's agent. It was none of his business how I spent the night. My mistress, in fact, was not in the mood for love, so I went to Madame Lebrun's house of pleasure in the Palais-Royal.'

'How long were you there?' Saint-Martin glanced at Georges, as if to suggest that he had already checked with Madame.

The duke's face grew pale. Distress worked the corners of his mouth. 'Only a few minutes. I decided I didn't want her services after all. I walked the streets of Paris until dawn, then returned to Versailles.'

'Any witnesses to this walk?' This was as preposterous a story as Saint-Martin had ever heard.

The duke glared at him.

'You came back to discover your wife had been murdered, is that correct?'

The duke's eyes narrowed, darkened. 'What are you implying, Colonel?'

'Your financial difficulties are common knowledge.' He leaned forward and met the duke's eye. 'Did you demand money from your wife Thursday evening and threaten her when she refused?'

'Careless words.' He paused for a moment, most likely calculating who had informed on him. 'I never meant to harm her.'

'Duc Henri, I expect you to allow us complete freedom to search your rooms, examine your account books, and interrogate your servants. You may consider yourself suspect of your wife's murder, for you had both motive and opportunity to kill her.'

'But you can't prove it.' His voice was hoarse and full of menace. 'Colonel, I shall make you pay for this.'

44

CHAPTER SEVEN

Seeking The Truth

Saturday, June 2

The sky over the road from Versailles to Paris had turned dark and cloudy. The threat of rain hung in the air. Still, a soft spring breeze blew through the windows of the coach and caressed Anne's cheek, encouraging her to savor a bit of good news in the midst of the day's distress. Her companion, Marie, had just reported that Baron Breteuil regarded Anne highly and appeared to have accepted her marriage to Paul at least as a *fait accompli*.

'Paul will be pleased,' Anne remarked. She cared less than he about the baron's disapproval but saw the advantage in keeping his goodwill. Then she glanced at the gray sky and recalled the depressed mental state of Denise de Villers. All joy left Anne's spirit.

'What did you and Paul learn at the prison?' asked the countess.

'The Marquis de Sully holds a personal grudge against Mademoiselle de Villers.' Anne explained that he had accosted the maid and she had defended herself. 'He's retaliating for the blow she gave him and for his shattered teeth. She's despondent, believes her cause is hopeless.' Anne's voice fell. For a moment she was overcome and could hardly speak. 'Denise is thinking of suicide.'

'Poor girl!' Marie slowly shook her head. 'I'll inquire among my acquaintances about that incident. But, apparently, there were no witnesses. And, if accused, the old villain would deny everything.'

'We must discover the real killer,' Anne insisted. 'There's

no other way to save the young maid. Richard de Beauregard could be our key.'

When the coach reached the countess's town house at mid-afternoon, Michou and Sylvie met them with news. During the morning in the garden of the Palais-Royal they had learned the name of Beauregard's short, fat acquaintance—Victor Hoche, assistant director of the Duc d'Orléans's art collection. He lived in the palace but could be found regularly in the late afternoon at Café de Foy.

At four o'clock Anne and Marie set out for the café to study Monsieur Hoche and his associates. As the two women arrived, several gentlemen and a few ladies came for afternoon coffee and another opportunity to display themselves. They had already dined in nearby restaurants. The men wore their hair brushed high and powdered. Their suits were of richly embroidered silk in pastel blue, red, and green. The women wore tall, fantastic hats and the recently stylish white muslin gowns.

Marie beckoned a waiter. 'Bernard, a corner table with a view over the room, if you please.'

'With pleasure, Comtesse.' He bowed, smiling as if he knew her well, and seated them side by side.

While waiting for Hoche to appear, Anne surveyed the room's elegant furnishings. Highly polished crystal chandeliers hung from the ceiling. Large gilded mirrors covered the walls. Fashionably dressed men and women sat around marble-topped tables in quiet conversation, reading newspapers, or playing chess. Such a civilized place, Anne thought. Hard to imagine anyone plotting murder here.

Marie followed Anne's eyes to the chess table. 'A chess club meets a little later in the room upstairs and attracts distinguished foreigners. I hear that the American ambassador Mr Jefferson is among them.'

Anne recalled meeting him a year ago at the institute, a tall, angular man, hungry for knowledge, intently observing the education of the deaf. Previously, he had believed the deaf couldn't think like other people, since they couldn't speak. Françoise and the students proved him wrong.

Suddenly, Anne felt the countess's elbow poke her side.

'The duke's clerk has arrived.'

Hoche joined a slender, stooped man on the opposite side of the room. On close inspection he reminded Anne of a bird of prey, thin-lipped, hook-nosed, beetle-browed. The two men ordered drinks and were soon conversing about serious matters. Anne couldn't read their lips—they were too far away. But, from their frowning, the shaking of their heads, she guessed that something upset them very much.

Marie signaled the waiter who had seated them. He came promptly. 'Bernard.' Her voice was low, barely a whisper. 'Would you please find out what Hoche and his companion are discussing?' She pressed a coin into his hand. 'And do so with your usual discretion.' She sent him off with a trusting smile.

'Watch him,' she said to Anne. 'He has a remarkable talent for eavesdropping.'

For several minutes, the waiter went about the room taking orders, serving drinks. Then, a patron near Hoche lifted an empty glass. The waiter approached quickly but without haste, took an order while hovering within earshot of Hoche. For a few more minutes the waiter served other patrons before returning to the countess with brandy for her and Anne.

'They're discussing the murder of Aimée de Saumur.'

'Like everyone else in this room,' murmured the countess, pressing another coin in the waiter's hand. 'Who is the other man?'

'A man of letters, Monsieur Gaillard.'

Marie turned to Anne. 'Bernard is too kind. By reputation Gaillard is a hack, a scandalmonger.' She smiled at the waiter. 'Thank you, my good man. Continue to eavesdrop.'

A half-hour passed while Anne related anecdotes from her recent visit to Bath. She had tutored a young deaf boy, the son of Sir Harry Rogers, a wealthy slave trader and sportsman. The experience was much more dangerous than she had bargained for. Rogers believed his wife was having an affair with her cousin, Captain Fitzroy, the same man who had assaulted Sylvie. Fortunately, Paul and Georges had come to Rogers's great house in pursuit of the captain and joined forces with Anne. 'The captain might have killed us all on the Bristol road, if we hadn't . . .' She stopped in mid-sentence as a young man entered the café. 'I believe Chevalier Richard de Beauregard has arrived.' She recognized him from one of Michou's sketches.

He hesitated at the door for a few moments until Hoche beckoned. Beauregard shook the hands of his companions and took a seat. They failed to return his nervous smile. Bernard soon approached to take his order and shortly afterwards returned with his drink. Conversation at the table grew lively, Hoche glaring at Beauregard, tapping his fingers irritably on the table. Gaillard seemed withdrawn, calculating.

A few minutes later, Bernard passed slowly by Comtesse Marie and murmured, 'Police . . . questions . . . idiot . . . keep us out of it.'

Marie acknowledged his message with a slight nod, looked down into her brandy glass, and asked Anne softly, 'What do you make of it?'

'Richard de Beauregard has reason to fear questions from the police,' she replied. 'His companions want to stay clear of him.'

With Duc Henri's threat of reprisal still ringing in his ears, Saint-Martin followed Georges to the guardroom on the ground floor of the palace. They would attempt to trace the duke's movements during the early hours of Friday morning. It seemed unlikely that a sleepy-eyed sentry would have noticed him, but it was worth a try.

They reached the guardroom as a late-afternoon dinner was being served. The night guards were sitting at a long wooden table. Saint-Martin waited in the background while Georges made the inquiries. Guard after guard shook his head. Finally, an older, sharp-eyed man nodded. Georges beckoned Saint-Martin to draw near and listen.

The guard, pleased by the attention, gave Georges a crooked smile. 'Yes, sir, I did see the duke yesterday. How could I forget!' He chuckled, recalling the incident. 'I was at the main gate. Just after the bell struck three, this fashionable gentleman rode up to me on an old, sway-backed nag without a saddle. So winded was the horse, that I thought it would drop and die at my feet. The night was dark, the gentleman's face covered, but I'd know him anywhere.'

'How?' Georges asked.

'I usually serve on the night shift. He often comes past me. I know his cracked voice, his lame walk, his fancy boots and gloves. Very taken with himself, he is. Easy to spot.'

Georges gave the man a pat on the shoulder. 'Thanks, you've been helpful.'

On the way out of the guardroom, Saint-Martin glanced at his adjutant. 'An angry duke could cause us trouble. We had better check his story at the Palais-Royal.'

By the time the colonel and Georges reached the Palais-Royal it was evening. They went directly to Madame Lebrun's brothel in the Valois arcade.

The establishment was above an elegant café. At the entrance in the arcade, the colonel took the lead, asking the doorman for the mistress of the house. The servant hesitated for a moment, anxiety gathering in his eyes. In full uniform, unsmiling, the two visitors presented an intimidating appearance. The servant studied them closely, realized he had no choice, and led them upstairs to a first-floor parlor.

In a short while, Madame Lebrun arrived, a fine-featured courtesan, painted and powdered for her clients. She greeted the two policemen with apprehension. As the colonel explained his mission, she began to smile cautiously. 'Duc Henri de Saumur is well known here and no longer welcome.'

'And why not, may I ask?'

'He owed much, paid nothing. When I demanded payment, he replied I should be satisfied that he deigned to frequent the establishment. Finally, I threatened to bring him before a magistrate. He assured me he would pay. Just wait, he said, until he received his wife's inheritance. I said to him, your wife is young and healthy, I'll be dead before she is.'

Madame clasped her hands, aghast at what she had said. 'God forgive me!' She hurriedly crossed herself, then spent a moment regaining her composure. 'I ordered him out of the house.'

'Did he protest?' asked Saint-Martin, himself a little

unsettled by her reference to the murdered woman. Had Lebrun insinuated a lethal idea into the old duke's muddled head?

'He looked at me as if he couldn't believe what I had said. Then he became haughty and threatened to cane me for an upstart procuress. I called my footmen and they threw him out the door. The last I saw of him, he was walking away into the palace garden, shaking his cane and shouting obscenities at me.'

Saint-Martin bowed and thanked the woman for her help. The two men showed themselves out and started across the garden toward their residence on Rue Saint-Honoré. The colonel turned to his adjutant. 'Duc Henri lied about not wanting the services of Madame Lebrun's brothel. He was in fact too humiliated to tell us he had been thrown out like a penniless vagabond.'

'Come to think of it, sir, he must have also stolen a carter's nag for the return trip to Versailles.'

'Yes, Georges. We have a credible suspect, a troublesome one, I fear.'

Late in the evening in the provost's residence on Rue Saint-Honoré, Anne inspected a blue silk gown, then set it aside. She was preparing for the move to Versailles. Marie was helping her. The trunk standing open between them was almost full. Their visit to the palace would be brief, but they needed to provide for many different occasions.

A servant appeared at the parlor door. 'A man calling himself Bernard says he must speak to Comtesse Marie de Beaumont. He's waiting in the front parlor.'

'I'll see him immediately.' She turned to Anne. 'Come along. This will be useful.'

The two women found the waiter disguised in a knee-length cloak. A hood concealed his face. He threw back the hood as the countess entered the room. When he saw Anne, he momentarily froze, then recognized her and relaxed.

'Comtesse, I've come from the café. This much I've pieced together from what I've heard and from reports by trusted friends. Chevalier Richard de Beauregard went to the apartment of the duchess early Friday morning before dawn. His

50

companions seemed to think he killed her and thereby ruined certain plans they had made. He insisted he left her alive— the maid must have killed her. He wanted his companions to tell the police that one of them was with him at the time. They said it was too risky. The police might catch them lying. Someone could have seen him near the private stairway or heard him in her apartment.'

'What do you think they meant by "ruining certain plans"?'

'I don't know. They didn't say. Probably a crooked scheme to get rich.'

'Thank you, Bernard, and good night. You've been very helpful.' She gave him a coin, he bowed and left the room.

Anne waited until an outer door slammed shut, then asked Marie, 'How could Bernard gather so much valuable information? It's amazing. Hoche and his companions must take precautions. They know that spies are everywhere.'

'That's true,' she replied. 'But Bernard's appearance is so nondescript, his manner so self-effacing, that even Hoche, an accomplished intriguer, didn't notice him. Bernard also hears unusually well and has learned to read lips. And, he has created a network of other waiters and domestic servants to spy for him. My late husband discovered him years ago and employed him in various delicate investigations. Since then, I have also used him occasionally.'

She patted Anne's hand. 'You seem shocked, young lady. In our society people are rarely what they purport to be and their promises are often suspect. In important matters, men and women like Bernard help me to reach the truth.'

'We'll do what we must to save Denise de Villers,' said Anne, 'even dance with the devil.'

CHAPTER EIGHT

A Ducal Suspect

Sunday, June 3

S aint-Martin and Georges reached Versailles shortly before
Sunday Mass. They had learned that Duc Henri custom-
arily appeared in the palace chapel of Saint Louis when the
King came to worship. It might be wise to observe the duke
in the company of others, especially his peers. Did he have
their respect? Would they support him if he were arrested and
charged with murder?

Choir members had filed into the organ gallery above the
altar. It was a special occasion, Trinity Sunday, and the royal
family would attend. To honor the Queen the choir would
sing a Mass by Joseph Haydn. The colonel was pleased, for
he shared her love of Austrian sacred music.

The chapel's lofty, airy interior of white stone and gilded
decoration drew in brilliant light from the midday sun. The
colonel, who knew the chapel well, marveled at its remarkable unity of design. All its elements worked together in
harmony.

'This is a place worthy of God!' he murmured.

His adjutant sniffed. 'The King should have spent the money
on the servants' quarters.'

They stood in a side gallery among high-born, silk-clad
courtiers. 'Posturing peacocks!' muttered Saint-Martin to
himself. In the nave below, a less distinguished crowd milled
about like cattle, gawking at those above them. A few minutes
before the Mass was to begin, a commotion erupted in the
royal gallery at the rear of the chapel. Heads turned to watch
the King and Queen appear with their children and attendants.

Saint-Martin had seen the King before on several occasions,

the last time nine months ago with Anne. He had seemed his bumbling, corpulent self, unmindful of the political storm looming on the horizon. The intricacies of a lock he was repairing had probably engaged his mind.

Today, pasty-faced and mopping his brow, also fatter and more lethargic, he looked unwell. In April in this palace, the Duc d'Orléans and the French nation's elite had rudely rejected reforms proposed by the King's ministers and had demanded a meeting of the traditional Estates-General. The clergy and the nobility intended to force the King to share power with them. Their challenge seemed to have broken the King's spirit. He relied now more than ever on the Queen's much sturdier will.

With her beauty and regal bearing she dominated the royal gallery. Her complexion was unusually clear, almost transparent, her eyes sky-blue and candid. When she walked, she seemed to glide through space. Now she stood tall, full-figured, erect.

Georges stared sullenly at the royal family. He had not seen them before.

'She truly looks the part of a Queen,' murmured Saint-Martin. 'If only she would also play the role, be wise and understanding, devoted to duty.' He sighed. 'Instead, she wastes her talents on private amusements and worthless favorites like the Polignac clan.'

Georges nodded. 'And spends money like it's hers to burn.' He added softly, 'In the city they call her Madame Deficit. She's ruining the country.'

'That's unfair.' Saint-Martin had begun to feel he ought to defend the Queen. 'France would be in the present crisis even if the Queen were thrifty. Our financial system is badly organized. The poor bear the brunt of taxation. The wealthy privileged classes pay little or nothing.'

The adjutant wrinkled his nose, unconvinced.

'Be generous, Georges. Consider her good qualities. I've heard she's a caring mother of her children, distressed that one of her daughters is gravely ill and not expected to live more than a week or two.'

Georges's lips tightened, his head inclined a little in a

skeptical attitude. He didn't sniff, as he usually did in the face of pomp and splendor, but remained ominously silent. Finally, he could not contain himself. 'Poor France!' he muttered. 'Ruled by a dolt, his wife an ignorant foreigner. She at least looks like a monarch. What will become of us?'

He retreated into silence for the duration of the religious service. The best efforts of organ, choir, and liturgical drama, with its clouds of incense and sonorous chants, failed to engage his spirit. 'There's the old fart,' he whispered, pointing to Duc Henri among the crowd of courtiers in the side gallery opposite them. 'Look at him preening himself, ogling the royal family. He makes me sick.'

'Georges, what matters to us is whether he killed Aimée de Saumur. We must intercept him after the Mass.'

That proved to be difficult. The duke pressed through the crowd leaving the chapel, greeting everyone whether they acknowledged him or not. Many rolled their eyes when he had passed.

The colonel turned to his adjutant.'The duke's peers seem to share your opinion of him. However, that he's foolish doesn't mean he's harmless.'

Eventually, they caught up with him in the Grande Galerie, a hall of mirrors. Saint-Martin bowed with respect, addressed him politely. 'Duc Henri, would you please come with us? We have a few questions for you.'

The duke stiffened. 'Sir, I have more important things to do.' He began to walk away.

Saint-Martin put ice in his voice. 'You lied to us yesterday. Must I call the guard?'

The duke stopped in his tracks. An old instinct urged him to call for a duel. His hand reached for the hilt of his sword. However, a glance at Saint-Martin's supple, athletic body and steely eyes made him give up the idea. Curious onlookers had begun to gather, and they did not appear sympathetic to the old man. Scowling, he withdrew his hand from his sword.

Saint-Martin nodded to Georges and they escorted the duke between them to an office which Baron Breteuil had set aside in the ministerial wing of the palace. Saint-Martin and the duke took seats opposite each other at a table while Georges sat to one side, prepared to take notes. The duke looked like a trapped animal. His eyes shifted nervously and without focus. Was he fully rational? Saint-Martin wondered.

'Yesterday, Duc Henri, you falsely said you were walking the streets of Paris at the time your wife was being murdered. In fact you had returned to Versailles a little after three in the morning on a wheezing old nag. You had plenty of time to kill her. What did you do instead?'

'Honor prevents me from telling you.'

'Sir, I have the King's authority to compel you to speak.'

The old man raised his chin in a pathetic, haughty gesture, looked out the window, remained silent.

'You leave me no choice. A guard will take you to the provost's prison. I shall notify Baron Breteuil that you are suspected of the murder of your wife.' The colonel turned to his adjutant. 'Monsieur Charpentier, call the guard.'

Georges laid down his pen and started for the door.

'Wait,' said the duke, then stuttered, trying to find words. Beads of perspiration gathered on his brow. 'You force me to compromise my honor.' He squirmed with discomfort, grimaced nervously. 'I spent the hours at issue in the company of a . . .' His voice fell so low he could not be heard.

'Speak up!' The colonel was rapidly losing patience.

'Someone in the laundry,' the old man mumbled.

'Her name?'

'I don't know.'

'What does she look like?'

'Young, small, I suppose. It was dark.'

Georges, who had been returning to his seat, stopped, glared at the duke, and clenched his fists. Saint-Martin raised a warning hand, lest his adjutant fall upon the duke and beat him.

'Duc Henri, you must accompany us to the guardroom and stay there while we attempt to find the young woman. We shall also search your rooms.'

Georges quickly wrote a note authorizing the search and brought it to the duke. He tore it up and threw it on the floor.

'I shall not go to the guardroom like a common criminal.'

He leaped from his chair with surprising agility and strode toward the door.

Georges blocked his way.

The duke drew his sword. 'Swine! I'll kill you.'

But Georges was quicker and brought the flat of his blade down on the duke's arm. His sword fell with a clatter on the tile floor. He howled in pain, his arm hanging useless at his side.

Georges seized the duke's good arm, pinned it to his back, and shoved him toward the door.

'Good,' said Saint-Martin, rising from the table. 'Let's be on our way.' To Georges, he murmured, 'This is beginning to look like a very nasty business.'

After leaving the duke in the guardroom, Saint-Martin and Georges proceeded down a flight of stairs to the basement laundry. Since it was Sunday, there wasn't much activity. A few women were seated at a table sewing and chatting.

When the two men approached, the women glanced up nervously. The colonel addressed them with courtesy, attempting to put them more at ease. As he mentioned the early-morning hours on Friday, he could see concern mounting in their faces. 'An incident occurred here in the laundry at that time. An elderly gentleman attacked a young woman.' The duke had not admitted attacking her, but Saint-Martin was sure that's what had happened.

The women lapsed into heavy silence. Finally, after a few minutes, the one who seemed to be in charge spoke up. 'We know nothing.'

Georges whispered in the colonel's ear. 'That one knows.' He nodded toward a woman at the far end of the table, head sunken, shoulders hunched over. He walked over to her. 'What's your name?'

'Birgitte.'

'Do you have a daughter who works here?'

'No, I don't . . .' She stiffened, her face filled with tears. Then she leaned over the table, her body racked with grief.

Thérèse, the woman in charge, stood up, faced Georges and the colonel. 'It was her son.'

Duc Henri had stumbled into the laundry after three in the morning. Been drinking. The boy, Daniel, had just risen to begin the fires for the day. He was in his nightshirt. The duke ordered him into a storeroom and abused him until dawn, then beat him and threatened to kill him if he complained to anyone. While looking for her son, Birgitte confronted the duke, was also beaten, and warned to send the boy away. If she said anything, she would be punished and lose her job.

'Has Daniel returned to his village?' asked Saint-Martin. 'I shall have to speak to him.'

Thérèse nodded and offered to take him there.

'The duke is still a suspect, sir,' said Georges, as the two men climbed up the stairs out of the basement.

'True, he would profit by his wife's death. But he couldn't have killed her himself. She was already dead by the time he ended his assault on the boy and his mother. He could have engaged someone else to kill her, a person familiar with the household's routine.'

The two men reached the ground floor and prepared to take leave of each other. 'For the present, Georges, I must further investigate the duke's assault on the boy. Thérèse will lead me to his home and I'll question him. You search the duke's rooms. We should find enough evidence to convict him of more crime. Then I'll ask Baron Breteuil to find space for him in a nearby royal prison.'

At the duke's apartment Jules Blondel opened the door for Georges, who quickly surveyed the small, sparsely furnished private rooms used for dining, sleeping, study, and visitors. An air of decay hung over the place. The wallpaper was stained and faded, the drapes mismatched. A narrow hallway connected the duke's apartment to his murdered wife's. They had shared a kitchen, a dining room, and a parlor.

Georges's search began in earnest in the study. Blondel was calm and helpful, unlocking drawers and cabinets, identifying works of art, opening account books, and so on. He explained that the Crown owned the art and the furnishings. The bulk of the duke's personal possessions consisted of a large wardrobe full of expensive clothing, shoes, and wigs. In a nearby cabinet were a few snuff boxes, watches, knives, and similar small objects of some value.

The account books, the wardrobe, and the cabinet confirmed what Georges already knew—the duke was a spendthrift, self-indulgent to the point of madness, but not patently criminal. They moved on to the bedroom, as ill-furnished as the others.

'Monsieur Blondel, are you aware that your master's sexual appetite included young boys as well as women?'

'I've not been concerned with that side of his life.'

'Does he have a secret cabinet?'

'Yes, I'll show you, but I've never been in it, and I don't have the key.'

Blondel led him to a locked door. Georges studied the lock. 'This won't be difficult.' With tools from his belt, he went to work and in a few minutes opened the door. He stepped inside a room lighted by two windows looking into a narrow, otherwise windowless courtyard. The walls of the room were covered with erotic pictures and shelves of books and devices of similar subject matter. Georges pried open the drawers of a chest-high cabinet and searched until he found the duke's journal. He skimmed several pages, then muttered to himself, 'This should cook his goose.'

The duke had kept a meticulous record of his sexual activity. There was much pedophilia, though mostly paid for rather than forced. Compared to early entries, the duke's recent handwriting had markedly deteriorated, further evidence of dementia. Georges snapped the journal shut. Colonel Saint-Martin would know what to do with it.

'This is what Georges found,' said Colonel Saint-Martin as he leaned across the table and handed Breteuil the duke's journal. The baron was in his office even on Sunday. Saint-Martin had just reported on Duc Henri's erratic behavior in Paris and his attack on the boy in the laundry. With help from Thérèse, the colonel had found the boy in a village near Versailles, verified his injuries, and brought back his statement.

As the baron grew absorbed in the reading, his naturally

58

florid color darkened, his lips curled in distaste. 'Duc Henri's a sick man, Paul, and dangerous as well. I've been concerned about him for some time. He used to escape notice, but now he's a public embarrassment. The Queen will not tolerate what he did to the laundry boy.'

'What are you going to do with him? Put him on trial? That's risky. The duke would claim the boy was willing.'

The baron laid down the journal. 'We shall have to put him in a royal prison immediately and hold his assets in trust. You will have access to him if needed. I'll ask the King for a *lettre de cachet*.' He glanced at Paul, whom he knew disapproved of secret arrests. 'As you say, Paul, a trial might prove inconclusive. It would also take months and taint the Court with scandal. In the meantime, Duc Henri could ruin a dozen boys and waste his wife's inheritance.'

On this occasion Paul had to swallow his principles. He couldn't think of a better plan than the baron's. 'Can you do something for his victim?'

'I'll send a doctor. If the boy's well enough, we'll bring him back and find something for him to do. He should feel safe with the duke in prison.' The baron cocked his head. 'How far have you come, Paul, in the investigation of Aimée de Saumur's death?'

'As of now, Duc Henri is a strong suspect. He might have hired someone to kill his wife.' Paul went on to report the evidence pointing to Jules Blondel and Richard de Beauregard. They had motive and opportunity.

'I must warn you, Paul, the Queen is in a very anxious frame of mind, her daughter dying, her favorite lady-in-waiting murdered. After Mass this morning she inquired again, spoke sharply. I said the investigation was proceeding, but I had nothing else to report. "Get on with it," she exclaimed.' He shook his head. 'Time is running out.'

'Unfortunately, I have encountered a major obstacle. Yesterday, while visiting Denise de Villers in prison, Anne and Marie discovered that the provost may not be an impartial judge in the maid's case.' He recounted the incident in which Sully lost his porcelain teeth. 'I fear that he has seized upon this case as an opportunity for revenge.'

'I recall the broken teeth and how disturbed he was at the time. An accident, he called it. He never mentioned the maid. If confronted now, he would deny any wrongdoing. Without proof, I cannot ask the King to take him off the case. It's in his jurisdiction, and he would fight to keep it.' The baron paused, lowered his voice. 'Remember, Paul, over the years Sully has built up powerful support in the palace. Even those who hate him, fear him.'

CHAPTER NINE

The Scent of Conspiracy

Sunday afternoon, June 3

'This should suit us,' remarked Comtesse Marie politely, as Marthe Bourdon showed them through the apartment's private dining room and its salon.

Anne nodded in tentative agreement. The new accommodations were spacious, luxurious, but hardly congenial. The tormented spirit of the murdered duchess seemed to hover over them. Anne also felt apprehensive. The servants were potential suspects of murder. If one were guilty and feared being found out, he could become desperate. God only knew what might happen. That Paul and Georges would be in Saumur's rooms made her feel a little more secure.

The tour of the apartment ended in the bedroom. While the countess inspected the windows, the furniture, the walls, and the ceiling with a searching eye, Anne stared at the floor, imagining blood spots there, though she saw it had been thoroughly cleaned.

Baron Breteuil and Marie had decided that the apartments of the duke and the late duchess were more suitable than any other rooms at his disposal. They stood empty since the duke's sudden departure. Only the cook, the housekeeper, the steward,

60

and a few maids remained to assist the new temporary residents.

Marie had suggested to the baron that the investigation might even benefit by her living at the scene of the crime. The provost's earlier search did not inspire confidence, given his enmity toward the deaf maid. He would have looked chiefly for whatever implicated her. Marie and Anne would dig for evidence that might have been missed or ignored and keep an eye on Madame Bourdon and Jules Blondel while they sorted royal from private property.

The countess gave Anne a final, questioning glance. 'Do you find the apartment suitable?'

Anne put aside her mental reservations. 'Yes, I see opportunities for our investigation.'

'Marthe,' the countess continued, 'we shall move in tomorrow afternoon. Lay out fresh linen, towels, and the like. Leave everything else as it is.'

Madame Bourdon promised that she would have the rooms ready. Footmen would bring their trunks up from the courtyard. With a slight curtsey she left the two ladies and returned to the kitchen.

When Marthe's retreating steps disappeared, the countess turned to Anne. 'What do you make of our housekeeper?'

'Frosty! Her face wore the mask of a proper servant, but her eyes couldn't conceal her displeasure. She may have thought that the baron's installing us here was indecent, disrespectful to the dead duchess. Madame Bourdon appears to have a keen sense of what is proper.'

The countess nodded. 'Breteuil's brusque manner *could* offend people who think that a dead person's home, as well as her kinsmen, should go into mourning—be draped in black and left empty for a decent period. But the home of the duke and duchess was in the Loire valley. This is the King's home, they were merely his guests. We will also be staying here at his royal pleasure.'

She pointed to the bed. 'I'll sleep there. Madame Bourdon will set up a proper bed for you.'

Anne shook her head. 'I prefer to use the deaf maid's room, sleep in her bed, follow her routine. I can better understand her and the people she worked with.' At first, it annoyed Anne to see how easily Comtesse Marie claimed the role as well as the bed of the murdered duchess, mistress of this place. In the next instant, Anne felt ashamed that she could be annoyed by one of her best, most generous friends.

They were ready to leave when Georges and Paul arrived. 'A *fête champêtre*, a party is about to begin in the palace garden,' Paul announced. 'Would you join us? I've been told that Chevalier Richard de Beauregard will be there.'

The two women glanced at their clothes. Both were wearing pastel silk gowns suitable for a garden party, pink for the countess, blue for Anne. They had also brought along broad-rimmed hats and matching pastel parasols to ward off the sun.

'Yes, I believe we can manage,' the countess replied.

On the way to the garden Paul recounted his meeting with the baron and the imprisonment of Duc Henri. 'He remains a suspect, since he could have arranged the murder. However, that would have required planning, and an accomplice familiar with the maid's routine. The duke's muddled mind might not be up to the task. Among other suspects, Beauregard ranks first. He gave a false statement to the provost and has tried to persuade Hoche and his companion to lie for him.'

The *fête* was in Apollo's grove to the north of the Latona Fountain, a short walk from the palace. Dozens of courtiers had already gathered and more were trickling in. Servants were opening baskets and laying out food and drink on linen-covered, shaded tables.

The grove had recently been transformed into a picturesque landscape with artfully planted trees and shrubs. Anne was reminded of English gardens she knew, most recently Combe Park near Bath. At the center of a sculpted marble group the god Apollo reclined on the shore of a shallow pond. Nude nymphs attended him. To the left and right, sea monsters with the heads of bearded men groomed his horses. Behind him was a grotto carved into a massive rocky formation. In the grassy areas under spindly young trees, silk-clad men and women, pampered by their servants, drew close to nature. A few were playing blind man's buff.

The baron had provided Paul with an invitation for himself

and his guests. They began to mingle with the others. Comtesse Marie recognized an old acquaintance and introduced her companions. Anne's connection to the Institute for the Deaf served to start a conversation. It soon touched upon the deaf maid accused of murdering Duchesse Aimée.

'Do you have an opinion on the matter?' the countess asked her acquaintance.

'Indeed I do,' she replied with heat. 'The maid must have done it. Who else?' The woman seemed oblivious to the servants nearby preparing her food. 'Servants would gladly cut our throats if they thought they could get away with it. I'm most pleased the provost intends to be firm in this case.'

The conversation wandered to less contentious topics before returning to the unfortunate Duchesse Aimée. 'I understand,' Comtesse Marie said tentatively, 'that she had involved herself with the Chevalier de Beauregard.'

That was enough to enthuse the acquaintance. 'She was supposed to advance him in the Queen's favor, hardly an unusual aspiration among young men at court. He wanted especially to attend to the dauphin and his brother and took every opportunity to play with them. I believe they liked him. He's a high-spirited and charming young man, adept at inventing games. But, a few days ago, he and the duchess had a falling-out, as she usually did with her young men. Beauregard was suddenly dismissed.' She shook her head at what seemed irrational behavior. 'Oh, there he is.' A welcoming smile flashed on her face. 'I'll present him to you.'

He bowed to each of the women, but favored Anne with a sensual wink. His beauty was truly extraordinary: clear skin, perfect white teeth, black wavy hair, long black eyelashes, regular features, and a well-shaped body. A French Adonis, Anne thought. And so he thought of himself, for he walked with a preening step. Even the small scar on his chin, a mark of honor from a duel, seemed to add to his beauty.

He spoke briefly with the women, then moved on to a group of young men his own age. They seemed cool toward him and drifted away. For a moment he found himself alone. Paul and Georges hastened to his side.

'We have a few questions to ask, Chevalier de Beauregard.'

Paul showed his authority from the baron. 'Please come with us to a more private place.' Beauregard seemed stunned, but he followed the colonel, while Georges brought up the rear. They found an isolated bench and sat down. Georges stood off to one side with his notebook.

'Monsieur,' the colonel began, 'how would you describe your relationship with Duchesse Aimée de Saumur on the eve of her death?'

'We had parted, like friends.'

'Had she found another lover?'

'No. She had merely grown tired of me.'

'Were you angry that she hadn't advanced you in the Queen's favor?'

'Disappointed, not angry. She did what she could. The Crown is cutting back on expenses.'

Saint-Martin looked the young man in the eye. 'You gave a false statement to the provost. We have learned that you didn't spend early Friday morning with Monsieur Hoche or his associate. Where were you when Duchesse Aimée was being murdered?'

The young man stumbled, grasping for words. 'I was in my room fast asleep. The provost's questions caught me unawares. Aimée's death had shocked me and I had no alibi. I answered hastily, misled him.'

'We have also learned that you went to her room shortly before dawn.'

Beauregard hesitated, clearly wondering if Saint-Martin was bluffing. 'Whoever informed you must have been mistaken.'

'I don't think so. But that will be all for now. I shall have more questions later.'

Saint-Martin and Georges watched the chevalier as he strolled back to the *fête*. 'We'll have to dig a little deeper, Georges. Search his room while he's engaged here.'

Georges found the chevalier's room on the palace's top floor off a drab, narrow hallway. No one was moving about. In less than a minute, Georges picked the lock, stepped into the room, and locked the door behind him. The room was dingy, cramped, hot and stuffy. A single small window open to an air shaft admitted meager light. Georges searched vainly thr small chest of drawers and the mattress. He could fi secret compartment under the floor or behind the walls scanned a shelf of books above a simple writing table. As he expected, a worn copy of Choderlos de Laclos's *Les Liaisons Dangereuses*, a popular tale of seduction, was among them.

While Georges was fanning its pages, a note fell out, unsigned and undated. Georges guessed Hoche had recently sent it. Beauregard was being summoned to a meeting in the Palais-Royal last Thursday, May 31, at six in the evening. A friend would meet him at the servants' entrance and lead him to the room. He was to bring along his discovery.

What discovery? Georges wondered. A sheet of used blotting paper lay on the table. He held it up to a mirror and attempted to make sense of the jumble of words. Most were too faint. But a few were clear enough and caught his eye: 'MA . . . Comte Fersen . . . rooms' were close together on the same line and had been emphatically written, then carefully blotted. Axel von Fersen, the Queen's handsome friend, a Swedish military officer in French service, often came to the palace from his frontier garrison. What exactly had fascinated Beauregard?

This had the smell of a conspiracy, thought Georges. What could be its aim? Was it related somehow to the death of the Duchesse de Saumur? The answers to those questions were in Paris, hidden in the vast, rambling palace of the Duc d'Orléans, like needles in a haystack.

Back at the *fête*, the countess introduced Anne to a few more acquaintances. Out of respect for the countess, they spoke to Anne politely. But their eyes flickered with curiosity—because of her morganatic marriage to Paul, she supposed. And, she was also English and Protestant. Later, there would be much tongue-wagging about her.

And about the countess herself. Her acquaintances in the palace surely regarded her as eccentric, for she lacked their servility to social convention. As she moved through the crowd, she drew the conversation away from common gossip and veiled backbiting to the 'mysterious murder' of the Duchesse

Aimée. Could someone other than the deaf maid have done it? she repeatedly asked.

The courtiers were content to leave the matter in the provost's hands. The maid's fate didn't trouble them in the least. Their attitude became so depressing that Anne and Marie left the crowd.

They were walking along the shore of the pond when a young woman came toward them without an escort. Comely and bright-looking, dressed in a simple yellow silk gown covered by an apron, she had to be one of the maids serving food to the guests. Her eyes darted toward the crowd gathered around the tables in the distance. Her lips worked nervously.

'Comtesse, I overheard you ask who really killed Duchesse Aimée.' She lowered her voice. 'Her lover Richard de Beauregard could have done it.'

'Oh!' The countess raised an eyebrow. 'He claims he was in his room all the time.'

'He lies,' said the young woman with asperity. 'Between three and four o'clock that morning I was working in a linen closet in the light of a small lantern. The Queen's daughter Sophie had been ill during the night and needed fresh bedding. Across the hall was the door to the private stairway from the duchess's bedchamber. Suddenly, I heard someone coming down the stairs. I doused the light and watched through a crack in the closet door. The chevalier stepped out into the hall, looked left and right, then hurried away. That was about the time the duchess must have died.'

'How well do you know Beauregard? I thought the private stairs were a secret.'

'He used to dally with me. I heard him boast to one of his friends about the stairs and about how he used them for trysts with the duchess. I didn't believe him at first, but then I searched in the hallway and found the stairs myself.'

'That friend of his, could you describe him?' Anne asked.

'Short, fat, maybe fifty years old. Had a stubby nose, a small mouth.'

Anne exchanged glances with the countess. Victor Hoche, the Duc d'Orléans's man.

With some reluctance the young woman gave her name, Catherine, and said she was a maid in Princesse Lamballe's household. The countess thanked her and agreed to use this information very carefully.

As Catherine slipped away, Anne observed, 'I don't fully trust that girl. She's been bruised by Beauregard and may be getting even.'

At supper in Comtesse Marie's town house on Rue Traversine, Anne and her friends gathered for discussion around a dining-room table, Marie at one end, Paul at the other. Georges and Anne, Sylvie and Michou, sat opposite each other. Gilded sconces threw a lively golden light on their earnest faces, as they shared the day's experiences. A bounty of bread, wine, pâté, fruit, and cheese lay before them, but the atmosphere in the room was more like a council of war than a feast.

Anne observed an amazing transformation in the countess. For more than a decade, this elegant great lady had lived apart from polite, fashionable society. She found her personal satisfaction in managing her estate at Beaumont, in philanthropic work for Abbé de l'Épée, and in the company of a few select friends. Through correspondence and occasional visits, she had kept just enough contact with acquaintances at the Palais-Royal and Versailles to know what was going on. Her Latin motto, she had told Anne, was *'bene vivit qui bene latuit'*, meaning, 'she lives well who has hidden well'.

But, since yesterday, Denise de Villers's cause had deeply stirred the countess and brought high color to her cheeks. Her once cool gray eyes now glowed with passion. Her speech had an urgent tone. She was prepared to devote her considerable resources to reaching the truth.

Anne caught Paul's eye in a moment of shared understanding. He too had been watching his aunt with a mixture of awe and pleasure. She had generously taken on a disagreeable and thankless task at the palace.

After servants had cleared the table, Paul lifted his voice to gain everyone's attention. 'Anne and Comtesse Marie have heard from Catherine, a maid in Princesse Lamballe's household. She has placed Richard de Beauregard close to the

Duchesse de Saumur at the time of the murder. However, the young woman may lack credibility.'

The countess glanced toward Anne. 'Tomorrow, after moving into our rooms at the palace, we shall call on the princess and learn more about Catherine.'

'Now, concerning Beauregard,' Georges remarked. 'I can assure you he lives like a pauper. He must have hoped to get money either from the Queen or from her enemies. Hoche would be willing to pay well for a scandal that he could feed to the journalist Gaillard.'

'Not common gossip,' Paul added, 'but convincing evidence of secret wrongdoing.'

Anne grew curious. 'Paul, what kind of secrets are you hinting at? Surely not the military or political kind. Hoche works for the Duc d'Orléans, not for a foreign power.'

'Personal secrets,' Paul replied. 'Beauregard hoped to observe the Queen at private, even intimate moments.'

'With Comte Axel von Fersen?' asked Georges, an insinuation in his voice.

'I should think so,' replied Paul. 'I believe we understand the likely direction of Hoche's mind.' He paused for a moment. 'We have to determine if Beauregard killed the duchess as part of a conspiracy involving the Palais-Royal.'

'Could she have discovered his intention?' Anne asked. 'Threatened to expose him and his companions? If so, she may have sealed her death warrant.'

'Possibly,' Paul replied.

Sylvie spoke up. 'Couldn't the police search Hoche's rooms for evidence?'

Paul shook his head. 'The police of Paris may not enter the duke's palace, much less search in it.'

Thus far, Michou had followed the discussion with help from Anne and Sylvie. Now, she raised her hand, caught the attention of the others, and began signing to Anne. 'Sylvie and I could seek permission from Monsieur Hoche to sketch in the duke's picture galleries. I could offer to paint a miniature portrait of him. He's vain and would probably accept. While he sat for me, Sylvie could search his rooms.'

Anne thought the suggestion had merit and encouraged

Michou with a smile. 'You could sketch in the galleries, alert for opportunities to spy on him. But searching his rooms requires skill and experience.'

'A task for Georges,' Paul added. 'Conspirators as clever as Hoche are cautious and well protected.'

CHAPTER TEN

A Kind Young Man

Monday, June 4

At nine in the morning, the two women approached the duke's palace in the Palais-Royal. Sylvie felt her heart begin to pound. Her strength and courage were about to be tested. To outward appearances, she and Michou were going to sketch paintings in Monsieur Hoche's care. In fact, they would attempt to uncover his secret dealings with the Chevalier de Beauregard.

Last night at supper, Michou had proposed the idea. Sylvie had embraced it and was now taking the lead. Was she foolish for trying? Young and inexperienced, she was unsure of her own ability. She also felt fragile, as if she would fall apart at the first challenge. The high stakes of this mission fueled her anxiety. At issue was the life of Denise de Villers.

Once inside the palace, Sylvie and Michou made their way to Hoche's office. Comtesse Marie had armed Sylvie with a note explaining she was a young woman of noble birth and the countess's goddaughter. Her deaf companion, Michelline de Saint-Esprit, was a talented artist and the countess's protégé. Would Monsieur Hoche please allow them to sketch in the galleries at appropriate hours?

It had not been easy to walk through the palace. Footmen in the duke's livery had stopped them again and again. Sylvie understood the need for this caution. The palace was only a few steps south of the shopping arcades and the garden, where

69

every kind of knavery took place. Thieves and prostitutes would gladly ply their trade in the palace if they could.

In a pale-red patterned silk gown, her hair brushed up and lightly powdered, Sylvie had made a conscious effort to recover the ingrained self-assurance of her class. Since infancy she had been groomed to be the wife of a count or duke. Captain Fitzroy's assault on her had cruelly shattered that prospect. Malicious rumors had echoed the captain's claim, she had been willing enough and her godfather Baron Breteuil had beaten her. No suitable man of her class would marry such a tainted woman!

For months, life had not seemed worth living, and she had tried to end it. Then, she encountered Michou. Deaf from birth, a foundling, she was familiar with rejection, had overcome it, and had become wise and compassionate. She reached out to Sylvie, became a friend.

The two women discovered ways to share their talents. Sylvie improved Michou's slender ability to read. In return, she helped Sylvie experience the joys of an artist's eye. Their friendship had given her life a new direction. The trappings of nobility no longer meant much to her. But they must matter to Monsieur Hoche. So, she walked through the great rooms, tall and erect, and persuaded herself she belonged in a duke's palace.

She glanced at her companion. Michou could never be more than a commoner, and her petite figure was easily overlooked in a crowd. But any perceptive observer would detect the intelligence in her large green eyes. Formerly shy and timid, she had gained confidence since entering the Institute for the Deaf and receiving recognition for her miniature portraits.

She also dressed smartly. For this occasion she wore a neatly fitted yellow silk gown and had gathered up her glossy auburn hair in a stylish chignon. She carried her sketch pad, pencils, and other tools of her art in a black leather portfolio. Haughty footmen in livery no longer intimidated her.

Hoche's office was near the center of the palace, where the duke had recently moved his art collection. The former galleries in the west wing had been demolished to make way for a great new theater, La Comédie-Française. Amidst the resulting confusion Hoche would be a harried man and should be approached tactfully. Sylvie had learned that he held a modest position in the palace hierarchy, assistant to the collection's director, an elderly courtier who expected him to do all the work.

'Yes? What do you want?' Hoche looked up crossly as the two women were shown into his office. He was sitting at a cluttered table with his back to a window. Shelves of file boxes covered the walls. A young man stood at a tall desk off to one side, pen in hand. He glanced at the women, then returned to his work. Sylvie recognized him from casual meetings in the garden of the Palais-Royal. They had exchanged smiles, but she didn't know his name.

Sylvie handed Hoche the countess's note. As he read it, the irritation on his face vanished, replaced by favorable regard toward the young aristocratic woman before him. He waved the two women to seats, then threw a questioning glance at Michou.

'My companion is deaf—as the note says. I must interpret for her when lip-reading becomes difficult. She has a remarkable gift for miniature portraits.' Sylvie handed Hoche one of herself. 'She recently painted it.'

He held the miniature up to gain a good light, gazed at the image for a few moments, then at Sylvie. His eyes shone with delight. 'As good as any I've seen.' He passed the miniature to his clerk. 'André's an artist too, paints portraits.' The clerk also studied the miniature and compared its image with Sylvie. His eyes lingered, feasting on her.

Hoche gave him a withering glance. The young man handed the portrait back to her, stealing a quick last look, and returned to his copying.

Sylvie went on to explain Michou's wish to sketch when the galleries were empty. 'I can promise you exquisite results.' She nodded to Michou, who drew a sketch from her portfolio and handed it to Hoche. 'Diana the Huntress,' Sylvie remarked, 'with me posing as the goddess.'

Hoche leaned back, cocked his head, studied the sketch with interest. After a while, he inspected Sylvie more closely, appearing to recall something about her. His eyes sparkled, grew wanton, as if teased by lecherous fantasies.

71

Swine, she thought. His disrespect triggered a rush of anger. Painful, sordid images of Captain Fitzroy's assault crowded into her mind. Hoche must have heard scurrilous tales of that event and thought of her as an easy mark.

She struggled to maintain her poise, pretended to be indifferent to his opinion of her. Fortunately, she also sensed that she had power over him. Her nerves steadied, her confidence returned. He could be used in the investigation.

'I'm intrigued by your little friend's talent,' Hoche finally said. 'I might buy some of her work. Come to the servants' entrance on the ground floor. Mornings are best . . . at nine. Show the doorman this pass and he will let you in.' He scribbled a note, signed it with a flourish, and handed it to Sylvie. 'You may go directly to the galleries and work until they become crowded.' He rose from behind the table, escorted the women to the door, and beckoned his clerk. 'André will show you through the collection.' With an enigmatic smile Hoche pressed Sylvie's hand, bowed, and sent them off.

'I'll soon see more of that man than I've bargained for,' Sylvie signed to Michou as they walked toward the galleries.

'Don't worry,' Michou replied. 'You're strong. Vanity has crippled him.'

During their meeting with Monsieur Hoche, Michou had paid more attention to his clerk than to Hoche himself. André was a slim, dark, presentable man about thirty and clearly unhappy. His shoulders bent in resignation, his clothes were shabby. Hoche was neither a kind nor an understanding master and probably paid poorly.

In the galleries, the clerk's eyes brightened. He held his head high and walked with a confident step. Dutoit, he announced, was his family name.

He came alongside Sylvie, who was translating for Michou. 'I'm thinking of a painting which might catch your fancy.' He touched her arm. 'It's this one.' They stopped at an idyllic landscape radiant with clear, silvery daylight.

'*The Three Ages of Man*,' he said. 'An allegory of life, by the Venetian painter, Titian. It's read this way.' He pointed to the right foreground, where dormant nature awaited spring

72

sunshine and rain. Two naked sleeping babies were curled up in each other's arms like puppies in a litter. A winged chubby infant cupid rudely climbed over them, gazing down, his hands touching the tall trunk of a branchless tree. Two small withered plants stood forlorn in the brown stony ground.

In the left foreground, a muscular, suntanned nude young man sat on the grassy ground beneath lush green foliage. His long black hair fell in wavy locks over the side of his handsome face. He rested his left arm on the shoulder of a beautiful fair-skinned young woman in a crimson gown sitting opposite him. A band of flowers graced her light blonde hair. A gauzy white scarf hung loosely over her shoulders. She leaned across his legs, a reed flute in each hand. Her tune still lingered in the air. They looked deeply into each other's eyes, as if entranced.

André turned to Sylvie. 'Young lovers in springtime, don't you think?'

She signed the question for Michou but didn't reply, just stared at the young couple.

André drew the women up close to observe a detail in the painting's middle ground. 'And here's how it ends.' A bearded old man sat staring down at a skull in his right hand. Another skull lay at his left side. 'Love, like life,' André intoned, 'slips through our fingers.'

Michou grimaced. A melancholy thought. She wasn't sure it was true. To her a love-filled life seemed somehow eternal. But, whatever its message, the picture was beautifully painted. On another day she would study it closely.

Then she glanced at Sylvie. At first the picture had seemed to engross her. Now she shuddered and turned away from André. Her back stiffened, her breath came in short gasps, her face worked as if she were fighting back tears. 'I'll sketch the girl,' she managed to say, avoiding his eyes.

Puzzled, he stepped back and stared at her. Slowly an awareness came over his face. He met Michou's gaze. Sadness and regret filled his eyes. He knew about Fitzroy's assault and realized the picture had triggered painful feelings of lost innocence.

'*Je suis désolé*,' he said softly to Michou, articulating clearly for her. She read his lips. He seemed stricken with remorse. Michou concealed her own concern—her friend's emotional health was so frail. She had barely recovered from her attempted suicide. For several minutes, Michou carefully watched Sylvie, who bent forward studying the picture, a sketch pad in her hand. Finally, she began drawing. With a few gestures Michou told André that the young woman's mind was now occupied. She would be all right.

He breathed a sigh of relief and led Michou further into the gallery. She inspected several paintings before settling on a portrait of an elderly pope seated in an ornate chair.

'Clement VII,' André remarked. 'They say Titian also painted this one, but I'm not sure.' He went on with an explanation that Michou could hardly follow. She could see for herself that the pope looked timid and frightened. Apparently, a monk called Luther had stirred up trouble in the church. War broke out and the pope was on the losing side. He had to watch while enemy soldiers looted Rome for eight days.

Michou studied the pope's face. Long nose, deep-set, cunning eyes. A worrier. Also a weak, faithless, cruel man. An intriguing subject. Like a theater manager she had worked for a few years ago.

She gestured to André, 'I'd like to sketch him.'

'You might as well get started.'

The three of them were alone in the gallery. André found small wooden chairs, lingered near Sylvie for a moment, but realized she still wanted to be left to herself. Finally, he rejoined Michou.

She sensed him bending over her as she sketched, felt the warmth of his body. He studied her work, nodding with approval. After several minutes, he smiled wryly and pretended to slash his throat. 'Monsieur Hoche expects me back in the office.' He bowed to the women and left.

Michou glanced over her shoulder to make sure they were now alone, then showed Sylvie a page in her small sketchbook. André was there in fast, light pencil strokes, standing chained to his desk, sweat dripping from his face. 'I studied him while you spoke with Monsieur Hoche. The young man doesn't like his master but is obliged to hide

74

it. He also has an eye for you. He's our man, the key to Hoche's secrets.'

Sylvie blushed a little. 'I was rude to Monsieur Dutoit. Couldn't help it.' Her eyes began to fill with tears.

'He's a kind man,' Michou signed. 'I believe he understands.'

Sylvie nodded thoughtfully. 'Yes, he can be of use to us. As Hoche's personal clerk, he may know where private papers are kept and have overheard conversations between Hoche and the Chevalier de Beauregard.'

'But,' Michou asked, 'how can we persuade him to spy on his master? He would run a great risk.'

CHAPTER ELEVEN

The Queen's Enemy

Monday, June 4

Wisps of an early-morning mist hung over Colonel Saint-Martin's garden. He and Georges were having breakfast outdoors near a terrace of rose bushes in full bloom. Fine beads of moisture clung to the petals and glistened in the sun's slanting rays. Georges caught himself taking notice of this jewel-like beauty. Nature's wonders often escaped him. Too restless. He was always in motion.

A servant brought fresh coffee. Georges poured for himself and the colonel sitting opposite—silent, eyes cast down, arms folded on his chest. Resting? Thinking, more likely. The man had a great deal on his mind. A murdered duchess. A rejected lover and his confederates. A demented duke and his valet. An ambitious deaf maid. Other suspects as yet unknown.

Birds twittered in the branches of the tree above. The rhythmic clip-clop of horses' hooves in the distance worked hypnotically. Georges nearly dozed off. The colonel stirred, looked up.

'Have you solved the case yet, sir?' Georges tilted his head skeptically.

His superior smiled, indulging Georges's ironic brand of humor. 'Not quite,' he replied. 'Yesterday, we learned that Richard de Beauregard might have conspired with a pair of dubious characters to exploit his intimacy with the victim. He may also have been observed near the scene of the crime.'

Georges added, 'Something went wrong. He quarreled with the duchess and hit her.'

The colonel shrugged. 'One plausible scenario among others. We must find proof.' He raised the cup to his mouth and drained the coffee. 'This morning, Georges, I want you to visit the Criminal Investigation Department on Rue des Capucines. Find out what they know about Beauregard's associates, Hoche and Gaillard. I have official business here in the office.'

A few minutes later, Georges was on his way. In the middle of Place Vendôme, he paused and tipped his hat in mock reverence to the colossal bronze statue of Louis XIV astride his horse, high atop a tall pedestal. Clad in the garb of a Roman emperor, he stretched out his right arm in an imperial gesture over the people. For years, this image of the Sun King had festered in the back of Georges's mind, ever since he first walked through this elegant square.

'Sire,' murmured Georges, staring up at the haughty monarch. 'I must give you credit. For decades, you sucked the lifeblood out of your people to wage war and build grand palaces. Your own glory was all you cared for. But, here you are, honored by them like a demi-god. They should have whipped, pilloried, and hanged you.'

Throughout this tirade the King remained silent, aloof. Georges shook his head and moved on, turning his thoughts to his mission. From his pocket he drew a copy of Baron Breteuil's instruction to the Paris police. They were to help gather information pertaining to the murder of the Duchesse de Saumur. Georges felt encouraged. He briskly walked the remaining short distance to the Hôtel de Police.

Inside, a clerk directed him to Inspecteur Quidor's office. While waiting outside, Georges recalled his old acquaintance.

Years ago, they had worked together for Lieutenant-General Sartine, the past master of criminal investigation. Georges eventually joined the Royal Highway Patrol.

Quidor remained with the Paris police, purchased the post of inspector, and prospered. Most recently, he had led the far-flung pursuit of the thieves of the Queen's necklace. Despite spending much money and time, he had not recovered the jewels, and the principal culprits were still at large. Georges valued Quidor despite his failure. He really knew criminal Paris. That could be helpful in the Saumur case.

The door opened and Quidor emerged, short, burly, pug-faced.

'Charpentier! Good to see you. Come in.'

The two men shook hands and drew chairs up to a dirty window overlooking a dull interior courtyard. There was nowhere else to sit in the small room. File boxes filled the shelves from ceiling to floor. Piles of loose paper rose danger-ously on the inspector's desk. Georges declined a glass of wine and went directly to the point.

'Monsieur, are you acquainted with a certain Hercule Gaillard, a journalist?'

Quidor's eyes rolled upward. '*Frondeur*, slander-monger, and extortionist. In fact he lives in my district near the Louvre. Once, years ago, I put him in the Bastille. I wish it were his permanent address. Unfortunately, he has learned from his mistakes and engages others for his dirty work. It's hard to pin a crime on him.'

'We may have to try. He's probably an accomplice in the murder of the Duchesse de Saumur.' Georges described Gaillard's connections with the chief suspect, Richard de Beauregard.

Quidor frowned. 'Gaillard may have departed from his usual manner of operating. To the best of my knowledge he has not been involved in murder before. But there's always the first time.' He looked askance at Georges. 'I've heard from Baron Breteuil. We're supposed to be helpful. What would you like me to do?'

Georges handed him a file. 'This is what we know about the duchess's servants and acquaintances who had opportunity to kill her. I'd like your agents to check their prison or court records, previous employment, and anything else that might yield a motive for murder. And put your best spy on Gaillard for a few days, like a flea on a dog's back. I need to know his routine, his vices, and the people he meets.'

The inspector held up the file and breathed out a sigh. 'It won't be easy. You're casting a wide net. The Crown's financial crisis is drying up my money. Tracking Gaillard will be expensive. Good spies are scarce.' He shook his head. 'The baron expects too much of us.'

Georges hesitated, stroking his bald pate. He understood that Quidor was bargaining. 'This matter lies close to the Queen's heart. The baron must take it seriously. He'll be thankful when it's resolved.'

'Of course,' muttered Quidor, sounding unconvinced. 'But I'll help you as a favor. I may call upon you someday.' He rubbed his chin, smiled a little. 'I can tell you already that Gaillard frequents Café Marcel on the Boulevard.'

'I'm in your debt, monsieur. I know the place and shall go there for a personal impression of the rogue. And what can you tell me about Victor Hoche who works for the Duc d'Orléans?'

'Hoche lives in the duke's palace out of our reach. He's a vain, sensual man, frequent patron of expensive restaurants and luxurious brothels. Lives beyond his means. We'd like to know how he does it. I learned just before you arrived that he will be at Madame Lebrun's brothel tonight, presenting a *tableau vivant*. Something piquant, I'm sure.'

'You've been helpful. This is a step forward. Thanks.'

'Anything for a friend.' Quidor patted Georges on the shoulder and walked him to the door. 'In a few days I'll have more for you.'

'By the way,' Georges asked. 'Do you know the provost's agent, Jacques Bart?'

Quidor nodded. 'A decent fellow. I saw him Saturday afternoon, coming out of Madame Bouffant's millinery shop in the Palais-Royal. "Business or pleasure?" I asked him, because of the pretty shopgirls inside. "Business," he growled and glanced back at the shop. That's odd, I thought, he's unhappy about something.'

Georges tucked that morsel into his memory, thanked his colleague, then rose from the table.

'Before you leave, would you like to look at our files on Hoche and Gaillard?'

'Surely.'

'Follow me.' Quidor led him into a room with a long work table. A clerk brought in boxes of files. For a couple of hours Georges scanned reports from police agents, transcripts of intercepted letters—some of them to foreign addresses—copies of business records and expenses.

Hoche's files were thin and unremarkable, except for his financial history. The man did spend beyond his means. Georges took note of the brothel that Hoche seemed to prefer. Madame Lebrun informed regularly for Quidor. Georges wondered if she might be persuaded also to work for him.

The files labeled *Gaillard* were the heaviest and most promising. Georges fingered rapidly through the materials that had sent the journalist to the Bastille. The word *'frondeur'*, or troublemaker, appeared frequently in the quarrel between the Crown and the Paris Parlement. During the last years of Louis XV's reign, Gaillard had openly supported the magistrates' right to veto the Crown's legislation if it violated the kingdom's traditional constitution. They were exiled to the countryside; he was imprisoned.

When he emerged from the Bastille early in the next reign, he turned away from politics. His writing, usually anonymous, dwelt on scandals, either financial or sexual. Rumors about the Queen's immorality figured prominently. She was the 'Austrian whore'. A few files contained complaints from prominent people who claimed Gaillard had tried to extort money from them.

A renewed interest in political issues appeared in several recent anonymous broadsheets and books attributed to him, often written or published abroad. At first he seemed cynically detached from the institutions he criticized or the persons he vilified. More recently, his attacks, those aimed at Marie Antoinette in particular, reeked of personal hatred.

Georges closed the files and leaned back, hands clasped behind his head. Had he come any closer to linking Gaillard with the death of Duchesse Aimée? Perhaps. It was easier now to imagine the journalist and his confederates using the unwitting duchess in order to ruin the Queen's reputation. Aimée might have uncovered the plot and threatened to expose it. Perhaps the conspirators had ordered Beauregard to kill her.

In the ground-floor office on Rue Saint-Honoré, Colonel Saint-Martin looked up from his desk. He heard Georges's voice, then his steps in the hall. Finally, the adjutant bustled in.

'Colonel, you'll have to don civilian clothes.' Georges paused to register the effect of his impertinence. Saint-Martin dutifully raised an eyebrow.

His adjutant smiled. 'Inspecteur Quidor told me that Gaillard will soon be at Café Marcel for a late-morning drink. I think we should observe him . . . unawares. You'll have to do without your sword and fancy suit. Just pretend you're bourgeois, my business partner from Rouen.'

Saint-Martin rarely objected to this teasing, a good anti-dote to the blind pride that afflicted so many in the privileged classes. And he liked the idea of playing the spy, a hidden vantage point for studying a suspect. Even the Emperor Joseph went about Vienna incognito, the better to observe his own people.

'You will be proud of me, Georges. I'll borrow clothes from one of the servants.'

An hour later, dressed in plain brown suits, the two men reached Café Marcel. Georges seemed a little anxious, probably still concerned that his colonel would stand out despite the disguise. Working with Georges, however, had taught him bourgeois mannerisms and speech. He was confident he could act the part.

They found a side table in the bar room close to a rack of newspapers. Once seated, Saint-Martin felt comfortable, even though this was his first visit to the place. He nodded to Georges who took the lead and ordered tea from a waiter passing by.

'Who comes here?' Saint-Martin asked, surveying the crowd.

80

'During the day,' Georges replied, 'you'll see mostly businessmen. Many are connected to the nearby concern that produces a famous painted paper for the rooms of luxurious homes. In the evening, fashionable men and women come from the Théâtre des Italiens.'

By noon, middle-aged men in grey, black or brown suits had almost filled the café. They sat at small tables close together, reading newspapers or conversing freely. Saint-Martin overheard their talk about prices, markets, wages, rates of exchange, bankruptcies, and the like. He groaned inwardly at their obsession with money. Their voices, gestures, and facial expressions lacked any grace or wit, any flights of imagination or intellect, any concern for the common good. Or for honor.

Saint-Martin felt his gall rising. These cunning tricksters would as soon cheat a customer or defraud a partner as look at him. Calm down, the colonel told himself, sensing a prejudice was carrying him away. He hoped his sentiments didn't show on his face.

He and Georges were drinking tea and reading newspapers when Gaillard arrived. He was a slope-shouldered, middle-aged man. His clothes were shabby, his pockets stuffed with papers. For a few moments, his eyes darted about the room, taking it all in. Reassured by what he saw, he walked with a curious shuffling gait to the rack of newspapers, picked out a few and sat down at a table with two acquaintances who also had newspapers before them.

They read avidly with pauses for sips of brandy, brief remarks to one another, and trips to the rack for more to read.

Saint-Martin leaned toward Georges and whispered softly, 'Find out what intrigues them so much.'

When Gaillard returned a paper and reached for another, Georges approached the rack in his best good-natured manner. 'What's the news today?'

'English and Dutch papers just came in with reports on the recent Assembly of the Notables at Versailles.' Gaillard's lips curled into a crooked smile. 'All Europe knows the truth which we've only now discovered ourselves. For years, the King's ministers concealed the sorry state of royal finances.

But, the notables have forced the government to reveal its annual deficit—more than a hundred million *livres*—and a royal debt out of control.'

Georges opened his mouth in feigned amazement. 'I usually don't read the papers. Didn't realize things were so bad.'

'Well, let me tell you how bad they are.' Gaillard clutched the paper and shook it, his sallow complexion turning livid. 'Half the King's money goes to pay the interest on that debt. The military, the ministers and their lackeys, and the Queen's friends eat up the rest.' He nearly spat out the reference to the Queen.

He glanced around—he had the attention of the men at nearby tables. 'If any of you men of affairs were to manage your business like the King's ministers run France, you would soon be out on the street begging—or in prison.' Several heads nodded.

'What did the notables do in this crisis?' Georges asked innocently. A crowd was beginning to form around him.

'The Queen's man, Brienne, begged for their support. He didn't get a *sous*. It was a complete defeat for the Crown. The government is nearly bankrupt and has nowhere to go for relief except to the representatives of the people in the Estates-General. We'll soon put the Crown on a tight leash as they do in England.'

'Who can we trust to lead us?' asked a prosperous-looking man in a fine black silk suit. 'Brienne's no better than Calonne, the minister he replaced.'

'The Duc d'Orléans?' suggested another voice from the crowd. There was a buzz of conversation. Some men nodded, others shrugged or frowned.

Gaillard seemed to grow cautious. 'The duke opposes the Crown's failed policies and demands a meeting of the Estates-General. Only they can legislate the reforms to solve the problem.'

'Who is the King more likely to listen to, the duke or the Queen?' asked a brash auditor. 'She's against yielding any royal power to the Estates-General.'

'Indeed!' Gaillard's eyes blazed, his jaw tightened. 'She's Madame Deficit, part of the problem.'

82

'And what should be done with her?' asked Georges, his voice more provocative than he had intended.

'Lock her up in a convent,' offered a man from the crowd.

Gaillard stared at Georges, eyes narrowing with suspicion, then stalked back to his table and finished his brandy. For a moment, he sat sullen and still, then beckoned his companions, and they left the café. The crowd returned to its normal pastimes.

During this exchange, Saint-Martin had kept in the background, lest his speech arouse suspicions and betray his identity. He couldn't entirely conceal his cultivated accent. When the room grew quiet, he had looked around. Men were leaving their tables and drawing near to listen to Georges questioning Gaillard. Many were nodding.

The journalist had spoken openly, as if unconcerned that police agents might be present or as if he didn't care if they were. The government's capacity to hurt him was still great, but its will to do so had greatly diminished. Magistrates rarely prosecuted bold journalists if they observed minimal caution in their writing and speech. Privately, many men in positions of authority shared Gaillard's views, if not his passion.

Previously, Saint-Martin hadn't paid much attention to royal politics, so pointless and futile, a sordid game among ministers. The opinion of reasonable persons like himself had seemed irrelevant. For some time, he had realized that men like those in the café, who appreciated Gaillard's comments, represented a class growing rapidly in numbers and wealth. A sleeping giant was awakening, angry and impatient, while the King's ministers floundered from one desperate expedient to another.

Saint-Martin's thoughts came back to Gaillard. What was most striking was not what he said, much of which made sense. It was the venom in his words, his visceral hatred of the Queen. Gaillard might indeed have used Richard de Beauregard in the hope of somehow destroying her. The idea of a conspiracy leading to the murder of the duchess now seemed more plausible than ever.

CHAPTER TWELVE

Lovers' Quarrel

Monday, June 4

At noon, Anne and Comtesse Marie reached Versailles. True to her promise the previous day, Marthe Bourdon had engaged men to carry their trunks to the apartment. She was there to greet the new occupants, her manner stiff, her smile strained. Nonetheless, she would do her duty. When the men finished, she paid them off, then oversaw the maids unpacking the trunks.

An hour later, she approached the countess. 'The clothes are put away. Your rooms are in order. May I do anything else for you?'

'You've been very helpful, Marthe. That will be all.'

After the housekeeper left, Marie turned to Anne. 'I do wish she would unbend a little, but one should be grateful for her expert service.'

Anne nodded. 'She may relax as we become better acquainted. The murder has shaken the servants, even Madame Bourdon. The police have questioned her like the others and made her wary.'

The two women set out to meet Bourdon's older half-sister, the cook. Robinette Lapire was in her tiny room off the kitchen, mending clothes and watching her cat at play on the floor. He was tossing a small gray mouse about. Anne felt queasy. The mouse appeared to be alive. Robinette was smiling, apparently enjoying the cruel sport. Then she became aware of her visitors and shook a finger at the cat.

'Bijou! That's enough!'

He bit hard into his prey, breaking its neck, and stalked out of the room with the dead rodent in his teeth.

Anne glanced at Marie, whose remarkable self-mastery failed to suppress a grimace of distaste. They were both reminded of the duchess and the unknown person who murdered her. Bijou had merely obeyed his instinct to hunt. He felt no guilt, appeared proud of his deed. Duchesse Aimée's killer could not have acted simply from instinct like an animal. So, what had motivated him—or her? Panic? Greed? Hate?

At a gesture from Anne, Robinette put aside her needle and thread and joined her visitors at the large table in the middle of the kitchen. The countess had brought a small bottle of brandy to share. Robinette found glasses. Anne poured. They saluted each other and sipped the drink.

'Madame Cartier has told me a little about you already,' the countess began gently. 'But I would also like to know what your deceased husband did for a living.'

'A carter. Worked in Paris.'

'When did he die?'

'Years ago.'

'Any children?'

'One. Born dead.'

Throughout the visit, she remained tight-lipped and timid. Even the brandy failed to loosen her tongue. As the countess approached events leading up to Duchesse Aimée's death, the cook seemed increasingly anxious. Her voice could barely be heard. Finally, the countess smiled to the poor woman and sent her back to her room.

As Anne observed this interrogation, she wondered if abuse in the past, coupled with morbid awareness of her plain appearance, had bruised Robinette's spirit. She seemed to suffer from deep-seated feelings of inadequacy. By all accounts, she was an excellent cook and probably had more intelligence than appeared at first glance. Her small feline face was almost impossible to read. Perhaps she knew something about the murder that she was afraid to tell.

'We should inspect the duke's apartment where Paul and Georges will stay,' Anne suggested. They left the kitchen and passed through the hallway connecting the two apartments. Jules Blondel met them at the door and showed them the rooms. Paul had sent the trunks for himself and Georges with instructions to Blondel to unpack them. That had been done neatly and efficiently and the trunks put away.

The valet pointed out Duc Henri's wardrobe of fine clothes and a vitrine of his snuffboxes and other small *objets d'art*.

'Is this the sum of the duke's possessions?' the countess asked.

'Yes,' Blondel replied. 'Everything else you see belongs to the Crown. Baron Breteuil has ordered an inventory. I'm at work on it now.'

Anne found Blondel to be a handsome man in his yellow livery. His manner was polite and engaging. A disarming suspect, he had no alibi for the crucial hours of early Friday morning and was in dire need of money. He might have killed the duchess to steal her brooch and coins or to cause her inheritance to pass to his master and then some of it on to him. But these were merely speculations.

'We shall call on Princesse Lamballe,' the countess remarked, as she and Anne returned to their apartment. 'I've sent my card ahead. She will be expecting us.' Marie gently met Anne's eyes. 'Actually, she will be expecting me. I've indicated that you would like to meet with her housekeeper.'

Though Anne resented this social snub, she didn't reproach Marie, who couldn't change the rules. Also, there was little for Anne to gain by being presented to the princess, then sitting off to one side as a mute spectator. The countess would have a difficult, unpleasant task gleaning something of use. It was well known that Lamballe lacked both wit and an inquiring mind. Still, she had access to members of the royal family and would be better informed than most courtiers, who had to rely on simple gossip.

Anne warmed to her task. The housekeeper Madame Flon was said to be an efficient manager, like Marthe Bourdon, but easier to talk to. She was well placed to observe a wide range of life in the palace and might reveal a clue or two.

They met in the housekeeper's room over tea. Yes, she knew the maid Catherine. She had not yet caught her in a lie but had never truly tested her. The young woman had indeed dallied with Richard de Beauregard, had in fact fallen in love with him, and seemed heartbroken when he left her. 'Silly goose!' the housekeeper exclaimed. 'What else could she expect from a such Lothario?'

'Would she take revenge on him now?'

'Hard to say. She's a spirited girl. You'd better ask her.'

'I shall.' On an impulse, Anne asked, 'How well do you know Marthe Bourdon?' Anne guessed that housekeepers in the palace would have common matters to discuss.

A frown gathered on Madame Flon's forehead. 'We meet occasionally in the laundry and the central kitchen. But she doesn't join our circle for cards and gossip. Hasn't the taste or time for frivolous pursuits, she says. Religion is her distraction. Mass every Sunday, I hear. Says her prayers morning, noon, and night during the week.'

That's not the behavior one would expect of a murderess, Anne surmised. 'Where does she worship?'

'In Paris, I suppose. I don't see her in church in Versailles. But, then, I'm not there very often myself.'

Anne thought she'd better study this side of Madame Bourdon's life. Religion might point to a sterling character, but it could also serve as a disguise, cloak a person's evil deeds.

Meanwhile, Comtesse Marie had engaged Princesse Lamballe in an exchange of trivia. They sat at a small brown mahogany table in her study, a bright, airy room furnished in the rococo style. Shelves of leather-bound gilt-edged books lined the walls. The windows offered a view at ground level out over the palace's Cour des Princes, from which she could observe the arrival and departure of dignitaries. A maid had served tea and biscuits and had withdrawn.

The princess was a lovely, graceful woman with a gentle, melancholy air. Her green eyes were big and sad. For this occasion she wore a richly embroidered pink silk dressing gown with matching slippers. Around her neck hung a band of perfect pearls. The Queen treated her friend very well indeed.

At a lull in the conversation, the countess ventured to ask, 'And what is your opinion of the death of the Duchesse de Saumur?'

The direct thrust of the question startled Lamballe, but she rallied. 'The maid did it. Part of a plot against the Queen.' She drew in a deep breath. 'Since you left society several years ago to live in the country, you may not realize how bold her enemies have become and how dreadful their tactics. They probably recruited the maid to uncover scandal. The duchess learned of the plot. The maid killed her.'

Marie nodded to encourage Lamballe to continue.

'Scandal is the weapon they use to destroy the Queen in the public's eye. They even accuse her of the most monstrous crimes against nature.' Lamballe stopped for a moment, short of breath, almost overcome by the horrors crowding into her mind.

Marie knew why the princess felt so offended. Broadsheets had recently appeared in Paris accusing her and the Queen of a sexual relationship, described and even illustrated in obscene detail.

'Since April,' Lamballe went on, 'when the King began depending on her for counsel and her role in the government became more prominent, the attacks against her have grown much worse. And, mind you, they often come from within this palace. Certain high-born persons here have always hated and slandered her. In the present financial crisis they feel even less restraint, blame her for everything wrong in the kingdom.' The princess paused again, her face pale and drawn, and sipped from a glass of water. 'After what has happened to the duchess, I fear for the dauphin and his brother.'

With her mind's eye Marie silently recalled the King's brothers, the Comtes de Provence and Artois, schemers both of them, who were next in line for the throne following the Queen's two boys. The Duc d'Orléans, also in the line of succession, was equally suspect. And if not he, then his agents and others linked to him by self-interest like Monsieur Hoche and the journalist Gaillard.

'They dare to hint,' Lamballe continued, 'that the boys are not the King's children but were sired by . . .' Her voice failed. She leaned back in a near faint. Marie rang for a maid, then patted the princess's hand. The maid applied a cold, damp cloth to the woman's forehead until she revived. But there would be no more conversation. Marie expressed her regrets and left.

Anne was still in the housekeeper's parlor when there was a loud knock on the door. Marie stood there, face taut, and addressed Madame Flon in an urgent tone. 'Your mistress has fainted.'

The housekeeper showed no sign of concern. 'The maids are taking care of her, I presume.'

'Yes.'

'Then she will be well in a short while.'

At first this exchange confused Anne, until it became clear that the princess was in the habit of fainting in stressful situations.

Comtesse Marie also appeared relieved. 'Madame Flon, I am pleased to meet you. When I last visited the Court, your mother helped me dress for a dinner engagement. A woman of excellent taste and good humor! You appear to take after her.'

'Thank you, countess, you are kind. Mother recalls you fondly.' Madame Flon brought another teacup to the table, and Marie sat down, perfectly at ease. Anne started with surprise, still not accustomed to observing the countess in such a modest setting.

After a brief chat about Madame Flon's family, Anne turned the conversation to the murder of the duchess. 'I understand there was a card party here that evening and the Duchesse de Saumur attended with Chevalier de Beauregard.'

'Yes, I assisted in serving the guests.'

'Did you notice anything unusual between Saumur and Beauregard?'

Madame Flon looked thoughtfully up at the ceiling for a moment before replying. 'On previous occasions they had acted like two lovebirds. Thursday evening something must have gone wrong. She was frosty toward him.' Flon hesitated, not wishing to gossip.

'Yes? Go on, please. This may be important.'

'Shortly before three o'clock in the morning, she left the table. Said she was going to her rooms. He followed her to the door. She was angry. He looked worried. They exchanged sharp words. I heard her say, "I'll tell the Queen in the morning." She gathered her skirts and marched out. He stood staring at the door for a few minutes, then he left too.'

'You have been very helpful, Madame Flon. Please consider this conversation confidential.' Anne nodded to Marie. It was time to go.

'I've learned something from the princess,' remarked Comtesse Marie, removing her hat and fanning herself. She and Anne had returned to their rooms and closed the doors, making sure no one could overhear them. 'The Queen's enemies are circulating nasty rumors in the palace, as well as in Paris. They say that it wasn't the King who sired the Queen's two boys.'

Anne patted her brow. 'Oh, the gutter press can say whatever it likes. No person of good sense will believe it.'

'True. But the jottings on Beauregard's blotter suggest he might have taken the rumor seriously and tried to confirm it.' Marie beckoned Anne to a window bench to catch a breeze.

'I see,' Anne agreed. 'Through Duchesse Aimée, he had hoped to draw near to the Queen and search for incriminating letters or diaries.' Anne considered other possibilities for a moment. 'Could he bribe a maid?'

'Perhaps. But I believe the Queen's maids are loyal to her.' Marie waved a finger. 'He might have been aiming rather at the Queen's friend, Comte Fersen. He may keep a journal and save letters.'

'Where does he stay when he comes to Versailles?'

'He used to take rooms in the town. I'll find out if he has found quarters . . . closer to the Queen. In fact, Paul might know. He and Fersen served together during the war in America.'

They rose from the bench and started dressing for supper. Marie turned to Anne. 'And what did Madame Flon say before I interrupted you?'

Anne heaved a sigh. 'The maid Catherine cannot be fully trusted in matters of the heart. I'll have to question her.'

'Patience, Anne. We now know at least that Beauregard and the duchess quarreled.'

'Yes, but that's of little use until we find a credible witness to his presence near the scene of the crime.'

Night had fallen on the royal palace at Versailles. Anne made her way back to Princesse Lamballe's apartment. Candles and oil lamps gave only dim flickering light to the main hallways and the public rooms. Servants scurried about like mindless mice. Guards lounged in the shadows, indifferent to courtiers sauntering by. Much of the palace lay in complete darkness. Measures of economy, Anne supposed, as futile as emptying the ocean with a teaspoon.

She had learned from the housekeeper that the maid, Catherine, could be approached most conveniently after the evening meal, when servants had free time. She was at a table in the kitchen playing cards with several companions. As Anne drew near, the maid's lips parted with surprise.

'May I speak with you alone, Catherine?' Anne's tone was more like an order than a request.

Embarrassed and annoyed, the maid excused herself from the game, rose from the table, and went with Anne to an empty parlor.

'Pardon this interruption,' Anne began, 'but you must show me how you saw the Chevalier de Beauregard leave the duchess's private stairway. Before the police accuse him, they need to be sure of your testimony.'

Catherine frowned. Her mouth opened as if to object.

Anne cut her off. 'Would you prefer to show my husband, Colonel Saint-Martin?'

The maid grimaced. 'Follow me, madame.' She set off at a brisk pace.

They turned into a short, dark hall. Anne lifted her lantern. Two doors faced each other a few paces apart.

Catherine opened the one on the right, to the linen closet. There was just enough room inside for a person to stand and work at the shelves.

'I was about to leave when I heard someone coming down the stairs. I backed into the closet, leaving the door open a tiny crack. He unlocked the door across the hall and stepped out, carrying a lantern.'

91

Anne had brought along a key. She unlocked the door to the private stairway and gave Catherine the lantern. 'Act the part of Beauregard. I'll hide in the closet and watch you.'

The maid entered the stairway, closing the door behind her. She could be heard walking up, turning around, and walking down. She opened the door and stepped out into the hall. Her lantern, nearly shuttered, emitted only a sliver of light. She had also pulled the hood of her cape over her head.

Peering through the narrow opening in the door, Anne saw only a dark figure whose face was mostly concealed. She called out to Catherine, 'How could you say yesterday that you recognized Beauregard?'

The maid opened the shutters and pulled back her hood. 'Who else could it have been? He was the only one who used the stairway.' Her voice had a defensive edge.

'Others knew about it and could have used it,' Anne retorted. 'So you can't be certain it was Beauregard whom you saw.' Anne could tell that Catherine had rehearsed her response.

Catherine shrugged her shoulders. 'Yes, if you put it that way.'

'That will be all,' said Anne sharply. Someone had given the maid a reason to lie.

'Madame Flon, could we speak in your room?'

The housekeeper frowned. The tone of Anne's voice indicated something was amiss. 'Why, of course.'

When the door closed behind them, Anne asked, 'I need to know if the maid, Catherine, had any visitors between late this afternoon and now.'

'Let me think for a moment.' The housekeeper lowered her eyes, rubbed her cheeks, searching her memory. 'Why, yes, of course. Monsieur Bart, the provost's agent, visited Catherine, then asked about you and the countess. I didn't tell him much. A little later, Chevalier Richard de Beauregard also came looking for Catherine. He seemed nervous. Said she had asked for him. They were alone together maybe ten minutes. When he left, I'd say she had the upper hand. Looked very pleased with herself.'

CHAPTER THIRTEEN

A Risky Invitation

Monday, June 4

It was a mild spring evening at the Palais-Royal. Much of the garden was a construction site for the new circus. Elsewhere, especially in the arcades and in the Camp of the Tatars, it was lively business as usual. Lamplighters hustled with their torches, driving back the growing dusk. Flecks of light appeared in the upper floors of the tall, rectangular buildings enclosing the garden. Sylvie breathed in the faint, intriguing scent of countless meals being prepared.

She and Michou sat next to each other outside Café Odéon, watching the crowd passing by. If something exotic caught their eye, they would sketch it. A pair of dark-skinned turbaned men sat down near them and fascinated Michou for a half-hour. Sylvie concentrated on a pathetic elderly fop in a thread-bare coat who attempted in vain to strike up a conversation with fashionable young women.

Between sketches, the two friends discussed their visit to the duke's picture galleries that morning. Sylvie was still disappointed in her emotional reaction to Titian's painting, *The Three Ages of Man*. It had touched a spot in her mind that was still sore, a crippling sense of life's fragility.

'Remember how quickly you recovered,' Michou encouraged her, 'and how we may have found an ally in the palace.'

They spoke briefly about André without reaching any conclusion, then went on to discuss various other men in their lives. A lighthearted, lively, but silent conversation. Three months of intensive private instruction from Françoise Arnaud had given Sylvie a fair grasp of sign language. She enjoyed practicing with Michou.

They were sipping punch, when Sylvie sensed someone at her side.

André lifted his hat and bowed. 'Good evening, mesdemoiselles. Forgive me for disturbing you. But the way you observe the world intrigues me. As a fellow artist, may I join you?'

The young man's smile was gentle and good-humored. Sylvie nudged Michou and signed his request.

'As you wish,' signed Michou with a guarded look at André. She picked up her pad and resumed sketching.

Sylvie turned to André. 'Yes, you may, Monsieur Dutoit, if you can endure the company of amateurs.' He pulled up a chair facing them. Her invitation challenged the limits of propriety, she realized. However, she had lost her lofty social standing months ago and by now had ceased to regret it. Almost. She would nonetheless be prudent. André was largely an untested character.

Since meeting him this morning, she had made inquiries. His father was a respected cabinetmaker in Monsieur Riesener's workshop, one of the most prestigious in Paris. It produced fine tables and chairs and other masterpieces of marquetry for the greatest families of Europe. A younger brother was apprenticed there.

André had studied with the portrait painter Alexander Roslin, then struck out on his own. A few months ago, he took the job in the palace with Monsieur Hoche. Probably needed the money, Sylvie guessed. By all accounts, André was an honorable, if unconventional, man.

Sylvie showed him a few of her sketches in the satiric vein that came easily to her. Male foibles were her chief targets. André paused at a sketch of fops in fantastic striped silk suits, drawn as roosters with magnificent tail feathers. 'I detect a talent for caricature,' he chuckled. 'Woe to your enemies.'

A pleasant conversation ensued. He listened attentively to what she told of Michou and as much as she wished to tell of herself. At a reference to her noble family, he raised an eyebrow.

'You dress like a commoner—for good reason, I'm sure.' He left the matter there and led the conversation to other, less

94

delicate topics. She was grateful that he wasn't the prying kind. She soon felt sufficiently at ease with him to ask how it was to work for Monsieur Hoche.

'Useful,' he replied carefully. 'Hoche knows the duke's collection and the art world very well. He doesn't want to teach me, but I learn a great deal from him nonetheless.'

'What kind of man is he?'

André hesitated for a moment. 'Intelligent, ruthless, a *bon vivant*. Qualities he's proud of. More than that I shouldn't say. He lives alone in a comfortably furnished palace apartment. I've been inside a few times with reports or messages. The duke seems to trust him, leaves priceless things in his hands, asks him to invent diverting artistic entertainment.'

Sylvie raised an eyebrow. 'Diverting?'

'Yes, Hoche is preparing a Roman feast for this coming Thursday. He's left the lesser details to me.' He paused, met her eye. 'Would you come as Diana the Huntress? Hoche likes the sketch you showed him. Thinks you'd fit into the program he's planning. He'd pay a small stipend. Interested?'

'This *is* a surprise. I'll have to think about it.' She suddenly felt hot and flustered.

André rushed to reassure her. 'For decorum and for safety's sake, you might seek the company of your cousin, Colonel Saint-Martin. He has a long, distinguished pedigree and is known to be a cultivated gentleman. I'm sure Monsieur Hoche would add him to the duke's guest list, if you ask.' He hesitated, measuring his words. 'Hoche really wants you at the feast.'

Sylvie pondered for a few moments the risk implied in André's last remark. 'May I speak to my cousin and reply to you tomorrow morning?'

'Surely.' André rose from the table. 'Thursday morning, Monsieur Hoche will need to instruct you in the role of Diana.' With a bow and a warm smile, André excused himself. He still had work to do in the office.

When he left, Sylvie summed up the conversation for Michou. 'Well, what do you think?'

'He likes you.' She paused, a teasing glint in her eye. 'And you feel the same about him. You could soon be friends. But take care. He hasn't revealed much about himself.'

Michou's assessment prompted mixed feelings of pleasure and caution in Sylvie's mind. Who knew what evil might lurk under André's pleasing surface? 'You're right, Michou, he's a stranger.' She hesitated a moment. 'Still, he's opening up an excellent opportunity to investigate Monsieur Hoche. I believe my cousin would like to go to Hoche's party.'

Late in the evening, Saint-Martin and Georges set off for Madame Lebrun's brothel in the Palais-Royal. With help from one of Quidor's agents, Georges had made arrangements with a locksmith in the Valois arcade. Their plan was to steal Hoche's keys and duplicate them while he was presenting his program, then search his apartment at the next opportunity. Saint-Martin had raised a hand to protest. But Georges had said, 'Leave the details to me.'

On route to the brothel, they stopped at Comtesse Marie's town house on Rue Traversine. Michou and Sylvie reported their conversation with André. Smitten by Sylvie, Hoche had invited her to the forthcoming Roman feast.

'Would you care to escort me?' Sylvie asked her cousin. 'You would have to wear sandals and a toga.' She kept a straight face.

'I would be delighted, my dear,' he replied in the same spirit. 'The duke wouldn't allow me in the palace in a policeman's uniform.' He switched to a more serious tone. 'Could you persuade André to include Georges in the party? Perhaps as an extra footman? It's a golden opportunity. Hoche will be preoccupied and away from his apartment.'

'I'll try.'

'If you're successful,' Georges added, 'I'll need a good partner for the search.'

'We'll have to ask her,' remarked Saint-Martin, having guessed whom Georges had in mind.

'The neighbors will suspect we're regular patrons,' remarked Georges as they climbed to the first floor above the shops in the Valois wing. They had come here in uniform just two days ago inquiring after Duc Henri. Now Georges wore a fine woolen buff suit with black trim, the colonel a pastel-green patterned silk suit.

Saint-Martin nodded distractedly. He was paying more attention this time to the place. The entrance hall was nondescript, but inside the brothel itself no expense had been spared. Over the windows hung richly embroidered damask drapes. He recognized the hand of master craftsmen in the plasterwork on walls and ceilings, the gilded sconces and crystal chandeliers, and the mahogany furniture. It was elegance worthy of a prince's palace.

A handsome black servant in scarlet livery with silver trim showed the two men into a parlor and took the colonel's card on a silver tray.

In a few minutes Madame Lebrun entered the room with a guarded smile. 'We meet again, Colonel. What, may I ask, has become of Duc Henri?'

'He has left Paris for good and will trouble you no more.'

'Good riddance! Unfortunately I'll never see the money he owes me.'

'I fear that is true, madame. But we haven't come here just to report on the duke.'

'Then, gentlemen, how can I serve you?' Her smile grew warmer.

'Tonight, we're investigating the affairs of Monsieur Victor Hoche.'

The woman gasped, waving her hands in protest.

'No,' the colonel assured her. 'Monsieur Hoche is not charged with a crime.' Not yet, he thought. 'Simply tell us, madame, how he spends his time here.'

She quickly recovered her composure. 'As Inspecteur Quidor should have informed you, the pleasures of this house are always orderly and discreet. When Monsieur Hoche arrives in a half-hour or so, he and other guests will join our women for a few drinks and a buffet supper. Next, they will move into our little theater, where the women will dance for the guests. Then there will be a special program. Monsieur Hoche, a noted connoisseur, has organized *tableaux vivants* inspired by great works of art and executed by himself and our women. Afterwards, our guests will retire to rooms upstairs for more intimate pleasures.'

'All in the best taste, I'm sure, madame. We wish to observe Monsieur Hoche in the least intrusive manner possible. Monsieur Charpentier, my adjutant, will don your livery and serve the guests. He has much experience in this line of work and will meet your expectations. I shall remain in the background watching.'

Madame Lebrun appeared outwardly satisfied with these arrangements. But her eyes betrayed more than a trace of anxiety.

Saint-Martin entered the parlor, where Georges was dressing for his role. They were alone.

'Tell me exactly what you intend to do,' the colonel asked with a nagging concern. Though he trusted Georges, he had only a general idea of his plan.

Posing at a mirror, Georges grimaced at his image, resplendent in the brothel's scarlet livery, then turned to his superior. 'Before his stage performance, Hoche will change his clothes and hang them in a small dressing room out of sight of the stage. I've arranged with madame to take the place of the footman who usually keeps watch in that area. While Hoche is busy on stage, I'll sneak into the room, take his keys, and pass them to Quidor's agent outside. The locksmith in the Valois arcade will immediately make duplicates. The agent will bring the keys back to me. I'll replace the originals in Hoche's clothes. *Voilà*! He'll never know.'

Saint-Martin's concern grew, his chest tightened. The plan didn't allow for accident or human error. 'Why not simply pick the locks to his apartment?'

'Unfortunately, the duke has installed clever new locks throughout the palace. They would take me too much time to pick, and in the end I might fail or get caught. But the Valois locksmith knows the new locks—he installed them—and can copy the keys in a matter of minutes, at least for the police. So, it's best to duplicate Hoche's keys.'

A dozen guests soon arrived, greeted cordially by Madame Lebrun. They were a mixed lot—a few British gentlemen on tour and a sprinkling of Germans, Italians, and Spaniards, and a solitary Frenchman. They had in common expensive, fashionable suits, sophisticated tastes, and fistfuls of gold *louis*. Madame Lebrun introduced the colonel as Monsieur Martin who had returned to Paris after many years in America.

In the parlor they met the women, all of them fashionably dressed and coiffed. Some were more attractive than others, but all had the elegant, graceful demeanor of well-groomed courtesans. It occurred to Saint-Martin that certain very rich, powerful, hidden patrons owned this house and engaged Madame Lebrun to operate it.

Hoche strutted about like a peacock at home in the place. A lively young woman with sparkling black eyes, light brown hair, and a clear, creamy complexion approached him with a friendly smile. Her rendering of 'Victor' seemed to thrill the man. He called her 'Nanette'. With much tittering and grimace, they discussed their roles in the forthcoming *tableaux vivants*.

Madame Lebrun had momentarily left her guests and stood alone off to one side of the room. Saint-Martin seized the opportunity to speak to her. After complimenting the good taste he had observed in her establishment, he asked what she knew about Hoche's connection to the Chevalier de Beauregard.

She gazed off into space, searching her memory. 'The young man often joined Monsieur Hoche and me for dinner. Their talk was about gambling, women, food, clothes, and the like. Beauregard sometimes asked for money.'

'Did they ever mention Versailles, the royal family, the Duchesse de Saumur?'

Again she reflected for a moment. 'When they thought I wasn't paying attention, they spoke about the Queen's lover.'

'Really?' The Queen's enemies had linked her to a variety of lovers, male and female. 'And which one might that be?'

'Oh, a courtier I hadn't heard of before. They called him "*le beau Fersen*".'

Saint-Martin started at this news. 'Fersen is one of the Queen's favorites, but I hadn't heard he's her lover.'

Madame shrugged, as if it didn't matter who was the Queen's lover. By common report the King's Austrian consort was a promiscuous woman. 'Monsieur Hoche told Chevalier Beauregard to find solid proof and he would be well paid.'

This was the clearest indication yet of a conspiracy, thought

Saint-Martin. Madame Lebrun had become its unwitting witness. 'I'm concerned that Hoche might wonder how much you know about his secrets. You must take care.'

She listened to him soberly, the danger of her situation beginning to sink in. At this moment someone hailed her. She turned from Saint-Martin without a word or backward glance and joined the gentlemen at the buffet table. The colonel was unable to catch her eye again.

Would she expose him and Georges? Or tell Hoche to beware? That could seriously complicate relations with Quidor and the Paris police and hinder an already difficult investigation. And what would Anne think? He felt a pang of guilt. He hadn't considered her feelings when he approved Georges's plan to visit a brothel.

A call to the theater jolted him out of these anxieties. He numbly followed the crowd and took a seat in the back row. The light dimmed before he could take notice of the place. The sound of flutes, cymbals, and drums came from a loft above him. Three shapely young women appeared in scanty gauze costumes with laurel in their hair and small cymbals in their hands. They danced with abandon, stamping and whirling like ecstatic followers of Dionysus. The tempo grew frenzied, the music ear-shattering. The guests responded with loud shouts of appreciation.

For several moments Saint-Martin felt the dance's seductive power. His brain told him that the brothel was cleverly tricking its clients into blindly spending great amounts of money on sensual, ephemeral pleasures. But he had to admit the dancing was artistic in its way, thanks to Hoche, who knew ancient customs very well.

After the dance, a curtain was pulled across the stage. Clothed in a knee-length white tunic, a laurel wreath on his bald head, Hoche announced that the evening's scenes would come from paintings by great French artists. He pulled the curtain to the side, exposing a nearly nude Nanette seated in a sylvan setting, removing her sandals, a bow and a quiver of arrows at her side. Three nude young women attended her.

'François Boucher's *Diana Resting after the Hunt*,' came a voice from the audience.

'That was too easy,' shouted another.

And so it went on through a half-dozen scenes, each composition true to the original work of art but creating a more erotic effect. Saint-Martin slumped in his seat, increasingly uncomfortable in his role as a voyeur. He also began to worry about Georges. Would Hoche catch him?

Finally, Hoche announced the last scene, a work in progress by the sculptor Clodion. After a lengthy pause, the curtain parted, revealing Hoche together with Nanette, he a satyr, she a nymph. A pan flute filled the air with a rustic melody. The audience broke out in spontaneous applause, so realistic was the *tableau*.

Hoche had fitted out the lower half of his body to resemble a goat's legs and hooves. His upper torso was naked, his ears pointed. He reclined languorously on a rocky formation. His right arm reached around Nanette's waist and drew her close. Naked, straddling his left leg, she leaned over him. From a cup in her left hand she slowly poured wine into his leering, open mouth. He drank the liquid in great joyous gulps, the excess spilling over his upraised face and on to his body. The scent of wine wafted through the room.

Against his will, Saint-Martin felt stirred by the scene, a compelling if brief depiction of sensual pleasure. Its actors lived fully in their roles. Then Madame Lebrun came out of the dark and pulled the curtain shut. An expectant silence came over the room. A minute later, Hoche appeared with Nanette, he in his tunic, she in a diaphanous dressing gown. They bowed to uproarious applause. The crowd dispersed. The women reappeared in luxurious costumes. Couples wandered off.

Saint-Martin left the theater, wondering what had happened to Georges. He had served at the buffet table, then disappeared. At least there had been no commotion to indicate that his plan had gone awry. As Saint-Martin walked past a darkened parlor, a low familiar voice drew him in. 'Colonel!'

'Georges!' The adjutant was in his own clothes.

'My plan worked perfectly.' He rattled keys in his pocket.

'Splendid! And Madame Lebrun gave me some useful pieces

of information.' Saint-Martin explained that Fersen seemed to be the conspirators' target.

'How was she persuaded to be so forthcoming?' asked Georges, as they left the brothel.

'I told her I must report to Inspecteur Quidor. I would like to tell him that Madame Lebrun ran an orderly house and had cooperated fully with my investigation.'

'Smart woman.' He rattled the keys again. 'We'll soon pay a visit to Monsieur Hoche.'

CHAPTER FOURTEEN

A Discovery

Tuesday, June 5

Shortly after dawn at Versailles, Anne awoke in the deaf maid's room. A thin shaft of light struggled through the small high window above her. For a moment she lost her bearings. The walls of the cramped dark room pressed in upon her. She felt trapped in a box. She reached out. Paul was not at her side, the first time since their marriage. She ached for him.

Then she remembered her new role. She rose from the bed, washed, dressed, and donned an apron. Following the maid's custom, she went to the kitchen, nodded to the cook and petted her cat. Silently, she began to prepare a breakfast tray for the countess.

A few minutes later, Madame Bourdon walked in, fully dressed for the day. When she saw Anne, she stumbled and dropped the empty basket she was carrying. A look of disbelief, tinged with anger, flashed over her face. She quickly picked up the basket. 'How clumsy of me. For a moment I didn't recognize you.'

Indeed! Anne thought, how revealing. I'm wearing Denise's apron, doing the maid's work at the customary time in the usual place. For an instant, the housekeeper must have thought Denise had been freed and had returned to the apartment. In Marthe's mind the maid was a murderer who belonged in prison. Anne glimpsed a fleeting malign smile on the cook's face. She had also understood Marthe's reaction.

Anne finished the tray and carried it to the bedroom. Marie was sitting at a table by the window. 'You were gone ten minutes.' She glanced up at a clock on the wall. 'When you left for the kitchen, I slipped into your room, put a brooch in your mattress, and returned here. I still had time to flee by the private stairway before you came with the breakfast tray.'

'The killer could have done the same,' Anne remarked, 'but he had to know the maid's routine.'

While they ate, they studied the provost's report concerning the apartment, then Madame Bourdon's inventory of Duchesse Aimée's possessions. 'What's missing in these documents?' Marie slapped them with the back of her hand.

'Any personal papers,' Anne replied. 'In his search of her desk Jacques Bart found only household messages, formal invitations, and the like.'

Marie reflected for a moment. 'Perhaps she didn't keep a diary but she certainly received personal mail. The house-keeper might know.'

Anne shot Marie a warning glance. 'I would rather ask Denise. Let's go to the prison.'

An officer led Anne and Marie to the provost's door. They had asked to visit the imprisoned maid. Impossible, the officer had said. Only authorized persons could visit prisoners. Having anticipated that reaction, Marie showed him an authorization from Baron Breteuil. The officer tried to persuade them to come back another day. Marie insisted.

Finally, they were ushered into the provost's office. The Marquis de Sully remained seated at his desk, a frown on his face. 'Why do you wish to see her?'

'We have questions to ask,' the countess replied.

'This is incredible,' he finally exclaimed. 'Is the baron destitute? Must he employ women to investigate such a serious matter?'

The countess adopted a gentle tone. 'He realizes that this young maid might speak more freely to women about certain matters, especially since one of us is fluent in the language of the deaf.'

'Will you make her reveal where she's hidden the missing coins?'

'We have other concerns,' Marie replied.

'I thought so.' His voice was heavy with scorn. 'If the King would let me, I'd use a thumbscrew and get the truth out of her.'

Marie stared at him with barely disguised contempt.

Sully received her reproach stonefaced, then growled to the officer. 'Bring the prisoner upstairs.'

A guard led Denise into the small, bare visitor's room, manacled again. She wore the same shapeless, coarse woolen gown as three days earlier. There were dark rings under her eyes. She shuffled toward them in her wooden shoes. Hadn't had enough exercise or slept well, Anne thought. But she had rallied from her earlier depression and held her head high.

This time, Anne paid attention to the guard, a short, stocky, rough-looking man with a scarred, low-browed face, wiry gray hair, thick chest, broad shoulders, and muscular arms. His left hand lacked a couple of fingers, and he walked with a limp. A hardened veteran of many battles. He freed Denise, then, stepping back, he scrutinized Anne with a penetrating, unsettling eye. What was that about? Anne wondered, as he left the room. She couldn't recall ever seeing him before.

Denise's wrists were red and raw. Marie produced a jar of ointment and applied some to the injured area, then sat the young woman down and began brushing her hair. Denise smiled her gratitude.

'Did Duchesse Aimée ever write in a journal?' Anne signed.

'Yes, nearly every evening and at other times, I'm sure. It's a beautiful leather-bound book. Sometimes she read it while I put up her hair. I could feel how much it meant to her. She used to caress it like a dear friend. I never tried to peek—that seemed indecent.'

'Where did she keep it?'

104

'I don't know, I never saw her take it up or put it away. But I'm sure it never left the bedroom. That's the only place where I saw her reading or writing in it. She once said she didn't trust anybody but me.' The maid paused for a moment, brow furrowed with thought. 'It might be on a shelf among her books. They are all bound the same way.'

'You've been very helpful, Denise. Trust us, we're working for you.'

As soon as Anne and Marie returned to the apartment, they started searching the bedroom for the duchess's journal. There were three encased shelves of leather-bound books on a wall above a row of cabinets. The two women took the books down, one by one, and carefully leafed through them. The journal might be bound together with pages from another book.

Anne could tell from the wear and tear on books she was skimming that the duchess was fond of serious literature—the plays of Molière and Racine, the fables of La Fontaine, the essays of Montaigne, the works of Voltaire. The most worn volume was Blaise Pascal's *Pensées*. Anne knew it only by name, so she showed it to Marie. 'What's it about?'

'The meaning of existence.' Marie fanned the pages, stopped at marked passages, and read some of them aloud. 'You must know this one.' She looked up at Anne. 'The heart has its reasons which reason cannot comprehend. We know this in a thousand ways.'

'How true!' Anne thought of the love between her and Paul which the baron could not understand. Come to think of it, neither could she. Their story seemed so unlikely. They were attracted to each other during the summers when, as a girl, she performed in Comtesse Marie's château theater. The war separated them, she in England, he in America. Last year, her investigation of her stepfather's murder in Paris brought them together again. Their love reignited and overcame huge differences of social class, religion, and culture. And yet somehow their union seemed meant to be.

Marie laid the book aside with a wry smile. 'Pascal explores the paradoxes of good and evil in the human heart, describes the dark light of faith, challenges us to believe in God.'

'A deep thinker, Monsieur Pascal,' observed Anne. 'I can't imagine why Aimée was drawn to him.'

'I'm surprised as well,' Marie admitted. 'Outwardly, Duchesse Aimée lived like a hedonist, one young lover after another. Her mind seemed as shallow as a teacup. She practiced religion as little as society allowed. But appearances can lie. During her youth, she lived among Jansenist magistrates of the Parlement of Paris, men with a taste for Pascal. And, later, here at the Court she probably found a few reflective men and women. She must have cultivated a secret inner life wrestling with the mystery of God.'

Anne stepped back and studied the empty bookshelves. 'The paneling looks odd to me.' Behind the shelves there might be empty space.' She tried tapping the wall. It sounded hollow. She removed several panels, revealing bundles of letters and a row of small leather-bound books. The missing journal! Anne counted twenty-six numbered volumes, one for each year since 1762.

'The story of her life is here,' exclaimed Marie, fingering a volume and raising a fine cloud of dust. She put it back and picked out a cleaner one. 'This is the most recent.' She brought it to a table by the window where the light was better, and turned immediately to the last entry. Anne sat next to her, reading over her shoulder.

The entry was written in a tense, hasty hand and dated early Friday, June 1, 1787.

Card party at Princesse L . . . Much trivia. Boring. Left at 3 in the morning. Before the party, I had told Richard it was over between us. I would speak to the Queen about his prying into the correspondence between her and Comte Fersen. Richard protested, I would ruin him. I said that couldn't be helped. Heard at the party that Jules Blondel pilfered from us. I will check his accounts later in the morning.

There followed a passage in shorthand or code. Then the entry resumed.

I am alone. Feel tricked, trapped, and very angry. Can't sleep. Only Bijou keeps me company. Dear Diary, this is too much. What shall I do? My husband, a vile monster, covets my inheritance. My lover is a treacherous opportunist. My steward is reputed to be a thief. My housekeeper mocks me behind my back and should be discharged. My Queen is the most hated woman in France. My King is an obese clod. The only person I care for and trust is my deaf maid. Should I give my wealth to the poor, quit the palace, and enter a convent?

There was more shorthand. Then, an ominous concluding line.

4 a.m. I hear someone at the door . . .

'The killer, most likely.' Marie met Anne's eyes. 'Aimée was close to being desperate. Poor woman! I've felt that way at certain moments in my life. The loss of my husband was very hard.' Marie was thoughtfully silent for a short while, staring at the open page. Then she closed the journal. 'I should read these volumes carefully for the light they may shed on who killed her and why. They must be kept hidden.'

Anne agreed, with a nod. 'But the entry we've just read offers nothing new concerning Beauregard. We've already suspected he was attempting to gather evidence of royal scandal and pass it on to Hoche. What's new is the threat to dismiss Jules Blondel for pilfering. He might have become desperate enough to kill her.'

The two women rose from the table and returned the journal to its hiding place.

'We ought to visit Monsieur Blondel,' said Anne, 'and examine his account books.'

Jules Blondel sat in Duc Henri's study, account books stacked on the table in front of him, a pen in his hand. He looked up as Anne and Marie entered. 'I've just put the finishing touches to the inventory that Baron Breteuil has requested. Everything appears to be in order and ready for his clerk to inspect.' He placed the pen on a tray and rose to greet his visitors. They took seats on the opposite side of the table. His face was calm, a pleasant mask, but his eyes flickered nervously.

Anne could understand his predicament. His master had gone off to prison, owing the valet back wages. Would he ever be paid?

At their request Blondel showed the women a summary statement of the duke's accounts. His assets consisted of a large wardrobe of fine clothes, a few small precious objects, and a meager allowance from his murdered wife. His obligations to bankers and merchants exceeded his assets by several times. The prospect of Blondel ever recovering his wages looked bleak.

'May I see the most recent entries?' Marie asked evenly.

The steward blinked, then brought an account book around to the countess and opened it in front of her.

'Monsieur Blondel, in the entries for last month I notice the duke selling some of his possessions—suits of clothes, shoes, a snuffbox, a toothpick.' She met his eye. 'Who carried out these sales, surely not the duke?'

'He asked me to do it, Comtesse. Said it was beneath his dignity.'

'I thought so. Can you imagine Duc Henri haggling with a *brocanteur* over the value of a toothpick?'

'It was an exquisite toothpick, countess. Finely carved ivory grip, tempered steel pick. An elegant little silver case.'

Anne smiled inwardly at Blondel's courteous retort and found herself beginning to like the man.

He soon excused himself. He had to run an errand in Paris. When he left the room, Marie said softly to Anne, 'While he's gone, I'll look more closely at his figures.'

'And I'll follow him. He may return to the same *brocanteur*.' Anne jotted down several recent entries. 'I'll give these to Georges to investigate. Blondel may keep some of the proceeds for himself. That may be what disturbed Duchesse Aimée.'

Disguised in a household maid's plain gray woolen garb, Anne followed Blondel into Paris. He entered a *brocanteur*'s shop in Rue Saint-Marc with a small, full bag. When he came out after several minutes, he stopped, looked anxiously over his shoulder. The bag was folded in his hand. He walked down Rue Montmartre. Near the rear of the great merchants' church of Saint-Eustache, he turned into a narrow alley. In a few seconds Anne was at the spot, but he was already out of sight. He couldn't have reached the ornate north entrance to the church at the far end of the alley. Not enough time. He must have entered one of several other doors.

She backed into a café across the street and took a seat by the window where she could watch the alley. The proprietor soon frowned at her, so she ordered a glass of wine. She had waited perhaps a half-hour when Blondel emerged from the first door on the right and walked back to Rue Montmartre.

Anne chose to gamble. She let Blondel retrace his steps and disappear. Ten minutes later, a young woman came out of the same door carrying a basket and walked down the alley toward the church. She was obviously pregnant, and possibly the person Blondel had visited.

Anne followed her into the quiet, cool interior, leaving the hot, noisy chaos of the city outside. The young woman made her way slowly past side chapels, where flickering votive candles witnessed to the hopes of previous visitors. The woman stopped now and then to gaze at a statue or a painting and mumble a prayer. Tinted light from the large colored windows illuminated the church's vast spaces. Tall stone pillars soared to the loftiest vaulting Anne had ever seen.

The young woman made her way to the Lady chapel at the far end of the church. For a few minutes she sat on a bench, hands clasped, staring up at a gracious marble statue of Mary the Virgin gazing tenderly at the child in her arms. The infant appeared to look out over the world, his right hand raised in a blessing. Finally, the young woman heaved a sigh, lit a candle, and left the church by a side door to the central markets. Anne followed her out.

For a moment, the young woman stood still, adjusting her eyes to the bright sunlight, then walked up and down the passageways among the stalls, comparing prices. The market was crowded at this late hour of the morning. Anne struggled to keep the young woman in view. Finally she bought some greens, carrots, peas, bread, and cheese.

Suddenly, Anne grew alert. Two boys of the type known locally as market rats had begun to show interest in the young woman. At a vegetable stall she took a small purse from her pocket. Instantly, one of the boys jostled her, nearly knocking her over. While she was distracted, the other boy snatched her purse and darted away.

Anne had anticipated the thief in time to place herself in his path. As he dashed past, she tripped him and wrestled the purse from his hand. He slipped away into the crowd. The incident was over in seconds. Anne returned to the young woman, who was leaning against the stall, pale and gasping for breath.

'Are you hurt?' Anne asked, returning the purse.

The woman shook her head, then looked down. She had dropped her basket, spilling its contents.

Anne picked up the fallen goods and returned the basket.

'Thank you,' replied the woman feebly and started to walk away. After only a few steps, she began to wobble.

Anne rushed to her side and supported her under the arm. 'May I help you to your home?'

The woman hesitated for a few moments before nodding toward Rue Montmartre.

By the time they reached the alley, she seemed exhausted. At her door she pulled a ring of keys from her bag but dropped it. Anne picked it up, unlocked the door, and helped the woman into a dingy hallway reeking of urine. Leaning heavily on Anne, the woman stared ahead to a steep flight of rickety stairs illumined by a skylight. 'The garret,' she whispered hoarsely.

Slowly, painfully, Anne helped the woman up three flights, unlocked her door, nearly carried her into a small, low room, and lowered her on to a bed. She lay on her back for several minutes, eyes closed, breathing in short gasps. Anne patted her hand, caressed her forehead, until she seemed to relax.

Her eyes opened. 'I'm very grateful. I thought I was going to die.' Her voice grew stronger. 'My name is Blanche Moreau. Who are you?'

'Anne, Anne Cartier.' She had earlier decided to be honest

with this person, though now she wondered how much truth would be helpful. 'You should rest for a while. I'll prepare something for us to eat. Then, if you're feeling better, we could have a talk.'

Within an hour, Anne managed to prepare a vegetable soup, cut the bread and cheese, and set a small table for two. Blanche lay fast asleep. She was a petite young woman with fine features. To judge from the few words she had spoken, she was also cultivated. How had she come into this miserable situation?

'The heart has its reasons . . .' Pascal's words came back to Anne in a dark and chilling sense.

Blanche awoke just as the meal was ready. For a moment, she seemed confused by the scent of cooked food and the presence of a stranger. Then she recalled what had happened and noticed two places set at the table. 'I'm grateful to you, but I really think I can take care of myself now.' She appeared not to wish to have a conversation.

'Would you rather speak to a police inspector?' asked Anne evenly.

'What do you mean?' Anger flashed in Blanche's eyes. Her face flushed.

'Your friend Jules Blondel is taking property that belongs to Duc Henri de Saumur and selling it to a *brocanteur*. He gives the proceeds to you. In the eyes of the police you are also guilty. I learned this rather easily. You can imagine the police will soon discover it, too.' Anne was aware that she didn't have the evidence against Blondel in hand, but she was convinced Georges would find it. 'To the police,' she went on, 'it doesn't matter that the duke owes his valet a year's wages. He's a thief.'

Blanche fell silent, staring at the wall.

Anne waited.

Finally, she met Anne's eye. 'I've suspected as much for several months, but I'm so desperate. I just took the money. No questions asked.'

'How did things come to this pass?'

Blanche rose, walked to the table. 'While we eat, I'll tell you my story.'

She was an only child. Her mother had died a few years ago. Her father, an improvident lawyer, was killed in a coach accident last winter. She was left alone with his debts. When the creditors were satisfied, there was nothing for her.

Jules Blondel, who had once worked for her father, offered to help her. As the duke's valet, he could save enough money for them to be married. They fell in love. Their future seemed bright. Unfortunately, the duke didn't pay him. Worse yet, she became pregnant. 'Now I don't know what to do. I realize the risks he's taking for me, and I'm grateful. He thought that when Duchesse Aimée died, the duke would inherit her money and pay him and the other creditors. But today, Jules said the duke's been sent to prison and the government is holding her money in trust.'

She gazed at her soup, stirred it idly. 'I don't see how Jules and I can ever get married. Sometimes, when I'm really miserable, I'm not sure I love him any more. Then we quarrel.' She grimaced with discomfort, shifted her position. 'This pregnancy has become difficult. I'm often sick.'

Anne listened sympathetically. This wasn't the time to mention that Blondel was a suspect in the duchess's murder. When the meal finished, she offered Blanche what little encouragement she could think of, then took her leave.

As she walked down the stairs, she reflected on Blanche's story. It was now easier to understand Blondel's state of mind. An honorable man, he could not simply abandon her. But this situation drove him to increasingly desperate measures. If Duchesse Aimée had threatened to expose him, he could very well have killed her. The image of a pale, faint Blanche Moreau crowded into Anne's mind. What would become of the young woman? A feeling of sadness gripped Anne. Jules Blondel might soon find himself in prison, charged with embezzlement—and perhaps murder.

CHAPTER FIFTEEN

Desperate Measures

Tuesday, June 5–Wednesday, June 6

Sylvie's heart pounded as she and Michou arrived at the duke's palace promptly at nine. Colonel Saint-Martin's note earlier that morning still jangled her nerves. The visit to Madame Lebrun's brothel had uncovered new evidence of a conspiracy. Hoche's keys were in Georges's hands. It was now up to Sylvie to enlist André Dutoit in a search of Hoche's apartment. She really didn't feel equal to the task.

The two women had hardly begun sketching when André appeared at Sylvie's side. 'Have you decided to attend the Roman feast?' he asked.

'Yes,' she replied. 'And Colonel Saint-Martin will accompany me.' She paused for a moment, searching the young man's face for reassurance, then continued tentatively. 'The colonel asks that his adjutant come as well, perhaps as a footman.'

André gazed into Sylvie's eyes and replied without hesitation, 'Yes, I can use extra help. Monsieur Hoche has given me wide discretion in such mundane details. The feast's artistic preparation has overwhelmed him. He can think of nothing but Roman recipes, living statues, fantastic entertainment, and the exhibition of ancient gems he must assemble.'

Sylvie smiled her satisfaction, opened her sketch pad, and set to work on Titian's *The Three Ages of Man*. The picture's melancholy message no longer bothered her. André quickly sensed her new mood. Soon they were exchanging comments on the picture. She was disappointed when he said he must return to the office. He took a few steps away, hesitated, then returned.

113

'Would you and your friend—' he gestured toward Michou '—join me for tea at Café Odéon later in the morning? I'll have a little free time while I run an errand.'

Sylvie tapped Michou on the shoulder and relayed the invitation.

Michou nodded and gave André a shy smile.

'And I would also be delighted,' said Sylvie.

'Then come to the office when you're finished. We'll go together.' He bowed to the women.

Sylvie noticed a new spring in his step as he went on his way.

At the Café Odéon a waiter showed them to a table for three and took their order. Michou chose a seat facing André, the better to observe him.

'Before I forget,' he began, turning to Sylvie. 'Monsieur Hoche wants to speak to you about your part in the Roman feast. Come to the office a little before noon. He'll also lead a rehearsal tomorrow morning.'

While the tea was being served, they carried on a light-hearted conversation, Michou joining in with signs, gestures, and hastily written notes. She could understand André better now, she was pleased to see, since he had learned to speak distinctly to her and give her good visual clues.

Her fluency seemed to fascinate him. Finally, he remarked, 'Mademoiselle, I can't help but notice how well you communicate.' He hesitated, as if embarrassed. 'I don't wish to be rude, but may I ask, have you always been deaf?'

Michou nodded with a smile, though stung by the direct thrust of the question. She sensed it was well meant. 'I used to sign and read lips barely enough for simple conversation with hearing people. I couldn't read or write and was very shy. At the Abbé de l'Épée's institute I'm learning to read and write and to sign and read lips much better. I understand what you say—much of it, and can guess the rest. I'm not so shy anymore.' Michou glanced gratefully at Sylvie. 'She often helps me.'

'I've asked you,' André rushed to explain, 'because my youngest brother is ten years old and deaf from birth. You

114

make me think he might also benefit from instruction. But we have little money.'

Sylvie seized the opportunity. 'I think something could be arranged.' She described Comtesse Marie's patronage of the institute. 'She helps many of the students. I can't promise for her, but, if you'd like, I could ask.'

He fell silent for a long moment, hesitant to seek a favor. 'I don't want to trouble you.'

Sylvie raised her hands to protest. 'I'll do it for your brother. You owe me nothing.' She promised to inquire at the institute if there was room for another student and if money could be found. 'Please call on us at Rue Traversine later in the day. I should have more information by then.'

'Thank you so much. I'll come in the evening after my work at the office. Now I must dash off on my errand.' He rose, bowed, and kissed the hand of each woman, then hurried away.

Michou tapped Sylvie's shoulder. 'A kind man, that André,' she signed. 'I'm beginning to trust him.'

For an hour Sylvie sat on a bench outside Hoche's office, waiting impatiently for a sign from André. She had thought of wandering off alone into the collection, but she felt too distracted to enjoy it. Several times, Hoche ran past her on his way to the great gallery. Carpenters, painters, and other craftsmen were transforming the room into the atrium of a Roman villa.

Finally, André signaled her to get ready. Hoche's last visitor, Duc Louis-Philippe d'Orléans himself, left the office with a smile on his face. He must have been pleased with what he had heard and seen.

'Mademoiselle Chanteclerc, I'm happy to see you.' Hoche met her at the door with a bow. He showed her to a chair in front of his table and sat facing her. André retreated to his tall writing desk, took up his pen, and began copying from a low pile of paper.

Hoche's face flushed with exhilaration as he described his plans for the Roman feast. The duke would be there, along with some thirty guests, most of whom were amateur connoisseurs of antiquities. They were to celebrate the sale of the duke's entire collection of 1,500 engraved gems before it left for Russia. Empress Catherine had purchased it for 450,000 *livres*.

'A bargain price,' Hoche declared, a note of disapproval in his voice. Thursday evening, he would display a selection of the most precious of the ancient Roman gems.

'How will you celebrate the sale?' Sylvie felt apprehensive about Roman feasts—orgies of eating and drinking, followed by unspeakably bad behavior. Hoche looked like a man who would enjoy them.

Hoche seemed to anticipate her concerns. 'The feast will be a model of decorum.' He described an hour of brief acts that would take place in the atrium during a Roman-style meal. The guests as well as the duke would attend in Roman costumes.

'And my role?' asked Sylvie, a bit relieved. There was nothing shocking in his description.

'To play Diana the Huntress,' he replied. 'You will dress as the Diana at Versailles. An artist will apply cosmetics to heighten your likeness to the marble goddess and you will stand motionless on a pedestal in the atrium. There will be several other living statues as well, taking turns at suitable intervals. When you've done your part, you may rejoin your escort for the Roman meal.'

Hoche paused, eyes hooded. 'Colonel Paul de Saint-Martin is your cousin, is he not?'

'Yes,' she replied simply. Or, more than a cousin? Is that what Hoche was hinting at? She resented his insinuation but told herself not to be upset. Her task was to win his confidence.

'That is all.' Hoche reached into the papers on his table and drew out a sheet. 'Come with your costume to a rehearsal at mid-morning tomorrow.'

As she left, she exchanged sidelong glances with André. He appeared to give her a nod of approval.

Sylvie looked out the window of her top-floor room in the house on Rue Traversine to the roofs beyond. The sun was setting. A forest of chimney pots threw long shadows over the weathered tiles. She shivered, though the evening air was soft and warm.

The prospect of meeting André had stirred up feelings she had almost forgotten. Ever since Captain Fitzroy attacked her, men had largely vanished from her life. For several months she had avoided occasions where she might have to converse with them. She had also dressed in dull brown shapeless woolen gowns, given up cosmetics, covered her hair with a plain bonnet—in a word, done what she could to escape the attention of men. For company she had Michou, who introduced her to simple, more satisfying pleasures than she had ever known in aristocratic society.

However, André was interested. That was obvious. His eyes sparkled when he noticed her. And she liked him. He smiled easily out of Hoche's reach.

A rap on the door startled her. A maid announced Monsieur André Dutoit's arrival. Sylvie stepped up to a mirror, tried out a smile, brushed an errant lock of hair from her forehead. 'That will have to do,' she murmured.

They met in a small parlor near the entrance from the court-yard. He glanced about, as if looking for someone. Sylvie realized he missed Michou, who had always been present at their previous meetings. This evening, however, Michou had excused herself, said she had work to do. Sylvie understood she was supposed to meet André alone.

André bowed and greeted Sylvie politely. They sat at a proper distance facing each other.

'Is Michou well?' he inquired, appearing genuinely concerned. Reassured by Sylvie, he went on to say, 'A remarkable person. Seems so wise.'

'And a good friend,' Sylvie added. 'As I promised, I have information for you. The abbé has found money and a place for your brother. Could you and he visit the institute in the morning at seven to see if it suits him?'

'Yes, I'm delighted. I'll go there before work and bring him along.' He paused for a moment with an afterthought. 'Do the abbé's students find employment? Can they support themselves?'

'Yes, many of the young men enter the printing trade. Young women work in the textile industry. Or, if they are gifted like Michou, they find opportunities in painting and decorating. Some are sought after as maids in fine households.' She hesitated before going on. 'Denise de Villers, whose name you may recognize, was hired to work in the royal palace at Versailles.'

'Why should I know her?'

'She's the young deaf woman accused of murdering her mistress, the Duchesse de Saumur. Many people have already burned her at the stake on Place de Grève, but I'm convinced she's innocent.'

André wrinkled his brow. 'Monsieur Hoche speaks about the murder, claims the maid's guilty, but hasn't mentioned her by name.'

Sylvie gave him a quick summary of the case. 'We regard Chevalier de Beauregard as the chief suspect, and Monsieur Hoche may be involved as well.'

André's expression became somber. 'I'll need to think about that.' He was silent for a moment, then he brightened. 'I look forward to meeting you again tomorrow. You've been very helpful.'

When he had gone, Sylvie returned to her room, leaned out the window and looked down at the courtyard. He emerged from the house walking slowly, head bent forward. A warm feeling flowed through her body.

Promptly at seven the next morning, after a short, brisk walk, Sylvie and Michou reached the Institute for the Deaf, a plain four-storey building on Rue des Moulins. André was already there with his brother, a fair-haired, slim lad. Anxiety clouded his eyes. Michou smiled, spread her arms wide in welcome. His face shone with relief. She took him by the hand and led the way into the institute.

Sylvie found herself walking side by side with André, relating bits of information about the institute's director, Abbé de l'Épée, and his students. This building was his own home. Almost a hundred students crowded into its rooms for instruction. Distinguished visitors, like Jefferson, also came

118

to observe the abbé's methods at work. Most of the students lived together in several houses in the city.

The old, bent director was in his office upstairs. Sylvie had earlier mentioned to him that André might help prove Denise de Villers's innocence. The abbé greeted the brothers warmly and excused himself for remaining seated. Michou and Sylvie, he said, would take the visitors on a tour of the institute.

As they wandered through the building, observing teachers and students at work, Sylvie explained to André how the abbé had transformed the simple, local sign language into an instrument for communicating even the most abstract, complicated ideas of science and philosophy. His students often gave public demonstrations of their proficiency in French and several foreign languages.

'You see they are happy here. Your brother should fit in well. He already knows the most basic signs he needs to get started. He'll make rapid progress.'

Though a little shy, the boy exchanged signs with a few boys his age and appeared eager to join them. Michou introduced him to the others. Soon, he was involved in their exercises, Michou at his side tutoring him.

Sylvie and André walked out into the small, quiet garden behind the building. As they sauntered between lush beds of early roses, André seemed to have something weighing on his mind. Reluctant to probe, or to rush him, Sylvie spoke casually about Françoise Arnaud and other instructors who would look after his brother.

'He'll be in very good hands,' she remarked.

André nodded distractedly, then abruptly asked, 'Please tell me more about Mademoiselle de Villers.' His expression had grown strained. He walked stiffly. Sylvie could guess the direction of his thoughts.

'She studied here for several years, a very gifted, attractive young woman of excellent character and a sense of her own worth.' Sylvie explained the charge against Denise and her present precarious situation. 'Provost Sully bears her a secret grudge. His influence at the palace is great. He *will* have his revenge. It's entirely possible that she may shortly burn on Place de Grève for a crime she didn't commit.'

'And Monsieur Hoche and Chevalier de Beauregard? How are they involved?'

'Beauregard was Duchesse Aimée's lover and probably the last person to see her alive. She had just broken off their relationship and was about to denounce him to the Queen for reasons we do not know. Hoche was using Beauregard for his own devious purposes and protecting him. They are often seen together. Hoche may have hidden evidence that would implicate Beauregard in the duchess's murder and save Denise.'

André fell silent, staring rigidly ahead, hands clasped behind his back. Sylvie waited, her chest tightening. Gravel crunched beneath their feet. Birdsong echoed off the walls of the adjacent buildings. The garden filled with a sense of expectancy. Finally, he drew a deep breath and faced Sylvie.

'How can I help?'

CHAPTER SIXTEEN

A Suspect Valet

Wednesday, June 6

'An emergency south of Paris,' his message had said. Anne sat anxiously waiting for Paul at the breakfast table in the garden. She hadn't seen him since Monday. When she returned home from Blanche Moreau's room yesterday, the message was on her table. He would be home very late and would sleep in a guest room rather than disturb her.

'Good morning, Anne.' Fatigue lined his face—and the day had only begun. He was dressed to travel with her to Versailles. As she poured coffee, he recounted yesterday's crisis. Angry peasants had destroyed a landlord's mill, killed his livestock, and beaten his steward. Paul's troopers had arrested a few leaders and restored order but reported that the peasants remained surly and openly disrespectful. Paul met with his officers and men in Villejuif and organized more patrols in affected districts to prevent further violence.

'The situation in the countryside is volatile,' he continued in a somber voice. 'Constant quarrels over rents and fees. Landlords and their lawyers press the peasants into ever deeper misery. There's really little the highway patrol can do about it. I'll lay the problem in Baron Breteuil's lap.'

Anne coaxed a smile from his lips. 'Do you have anything else of interest to tell me, Paul?' He looked down for a moment, then cast her a quick, insouciant glance. 'Georges and I visited Madame Lebrun's brothel Monday night.'

Anne started, then noticed a sparkle in his eye. He was teasing her. She retaliated with a frown.

'Seriously,' he said in a penitent voice. 'I met a potential witness.' He went on to speak of his conversation with Madame Lebrun. 'She strengthened my belief that we're dealing with a conspiracy. Hoche engaged Beauregard to uncover evidence of scandal in the Queen's relationship to Comte Fersen. And there's more. While Hoche was entertaining the guests, Georges made copies of his keys. We're close to searching his apartment.'

Paul reached into the bread basket for a brioche. His spirits seemed to rise. 'Tell me, Anne, what you learned at Lamballe's apartment.'

'The duchess and Beauregard had quarreled only an hour or two before her death. Beauregard apparently bribed the maid Catherine to deny seeing him exit from the secret stairway.'

Paul breathed out an exasperated sigh. 'For a few *livres* she would perjure herself even though the deaf maid's life hangs in the balance. Nonetheless, Beauregard's still our prime suspect.'

'We also have a new credible suspect, Jules Blondel.' Anne went on to report the discovery of the duchess's journal. 'She had suspected Blondel and was about to examine his account books. From his entries, Marie has singled out several dubious transactions he made for Duc Henri at a *brocanteur*'s shop on Rue Saint-Marc. I left them with Georges to investigate.' She went on to describe her conversation with the pathetic

Blanche Moreau. 'Blondel seems desperate,' Anne concluded, 'and may be dangerous.'

Paul nodded. 'We shall watch him carefully.'

Upon arrival in Versailles, Anne found Marie at her bedroom table in a blue silk dressing gown, an empty breakfast tray off to one side. Duchesse Aimée's journal was propped up before her. She seemed engrossed in reading, unaware of Anne at the open door.

Anne cleared her throat.

Marie looked up, blinked, smiled. 'What have you discovered in Paris?' she asked, laying the journal aside.

Anne related the gist of her conversation with Blanche Moreau.

Marie sighed. 'Blondel seems to be a decent man who has judged badly. Unfortunately, he has turned to crime to deal with the consequences. Yesterday, I went over his accounts again and found a few more suspicious entries. They've gone by courier to Georges.'

'Is Blondel aware of my visit to Blanche?'

'Not yet. He returned here late yesterday afternoon, his usual calm, unconcerned self.'

'He'll be angry when she tells him.' Anne hesitated, loathe to arouse anxiety. 'Do we need to be concerned that he lives here with us?'

'I think so,' Marie replied. 'Paul will take him into custody as soon as he appears dangerous.'

After Marie completed her morning toilette, the two women walked through the town to the provost's prison to visit Denise de Villers again and inquire into her relations with Blondel. Supposing he killed Duchesse Aimée, could the maid have given him any reason to shift the blame to her rather than to the cook or the housekeeper or someone else?

The same guard as on previous visits showed them to the visiting room and left to fetch Denise. In a few minutes she arrived, manacled as before. The guard freed her, this time without being asked, even showing care lest he cause pain. Denise appeared to have won sympathy from him.

Anne rubbed ointment into the young woman's sore wrists while Marie brushed her hair.

'You both are very kind,' the maid signed, a sweet smile lighting up her wan face.

'Tell us what you can recall about Jules Blondel,' Anne asked.

Denise reflected for a moment. 'During the last month or two he paid more attention to me than before. He smiled, lightly touched me, and very recently found excuses to come to my room. When we were alone together working in the kitchen, he sometimes seemed sad and lost. I felt sorry for him, patted his hand.'

Anne wondered, why was Blondel courting Denise? At the beginning, he might have sought romantic relief from his strained relationship with Blanche. Later, perhaps fearing the duchess had uncovered his thefts, he decided to kill her and pass the blame on to Denise.

'Denise, can you think of any reasons why he would want to incriminate you?'

She frowned, her brow lined with the effort of recalling impressions of Blondel. 'I can't think of any,' she signed. 'We never quarreled or argued.'

'Did he show any ill will toward the duchess?'

Denise thought again, then slowly shook her head. A shadow of despair crossed her face.

As Anne and Marie were returning to the apartment, they saw Blondel dash from the palace and leap on board a coach bound for Paris. A message from Blanche Moreau had just reached him, Anne was sure.

In the kitchen Marthe Bourdon and the cook were polishing silver. As Anne entered, the housekeeper looked up, her hand gripping a spoon.

'Have you seen Monsieur Blondel?' asked Anne.

'He received a message from Paris a few minutes ago,' the housekeeper replied, 'and left immediately.'

'Did he say what was the matter?'

'I asked. He said, "something urgent."'

Anne suspected Blanche had warned him of their growing

peril. Since she was too weak to travel to Versailles, he had to go to her. What would they do now?

Anne joined Marie in her room and shared her suspicion. 'Blondel will be angry—and perhaps dangerous.'

Marie agreed. 'I don't want him to return to this apartment.'

Colonel Saint-Martin was at the writing table in Duc Henri's study when Georges walked in. Early in the morning, he had gone to the *brocanteur*'s shop to examine the record of Blondel's sales. Saint-Martin waved his adjutant to a chair. 'Well?'

'As we suspected, sir. Monsieur Blondel is a thief. To get the *brocanteur* to cooperate I had to threaten him with a visit from Quidor and his agents. The prospect of police auditing his books loosened his tongue. He had paid Blondel a thousand *livres* for the duke's toothpick and other things that Comtesse Marie had checked. The duke's account books indicate he received only eight hundred *livres*. Blondel must have kept two hundred *livres* for himself. And that's probably not all he kept. He had sold other items earlier.'

Saint-Martin shook his head. 'That's unfortunate. I rather like the fellow. But he's become desperate and must think he's recovering unpaid wages. We need to interrogate him, and his pregnant friend.'

'Where? In the provost's prison?'

'Not yet. That Blondel murdered Duchesse Aimée is still too conjectural to bring to the provost's attention. And I don't want to charge Blondel with theft prematurely and ruin his life and that of his friend Blanche. It's still possible for them to make amends.' Saint-Martin leaned back, arms crossed on his chest. 'We cannot allow Blondel to remain in this apartment, and we must also prevent him from fleeing. What do you recommend, Georges?'

The adjutant studied the shiny brown mahogany surface of the table in front of him, then looked up. 'The captain of the palace guard could hold him and Blanche in secure rooms on the ground floor of the palace. And we could interrogate them there.'

Saint-Martin nodded. 'First, we must catch them.' He wrote out an order and handed it to Georges. 'Pick up Blanche

Moreau and Jules Blondel, peacefully if possible. Quidor's agents will help you.'

Saint-Martin was having afternoon tea with Marie and Anne, when Georges returned to the palace. Marie invited Georges to the table and poured a cup for him. He watched her with wide-eyed surprise and thanked her. She was the first countess to have ever served him anything.

Saint-Martin offered him a brioche. 'What do you have to report?'

'Blondel and Moreau are in the guardroom, sir, ready for interrogation. I found them together in her garret. They came without protest. I think they were expecting me.'

After tea, the two men went downstairs. The captain of the guard showed them into a small waiting room. Georges took a seat off to one side and opened his notebook. Saint-Martin sat at a table to lead the questioning. 'Captain,' he said, 'bring in Mademoiselle Moreau first.'

Blanche Moreau entered the room, the captain at her side. He pulled a chair up to the table for her, then left the room. She smoothed her plain brown woolen gown, folded her hands in her lap, and cocked her head defiantly. Her eyes flashed with anger.

Saint-Martin began softly. 'You've admitted that Monsieur Blondel was supporting you with money from the illegal sale of Duc Henri's possessions. In the eyes of the law you are an accomplice to his crimes. Do you agree?'

She glared at him. 'Your wife helped me at the market and won my confidence, then tricked me. She'll be my ruin.'

The colonel tapped on the table. 'A young maid's life is at stake, mademoiselle. We must get to the truth any way we can.'

'What do Jules and I have to do with the death of the duchess?'

'That's what I want you to tell me.' Saint-Martin leaned back and regarded her soberly. Blondel might have admitted to her that he had killed the duchess. If Blanche held any ill will toward him for her present misfortune, she might implicate him.

'Jules was simply trying to recover his wages. We're desperately poor. That's all. He had no reason to kill the duchess.'

'Shortly before her death, the duchess threatened to discharge him and have him arrested for theft. Did he ever tell you that?'

'Yes,' she replied hesitantly.

'Then her death must have come as a great relief to both of you.'

She cast her eyes down, said nothing in reply.

Saint-Martin forced her to meet his eye. 'Had Jules ever threatened to harm the duchess?'

'No, absolutely not!' She folded her arms on her chest and glared at him.

The colonel rose, leaned toward the woman. 'Mademoiselle Moreau, you should reflect on whether Jules Blondel has dealt fairly with you, putting you at risk of going to prison. How much loyalty do you owe him?'

She remained defiant, refusing to speak.

Saint-Martin called for the captain, then turned to the woman. 'You'll go back to the guardroom for now. We'll speak to you again at another time.'

The captain brought Jules Blondel into the waiting room. He was without manacles and still wearing the duke's yellow livery. His face was composed but his eyes smoldered with resentment mixed with fear. Saint-Martin pointed to the chair facing him.

'Monsieur Blondel,' he began, 'do you admit having kept for yourself money that belonged to the Duc Henri de Saumur?'

'That money was my back wages. I didn't take more than was my due.'

'That's for a magistrate to decide. The duke had other creditors besides yourself, some of them struggling shopkeepers and artisans. You stepped ahead of them.'

Blondel opened his mouth, about to protest. The colonel cut him off. 'Did you realize that Duchesse Aimée might disapprove of what you were doing?'

Blondel hesitated momentarily, uncertain how to respond, then shrugged his shoulders.

'If it didn't matter, why did you trouble to write counterfeit receipts and enter false figures in the account books? It was easy to fool the duke, but not the duchess. What would happen if she found out?'

His lips tightened. He replied in a low, soft voice. 'She would dismiss me from her service and turn me over to the police.'

'And what would happen to Blanche Moreau and the child she is carrying? Your child, by the way.'

'I don't know,' he replied. 'She's destitute, with nowhere to go. Perhaps someone would have pity on her.'

'Or. . .' Saint-Martin paused for a moment of heavy silence. 'She might throw herself into the Seine. She's a proud woman, too proud to beg or sell herself, isn't she?'

Blondel averted his eyes, looked down at the table.

'You were caught between two women, one who would have you imprisoned and the other who threatened to kill herself. You were a desperate man early that Friday morning when you heard Duchesse Aimée return from a party. While playing cards, she had mentioned to a friend that she would confront you later in the morning. A servant overheard and immediately sent you a warning.'

Saint-Martin glared at Blondel, who was sitting stiffly erect, his hands gripping his thighs. 'You were at a loss what to do. Finally, you decided to confess your crime, explain why you had done it, and beg for her understanding. In a nutshell, you would throw yourself upon her mercy.'

His lips parted, Blondel still said nothing. He appeared spellbound.

'So you went to her room at four in the morning, knowing that she would most likely still be dressed and awake. The cook may have told you that the duchess would breakfast at dawn. She was surprised but let you in. Asked what you wanted at that hour. Heard your confession to the end. Then she stared at you with anger and contempt, dismissed you on the spot from her service, and turned as if to pull the bell rope. You feared she would call the palace guard. In panic, you seized a poker and—'

'No! I did not kill her. I felt the urge but I left her alive and returned to my room.'

127

'By what route, the private stairs?'

'No, the servants' hallway.'

'Can anyone verify your alibi?'

'No one saw me.' He hesitated. 'None that I'm aware of.'

The colonel glanced sideways. 'Any questions, Monsieur Charpentier?'

'None, sir.'

'Then take Monsieur Blondel to the guards' quarters, where he'll remain until further notice.'

'Sir, how did you conjure that scenario out of our slim body of evidence?' Georges thoughtfully palmed his bald head. 'Blondel usually keeps a good servant's mask on his face. But as you told his story, the mask fell and his face became an open book. He agreed with everything you said, except for his killing Duchesse Aimée.'

The two men were sipping brandy in Duc Henri's study. Georges had found an opened bottle hidden in one of Blondel's boots and had poured into two glasses.

The question hung in the air while Saint-Martin swirled the liquid, sniffed its aroma. A brandy, he thought, from the duke's collection of fine spirits. And hardly the first bottle the valet had stolen.

The colonel took a reverent sip from his glass, then replied easily. 'If I really know a man's character and the circumstances of his life, I can usually predict what he would do in a given situation. I was sure Blondel met the duchess shortly before her death. I wasn't sure he killed her.' He peered over the rim of his glass and lowered his voice. 'I'm now inclined to bet he didn't.'

Evening approached the palace of Versailles. Anne, Paul, and Georges gathered at the supper table. Comtesse Marie was away, dining in Princesse Lamballe's apartment with a select company from which useful gossip would flow.

Marthe Bourdon brought a tureen of thick pea soup to the sideboard. Bread and cheese were already on the table. She served the soup, then a bowl of greens.

Anne made a point of observing her. She had surely heard

the news about Jules Blondel and his friend Blanche, but she appeared outwardly unaffected. His trips to the *brocanteur* had probably aroused her suspicions. She would have little sympathy for a servant marked as a thief. Blondel's fall also meant more power for Marthe, charged now with the duties of steward as well as those of housekeeper. Inwardly, she must relish the change.

When Marthe had withdrawn, the men reported on their interrogation of Blondel and Moreau. Anne felt a pang of guilt for having taken advantage of the pregnant young woman's distress. It helped ease her conscience that she meant to serve justice and to save Denise.

The conversation shifted to the reading of recent entries in Aimée's journal. Anne had joined Marie in the slow, tedious work. 'Many passages are cryptic, usually those dealing with intimate matters.' Anne sighed. 'Names are disguised. Marie clarified the text by chatting with Princesse Lamballe and other women in the palace.'

'So, what have you discovered?' asked Paul.

'DuchesseAimée had so ingratiated herself,' Anne replied, 'that she became a trusted courier between the Queen and Comte Fersen. The Queen often gave a written message to Aimée, who took it to Fersen's apartment in the town, and brought back his response.'

Paul leaned forward, his eyes widening with interest.

'On Thursday morning, Duchesse Aimée caught Chevalier Beauregard at her desk going through her papers. He had a fake message from Fersen in his hands which she had laid out to trap him. She had already become suspicious. Fersen had earlier complained to the Queen that someone had tampered with the seal on one of her messages.'

'And perhaps delivered its contents to Monsieur Hoche,' Paul remarked.

'For a price,' Anne added. 'Beauregard swore he had done nothing wrong. Claimed he had picked up the Fersen message merely out of curiosity. He apologized. Aimée told him she would think it over and reach a decision in the evening.'

Anne paused to cut bread and pass it around the table. Georges poured the wine.

Paul lifted his glass. 'We already knew that the duchess had grown tired of him and had decided to send him away.'

'There's more,' Anne continued. 'Princesse Lamballe has revealed to Marie that the mysterious "Josephine" in Duchesse Aimée's journal is the Queen herself, the same name Comte Fersen uses in their correspondence.'

Georges emptied his glass and set it on the table. 'From the marks on Beauregard's blotter we learned that he wrote to someone, probably Hoche, about Fersen and the Queen. So, among Hoche's papers there should be evidence of Beauregard's attempts to spy on the Queen and Fersen, as well as his early-morning visit to Duchesse Aimée's room.'

He turned to Paul. 'Colonel, during tomorrow's Roman feast, while Hoche is busy in the great gallery, I would like to search his study.'

'Yes, it's the right time.' Saint-Martin reached into his pocket and pulled out a folded sheet of paper. 'Sylvie has informed me that Hoche's clerk, André, will cooperate. Hoche has entrusted him with engaging extra servants. He will hire you, Georges. André himself will serve as a waiter and track Hoche's movements for you. You must plan carefully. The Duc d'Orléans polices his own palace. It would upset him if you, an officer in the Royal Highway Patrol, were caught in the act of burglary. But you know the palace and are the best man for this task.'

Anne recalled that when Georges had worked for Lieutenant-General Sartine many years ago, he had secretly searched the palace for evidence of a conspiracy against the Crown.

'Don't worry, Colonel!' Georges squared his shoulders, stuck out his chin. 'I have the keys, André will give me a description of the rooms.' He paused, engaged Anne's eye. 'But I'll need a reliable partner, a person familiar with our investigation and utterly discreet. I can't trust Quidor's agents in a matter so closely touching the royal family. I need Madame Cartier.' He hesitated for a moment and added, 'André could also hire her as a servant.'

Paul frowned, remained silent for a moment, then glanced at Anne. 'Do you want to do it?'

'I'll think about it overnight.' She was pleased he had asked her.

Paul looked at the paper in his hand, then gazed at Anne. 'Sylvie also would like me to come as her companion—if Madame Cartier would agree.'

'Of course.' Anne chuckled. 'Sylvie couldn't find a better escort.'

CHAPTER SEVENTEEN

A Warning

Thursday, June 7

S till in Denise's role, Anne rose at dawn, quickly washed with cold water, and hurried to the kitchen. Robinette had already stirred up the fire and was cutting bread. Anne greeted her with a smile, petted Bijou, and set about preparing a large breakfast tray.

The cook smiled in return and managed a clearly enunciated *bonjour*. She usually spoke in a nervous mumble. Apparently, some of her initial anxiety about Anne had disappeared. When she turned back to the stove, her shoulders were relaxed.

Then Marthe the housekeeper entered the room and the atmosphere abruptly changed. The cook's entire body stiffened. Even the cat slunk away. How remarkable, Anne thought. There was nothing outwardly threatening about Marthe. She gave the cook an unsmiling sidelong glance, bid Anne a polite good morning, and began taking stock of supplies in preparation for a morning visit to the central kitchen next to the palace.

Something strange was going on between Marthe and Robinette even though they behaved correctly toward each other. No complaints or harsh words, no shaking of heads or gimlet glances. At least none that Anne had noticed. She wondered if the root of the problem lay within the cook. It was perhaps time to probe gently for the truth. But first she would serve breakfast.

Georges and Paul had already come to Marie's room when Anne arrived with the tray. The mood was somber. They were seated at the table by the window, but no one was speaking.

'A messenger delivered this a few minutes ago,' Paul said, handing her an official-looking note. 'The provost demands a full report of the investigation this morning.'

Anne read the closely written text. It acknowledged this was short notice.

But the Queen has summoned me for this afternoon. Writing a report should not unduly inconvenience you, as I understand that you have uncovered very little that is germane to this case.

Marie complained, 'It's not a week since Denise discovered the duchess's body right here.' She nodded toward the spot. 'And we have two strong suspects, Blondel and Beauregard.'

'But no proof that either man is guilty,' Paul countered. 'I have little to report to the provost.'

'Perhaps we'll find evidence this evening in Hoche's study,' Georges offered hopefully. He glanced at Anne. 'Are you going to join me?'

'Yes.' She turned to Paul. 'I'm familiar with the duke's palace and know what to look for. At this point, we must run the risk of being caught and compromising ourselves.'

'I agree . . . for the maid's sake.' His voice sounded strained.

While Anne served the others, then ate her own breakfast, an idea had nagged at Anne's mind. 'Thus far,' she began, 'we've almost ignored Robinette the cook.'

'Jacques Bart interrogated her and found no ill will or hostility,' observed Paul, 'nor did we.'

'Aimée's journal doesn't even mention her,' added Marie. 'I've showed Marthe's household account books to the baron's clerk. They are carefully kept and reveal no thieving either by the cook or by Marthe. So, the cook had no reason to fear, as Blondel did, that the duchess would discharge her.'

'Still, the cook may have a hidden scandal in her past, a secret crime elsewhere years ago,' Anne suggested. 'The duchess may have discovered it. That could also explain Robinette's odd behavior early this morning in the kitchen. She seemed strangely troubled by the presence of the housekeeper, who might know her secret.'

'A far-fetched idea, madame,' Georges remarked, a trace of sarcasm in his voice. 'After all, they are half-sisters! Robinette is plain as a post, has the spirit of a doormat, hasn't achieved much in life. Marthe is a proud, handsome woman and a successful servant. The cook's likely to envy and resent her sister, who probably pities or despises her in turn. *Voilà!* A conflict between kin simmering just below the surface. What does that have to do with the death of the duchess? Take care, madame, you might find yourself on a wild goose chase.'

'Thanks for the warning, Georges.' Anne allowed a bit of sarcasm to creep into her voice. 'Robinette may lack beauty and spirit, but I believe she's cunning—like her cat.' Anne loaded the breakfast tray and left for the kitchen, hoping that Marthe Bourdon would have gone shopping and the cook was alone.

They sat in Robinette's room, with a small table between them and two wooden chairs to sit on. A narrow bed occupied the rest of the room. The sole window had a wide sill. Bijou perched on it watching birds fly by. The cook poured tea.

The conversation turned at first to Bijou, whose ears twitched at the mention of his name. Several years ago, Robinette had found him, then just a kitten, and raised him in the palace to be an excellent mouser.

'Who taught you to cook?' Anne sensed that Robinette would not mind giving out some personal information.

'My father.' Her words were cool, as if he had meant little to her. 'He worked for the Bourdon family's *hôtel garni*. I had to help him. When he died, I took over.'

'You've been together with Marthe Bourdon a long time. You must know each other well.'

'Yes, you can say that. She's a strict housekeeper. With her you always know what you're supposed to do.'

Anne noted that the cook ignored the opportunity to say she and Marthe were friends. There was distance between them. 'Has she ever been married?'

Robinette seemed momentarily startled by the question. 'No, she hasn't.' An ambivalent inflection crept into her voice. Anne wondered if the formidable Marthe had had a serious romantic episode in her life. It might have left an emotional scar and account for the cool rigidity of her character. People kept at a safe distance couldn't hurt her again.

Robinette put her tea aside, picked the cat off the sill, and watched it curl up in her lap.

Anne understood the woman would say no more about issues of love in Marthe's life. But Anne's own experience prompted her to observe, 'Even strong women may hide badly bruised hearts.'

'That's true.' Robinette spoke as if she meant it. She hesitated briefly, then asked, 'You've visited Denise, haven't you?'

'Yes, three times. She's bearing up under the strain as best she can.' Anne went on to describe her distressed appearance and the cruel hardships she had to endure.

''Tis a pity. She's a good girl. Loved to play with Bijou.' The woman looked up from the cat. 'What will happen to her?'

Anne had to tell the brutal truth. 'She'll die a horrible death, unless we discover the person who killed Duchesse Aimée.'

Robinette nodded slowly, cautiously. 'That's what I feared.' She shuddered. 'May God have mercy on her.'

Anne took note of that sentiment but wondered how sincere it was. Robinette's eyes were dry, enigmatic. Anne tried to probe in another direction. 'How did you feel about Duchesse Aimée?'

'Never whipped me.' The cook's brow strained with the effort of recall. 'Hardly knew her. I've cooked here for five years. She never came into the kitchen. Hated the smell. Spoke maybe twice with me. Didn't know my name.'

The two women exchanged a few more remarks. Anne thanked her for the tea and left.

Georges might be right, she thought on the way back to her room. Whatever troubled the relationship between the cook and the housekeeper appeared to have nothing to do with the crime being investigated.

At mid-morning Paul left the palace apartment, his report to the provost in a portfolio under his arm. Anne had returned to Paris with Georges to prepare for their part in the Roman feast. Paul felt increasingly uneasy about the plan to gather evidence in Hoche's apartment. It was an affront to the duke and a challenge to his authority. The consequences of failure could be serious. Paul's imagination took flight. Scandal, arrest and conviction for burglary, the pillory. Even prison. 'Enough!' Paul murmured to himself and curbed his errant thoughts.

On the stairway to the main floor he recognized a tall, slender figure walking toward him. 'Comte Fersen! What a pleasure to see you again.' Their paths crossed infrequently since returning from America to France some four years ago. Fersen became the colonel-proprietor of a regiment near the Belgian frontier, while Saint-Martin entered the Royal Highway Patrol.

The Swede breathed an audible sigh of relief. 'I was about to call on you.'

'I'm on my way to the provost's office,' said Saint-Martin, wondering where his friend had spent the night. Apparently in the palace. The combination of his handsome features and his melancholic personality seemed to attract well-born, beautiful women.

'I'll walk with you,' Fersen said. 'It's safer to talk in the open.' He began tentatively, as if not fully sure what to say. 'I understand you are pursuing the Duchesse de Saumur's case.'

'Yes, I'm going to report on my progress this morning.'

'Has there been any?'

Saint-Martin was taken aback. He hadn't felt that the palace was looking over his shoulder, but apparently it was. Blondel's detention in the guardroom could not be kept secret. 'Yes, I've found two possible suspects in addition to the maid.'

The Swede lowered his voice though no one but Saint-

Martin could possibly hear him. 'I'm also interested in one of them, the Chevalier de Beauregard. He may have tampered with my mail. He denies it. Certain pieces have been furtively opened, others are missing.' His eyes seemed to waver with anxiety. 'In the course of your investigation, would you please look carefully into this matter?'

'I would be happy to help you, my friend. However, this seems to fall within the provost's jurisdiction.' Saint-Martin felt sympathetic, but he wished to avoid unnecessary conflict with Sully.

'Unfortunately, he's a gossip monger and cannot be trusted. You are a man of honor and discretion. The matter is intimate—and very serious.' His eyes registered a rising level of distress. 'It involves a lady of great distinction.'

Alarm bells rang in Saint-Martin's mind. Fersen's 'lady' was none other than the Queen. 'I'll alert my adjutant, Charpentier. In our investigation of the chevalier, we shall watch out for your missing messages.'

Fersen thanked the colonel, then added, 'By the way, Beauregard quit the palace early this morning. The Queen has banished him.'

'Has she indeed!' A kind of death sentence, reflected Saint-Martin. It killed the young man's prospect of royal favor and probably ended his usefulness to Hoche and Gaillard. 'Where has he gone, do you know?'

The Swede's eyes darkened, his voice thickened with anger. 'When he climbed into a coach for Paris, he was heard to say to the driver, "the Palais-Royal".'

Saint-Martin parted from Fersen outside the prison, mulling over his last remark. The duke's palace at the Palais-Royal was the main camp of the Queen's enemies. Beauregard would go to Hoche. Would he stay in his apartment? If so, that could complicate any attempt to search it for evidence. Georges and Anne must be warned of the new danger and informed of Comte Fersen's concerns.

A guard showed Saint-Martin into Sully's office. The provost was sitting at his table, his agent Bart standing next to him holding a file box. They appeared to have just ended a discussion. To judge from their faces, it had been unpleasant, perhaps contentious. Sully looked sour, Bart seemed to smoulder with repressed anger.

What kind of man could work for Sully? Bart had a common round face with no distinguishing features. The rest of him was average in every way. From a distance, he was a man easily overlooked, a chameleon who blended into a crowd or disappeared in the shadow of a doorway. On closer inspection, he appeared intelligent. Was he servile enough to please his master? Saint-Martin wasn't sure.

Bart returned the file box to a vacant place on a shelf, and left the room. The provost's eyes followed him, then turned to Saint-Martin. 'Have a seat, Colonel. What do you have to report?' The provost's tone was unfriendly. He worked his mouth as if seeking relief from poorly fitting artificial teeth.

Saint-Martin explained what he had done thus far, and his reasons for suspecting Beauregard and Blondel. The latter's selling of Duc Henri's property in lieu of wages called for further study before making an arrest. 'I realize,' he concluded, 'that I must still find evidence directly implicating one of these men in the killing of the duchess. The investigation continues.'

Sully raised an eyebrow at Blondel's detention but didn't pursue the point. 'Colonel, as I told Her Majesty this morning, I see no reason for further delay. Your investigation has unearthed evidence of scandal and crime by Duc Henri, Chevalier de Beauregard, and Monsieur Blondel. But you haven't proved that any of them killed Duchesse Aimée. Mademoiselle de Villers remains our prime suspect, transparently guilty. Baron Breteuil has thus far prevented me from charging her. But I fully expect Her Majesty to force his hand soon.'

For a few moments, Saint-Martin silently studied Sully's face. It was implacable. If he had his way, Denise de Villers would soon be dead.

Saint-Martin found Baron Breteuil leaving his office in the palace.

'Paul,' said the baron as they stepped out into the courtyard

'I'm going for a ride in the park before dinner. Come along. We'll talk on the way.' He signaled a groom, who went off to the stables. A few minutes later, he returned with two horses and riding gear. The two men donned boots, mounted, and set out at an invigorating canter.

They rode along the Grand Canal to its farthest extremity, l'Étoile Royale, where they dismounted and looked back. A long mile away over the canal's glittering surface rose the great palace, imposing, intimidating even at a distance. For several minutes, the two men took in the sight, each absorbed in his own thoughts.

'As I gaze at the palace and its garden,' said the baron finally, 'I could believe that the kings of France, the greatest monarchs in Europe, will reign gloriously forever. But, when I return to my office and soberly consider the state of the kingdom, my faith wavers.' He shook his head. 'Our present King is bankrupt, his spirit broken. The notables of the realm are openly critical of his reforms and, I believe, inwardly rebellious. The Queen is brave but utterly incapable of governing in her husband's stead. The man she has put in charge, her favorite, Archbishop Brienne, has no standing, no influence. His ministry will accomplish nothing. In a year or two, he will be pushed aside. And then what?' He glanced at Paul.

'In the Palais-Royal,' Paul replied, 'some say the Duc d'Orléans will rule as regent and confine the royal family to a distant château.'

'That's hardly a better alternative for the country, Paul. Orléans is weak and incompetent. Other devious men would use him.' The baron shrugged the issue away. 'Let's talk instead about Denise de Villers. Have you any hope of proving her innocent?'

Paul repeated what he had told the provost. 'I need more time than he cares to give.'

Breteuil sighed. 'The Queen has summoned me to her study this afternoon for my views on this matter. She has already heard from Sully. I may be able to win you three more days, till Monday at the latest. Then he will put Mademoiselle de Villers on trial. Duly convicted, the maid will be moved to Paris and imprisoned in the Conciergerie to be at Parlement's disposal.' He hesitated, studying Paul's face. 'You and your adjutant will return to your ordinary duties with the highway patrol.'

At that moment Paul felt powerless. An inexorable fate seemed to control the actors in this drama. His own best efforts appeared futile. 'I shall continue the investigation for as long as possible.' Even as he spoke, he wondered if he were tilting at windmills, like that other chivalric soldier, Don Quixote de la Mancha.

CHAPTER EIGHTEEN

A Roman Evening

Thursday, June 7

The evening feast was about to start. The duke's palace had come alive with men and women in the garb of ancient Rome. Like other female servants, Anne was dressed in a white sleeveless woolen tunic, pulled up to the knees, girded at the waist. She wore sandals on her feet. A footman had put a tray of drinks into her hands and sent her on a tour through the public rooms.

She felt like an actress on stage again, excited, playing a role, enjoying the crowd. Scenes from years of performing at Sadler's Wells came back vividly and threatened to distract her. She imagined herself once more on a high tightrope, holding a balancing pole instead of a tray.

Also distracting was news that Paul had brought back from Versailles a few hours ago. The baron had warned that the investigation into Duchesse Aimée's death must conclude in a few days. Barring a miracle, Denise would then be sent to the Conciergerie, convicted of murder. Beauregard had left Versailles and might seek refuge with Hoche. Paul had also alerted Anne and Georges to Fersen's missing messages. They might be hidden in the duke's palace, most likely in Hoche's apartment.

Anne fought back her anxiety for Denise. Serving the drinks called for a clear head. In the exhibition galleries guests gathered in lively conversation or bent over display cases of engraved Roman gems, awestruck by their rare beauty, enjoying a last look before they were shipped off to Russia.

One of the gentlemen moved among the cases with easy familiarity, commenting in cultured French on the merits of the gems. His bearing declared him to be Philippe, Duc d'Orléans, host of this party. His toga's broad scarlet border hinted at his lofty political ambitions. There was talk in the Palais-Royal that he should be regent or king.

He appeared about forty years old, rather tall, red-faced, and heavy. His slack jaw and soft features betrayed a phlegmatic character. To his credit was a high, intelligent forehead and an amiable, courtly air. He motioned for Anne to come with the tray. As he took a glass of wine, a spark of interest, then a glint of desire lighted up his jaded eyes. This woman, he had concluded, was no ordinary serving maid. In an instant, he scanned her from tip to toe and seemed about to question her.

Anne grew nervous. Her hands weakened. The tray began to tremble. Becoming involved with the duke could keep her from searching Hoche's apartment. Fortunately, a distinguished-looking guest called out to him, would he comment on a particular gem, *Minerva Arming*.

'Yes, of course,' he replied. 'The goddess of war is one of my favorites.' He joined the gentleman at the display case. 'Compare this Minerva to Empress Catherine's portrait.' He pointed to a sketch hanging on the wall above the case. 'There's a remarkable physical likeness. And in character, too. I understand she's gathering her armies for another battle with the Turks.'

While the two men fell deeply into this discussion, Anne handed her tray to another servant and slipped away, vowing henceforth to avoid the duke. In the anteroom to the great gallery, guests milled about, chattering with anticipation. The women—mostly courtesans—were in high-waisted, long, flowing, sleeveless silk gowns, their hair coiffed in antique styles and crowned with diamond-studded diadems. The

140

diamonds were of the paste variety, Anne thought. Men wore long, mostly white, silk tunics. Men and women alike were shod with sandals laced up the calf of the leg.

Hoche had warned the guests that those not wearing Roman costumes would be turned away at the door. He set an example in sandals and tunic, a laurel wreath on his head, greeting guests with *salve amice* and similar bits of Latin.

Anne found Sylvie in the women's dressing room. Deft application of powder had hardened and whitened the lovely, soft texture of her skin. Her arms uncovered, her long tunic pulled up above the knees and girded at the waist, a quiver of arrows on her back, a bow in her hands, a crescent diadem in her hair, Sylvie looked every inch the huntress. She struck her pose for Anne, stepping forward with the left foot, glancing to the right at an imaginary prey and drawing an arrow from her quiver.

There was a knock on the door, and a voice summoned Sylvie. She was to perform at the beginning of the feast. Anne bent to Sylvie's ear to whisper, 'Are you nervous?'

She nodded without changing her expression. 'I'll be all right.' Anne gave her a smile of encouragement. Off she went with a confident stride.

A few minutes later, the guests were called to the entrance hall. Anne found Paul waiting, quite handsome in a white toga, a laurel wreath on his head. He bowed, then drew her to his side.

'Georges is waiting in that hallway,' he whispered, indicating with his eyes a door opposite them.

Anne nodded, breathed, 'Pray for us,' and left with the other servants. Once in the hallway, she spotted Georges. His thick body clothed in a plain gray tunic, he looked like he'd been routed from bed. Anne resisted the temptation to smile, for the set of his jaw was earnest, his gaze serious.

He came up to her. 'All the duke's footmen are occupied with guarding his collection. The hall leading to Hoche's apartment should be empty, but we can't be sure. The Chevalier de Beauregard may be here tonight. He was seen in the Café Odéon this noon.'

André soon appeared, his face drawn and tense. He sent

the other servants out, then turned to Georges and Anne. With a wink he ordered them, 'Be about your business,' and left. As they ascended the stairs to the upper floors, they heard the flourish of a horn, then the swelling sound of pipes, cymbals, and drums. Anne's heart beat faster. The entrance procession had begun.

The music was loud and shrill, presumably Hoche's idea of an ancient processional. He led the way, carrying the ivy-wreathed wand of Bacchus. The guests entered the *triclinium* with gasps of amazement. The large gallery was transformed into a Roman dining room. Temporary, painted walls recreated the interior of a villa in ancient Pompeii, offering vistas of fountains and plants in a colorful pleasure garden. A similarly inspired, artful arrangement of fresh flowers added to the illusion.

Three long tables partly enclosed an open area. Servants laid cushions at one of the tables for those guests who wished to recline in the Roman manner. The other tables were set in the modern fashion for the duke and the remaining guests. Paul counted about thirty in all, including the duke.

Just inside the room stood a figure on a low pedestal, concealed by a drape. At a gesture from Hoche, a servant pulled aside the drape, exposing Sylvie as *Diana the Huntress*. She was in mid-stride, hand reaching to the quiver of arrows on her back.

As the guests passed slowly by, some stopped for a moment, startled by the tableau's realism. Others attempted to make eye contact with Sylvie to draw her out of the pose. But she remained motionless—appeared not even to breathe or blink. When the guests had taken their seats, Hoche signaled the servant again to close the drape. The duke stood up, spoke a few Latin phrases of welcome. The feast, a Roman *convivium*, began.

Sylvie, now in a white sleeveless Roman gown and wiped clean of the powder, joined Paul for the *gustum*, the opening course. They reclined side by side. He patted her arm and whispered, 'Well done! You held the pose for at least five minutes.'

'It felt like eternity,' she flustered with a nervous smile.

While Sylvie was doing her act, Paul had closely observed Hoche. His porcine eyes had widened in a lecherous stare, his face flushed. A Bacchus in heat. Paul now warned Sylvie.

'I noticed.' She glanced in Hoche's direction. 'Perhaps he will be distracted and forget about me. He needs to stay here and direct the feast.'

Paul nodded. His thoughts wandered to Georges and Anne upstairs, searching through Hoche's apartment. He imagined them stumbling upon the Chevalier de Beauregard. Anxiety lightly tingled over his skin.

Servants in Roman costume soon arrived at their table with arugula and watercress salad, lamb-liver pâté in the form of a fish, and tuna with sliced hard-boiled eggs. With these dishes they served *mulsum*, a dry white wine tinctured with honey.

Sylvie showed little interest in the food, merely picking at her salad. Her eyes were discreetly focused on the duke in the place of honor at the next table. 'Paul,' she whispered 'Isn't he speaking English?'

'I'll find out.' Paul finished eating a piece of tuna, his ear cocked to the duke's conversation. 'Yes, he has English guests with him.'

'In the Palais-Royal, I hear men say he wants France to be more like England.' She grimaced with misgivings.

'He has many friends there, including the Prince of Wales,' Paul remarked. 'He likes the way sensible men of property govern that country. Their House of Commons controls the power to tax and keeps the King on a tight leash.'

Doubt persisted in Sylvie's face. 'My godfather the baron says Monsieur le Duc d'Orléans would like to govern us in the English way.' She whispered into Paul's ear. 'But he's not up to the task.'

'Baron Breteuil is a keen judge of men.' Paul studied the duke's face. Pleasant, but weak and irresolute. 'The duke trusts others to work in his interest, a recipe for failure.'

At the interval after the appetizers, Hoche stood up and clapped his hands. Into the open area rushed a troupe of dark-skinned acrobats, men and women alike clad only in scant loincloths. To the music of pipes and cymbals they built human pyramids, leapfrogged over one another, somersaulted, and danced on their hands. Their performance ended in a crescendo of whirling bodies.

When the way was clear, servants brought in the *mensa prima,* the main course. Hoche rose to tell the guests what to expect. The ham had first been boiled in water, dried figs, and bay leaves, then honeyed and baked in a pastry in the form of a suckling pig. On offer also were thrushes stuffed with an olive paste and roasted eels in wine and prune sauce. The vegetable dishes included boiled carrots with cumin sauce, a casserole of egg yolks, wine, and pea purée, spiced with ginger, and boiled lentils in a chestnut purée. A white Loire wine would be served.

André approached Sylvie and Paul with the ham. While pretending to discuss its merits, he murmured under his breath, 'Watch Hoche. I know him—he's upset about something. I'll try to learn more.' After serving Sylvie a slice of the ham, André went to Hoche's table, within earshot of the duke's.

Sylvie and Paul exchanged concerned glances, then studied Hoche for a few minutes. He acted the perfect courtier, a calm expression on his face, a glass of wine in his hand. If he had a problem, he wasn't showing it to the duke. 'Is Hoche about to leave the party?' Sylvie asked.

Before Paul could reply, André was back. 'The English gentlemen want to buy the duke's paintings. He's almost bankrupt and is showing an interest in their offer. Hoche thinks it's a bad idea. The collection should stay in France.'

Paul felt relieved. The paintings weren't his concern. Hoche didn't appear about to leave. Instead, he found solace in the duke's fine wine.

When the main course was finished and the servants had cleared the tables, Hoche clapped again. Two bearded 'barbarians', clad in faux Roman armor and wielding wooden swords, feigned a gladiatorial combat. With much grunting and groaning they beat upon each other. It was all to little effect until one of them, at a wink from his companion, fell to the floor and was dragged out by servants.

Sylvie had ignored this last entertainment, her eyes fixed on Duc Philippe. Shaking her head, she turned to Paul. 'If the duke can't manage his own money, how can he expect to govern this country any better than the present King?'

'He would never truly govern,' Paul replied. 'Men like Hoche and Gaillard believe they will use him as a puppet and govern France in his name. They have radical ideas about how that should be done.'

His cousin nodded thoughtfully, wrinkling her brow in an effort to grasp the implications of Paul's remark. It was difficult to concentrate. Servants came with fresh dishes of food. Other guests engaged them in conversation. Finally, she caught Paul's eye. 'These new men, Hoche, Gaillard, and their friends, intend to push us aside, like dead wood. And why not?'

At first, the serious turn of her mind surprised Paul. Earlier impressions of her as a light-hearted, playful girl still lingered in his mind. Now he realized this change grew out of her recent crisis. Though she still thought of herself as an aristocrat, she no longer believed in the claims of her class to power and privilege.

'Why not?' Paul echoed her question. 'Let these "new men," as you call them, try to persuade us that they know how to build a new, just, and humane society, a task far more problematic than dismantling the old one.'

A waiter approached them with a loaded tray. Paul patted Sylvie's hand and announced in a soft, almost reverent tone, '*Mensa secunda*, the dessert, is served.'

The waiter offered them bowls of warm egg pudding with honey and ground pine nuts, followed by dates stuffed with walnuts and fried in honey. Other servants poured *pastum*, a sweet raisin wine.

'The dates are delicious,' said Sylvie, chewing on one and reaching for another. 'I'm glad I came.'

Throughout the feast, as certain delicacies were served, Hoche read, then translated brief Latin excerpts from the recipes of Apicius, together with culinary remarks by Martial, Petronius, and Pliny the Elder. The guests appeared to pay little attention to him.

Wine flowed freely. 'Pretend you're indulging,' Paul counseled Sylvie, who was being offered the raisin wine. 'But drink very little. You may need your wits about you.'

Other guests had less reason to be prudent. The wine had its way. Speech became slurred and loud. Hoche set an example, acting out his role as Bacchus. At the conclusion of the dessert, unsteady on his feet, he announced more masterpieces of ancient sculpture.

The first would be *Venus aux Belles Fesses*. A drape was pulled, exposing a young woman as the goddess of love coming out of the bath. The classic pose obliged her to pull up her gown and glance backwards at her buttocks, exposing a breast and much else.

Paul recognized her, one of Madame Lebrun's courtesans, a handsome young woman, plump and well formed, as suitable in the role as any goddess he could imagine.

Surprised yet pleased, the diners sucked in their breath in unison. A buzz of amazement filled the gallery. This was a familiar, much copied Venus. The Swedish sculptor, Johan Tobias Sergell, had recently produced one with the likeness of his King's mistress, Comtesse Ulla von Höpken. Paul also recalled a splendid modern marble version in the royal palace at Marly.

In five-minute intervals, several other famous statues from antiquity appeared live on pedestals surrounding the guests— a *Discus Thrower*, a *Minerva Arming*, and a *Dying Gaul*. Especially striking was a young *Dancing Faun*. A cymbal in each outstretched hand, his right foot poised to stamp on a *scabellum*, a castanet attached to his sandal, the young man lived the part, his face full of thoughtless, joyful folly. Almost perfectly still, his agile muscular body seemed frozen in a moment of wild movement.

All the figures were nearly naked. But, since they didn't move, avoided eye contact, and were also lightly powdered to suggest skins of marble, they seemed no more scandalous than the pieces they portrayed. For about ten minutes or so, each of them remained frozen. The duke and his guests swarmed around them, admiring them and trying in vain to tease them out of their poses.

Finally, the drapes were closed and the feast came to an end. The duke told Hoche that he would be leaving, and professed in a loud voice to have been thoroughly pleased with the evening. The English gentlemen and many other guests left with him. Those who stayed behind were Hoche's friends bent on continuing with Roman revels.

In the interval caused by the duke's departure, the remaining guests stretched, milled about, and relieved themselves in nearby water closets. Paul and Sylvie kept watch on Hoche. Should he make for the exit, they had agreed Sylvie would try to hold him in conversation.

'Paul,' came a mocking female voice from behind. 'I didn't expect to see you here. Why isn't your English bride with you? I saw her among the servants. But perhaps that's as it should be.'

He swung around to face his cousin, Comtesse Louise de Joinville. During the feast, she must have been at a private party elsewhere in the palace.

'I've come for the orgy.' She shook her hips to the beat of an inaudible music. 'Are you going to join us?'

Taken by surprise, nettled, Paul was momentarily at a loss how to react to her taunts.

'And Sylvie. Are you well enough now to enjoy our *pagan* pleasures?' Louise appeared to have drunk deeply of the wine. Her face was flushed, her tunic had slipped off one shoulder.

'I'll leave *pagan* pleasures to you, Louise,' replied Sylvie evenly. 'Monsieur Hoche met me in the gallery a few days ago, showed an interest in my Diana, and invited me to perform. Paul was kind enough to accompany me.' She moved a fraction closer to him.

He recalled her last encounter with Louise. Sylvie had barely recovered from Fitzroy's brutal assault when Louise had openly mocked her. That had upset her fragile emotional balance and led to the attempted suicide. Angered, Paul was searching in his mind for a cutting remark to silence Louise, when he noticed out of the corner of his eye that Monsieur Hoche had disappeared.

CHAPTER NINETEEN

A Royal Secret

Thursday, June 7

U pstairs, the palace was eerily quiet. Only the faint sounds of pipes and cymbals reached Anne and Georges. They stood arms akimbo surveying Hoche's study in the faint light of a small oil lamp. Georges had opened the room with the duplicate keys and had locked the door behind them.

Earlier in the afternoon, André had drawn a plan of the apartment. 'Where do you think Hoche keeps his personal papers?' Georges had asked.

'In a room that looks like a study.' André had then explained it was the only room Hoche kept locked while his clerk was present. But, on one occasion, André had noticed the door was open a crack. Hoche was busy elsewhere. Curious, the clerk had gone in and looked around. There were many books and maps of ancient Greece and Rome, a plaster copy of *Venus Leaving the Bath*, a few locked cabinets, and a work table covered with neat stacks of paper. On the walls hung several engravings of scenes from Pompeii.

'We've checked all the places André mentioned,' said Georges, throwing up his hands in frustration.

He and Anne had gone through Hoche's table, drawers, file boxes, cabinets, and books and had found nothing even remotely relevant to the murder of Duchesse Aimée de Saumur or to any scandal. Anne grew more discouraged by the minute. 'Then there must be a hidden place.' She began to inspect the room's paneled walls.

Suddenly, Georges whispered, 'Someone is unlocking the outer door.' He and Anne had anticipated this danger and had picked a refuge. Anne shuttered the lamp, and they dashed

148

behind the heavy drapes that closed off a utility closet. With his knife, Georges quickly cut tiny holes at eye level. 'Let's hope they don't smell fumes from our lamp.'

A key turned the lock to the study door. Hoche walked in with a small oil lamp, followed by Gaillard. Both men appeared highly agitated.

'Did you have to?' hissed Gaillard.

'I had no choice,' Hoche replied. 'We must move quickly. I should return to the party, or they'll wonder where I am.'

There was a pause, a shuffling of feet. For a moment, Anne lost sight of the men. Then she saw them again at the opposite wall. Hoche worked on a sconce that opened a panel, and the men walked into a darkened room. A minute later, Hoche came running out, holding his hand over his mouth, and hurled himself into the water closet.

'Bacchus is throwing up,' whispered Georges, a grin in his voice.

The sounds of the man's distress echoed through the room. A few minutes of silence followed, then Hoche emerged, wiping his mouth, and returned to the secret room. From within came muffled voices, an occasional loud curse, and the sound of moving furniture. Finally, the two men dragged out a large object wrapped in a blanket, straining at the task. They shut the panel and left with their burden, locking the doors behind them. The apartment grew silent.

'What was that?' exclaimed Georges in a whisper, pulling aside the drapes. 'A body?'

'And why did it have to be moved secretly?' Anne opened the shutters of her lamp and hurried to the wall. She manipulated the sconce as she remembered Hoche had done. After a few tries the panel opened. She stepped inside and raised the lamp. Georges joined her. She realized he was allowing her to take the lead, like an apprentice in training with a master.

It was a narrow, low, windowless room. On the walls were shelves of file boxes. A strongbox stood in one corner, a table in another. The room appeared clean and in good order. No sign of violence.

'The object they removed—probably a body—is a mystery

we can't unravel tonight,' said Georges. 'But we can go through these files.'

They carried boxes to the table and went to work. Hoche had gathered a great deal of scandal, much of it from Madame Lebrun's brothel. What use he made of it wasn't clear. Numbers after the names could have been payments from victims of extortion. He could also have hired himself out as a spy.

'Georges, I've found something.' Anne opened a file labeled 'Beauregard' and began to sift through a packet of letters. Under the *nom de plume* Caligula, the chevalier described his seduction of the duchess and his growing favor in the royal household. He was playing with the Queen's children and occasionally receiving her smile. About a month ago, he began intercepting messages between the Queen and Comte Fersen, often copying passages.

A week ago, he found a note which the Queen had enclosed in a message to Fersen. She had neglected to indicate that she was enclosing anything. Beauregard apparently thought Fersen wouldn't miss the note. So, he passed it on to Hoche, together with a copy of the Queen's message.

While Georges sat next to her, Anne read aloud from the copied message. The Queen told Fersen that work was finished on the hidden stairway connecting her private apartment with his secret one on the floor above.

Then Anne read the Queen's note silently:

My dearest friend, I now have you close to me. You are also
near your son, Louis-Charles. I yearn for your warm embrace,
your sweet lips, and your loving self. As ever, your Josephine.

Anne hesitated to show the note to Georges. It was so intimate. She felt guilty for having read it. However, his curiosity had been aroused. He looked at her expectantly. She handed him the message and the note.

As Georges read them, his lips pursed in surprise. 'So, the Duc de Normandie is Fersen's boy. Fancy that! And we already know that Josephine's the Queen. I could easily verify the handwriting.' He lowered the papers, fixed his eyes on Anne.

'Secret apartment, hidden stairway, warm embrace. These things we expect from kings of France, though the present one is weak in these matters. Our previous Louis, the fifteenth of that name, was called "*le bien aimé*," the well-loved. Madame Dubarry and a stable of willing ladies answered to his beck and call. But we expect our queens to be chaste. This note . . .' He slapped it with the back of his hand. 'If it's made public, it'll ruin the Queen!'

Anne understood Georges's low opinion of monarchs and aristocrats. It wouldn't trouble him if the Queen's liaison with Comte Fersen were exposed, though he might resent Hoche and British hack journalists making money out of a French disgrace. Still, Paul had promised Fersen and would deem it a point of honor to return the stolen papers. 'The colonel's instructions are clear, Georges, we must take these papers with us.'

'That's risky.' He held the incriminating papers in his hand. 'Hoche is negotiating with British agents for certain intimate papers regarding the French Queen. The sums of money at stake are large, thousands of pounds sterling. If we take the note, the letters, any of these things, Hoche will soon miss them, may find out who took them, and would stop at nothing to recover them. His wrath might fall on André and Sylvie. They are vulnerable.'

'We'll have to take that risk,' Anne insisted. 'We can't leave the papers here.'

For a long moment, he stared at them with disgust, then handed them over. She tucked them under her tunic.

'We must also look for documents that could explain Beauregard's behavior the morning of the murder,' said Anne.

A few minutes later, Georges pulled out a letter. 'This is from Beauregard to Hoche that same morning, after the provost interrogated him. He's concerned that someone may have seen him leaving the private stairway from the duchess's room. He did ask her not to denounce him to the Queen, but he insists that she was alive when he left her shortly before dawn.' He handed the letter to Anne.

She read it carefully, then shook her head. 'Beauregard could be lying to Hoche.' She was unable to conceal the

151

disappointment she felt. She had hoped to find a clear confession of guilt. 'Do you think this letter can be of any use to Denise's cause?'

Georges mulled over her question. 'It's hard to say. True, it places Beauregard at the scene of the crime and very nearly at the time it was committed. But he denies killing the duchess. The provost is likely to accept his story. The material evidence points to Denise.' He sighed audibly. 'If we try to use this letter at Denise's trial, Hoche will accuse us of having stolen it from the duke's palace. That could stir up a hornet's nest of trouble.'

'I say, let's take the letter, Georges. We can decide later whether it would be wise to use it.' She slipped it under her tunic.

He shrugged. 'It's time to go. We've done what we can here.' They put the files in order and returned the boxes to the shelf. After locking the doors behind them, they left the apartment and made their way back to the great gallery.

A cacophony of pipes, cymbals, drums, and horns met them as they drew near. Through a crack in the door they saw that the party had become a bacchanal. Some of the guests had fallen over the tables in a drunken stupor. Others were dancing wildly in the open area like Dionysian rioters. Hoche was lying on a cushion with a half-naked woman, her back to Anne.

At that moment, André came by looking tired and haggard. Anne caught his attention. 'Where are the colonel and Sylvie?'

'For a while they were concerned because Hoche suddenly left the party. But he returned soon afterwards and met that lady.' He jerked his head toward Hoche's companion. 'The colonel then judged it safe to take Sylvie home. He has come back and is waiting in the anteroom. I'm to inform him if Hoche leaves again.'

'I think Hoche has just passed out,' said Georges. The man had rolled off the cushion and on to the floor. His female companion rose to her feet, stretched, ran her hands through her hair, and staggered toward André.

'Good God,' whispered Anne. 'That's Comtesse Louise de Joinville, Paul's cousin. I don't want to meet her.' Anne started to rush away, then stopped and looked back. 'Georges, you stay here and help André. I'll find Paul.'

Paul was pacing the anteroom when Anne arrived. He turned to her with obvious relief and held her in a warm embrace.

'It went well,' she said, 'but let's not talk about it now. Hoche may wake up and wander in here.' They left immediately for their residence on Rue Saint-Honoré.

When they were finally alone in his office, Anne handed Paul the Fersen papers. 'They are very compromising to him and especially to the Queen. Your Swedish friend has good reason to thank you.'

He read them quickly at his desk, then looked up at Anne. 'A cuckolded King, an unfaithful Queen, an illegitimate heir to the throne! This could shake an already feeble monarchy to its foundation.'

Anne sat facing him. 'Is it as bad as that?'

'Yes, worse, if possible. Who would take power if the King should fall? The Devil himself?' He was silent for a few moments, a troubled expression on his face. He sighed, then pointed to the papers. 'They testify to a long, loving relationship. I know Fersen to be a man of honor. Though he's never confided in me, I'll wager he's the Queen's true friend.'

'In our search, unfortunately,' Anne went on, 'we found nothing that would help Denise.' She described Beauregard's letter to Hoche and handed it to Paul. 'I had hoped he would confess to the crime.'

Paul nodded gravely. 'That was a desperate hope.' He put the papers in his desk drawer and locked it. 'I'll deal with them tomorrow.' He fell silent again, lost in thought.

'Yes?' Anne asked.

'Hoche. He gave me a great fright when he left the gallery. André followed him upstairs to the apartment. What happened inside?'

'We hid behind drapes. He and Gaillard carried away a large object, maybe a body.'

'Beauregard's, most likely. André followed them to the servants' door, where they put it on a small cart. A pair of rough-looking men pulled it away.'

'Did you notice Beauregard at the party this evening? Don't you think he should have been there?'

'Yes, if he were still alive.'

CHAPTER TWENTY

A Question of Honor

Friday, June 8

Rays of sunlight slanted through the bedroom windows, waking Anne from a troubled dream. Hoche and Gaillard had dropped a box they were carrying from the secret room. It sprang open. Denise fell out, eyes wide with terror, her hands at her throat, gasping for breath. The men pushed her back into the box. She fought them desperately, then slowly weakened. They overpowered her, forced the lid on again, and carried the box away as if nothing had happened.

Anne lay still, agonizing over the dream. Its implications for the maid were all too clear—and dire. Finally, Anne stirred herself, reached over and prodded her husband. He woke reluctantly, glanced at the wall clock, and scowled.

'Too early,' he complained. 'Just got home from the party a few minutes ago.'

It had been well after midnight, Anne admitted to herself, when they reached their residence on Rue Saint-Honoré. 'You've had enough sleep,' she said without pity, climbing out of bed. 'There's work to do.'

They dressed and went downstairs to the parlor for breakfast. Michou and Sylvie arrived at the same time as Georges. The table was already set—with an empty place next to Sylvie's.

'Before leaving the duke's palace I invited André to join us,' said Paul. 'We must discuss what happened last night and determine our next moves.'

A footman opened the door and André walked in, greeting

154

his companions with a tired voice. Lines of fatigue creased his forehead. 'The last revelers didn't leave the gallery until dawn,' he complained. 'I've hardly had time to shave and change clothes.'

Sylvie beckoned him to the empty place and gave him a sympathetic smile. He returned it warmly.

When everyone had helped themselves to the bread and coffee, Anne described how she and Georges had searched Hoche's apartment.

Georges turned toward André. 'Take care, young man. When Hoche regains his wits, he's going to be very angry and lash out at anyone nearby. We took certain papers from his secret room that are worth a great deal of money.'

Sylvie and André exchanged puzzled glances. 'Why so valuable?' asked Sylvie. 'Could they help free Denise?'

Anne and Georges pointed the questions toward Paul.

'Sylvie, the papers concern the Queen's friendship with Comte Fersen.' He retrieved a small packet from the portfolio at his side and held it up. 'They are intimate, confidential, and unrelated to Duchesse Aimée's death.'

Georges's head snapped back in protest. 'I disagree! They give Beauregard a powerful motive for murder. He's *still* a suspect, even though he may be dead. He took great risks to steal the papers and might have killed the duchess to prevent her from denouncing him. And, to keep them safely hidden, Hoche might have killed Beauregard.'

Anne nodded before she realized what she was doing. Paul frowned at her. The room fell unnaturally silent.

'That is true, Monsieur Charpentier,' admitted Paul grudgingly. 'These papers increase our suspicion of Beauregard. But we already have sufficient grounds to suspect him. What we need is evidence that, in fact, he killed the duchess.'

Georges remained darkly silent, stirring sugar into his coffee.

Paul's voice took on a sharp edge. His fingers tapped the packet. 'If I were to show these papers to Baron Breteuil, he would forbid me to use them. By discrediting the Queen, they would weaken royal authority at a critical moment in our country's history. No royal magistrate, including the Marquis de Sully, would dare to allow them in Denise's trial. What useful purpose could they serve, except to gratify the gutter press and amuse the enemies of our country?'

Anne noticed Paul hadn't mentioned his personal obligation to return the letters to Fersen. If they were of use, would he have compromised his honor and pursued justice for Denise? Was a Queen's reputation or a King's authority more important than a deaf maid's life?

Georges raised his cup, peered over its lip at his superior. 'Could your packet *persuade* the Queen to do the right thing for Mademoiselle de Villers?'

'Frankly, Georges, I've considered that possibility.' Paul threw a glance in Anne's direction. 'I could approach the Queen and threaten to present this packet to the King and to the rest of the world, unless she took steps to free Denise.' He paused to allow the others to ponder what he had said. 'She's a proud woman and would never submit to extortion. I would expect her to reply, "Do your worst, I shall let justice take its course."' He sought the eyes of his companions. 'What would I have gained? Nothing for Denise. Much ill will for me. A political crisis for the country.'

Georges persisted. 'Could you oblige Fersen to confront the Queen in return for the packet?'

'If I were to ask him, he would refuse to bargain—and resent my asking.' Paul surveyed his companions. 'Shall we move on to another matter? There's something sinister about the bundle that Hoche and Gaillard carried out. We shall soon hear that Chevalier de Beauregard has disappeared.'

Paul turned to André. 'Could you describe the cart and the men who pulled it away?'

The young man thought for a moment. 'They wore carpenters' aprons. Their cart had two wheels. More than that I couldn't see. The light was poor. I dared not draw close. I'll search records at the office for men who do hauling for Hoche.'

'Either Gaillard or Hoche must have known them, engaged them for the task,' said Georges. 'Perhaps Quidor can also help us find them. I'll pay him a visit.'

'This case is growing more complicated daily,' observed Paul.

Anne sighed. 'And we don't seem to be getting any closer to the killer of Duchesse Aimée.'

She and Paul reached their Versailles apartment at mid-morning to find Marie at her writing table still in a dressing gown. Duchesse Aimée's journal lay open before her. Marie had the look of someone completely absorbed in the story she was reading. Even as she greeted them, her mind seemed elsewhere. She waved them to chairs facing her, poured them coffee from a nearby pot.

She pointed to the journal. 'Some entries are so cryptic that I need a day to read a page. There are weeks when the duchess wrote nothing. I try to fill in the gaps. I don't regret the effort—it's a fascinating, often touching story.'

'Dear aunt,' said Paul. 'I can't recall ever having seen you so taken by a book.'

Marie smiled, lifted up Aimée's journal. 'I'm now seeing the Queen through the mind of a close friend and keen observer. Marie Antoinette emerges from these pages as a decent, even modest woman, and a caring mother of her children. Unfortunately, from the beginning, palace society has been poisoned against her—too free-spirited, and an Austrian. The King's aunts and his brothers and sisters are especially treacherous. The Queen needs a friend she can trust. And that's Comte Fersen. I understand her perfectly.'

'Speaking of the count,' Paul said, 'I must return the intimate papers that Beauregard stole. Anne will tell you more about them.'

'You will find him in his apartment above the Queen's, I'm sure.'

Paul raised an eyebrow. 'I thought that was a secret.'

'It still is, officially, but many people know about it. The count and the Queen played cards with us last evening. He stayed the night in the palace.'

'Do you also know that there is a secret staircase between her private rooms and his?'

'No. But I'm not surprised.'

'Won't this affair ruin the Queen's reputation?' Anne asked.

Marie grimaced. 'In the mind of many it's already as ruined

as it can get, although thus far no one has come forward with evidence of any infidelity. She's the victim of malicious gossip fueled by her own lavish spending, foolish indiscretions, and willful disregard of court conventions.'

While Marie was describing the Queen's predicament, Paul noticed a frown crossing Anne's face, as if she were seeing certain realities of palace life for the first time. She probably thought wealthy, high-born, well-bred men and women, all of whom professed to be Christians, wouldn't be so petty, so mean-spirited, toward each other.

Marie also glanced at Anne. 'Does this shock you? Recall the affair of the diamond necklace. Two years ago a gang of tricksters, pretending to act in the Queen's name, swindled Cardinal Rohan and a jeweler out of a huge, costly diamond necklace. The Queen's enemies accused her of having led the cardinal on. They spread the lie to the far corners of Europe.'

'Yes,' Anne agreed. 'In Britain it was reported with great relish. Many of the diamonds found a home there.'

Paul finished his coffee and rose from the table. 'I shall be on my way.' He took the packet of Fersen's papers from his portfolio, then stared at them for a moment. 'They may have cost the Chevalier de Beauregard his life.'

Fersen's rooms were on the same floor as Duchesse Aimée's apartment, but they were hidden away. Saint-Martin had to walk through a storeroom of discarded rugs and drapes to reach the count's nondescript door. A maid answered his knock and showed him into an antechamber.

There he saw the first signs of his friend's taste. Against the opposite wall stood a simple gray table, flanked by a pair of identical gray chairs. Over the table hung a gilded rectangular mirror. The walls were off-white, the moldings a light gray. This harmonious, understated elegance seemed to reflect the cool, rational side of Fersen's character.

'I'll see if my master's available,' said the maid without ceremony. The colonel took note of her—a sturdy, square-faced, bright-eyed woman, about thirty, good-natured but rather rough at the edges. She seemed out of place in this setting.

A few minutes later, she opened the door to what appeared to be a small study. Shelves of books lined one wall. A closed door led to another room. Fersen rose from behind a writing table, also gray and white with delicate gilded ornament. In the same style were a pair of upholstered chairs and a side table. Patterned gray velvet drapes framed the windows looking out over the palace's Cour d'Honneur. The room harbored distinctly private, muted pleasures.

Fersen wore a yellow silk dressing gown. His hair was brushed up and powdered. He had shaved and appeared nearly groomed for a round of palace visits.

His visitor gave a sidelong glance at the retreating maid.

Fersen smiled perceptively. 'Jeanne is an unpolished diamond, intelligent and loyal, my eyes and ears in the nether regions of the palace. Helps me follow the movements of my friends and enemies. Her family served my father years ago.' Fersen paused. 'What do you have for me, Paul?' Though his face was perfectly composed, his eyes betrayed anxiety.

'The messages which Chevalier de Beauregard intercepted—and tried to sell. I believe I have them all.' Paul pulled the small packet from his portfolio.

A sigh of relief escaped from the Swede's lips. 'I am grateful to you, as will be the Queen.' He hesitated a moment, gazing at the packet. 'I realize you had to verify the contents. May I count on your discretion?'

His limpid blue eyes fixed Paul in a demand for assurance. A great deal was at stake. The Queen might be put away in a convent for life. Her enemies would challenge the legitimacy of her son Louis-Charles, who could one day become the dauphin of France. His older brother was very frail and likely to live only a few more years.

Paul replied resolutely, 'Yes, you have my word of honor. And you can rest assured of the discretion of my wife, Anne, and my adjutant, Georges Charpentier, who at some risk to themselves discovered the papers.'

'Where?'

'In the Palais-Royal.'

Fersen did not seem surprised. 'And the thief?'

'Beauregard. He has disappeared.'

Fersen lifted an eyebrow. 'You know he tricked Duchesse Aimée, betrayed her.'

'And may have killed her.'

'Do you think so, despite the evidence against the maid?'

'He had opportunity to slip the brooch into her mattress when she left her room to make breakfast.'

Fersen nodded noncommittally. 'I must go now. The Queen expects me.'

Saint-Martin understood this was as far as Fersen cared to discuss the matter. As the Queen's best friend, he would share as much with her as she would listen to. And not a word more. Unlike other courtiers, he would not try to influence her. She would make up her own mind.

'We shall meet again, Paul. You must tell me about your recent adventure in Bath. I would like to meet your wife.'

Paul took his leave, feeling he had done little to improve the situation of Denise de Villers.

Fersen sat uneasy at his desk. The door opened and the maid stepped into the room.

He beckoned her forward and related the gist of his conversation with Colonel Saint-Martin. No danger there. She had often proven trustworthy, recently alerting him to Beauregard's treachery. 'What I've told you, Jeanne, is confidential.'

'I understand, sir.'

'Good.' He distractedly touched the packet, still overcome by a feeling of relief. He *could* count on Paul.

'Would there be anything else, sir?' Her tone was slightly impatient.

He flashed her an apologetic smile. 'Yes, there is.' Paul's investigation had raised a troubling issue. If the maid Denise were truly a scapegoat, her conviction and public execution could reflect badly on the Queen. That must not happen! Once the truth came out, the gutter press would accuse her of judicial murder.'

He leaned forward, spoke carefully to the young woman. 'Inquire in the palace. Find out as much as you can about Denise de Villers. Tell Benoit to do the same at the prison. Be quick. The provost is in a hurry to kill her.'

CHAPTER TWENTY-ONE

A Suspicious Death

Friday, June 8

After leaving Fersen, Paul returned to his own apartment and found a note from Baron Breteuil. They had to discuss what to do with Jules Blondel and Blanche Moreau. The provost was pressing a claim to jurisdiction in their case. Paul dreaded this moment. They were a poor young couple on the edge of ruin as a result of Duc Henri's callous disregard of his financial obligations. The investigation had exposed their desperate, illegal attempts to save themselves. Anne would feel badly if Blanche were to go to prison, lose her baby, become destitute. With a painful conscience, Paul hurried down to the baron's office.

Breteuil was standing by his window, gazing at a constant late-morning stream of visitors crossing the palace's Cour d'Honneur. His hands were clasped behind him, his head tilted back at a philosophic angle. He didn't hear the door open. Paul scratched lightly on it.

'*Bonjour*, Paul.' The baron waved him to a chair. 'You caught me wondering what I'm doing here. Dozens of people will enter this office today, whose lives I shall alter forever. Yet, in the few minutes they are with me, I shall scarcely learn who they are. In most cases I shall never see them again.'

'Perhaps Blondel and Moreau are lurking in the back of your mind.'

'Yes, I shall have to meet them.' He sighed. 'The provost insists that Blondel should be transferred from the guardroom to the prison for a hearing and, if warranted, a trial. Sully also wants to interrogate Moreau to determine if she should be detained and, if so, where.'

Paul seized this opportunity. 'With all due respect to the provost, sir, I believe it would be wrong to allow Blondel and Moreau to fall into his clutches. He seems too distrustful of servants and thinks the worst of them. Because Blondel is a potential suspect—he had motive and opportunity to kill Duchesse Aimée—I would like to detain him for further questioning at least until another suspect has been convicted of the murder. Even then it would be unfair to commit him to the harsh, degrading conditions of Sully's prison. In selling Duc Henri's property, Blondel was exercising a moral right to recover his wages. Duc Henri should not be allowed to force his servant into penury.'

The baron leaned back in his chair, his hands folded over his ample stomach. 'And what do you propose I should do?'

The baron's open mind encouraged Paul to speak frankly. 'The King holds the duke's property in trust. I believe you have the discretionary authority as Minister of the Royal Household to allow the sale of certain small bits of that property to cover pressing expenses, such as the valet's wages, minus what the valet has already received on his own initiative. That procedure could lift the taint of crime from what Blondel did. The provost would no longer have reason to be concerned about the matter. Until the murder investigation is completed, Blondel and Moreau would continue to live in the servants' quarters by the guardroom, work for their room and board, and be available for questioning.'

The baron nodded thoughtfully. 'Sounds reasonable to me. I'll reply in that vein to Sully.'

Paul left the office, feeling that a weight had been lifted from his chest.

In the apartment upstairs, Anne finished preparing a basket of food and clothing for Denise. The prison provided hardly enough to keep a prisoner alive. Marie had put away Duchesse Aimée's journal and was dressing for the day.

'Shall we leave soon?' Anne asked.

'Yes,' Marie replied. 'We'll arrange our visit to coincide with the provost's absence from his office. I truly dislike the man and wish to avoid even a chance meeting with him.'

Marie had learned that he would attend a protracted dinner at the palace. At noon she and Anne climbed into a coach and set out for the prison.

They had waited in the small bare visitors' room only a few minutes when Denise entered, followed by the same burly guard who had brought her before. Anne sensed immediately something was different. A bond had developed between Denise and this man. He was gentle toward her. She looked kindly upon him. He removed the manacles without being asked and stepped out of the room.

As on previous visits, Marie had brought salve for the maid's wrists and began to rub them. Anne brushed her hair.

Marie patted the wrists. 'They are much better, Denise.'

The maid understood. Glancing over her shoulder at the door, she signed, 'That guard has taken pity on me. When he's on duty at night, and no one is watching, he removes the manacles. And when the other guards . . .' She hesitated with embarrassment.

Anne caressed her cheek. 'Tell us, Denise.'

The maid smiled awkwardly. 'My cell is like a cage—everyone can see me. The other guards used to insult me with obscene gestures, stare and laugh when I had to relieve myself. This guard became angry, shook his fist at them, and they stopped. I don't know his name, so I call him Moses.'

Denise's attitude toward life in prison seemed to have changed, Anne realized. She now accepted her situation and tried to make the best of it.

Marie opened the basket and handed Denise the food and a bundle of fresh undergarments. 'I'll ask the guard to put your soiled things in this basket.' Marie studied Denise closely. 'Are you getting enough food?' Though Marie had paid Sully for decent meals, the money could have ended in his pocket. The maid was pale but didn't appear to have lost any more weight.

'Like other prisoners, I'm fed a thin broth and a piece of bread. But Moses sneaks me food from the guards' table.'

Anne and Marie exchanged glances. Sully was pocketing Denise's food money—more likely for revenge than greed. Better not to protest. He might press down even harder on Denise, stop Moses from caring for her.

163

Conversation shifted to news from the palace. Anne cast the investigation's progress in the best possible light. Yesterday's conversation with the cook came to her mind.

'What can you tell us, Denise, about Madame Bourdon and her half-sister, Robinette Lapire? Though they're blood relatives and have worked together for years, they appear to dislike each other. Robinette even seems to fear Marthe.'

'That's true,' Denise signed. 'Cook must envy or resent her half-sister's beauty and good fortune. That's human nature. Madame Bourdon treats her like a common servant rather than kin. Cook may fear she could be sent away at any time. That would be a calamity. She has no money, no family, no place to go.'

'Have the sisters ever quarreled?'

'Not that I know of. When they are together, cook guards her feelings. But I see bitterness and hate in her eyes when Madame Bourdon isn't watching.'

It was time to leave. Marie went to the door, had a few words with the guard, and pressed a coin into his hand. He came back in a few minutes with the basket. The two visitors bid Denise goodbye. Moses replaced the manacles and led the maid out.

On the way back to the palace, Anne suddenly had a feeling of dread in the pit of her stomach. The visit with Denise had been so pleasant that it had disarmed Anne's anxieties. Now, the brutal truth struck her. The investigation was failing and time was running out.

After breakfast Georges walked briskly to the Hôtel de Police. Inspecteur Quidor was in a conference room with other inspectors. Georges waited in an antechamber. A few minutes later, Quidor's comrades emerged, followed by Quidor himself. His face brightened when he saw Georges. With a grand sweep of his hand, he invited him into the large empty room. They pulled chairs up to a table and sat facing each other.

'My colleagues and I were discussing a report that had just arrived. A body has been found hanging in the duke's circus, the big new building under construction in the garden of the

Palais-Royal. One of my agents is standing guard to prevent anyone from disturbing the site. It's within the duke's jurisdiction, but a suspicious death is the King's business. So, I'm supposed to look into it.'

'The body belongs to Chevalier de Beauregard.'

Quidor looked up sharply. 'How do you know?'

Georges gave him a quick summary of last night's events, omitting any reference to Fersen and the Queen. At the mention of Gaillard and Hoche carrying out a heavy object, Quidor exclaimed, 'Aha! Now they're in the soup.' He leaped to his feet. 'Come with me, Georges. We'll study the site together.'

The circus was being built in the middle of the garden and appeared to be nearly complete on the outside. Semicircular at each end, the long oblong structure rose from a deep underground level to the height of a single tall storey above ground. Its flat roof was designed to support a garden.

Georges and Quidor entered the building and edged their way through a forest of scaffolding down to an open arena for equestrian sports.

'We'll be ready in two months,' said the master carpenter who was guiding them. At first, Georges found that hard to believe. He changed his mind as he noticed hundreds of men hammering and plastering. A thunderous noise attacked his ears. Dust filled his nostrils.

The carpenter pointed toward dense scaffolding near a side exit at ground level. 'The body's up there.' They set off in that direction. Soon, Quidor's agent came into view and waved.

The body was hanging by a stout rope from a truss, his feet a few inches from the floor. A block of wood had been knocked over.

'That's Beauregard, without a doubt,' said Georges. The body was fully dressed in street clothes. The agent pulled a pad from his pocket and began writing notes for a report. 'May I look around?' Georges asked.

'Of course,' Quidor replied. 'I'll join you shortly, after I instruct my agent. We'll need a wagon to take the body to the morgue at the Châtelet for autopsy.'

Georges and the master carpenter walked the short distance

to the side exit and looked back. The hanging body couldn't be seen. Georges examined the door. It had no lock yet. 'Is this door guarded at night?'

The carpenter shook his head. 'A watchman walks around the site, mostly looking for fire. He also checks on the tool-sheds and the piles of lumber and other building materials that might attract thieves. But he wouldn't pay much attention to this side of the building. There's nothing of value here.'

So, thought Georges, a body could easily have been wheeled up to this exit in the early morning hours when the shops were closed, the lights were out, and only the trash haulers were moving about. Small carts were plentiful at the site. Gaillard might have recruited a pair of workers familiar with the building, perhaps men he knew.

'Could you tell me,' Georges asked, 'who was working in this area late yesterday afternoon or early evening?'

The carpenter scratched his head. 'Maybe a dozen men. Don't know them all by name.'

'I'm thinking of an evil-looking pair, who would hire themselves out to haul a body here in the middle of the night.' Georges jerked his head in Beauregard's direction.

The carpenter grew wary, not wishing to be drawn any deeper into police business.

'I see that you know them. You don't have to worry. I have no reason to mention you in this investigation.' Georges stared sternly at the carpenter. 'Tell me their names and where I can find them.'

'Pierre and Jean. They worked yesterday but aren't here today. I call them when I need extra hands. Go to the slaughter shops on the riverbank. Ask for them among the butchers there.'

The butchers were slaughtering near Pont au Change, a district Georges avoided when he could. The stench was powerful, the sight, disgusting. Tanners also worked in the area and added greatly to its foul-smelling atmosphere. As he neared his destination, he paused, drew a deep breath of fresh air, then nodded Quidor and two of his agents forward. They walked by rows of hanging carcasses, piles of offal, and

166

puddles of blood, up to a line of butchers at a long, thick wooden table.

At first, they were too busy at their grisly work to notice the newcomers. But soon one of them looked up, then nudged another. In an instant the whole row was alert. And suspicious. The butchers were a tight fraternity, protective of each other. Among such men Georges chose to be diplomatic. He singled out the man who seemed to command the greatest respect and explained politely that he wished to question two men about an incident at the Palais-Royal's construction site.

Several stout butchers had gathered behind their leader, bloody cleavers at the ready and dark frowns on their faces. Quidor and his agents edged closer behind Georges. For a moment, he thought a riot would break out.

'The men you want, what are their names?' The leader cocked his head suspiciously.

'Pierre and Jean,' Georges replied. His voice threatened to tremble.

The man's forehead briefly creased with confusion, then cleared. 'Those men aren't butchers. Just do odd jobs for us. They're away on an errand. Be back soon. I'll point them out.' He gestured the other butchers back to their work.

Georges and his companions moved into the shadow of Pont au Change and observed the scene. After a few minutes he spotted two men hauling a carcass to the table. He glanced at the butcher. He nodded.

'There they are,' Georges whispered to Quidor, who pointed them out to his men.

What happened next amazed even Georges, who had often observed police in action. The agents approached their prey from the rear, chained them hand and foot, and led them shuffling from the market—all in a matter of minutes.

'Come along, Georges,' said Quidor. 'I'll interrogate them at the Châtelet. It's only a stone's throw from here. I hope to have Gaillard and Hoche in prison by nightfall. The autopsy should be ready tomorrow. Then we'll know what happened to Chevalier de Beauregard.'

'Good,' said Georges. But, he thought with regret, the strongest suspect in the murder of Duchesse Aimée was dead beyond a doubt.

CHAPTER TWENTY-TWO

Slander

Friday, June 8

Georges accompanied Inspecteur Quidor, his agents and their prisoners to the Châtelet, the city's ancient prison and hall of justice, a few steps to the east of the butchers. Quidor found a room, sat the prisoners down at a table, and began to question them. Hardened rogues, they maintained a surly silence.

'You run little risk talking to me,' Quidor said, leaning toward them and inviting their confidence. 'We know you hanged a dead man. You won't suffer much for that, especially if you cooperate. Tell me who hired you.'

The men glanced at each other. Pierre, the older of the two, shrugged. 'Gaillard, the scribbler. We do odd jobs for him. Said he had a body in the palace to get rid of. Pick it up when the garden and the arcades are empty. We got there about midnight. The body was wrapped in a blanket. A little fat man with Gaillard told us, "make it look like suicide." We didn't dare pull the cart through the streets. The watchmen would think we were thieves and search us. So, we took it to the circus just a few steps away. The body was already stiff. We hanged it anyway. Looked odd, but we thought it might relax a bit by the time it was found.'

Pierre spoke with the nonchalance gained by experience with dead bodies. Had probably been in the army. Hoche was the little fat man.

Quidor turned to Georges. 'Do you have any questions?'

'Yes,' Georges replied, then addressed Pierre. 'When did Gaillard contact you?'

'Three or four in the afternoon. We were at work in the circus.'

Georges nodded to Quidor.

'That will be all for now,' said Quidor and sent the prisoners away.

Georges remarked, 'It looks like Beauregard died at the latest about two in the afternoon. Rigor had almost ceased by the time we saw the body, twenty hours later.'

'He didn't die much earlier than that,' Quidor observed. 'My agent saw him at noon or shortly thereafter.'

'How *did* he die, is the question. Perhaps Messieurs Hoche and Gaillard can give us the answer.'

A bailiff reported they had just arrived separately at the Châtelet within minutes of one another, each accompanied by one of Quidor's agents. They had come willingly and were not manacled. News of Beauregard's death spread quickly. As his associates, they knew they would be questioned.

Hoche was the first. Judging from his carefree expression, Georges guessed the man had not yet missed his stolen Fersen papers.

Quidor shook his hand, invited him to sit down, spoke to him in respectful tones. After initial pleasantries, the inspector leaned toward Hoche, gazed at him sternly for a moment. 'When did you last see Chevalier de Beauregard?'

'At about two o'clock yesterday afternoon. He visited my apartment in the Palais-Royal. Seemed greatly distressed. The Queen had turned him out of the palace at Versailles.'

'I suppose you comforted him, gave him a drink,' observed Quidor evenly. 'When did he leave?'

'After about an hour,' Hoche replied. 'There wasn't any more I could do for him.'

The inspector sat back, exhaled impatiently. 'Monsieur Hoche, it's always best to tell me the truth. Several witnesses observed you and Monsieur Gaillard carry the chevalier out of your apartment in a blanket and load him on to a small cart.' Quidor signaled a guard. A few seconds later, Pierre was brought into the room.

Quidor addressed him and pointed to Hoche. 'Is this the man who said, "Make it look like suicide"?'

'Yes, that's him.' Pierre's lips curled with contempt for Hoche, a bungler. Quidor signaled the guard again, and Pierre was led away.

During this exchange, Hoche's expression changed from insouciance to dismay as he began to realize his lie was being exposed. He breathed heavily. Beads of perspiration gathered on his brow.

'Now let me hear the truth,' demanded Quidor, glaring mercilessly at him.

Hoche began by stuttering, stopped, then started again in a voice so low he could barely be heard. A guard brought him water. Finally, he told his story. Beauregard had arrived in such a nervous state that Hoche had offered him a bed and a dose of laudanum to quiet him down. Unfortunately, Hoche left the bottle in plain sight on a side table. When he returned an hour later, the bottle was empty and his distressed visitor was dead.

'At first, I didn't know what to do.' Hoche wrung his hands, bit his lower lip. 'The Paris police would investigate. Scandalmongers would paint this incident in the most garish colors. Duc Philippe would be embarrassed and become angry with me. I called upon Monsieur Gaillard for help. He recruited the two men who took the body away.' Hoche lowered his head with shame. 'It was all hastily done.'

During this interrogation Georges sat to one side, taking notes for Quidor. A fear lurked in the back of his mind that the inspector might wonder what else he and Anne had done in Hoche's apartment that night. Georges had told Quidor only that they had been investigating Hoche's possible complicity in the murder of the duchess. By chance, they and André had observed the rolled-up blanket being carried out. Georges had not mentioned finding Fersen's papers. Quidor had a mercenary mind and could not be trusted with such sensitive information.

Quidor put Hoche in the custody of a guard and sent him away, then called in Gaillard. The inspector and the journalist sat studying each other silently for a moment, like old adversaries who were about to wrestle again.

'What can you tell me about Beauregard's death?' Quidor began.

'I only know what Hoche told me and can't vouch for it.' The journalist essentially repeated Hoche's story. 'I arranged to dispose of the body. The duke wouldn't want it to be found in his palace. Hoche was near panic, helpless.'

Gaillard could not be enticed into saying any more, and a guard led him away. Quidor turned to Georges. 'I'll hold the two men here until an inquest is held. Tomorrow, the autopsy will report death by an overdose of laudanum. At the urging of Duc Philippe, the inquest will reach a verdict of accidental death. He would not want his name involved in a suicide or a murder trial.'

'I understand the duke,' Georges granted. 'Nonetheless, a trial might bring out the truth about the murder of Duchesse Aimée. Yesterday, in his unstable, irrational state of mind, Beauregard might have felt he was about to be arrested for the crime. Desperate, he demanded money from Hoche in order to escape from France. Beauregard might have threatened, if he were arrested and forced to confess to the murder, that he would also accuse Hoche of complicity. Under such circumstances, Hoche might have killed Beauregard with an overdose.'

Quidor appeared sympathetic. 'Georges, your speculation has merit, but it's nearly impossible to prove. In view of the duke's attitude, it's also moot.'

It was time to leave. Nothing more could be done at the Châtelet. Georges rose from the table. Nonetheless, he continued to believe that Hoche might know whether Beauregard had killed the duchess. But Hoche could not accuse Beauregard without implicating himself in a conspiracy against the Queen. The truth seemed more difficult than ever to reach.

Darkness was falling over Paris. The lamplighters were making their rounds. The coach from Versailles left Anne at the institute's door. It would park nearby and wait for her. She didn't know what Abbé de l'Épée wanted. His note spoke about discussing Denise's case. The servant who had delivered the note said the priest seemed distressed.

Inside, the building had quieted down. The students had left for their lodgings in the city. A few servants were about their business. Anne caught the smell of onion soup. Supper was being prepared. A servant showed her to the abbé's parlor next to his office. The old man was seated in a chair, a light cover over his legs.

His face brightened as she entered. 'Good evening, Madame Cartier. So good of you to come.' His voice was soft and weak.

She sat near him and asked, 'What can I do for you, monsieur?'

'A few days ago, your husband the colonel wrote to me for an estimation of Mademoiselle de Villers's character. It might work in her favor. He wanted to include it in his final report on the case. I have done as he wished. In his letter he also asked me if our former student Mademoiselle Cécile Fortier could be persuaded to retract what she said against Denise and clear her name. It seems Provost Sully intends to use those accusations to portray Denise as inclined to steal things.'

Anne was saddened. 'That could badly damage her cause. The magistrates in Parlement are likely to accept the provost's word on that point.'

The priest nodded. 'I have written to Mademoiselle Fortier, pleaded with her, but without success. She refused to meet with me, and sent a note standing by her claim that, when suspicion turned on Denise, she sneaked back into the room and secretly returned the lace collar.' The abbé shook his head and sighed. 'What's worse, at the provost's request, Mademoiselle Fortier has given him in writing her version of the incident and her opinion of Denise's character.'

As the abbé told this story, Anne felt her chest tighten with anxiety. The provost would prepare his charges against Denise in the next two days. Only Mademoiselle Fortier's public retraction could counteract the damage that she had already done. Anne studied the priest's face and anticipated his request. 'Do you want me to speak to Mademoiselle Fortier?' She wondered why the young woman would listen to her but not to the priest.

'Yes, I do,' he replied, then went on to deal with her objection. 'Hopefully, you can meet her face to face, study her attitude and perhaps find a way to change it. She used to be

172

jealous of Denise, envied her beauty, good taste, and fine manners.' He described Mademoiselle Fortier's humble origins, her plain appearance, and her fierce desire to improve her situation. 'I can imagine her smiling if Denise were to stumble in polite society, but unless I'm badly mistaken, she would not wish to see her destroyed.'

'How can I find Mademoiselle Fortier?'

'Just a minute.' The priest rummaged through the box of papers at his side. 'She has recently gone to work in a fashionable millinery shop in the Palais-Royal.' He handed Anne a slip of paper with the proprietor's name, a Madame Bouffant, and an address in the Valois arcade. 'In Cécile's new position she may feel too embarrassed to retract her story.' He waved a warning hand. 'I am only guessing, but you could find out.'

She gave the priest a reassuring smile. 'I'll do what I can.'

'Before you go, you might speak with Mademoiselle Françoise Arnaud downstairs. I've told her that you were coming. She knows Mademoiselle Fortier better than anyone else.'

Anne found Françoise at a table in her room on the ground floor, writing in her journal. She closed the book and invited Anne to a chair facing her. More than a week had passed since the two women had last met. In the meantime, Françoise had led efforts among the students at the institute to help Denise. They had added their appreciation of her character to the report the abbé had sent to Paul. More important, several of the older, more mature students had investigated the incident of the lace collar.

'We started from the premise that there were only three options. Either Denise stole the collar and later secretly returned it, as Cécile claimed. Or, Cécile lost it and later found it, as Denise suggested. Or . . .' Françoise paused, fixed Anne's gaze. 'Or, Cécile hid the collar, then claimed Denise stole it and later furtively returned it.'

'And what did you discover?' asked Anne, her interest rising.

Françoise signed with insistent hands and gestures. 'All

along, Cécile has asserted that she missed the collar immediately after Denise left the room.' Françoise rolled her eyes. 'No one ever saw Denise with the collar. Nor do we think Cécile lost it. One of the girls remembered seeing Cécile holding the collar in her hand *after* Denise had left the room.'

'Why didn't that girl speak up at the time? A great injustice could have been avoided.'

'She was unaware of the controversy. Her mother had called her home to Amiens to care for a sick sister. She's still there. I met her only a few days ago. She gave me a written statement.'

'That leads to your third alternative. Cécile hid the collar, then deliberately blamed Denise for stealing it.'

'Correct.' Françoise paused, her face heavy with sadness. 'I confronted her yesterday in her garret room above the millinery shop. She denied everything, claimed we were conspiring against her, ordered me out.' She spread her hands in a gesture of desperation. 'Madame Cartier, what can we do?'

Anne stepped into the waiting coach and told the coachman, 'Back to Versailles, please.' On the way, she closed the curtains, sank back in the cushioned seat, and cast about in her mind. How should she begin? It wouldn't be easy, she realized. Cécile would want to meet her, a complete stranger, even less than Abbé de l'Épée. She at least knew him, probably still respected him.

Furthermore, Anne was Denise's friend, a strong reason to distrust her. And Anne would ask Cécile to perform a humiliating act, that is, to publicly recant her story. Sully would try to hold her to her statement, would threaten to punish her if she recanted. At the least, he would brand her a notorious liar and ruin her reputation.

The abbé had appealed to Cécile's humanity and her Christian conscience. That hadn't worked. Anne had to discover a way to force her to do the right thing.

There wasn't much time. In two weeks or less, Denise's case would come before Parlement. Anne decided her first step should be to consult Marie. She would know the milliner Madame Bouffant.

It was past ten at night when Anne reached her Versailles apartment. Fortunately, Marie was still awake in bed, reading the duchess's journal. 'How far have you got?' asked Anne, slipping off her shoes and pulling up a chair.

'I've reached the point when Duchesse Aimée first met the Queen seven years ago. The two women liked each other instantly. The Queen chose her for a minor part in a play for a garden party at the Petit Trianon.' Marie laid the book in her lap and stared at it wistfully. 'As I grasp the sense of these obscure lines, Aimée comes alive in my imagination. I've come to think of her almost as a daughter—a part of her was generous, likeable.'

She looked up at Anne. 'What have you to report from the institute? How is the good man?'

'He seemed a little weaker. But he was at the end of a long day. He and Françoise and several students are working hard for Denise.' Anne described their investigation into the lace-collar incident. 'They have proved to my satisfaction that Cécile Fortier set out deliberately to ruin Denise's reputation. During the past few days, Cécile has rebuffed pleas by the abbé and Françoise to retract her charges.'

'I'm sorry to hear that.' Marie put the journal aside and sat on the edge of the bed. 'What more can be done?'

'Have you heard of a Madame Bouffant, a milliner in the Palais-Royal?'

'Madame Bouffant! Yes, I know her . . . by reputation.' She indulged an ironic smile. 'In her youth she was a celebrated courtesan. Later, she turned to millinery. I've been in her shop a few times. She's fashionable and has a distinguished clientele here at the palace as well as in the city.' Marie gazed at Anne inquisitively. 'What have you to do with her? A new hat, gloves, ribbons? I can recommend my milliner, who does better work for half the price.'

Anne shook the slip of paper. 'This has to do with the same young deaf woman, Cécile Fortier. She sews at Madame Bouffant's shop. Abbé de l'Épée has asked me to look into

Cécile's situation. Do you think if I were to speak to the milliner, explain the harm that her young woman is causing, she might threaten to discharge her, force her to recant?'

Marie put on a robe and carried the journal to its hiding place. With a sigh of exasperation she turned to face Anne. 'The Devil has his hand in this matter. You said Mademoiselle Fortier *recently* went to work in the milliner's shop.' Marie continued in a low, measured voice. 'If I told you that Madame Bouffant was once the Marquis de Sully's mistress and is still his friend, could you guess who found that position for the young deaf woman?'

Anne sank back in her chair, stunned. The provost had thought ahead, had carefully built his case against Denise. He had made sure that Mademoiselle Fortier remained firmly in his grip, unable to change her story.

CHAPTER TWENTY-THREE

Forceful Measures

Saturday, June 9

The sun neared its zenith as Anne's coach reached her residence on Rue Saint-Honoré. These twelve-mile trips between the palace and the city were becoming wearisome. Why had the royal government moved away from Paris in the first place? True, it was a dirty, crowded, and often violent place. But it was where most of the country's business was done. The King's ministers and servants were constantly running back and forth just like she was. Fortunately, the baron had given Paul free use of the royal stables, and the privilege extended to her. At least the ride was fast and comfortable.

In the ground-floor office Paul laid aside a sheaf of official paper and rose from his desk to greet her. 'I'm waiting for the autopsy report on Beauregard. Before noon Quidor will pick it up at the morgue in the Châtelet and bring a copy here.'

Anne embraced him, then took a seat. 'Has Sylvie brought back any news from the duke's palace this morning?'

'Duc Philippe dismissed Hoche last night,' said Paul as he returned to his desk. 'For some time the duke has been displeased with him entertaining at a brothel. His bookkeeping has also been careless, expenses improperly reported. Beauregard's suspicious death was the last straw.'

'With Hoche gone, what will happen to André?' Anne was also concerned for Sylvie, who seemed fond of the young man.

'Hoche's fall is André's good fortune. The duke discovered that André is a personable young man and knows the collections very well. For the time being, he will take over Hoche's duties in return for an assistant and a little more money.'

'That should please Sylvie,' Anne remarked. 'I expect she'll see more of him from now on.'

'I'm happy for her,' Paul said, his eyes drifting to the sheaf of paper on his desk.

'Now, about Denise de Villers . . .' Anne raised her voice slightly to hold his attention. 'I have information that might help her cause.'

He looked up, instantly alert.

'Françoise Arnaud and students at the institute have exposed Cécile Fortier's deceitful conduct in the lace-collar affair.' Anne described their investigation thus far. 'Unfortunately, Cécile claims she's being persecuted and refuses to retract. Can you think of a way to change her mind?'

'I shall try,' he replied, his expression hopeful. 'We must discuss this with Georges. He should be in his rooms upstairs.' A servant was dispatched to call the adjutant.

With his customary bustle he joined Paul and Anne at the office conference table. A servant came with coffee. Anne repeated for Georges what she had learned at the institute.

He rubbed his chin reflectively. 'Quidor might have compromising information on Madame Bouffant. If he would share it with us, we could threaten to ruin her business unless she forces Cécile to confess.'

Anne shook her head. 'Bouffant and Sully are friends. He would defend her.'

'I have another idea,' said Saint-Martin. 'Quidor could bring Cécile in for questioning about her false accusations. We might be able to persuade a magistrate, even Lieutenant-General DeCrosne, to charge her with malicious slander and punish her with a day or two in the pillory. That would effectively undermine her credibility. The Marquis de Sully would be irate but helpless.'

'Let's try it,' said Georges. 'What have we to lose?'

A few minutes later, Quidor arrived by coach in the courtyard. Standing by the window, Saint-Martin watched him shuffle stiffly over the paving stones to the front door. 'Quidor has had a rough ride from the Châtelet. He will be grumpy.'

'Good reason for me to leave,' said Anne. 'You'll find me at the institute.'

After waving her off, Saint-Martin hastened to greet the visitor, and led him into the office. With a solicitous smile Georges took his topcoat and hat.

Quidor managed a gruff *merci*, then pulled the autopsy report out of his portfolio and laid it on Saint-Martin's desk. 'No surprises here,' he remarked. 'Beauregard died from an overdose of laudanum at about two in the afternoon. No signs of violence on the body.'

Georges offered him a chair facing the colonel and a glass of brandy. He gladly accepted. 'To your health and mine,' he toasted. The drink went down in one gulp. He smacked his lips and sank back in the chair, the fatigue already beginning to vanish from his face. 'I've been chasing criminals since dawn. I don't know what Paris is coming to.'

Crime in Paris hadn't worsened, thought Saint-Martin. The city had grown. But there were only four inspectors in the criminal investigation department to deal with thousands of criminals busy night and day. Saint-Martin wondered if this was the right moment to propose more work. But it was probably as good a time as any.

'Inspecteur, I have a problem,' Saint-Martin began. 'It concerns the Marquis de Sully's prime suspect in the murder of Duchesse Aimée.' He described the lace-collar incident and the harm it caused to Denise de Villers's reputation. 'The provost intends to use Mademoiselle Fortier's accusation to prove that de Villers has a history of theft. The charge is simply false, deliberately invented by Fortier. A fellow student witnessed her deception. Moreover, de Villers's companions, teachers, and the head of the institute all vouch for her sterling character.'

Quidor nodded languidly, studying his fingernails.

Saint-Martin leaned forward, trying to catch the man's eye. 'The Marquis de Sully continues to insist that Fortier's accusation is sound, that de Villers is a habitual thief. I want the truth to come out.'

'So, what do you want from me?' The inspector's voice was flat. Not much in it for him. After all, he and his agents were busy and could see little profit in a quarrel among poor deaf students.

Georges spoke up. 'Do you know of any way to *persuade* Madame Bouffant to compel Fortier to retract her accusation against de Villers?'

'I grasp your meaning, Charpentier.' The inspector sighed with mock regret. 'I'm sorry to have to tell you, Bouffant's an honest, if high-priced, milliner. And, what's worse, she's fiercely loyal to the Marquis de Sully. He pays her rent.'

'In that case,' interjected the colonel, 'we'll try a different tactic. Would you lend your name and authority to a charge of malicious slander against Cécile Fortier? It's the only way to prevent the provost from wrongly ruining de Villers's reputation.'

'I gather that you and Georges believe she's innocent of the murder.'

'Yes, but we can't prove it yet.'

'Well,' Quidor sighed, 'Baron Breteuil has ordered the Paris police to assist you.' He glanced at the brandy bottle. Georges filled his glass. 'I'll pay a visit to the abbé's institute. I've never interrogated the deaf before. May need some help.'

'My wife is on her way to meet students and staff at the institute. She'll interview the most credible witnesses. With her help you can quickly confirm her findings, then go to Lieutenant-General DeCrosne with the charge of malicious slander. I'll speak to him and prepare the way.'

Quidor sipped the brandy thoughtfully. 'I've heard of Madame Cartier's talent for criminal investigation. Perhaps at the institute she could teach me a trick or two.'

Was he being ironic? wondered Saint-Martin, studying the inspector's face. He seemed sincere.

Georges leaned forward, a playful sparkle in his eye. 'If it'll help persuade you, monsieur, I'll lead you to the secret room in Hoche's apartment where he keeps his personal papers.'

Quidor smiled, finished his drink. 'Now, that's an offer I can't refuse.'

Quidor and Georges walked the short distance to the Palais-Royal, chatting about mutual friends and enemies. 'You know, Georges, your colonel is about to stir up a hornet's nest. Sully is as malicious as he is obstinate, and he has powerful patrons in the royal palace. He will never forgive a man who publicly humiliates him.'

'The colonel's no fool. He knows Sully and the mischief he can cause, especially at court among Baron Breteuil's enemies. But, as long as the baron is the Minister for Paris and the Royal Household, the colonel is safe.' Georges felt less secure than he sounded. In these uncertain times even the most powerful minister could fall from the King's grace, leaving his dependants helpless.

In Hoche's study Georges waved a hand over the room. 'There's nothing of interest here,' he told Quidor. 'But let's try this.' He manipulated the wall sconce and the secret door opened.

'That was well hidden,' remarked Quidor. 'I might have missed it.'

They pulled file boxes off the shelves, spread them out on the table, and went through the papers systematically. Quidor's spirits improved with every bit of evidence he uncovered. He held up a fistful of receipts. 'The duke will be chagrined to learn how Hoche fooled him.'

Georges also knew what Quidor wanted and found several pieces of evidence for him. At the end of an hour they had gathered convincing proof that Hoche had stolen money from the duke. He had also substituted paste diamonds and gems for the original precious objects. Gaillard had sold them to dealers in London, then shared the profit with Hoche.

As the search of the files neared its end, a puzzled expression crossed Quidor's face. 'This is odd,' he remarked. 'In his journal Hoche refers to secret work that Beauregard was doing for him at Versailles.' The inspector showed Georges a page. 'In the margin Hoche refers to a letter from an unnamed count to a person called Josephine. Have you seen it?'

'No,' replied Georges. A simple but necessary lie.

In the next few minutes, Quidor found several other references to messages between the count and Josephine, none of which were in the files. 'This is puzzling. What could Hoche have done with them? Hidden them elsewhere?'

Georges shrugged noncommittally, but he was worried. Quidor had an itch and would scratch until it went away. He would soon question Hoche again. Georges hoped Hoche understood he could gain nothing by exposing Fersen and the Queen without documentary proof. He might instead find himself more harshly confined in prison, or dead. Not that Georges pitied either Hoche or the Queen. The only thing that mattered was to keep Quidor's goodwill and to enlist his talents in the investigation into the death of the duchess.

Quidor closed the journal. 'I believe we're finished here, Georges. I'll have to ask Hoche later about the missing messages.'

At one o'clock, Saint-Martin glanced up at the sign, Le Grand Canard. The artist had portrayed a full-bodied, striding duck, its green head tilted up, its yellow beak opened wide like a trumpet. The colonel dismounted and hitched his horse to a post. Many coaches had parked by the inn. The mild, sunny day had drawn their owners to this lovely area of woods and meadows west of the city, its shaded lanes ideal for the pleasures of riding.

He had spent much of the morning searching for Lieutenant-General DeCrosne. 'He rides in the Bois de Boulogne,' an officer on duty at the Hôtel de Police had said. 'He may stop at Le Grand Canard.'

Inside the inn, Saint-Martin recognized the lieutenant-general rising from a table, having finished a light lunch. An empty wineglass, bits of bread and cheese, remained on the table. Several male companions appeared ready to disperse. Saint-Martin waited until DeCrosne had disengaged himself from the others.

'May I have a word with you, sir? It's important.'

A look of surprise came over DeCrosne's face, followed by consternation, as if he expected to hear news of a catastrophe. 'Colonel,' he blurted out. 'What is it?'

'A delicate matter has come up. I must bring it to your attention.'

DeCrosne frowned. 'Can't it wait until Monday?' He studied Saint-Martin's face. 'No, apparently not. Shall we walk into the woods until we are at a safe distance from the inn?'

Saint-Martin agreed, and they set off on a well-trodden path. They soon turned off into a meadow and sat on a lightly shaded bench. 'Now, Colonel,' said the lieutenant-general, with a courtesy in his voice that put Saint-Martin at ease. 'What's wrong?'

'It concerns the maid Denise de Villers, sir.' He described briefly the lace-collar incident and its relevance to the investigation of the duchess's death. 'Sully is using dubious written testimony by Cécile Fortier to portray Denise de Villers as prone to thievery. I believe that a fair investigation of the incident will show that Cécile maliciously slandered Denise. A credible witness has testified to her innocence. Inspecteur Quidor will confirm the truth of their statements.'

'And how am I to be involved in this matter?'

'As a magistrate, you could order Fortier to retract under threat of the pillory.'

DeCrosne thought it over for a moment. 'Colonel, your request has merit. Privately, I agree that Sully's excessive zeal to deter the lower classes from crime against their masters has warped his judgment. Hence, his plan to convict the maid, even though Mademoiselle Fortier's accusations do not deserve credence.'

'Then he should be stopped, sir.'

'Still, Colonel, I must take care in challenging him, especially in these financially stringent times. Is the issue sufficiently important to justify spending police money and effort on what would appear to some highly placed observers as a quarrel among poor deaf schoolgirls?'

'Sir, the cost of such a challenge would be small. The Institute for the Deaf has undertaken the necessary investigation. Inspecteur Quidor has only to confirm a few statements and prepare an investigative report, which I shall submit to you.'

'Granted, the cost might be small. Is the effort justified?'

'I believe the stakes are high. The provost's case against the maid rests in large part on her alleged greed and thieving habits. If that perception is false, if in fact she is a young woman of excellent character, it will be difficult to convict her of murder.'

The lieutenant-general raised a skeptical eyebrow. 'The brooch in her mattress?'

'I have found two other suspects with strong reasons to kill the duchess and the opportunity to do so. They could easily have put the brooch in that mattress while the maid was in the kitchen preparing breakfast.'

'I see,' murmured DeCrosne thoughtfully.

'If the provost has his way,' Saint-Martin continued, 'an innocent young woman will be gruesomely, publicly executed on Place de Grève, to the dismay of civilized men and women throughout France and the rest of Europe.'

'Do I detect an allusion to Jean Calas and the Chevalier de La Barre?'

'Yes, I expected you would.' The maid's possible fate had reminded Saint-Martin of those earlier victims of judicial blindness and savagery. Some twenty years ago, the Protestant Calas had been tortured and brutally executed in Toulouse for the murder of his son, who in fact had committed suicide. DeCrosne should know, for he directed the official posthumous vindication of Calas and the reparation paid to his family. DeCrosne, like every literate person in Europe, also knew of the young Chevalier de La Barre, cruelly executed in the same period for alleged blasphemy, for which a month in prison would have been sufficient punishment. In his widely read tracts, Voltaire had exposed these atrocities and covered French criminal justice with shame.

'Colonel, you've given me cause for concern.' DeCrosne rose from the bench. 'It's time I return to the city. Much work waits for me. This evening, I'll send a message to Sully warning him that Mademoiselle Fortier's accusation against Denise de Villers is possibly slanderous and is under investigation. I shall know by Monday morning whether to arrest her.'

The two men walked back to the inn, shook hands, and mounted their horses. As they rode off in different directions, Saint-Martin felt a rise of hope. The lieutenant-general of police, an honorable and just man, had engaged himself in the maid's case.

In the dining room of the Institute for the Deaf, Anne was near finishing an evening omelette with Françoise Arnaud when Georges and Quidor entered. 'Would you care to join us?' she asked. 'There's a pot of delicious ragout in the kitchen left over from dinner.'

The men admitted to not having eaten since breakfast. Françoise rose immediately and went out for the food.

While setting two places at the table, Anne explained that she had spent several hours interrogating students, the abbé, of course, and Françoise herself. Besides the Amiens girl, who could soon return to the institute, Françoise had brought forward two other witnesses, a boy and a girl. Previously, they hadn't wished to get involved—they didn't like Denise. But now they realized how wrong their silence was. They confessed to having heard Cécile boast that she had hid the lace collar to embarrass Denise.

At the time, Anne continued, Abbé de l'Épée, the staff, and the students felt alike that the lace-collar incident was best settled quickly and quietly. True, Cécile continued to insinuate that Denise was a thief. Nonetheless, the matter seemed likely to remain within the institute and do no harm. No one took Cécile seriously until she put her accusations in writing and made them public.

'Then,' concluded Anne, 'they became literally a matter of

184

life and death for Denise. Besides the three students whom Françoise discovered, I have found several more who will now testify to Denise's good character.'

'Can you provide me with written depositions?' Quidor asked.

'Yes, here they are.' Anne patted a pile of papers on a side table. 'You will find them carefully written and signed.'

Quidor reached over and began sifting through the pile, murmuring his approval.

A smile of satisfaction spread over Georges's face. Anne understood he took credit for teaching her what magistrates expected from investigators.

'These will do very well, madame,' remarked Quidor as he read a student's deposition. 'With your help in signing, I'll ask this person and a few others to confirm what they've written.'

'I anticipated your wish, sir, and asked them to wait until you've finished eating.' Anne felt a touch of pride.

At that moment Françoise and a pretty female student returned with tableware, bread, a large pot of rich beef ragout, and a jug of red wine.

Quidor ate the meal with relish, pronounced the wine to his taste, and declared he was ready to meet the witnesses. When they entered the room, his expression grew a little uncertain. Anne knew he probably shared the common view that a lack of hearing somehow weakened the intelligence of deaf persons and made them less observant.

This was most likely the first time in his long career that he had met a deaf community. His eyes widened in astonishment as he observed the students' unaffected self-assurance. Their signs and gestures were lively, even elegant, and fully answered his questions.

'I'll present my findings to the lieutenant-general first thing on Monday morning,' he said, shifting the depositions into his portfolio. 'I'm confident he'll do the right thing.'

Comtesse Marie discreetly suppressed a yawn. It was near midnight. She had sought an invitation to an evening in the Princesse de Lamballe's salon, though not to enjoy palace gossip and card games. She had heard that the provost would be there. Denise's case might be discussed and something useful learned.

The princess's guests were a distinguished sample of the aristocracy residing in the palace—in all, twenty men and women. They had come fashionably dressed in silk suits and gowns, hair powdered, cheeks rouged. The cadenced murmur of polite conversation filled the graceful room. Blazing crystal chandeliers cast a rich, golden living light that worked magically on the ladies' diamonds, rubies, and other precious stones.

Nonetheless, a common awareness of the Crown's financial crisis and the economies ordered by the King and Queen gave the gathering a somber tone. Several prominent persons who would have been invited had quit the palace. Others had been sent away, notably the Princesse de Polignac and her clan. Many of those who remained felt like passengers on a sinking ship.

A hush of anticipation came over the room. The guests began to whisper, 'The Queen is arriving.' A minute later, Marie Antoinette glided into the room in her inimitably gracious manner, smiling to some, speaking briefly with others, depending on the level of their dignity. Comte Fersen followed her at a short distance.

'The King, clumsy fellow, rarely attends a salon,' whispered a friendly acquaintance to Marie. 'He goes to bed early, alone.' Such irreverence toward the sovereign, Marie had discovered, was commonplace in palace circles, but always behind the King's back, never to his face. He was, in fact—she agreed silently—a clumsy fellow, but he wasn't stupid. He had a good measure of common sense and was keenly aware of the honor and respect owed to his office.

The Queen and Fersen sat in a circle of guests selected by Princesse Lamballe. Among them was the Marquis de Sully. Marie managed to stand right behind him, close enough to hear what was said. As the guests drank punch from delicate Sèvres cups, they conversed with a rather forced gaiety. Everyone knew that the Queen's daughter, Sophie, was dying. Fersen contributed a few anecdotes to the company but was

186

otherwise withdrawn. A slightly melancholic air hung over him.

Marie overheard nothing remarkable until Fersen and the Queen were about to leave. She leaned toward Sully. Marie moved back a step and looked away, so as not to appear to be eavesdropping. But she heard every word they spoke.

'Marquis de Sully,' asked the Queen, 'has the investigation into Duchesse Aimée's death concluded?'

Out of the corner of her eye Marie noticed the Queen's lips tightened with concern.

'Yes, Your Highness, it has, for all practical purposes. Colonel Saint-Martin is writing his final report this evening. Monday morning, I shall hold an official examination of the evidence and charge the maid with the crime. Her guilt is clear. I shall recommend to Parlement the following punishment . . .'

'Sir!' The Queen cut him off. 'Don't distress me with ugly details. Follow the law and do it quickly.' She turned away from him, his mouth still half-open. Fersen led her through the crowd. When they were gone, the remaining guests relaxed in a buzz of gossip.

Marie left the room, stunned, feeling as if Denise had just been convicted without even a word in her defense.

CHAPTER TWENTY-FOUR

Sunday in the City

Sunday, June 10

The pots on the kitchen stove hissed and gurgled. From outside the palace apartment came faint sounds of servants at their daily chores. Anne had awakened, still tired from yesterday's investigation of Cécile Fortier in Paris. Upon her return to Versailles she had stayed up another hour sharing news with Marie. It was discouraging to hear that the Queen left Denise's fate in Sully's hands.

Anne placed bread, milk, sugar, butter, and fruit preserves on a large breakfast tray. The cook came to her with coffee and freshly baked small brioches. She buttered one for herself and offered another to Anne.

'How lovely, Robinette! Is this especially for Sunday?'

The cook smiled brightly. 'Yes, slice it in half. It's delicious with butter and strawberry preserve.'

Round and sweet, the pastry reminded Anne of a similar, though lighter bun she had recently enjoyed at Sally Lunn's bakery in Bath.

'What will you do today?' asked Anne. 'Go to church?'

'No. I'd rather darn stockings. Maybe walk in the garden.'

'And Marthe?' Anne asked, though she already knew. She hoped to draw Robinette out. 'Will she go to church?'

'Of course,' she sniffed. 'Like any other Sunday.' Suddenly, she glanced over Anne's shoulder. Fear shadowed her eyes.

'Yes, I shall.' Marthe had quietly entered the kitchen in a dressing gown. Her face was calm, but her eyes betrayed her irritation. For a moment, she glared at her half-sister. 'Have you nothing better to do than pry into my affairs?'

Then she turned to Anne. 'When I entered Duchesse Aimée's service, she agreed that I would be free on Sundays. I hope your husband will honor that arrangement.' The tone of her voice was firm, determined.

'I'll ask him at breakfast.' Anne was sure she could have agreed for him, but she felt Marthe wanted his express permission.

'Thank you, madame. You may tell him, I usually leave at eight in the morning and return at eight in the evening.' She prepared a small tray of bread and coffee for herself and went to her room.

Anne looked for Robinette. She had vanished.

'I have no objection.' Paul stirred sugar into his coffee. Anne had told him of Marthe's request. 'I'll speak to her now, while I think of it.' He excused himself and left the room.

Anne and Georges sat with Marie at her window table enjoying the cook's brioches. Outside, the sun was rising into a blue sky. The outlook for the rest of the day was hopeful.

'It's time we paid more attention to Marthe.' Anne recounted the incident in the kitchen. 'I'll follow her into Paris today.' Before leaving the institute last night, Anne had learned that the woman once belonged to the parish of Saint-Roch and still attended religious services there.

'Good idea,' Georges remarked. 'I've wondered about her.'

'Can either of you suggest a disguise?' Anne asked.

Marie looked to Georges who was slathering a brioche with butter and preserves.

He laid down the pastry. 'Dress like a fop, a *petit-maître*. They're as common as flies where you're likely to go, especially on Sunday. People hardly notice them. You know how to act the part.' He gave her a crooked smile. 'One of Duc Henri's suits will do. You're about his size. And wear a wig.' He raised the brioche in a salute, then asked casually, 'Do you want help?'

'Yes,' she replied, thinking ahead. 'She'll go to the parish Mass at Saint-Roch and afterwards to the Palais-Royal, not to a den of thieves. But if something unexpected happens, it would be good to have you there.'

'With my tools,' added Georges. 'For good measure, I'll send word to Sylvie and Michou to meet us. They might be helpful. Marthe has never seen either of them.'

Exactly at eight, as the housekeeper left the apartment by the front door, Anne and Georges hurried down the private stairway. They reached the main palace exit shortly after she did and followed her at a safe distance. She boarded a coach that departed a few minutes later directly for Paris. Anne and Georges hired a waiting cabriolet and set off behind her.

From Duc Henri's wardrobe Anne had chosen a slightly worn pearl-gray suit with discreet black embroidery. Among *petits-maîtres* she would not call attention to herself. Georges also dressed as a fop in brown and black. Both wore wigs. Anne had dulled her complexion with powder, lowered her voice.

Next to her, Georges studied her disguise with a critical eye. 'Face to face, she'll recognize us. But we're safe at a short distance. Fortunately, she's a little near-sighted.'

An hour and a half later, her coach stopped in Place Vendôme. Several passengers got off, among them Marthe. Hardly looking to left or right, she walked east two blocks to the church, paused at the front entrance as if gathering courage, and went in. Anne and Georges waited for a minute, then followed her.

She took a front seat off to the left in the nave and stared straight ahead. Gradually, the church filled with worshipers. Anne walked up the left side aisle to steal a glance at her. She sat erect, stony-faced, eyes open but fixed on an inner vision. Anne returned to seats Georges had saved a few rows back and off to the right.

Soon, the bells of Saint-Roch sounded the beginning of Solemn High Mass. Marthe joined in the traditional movements of the liturgy—kneeling for prayer, standing for the Gospel, sitting for the sermon, crossing herself when others did. But she didn't seem to listen, didn't part her lips to pray.

At the conclusion of the Mass, Anne was left with the curious impression that Marthe had worshiped alone in the tightly closed chapel of her own soul. What kind of god dwelled there was a mystery.

Marthe remained seated until most of the congregation had gone. Finally, she walked forward past the chancel through the Lady chapel and into the Calvary chapel at the far east end of the church. Anne followed her, while Georges lagged behind.

The chapel was dark and empty of people. A huge, rocky, hill-shaped monument representing the crucifixion rose up against the front wall. A dramatic light from a hidden window in the ceiling drew Anne's eyes to a nude, writhing Christ on the cross, his gaze lifted to heaven. Staring up at him, Mary Magdalene sat on the ground to the left of Christ's feet. A serpent glided among the rocks beneath her. Off to the right were two gaping, awestruck Roman soldiers.

Carved into the foot of the hill beneath the scene of the crucifixion was a sepulchre with an altar in the shape of a sarcophagus. Its tabernacle, a truncated fluted column, reminded Anne of a life cut short. Her much beloved stepfather, Antoine, had been murdered in Paris almost two years earlier.

Anne shivered. The place spoke powerfully of death and desolation. She could see no sign of hope. Was she missing something? A hidden meaning visible only to eyes of faith?

After crossing herself, Marthe kneeled before the altar and stared up at the figure of the crucified Christ. For several minutes she seemed transfixed, her body rocking back and forth, her lips moving silently. The stillness of the room, the rhythmic movement of the kneeling woman, the faint scent of incense lingering from the Mass, worked hypnotically on Anne. Time stopped. She wondered, what memories brought Marthe to this place?

Suddenly, the woman threw herself flat upon the pavement, jarring Anne into heightened awareness. The prostrate figure moaned softly, her shoulders heaving with sobs. A few moments later, she grew quiet, then slowly rose to her feet. Anne barely had time to gather Georges and retreat to a safe hiding place behind a pillar in the nave. Marthe shuffled past them, offering Anne a clear view of her face. It was altered, ravaged, as if marked by the horror of the crucifixion. In a few more seconds she was out the front door and on to Rue Saint-Honoré.

It was mid-morning. Paul and Marie were studying Duchesse Aimée's journal together. Someone knocked on the outside door. And knocked again. No one responded.

'Marthe's on her way to Paris. Where's the cook?' Paul rose to tend to the door himself.

'She disappeared without a word after breakfast. Probably out walking in the park,' Marie replied. 'Can't blame her. She doesn't have much work to do on a Sunday.'

Paul returned with a message from the guardroom. Jules Blondel and Blanche Moreau had quarreled loudly and he had struck her. What should be done with them?

'I must look into the matter, Marie. Could you come with me? Mademoiselle Moreau is pregnant. A woman should look after her.'

'Yes, of course, Paul. I'll be ready in a minute.'

In the guardroom they found a sullen Blondel sitting manacled in one corner, a badly bruised Moreau in another. Two stern-faced guards sat at a table between them.

While Marie examined the woman, Paul asked Blondel what had happened.

'That bitch!' He jerked his head in Moreau's direction. 'She nags me to distraction. Says the rooms are damp and rat-infested, the food's bad, the work in the laundry is boring. She feels sick every morning. Nothing's right and it's all my fault. Finally, I had enough and I hit her.'

'Hard, and more than once,' snarled a guard from the table.

Blondel was a pitiful shadow of his former self. Gone was the perfect servant's cool, calm demeanor. He looked haggard and irritable.

Saint-Martin sent him away with a guard, then walked over to Blanche Moreau. She appeared listless, semi-conscious. The left side of her face was swollen and discolored, her lips broken and bleeding.

'Mademoiselle,' Saint-Martin asked gently, 'can you hear me?'

She didn't respond, her eyes half-open but unseeing.

He repeated his question.

Finally, she looked up at him and spoke with a thick, slurred voice. 'It was a bad day in my life when I first laid eyes on Jules Blondel.'

Marie brought a cup of water to the woman's wounded lips. She swallowed a few drops, then mumbled, 'He's a sweet-talker.' She drifted off, eyes closed.

'I find no damage to her body,' said Marie softly. 'He hit her only in the face. I don't think he broke any bones. She's fortunate. A blow to the temple could have killed her.'

At first, Marie seemed not to realize what her words had implied. Then the awareness crept over her face. Duchesse Aimée died from such a blow, though given with a poker.

They stepped out of the room to speak privately. The remaining guard had begun to show interest in what they were saying.

'Marie, I can now imagine Blondel might have exploded with violence in the duchess's room as he's done here. The person whom the maid Catherine saw leaving the private exit early Friday morning could have been Blondel, who had just killed Duchesse Aimée, planted the brooch in Denise's mattress, and kept the coins for himself. Hid them somewhere.'

'His motive?'

'Greed. He wanted more than back wages. He also expected Duc Henri would inherit his wife's money and perhaps give him some.'

'How will you drag the truth out of him?'

'I don't know yet. For the present, I'll send him to the provost's prison.' He opened the guardroom door and glanced at Moreau, apparently asleep. 'And what shall I do with her?'

'I've heard of a convent in the town, Paul. I'll ask the nuns to nurse her, keep her until the baby is born. I'll make the arrangements right away.'

After leaving Saint-Roch, Marthe Bourdon walked briskly toward the Palais-Royal. She seemed to have returned to normal, her demons hidden beneath a rigid, calm, purposeful mask. Halfway, she looked at her watch and stopped in a café. Anne pretended to study a shop window across the street. The chapel scene came back to her—Marthe, in agony on the floor. What loss, what tragedy had she suffered? And, did that have anything to do with the case under investigation?

Meanwhile, Georges had gone ahead to Rue Traversine to fetch Michou and Sylvie. They returned just as Marthe left the café and went on to the Palais-Royal. For more than an hour she looked at hats, scarves, ribbons, and the like in shops in the Montpensier arcade. Sylvie and Michou took turns following her. Georges and Anne held back at a safe distance. Promptly at two, she greeted a gentleman outside Café de Foy. Their embrace seemed polite rather than passionate.

He was a little older and a little taller than she. A prosperous businessman, to judge from his well-fed appearance and hearty manner. His lightly patterned green silk suit was of high quality. He might have dealt in fabrics, Anne thought. Then, again, he might come from almost any honorable profession. This was Sunday at the Palais-Royal, an occasion calling for one's finest clothes. Marthe had chosen a beautifully tailored gray silk gown with silver embroidery. She must have made it herself. She could hardly afford a dressmaker's price.

In the shadow of an arcade, Anne addressed Sylvie and

Michou. 'Marthe might recognize Monsieur Charpentier and me at close quarters in the restaurant. We'll eat something at a food stall nearby. You will follow Marthe and her gentleman into the restaurant, sit near them, catch what they say.'

Michou gathered that they were about to eat in an expensive restaurant. She frowned, pulled a *sous* from her purse, and held it up for Anne to see.

She smiled, gave Sylvie a handful of coins, then turned to Michou. 'Fear not, my dear. Baron Breteuil is paying for your meal.'

Michou grinned broadly and signed, 'Thank him for me.'

Sylvie led the way through the café to an intimate, richly furnished dining room on the first floor. It had a quiet atmosphere where respectable women could feel comfortable. She had often eaten there and knew the head waiter. He stared dubiously at Michou and appeared about to balk, though she was groomed and properly dressed. She did seem ill at ease in these luxurious surroundings.

'My guest from the country,' Sylvie remarked without apology. In a firm voice she ordered a table for two, nodding toward the one next to Marthe and her male companion.

Their conversation began with an exchange of remarks about the weather and news of the past week. Eventually, she asked about his business. He owned and managed La Normandie, a large *hôtel garni*, on Rue de Valois.

'It's prospering,' he said. 'Hardly an empty room in the building. Many of our guests come from abroad, especially from England.'

She listened politely, asking a question now and then to keep him on the topic.

'I need a trustworthy, efficient housekeeper,' he said, gazing at his attractive companion with an interest that wasn't entirely businesslike. 'Would you be willing to consider the position?'

'Your offer is intriguing, sir. I am thinking of returning to the city. You must tell me more about your hotel.'

He went on, interrupting his monologue with red wine and roasted lamb. She took little of either food or drink. By the end of the meal, his face was florid, his voice loud, and his eyes plainly lecherous.

Throughout the meal Marthe had remained calm, self-possessed, amiable, smiling at his *bons mots*. His predatory manner didn't seem to intimidate her. She promised to respond to his offer in a few days. The meal finished, they walked out into the garden and sat in the shade on rented chairs. A quarter of an hour later, he gallantly kissed her hand and they parted.

Meanwhile, Georges and Anne had joined Sylvie and Michou in the shelter of an arcade. With the housekeeper still in view, they shared impressions.

'It's time Marthe found another position,' Anne observed. 'Hmm, what's she doing now?'

She had stepped into a florist shop. In a few minutes, she came out with two red roses, their stems wrapped in paper. Then set off again.

Georges replied, 'She's heading toward the river.'

At Place de Grève she stopped in front of a tall old building facing the Hôtel de Ville, the city hall. Her trackers immediately concealed themselves in nearby doorways. That was fortunate, for she suddenly looked around to see if she had been followed. Her manner became furtive. Apparently reassured, she disappeared into a narrow passageway.

Anne waited a minute, then stepped out and surveyed the building. At ground level there appeared to be an office. Did Marthe have business to transact or was she visiting someone? Why enter the back way? And why act so secretively?

While the others remained out of sight watching the front of the building, Anne explored the passageway. She came to a small courtyard and the rear entrance. On the far side was a blank wall. She walked out into the yard to look around.

'And what do you think you're doing, sir?'

A short, stout, scowling, middle-aged woman was standing in the entrance, arms crossed on her ample chest. The concierge, Anne realized. And an eagle-eyed, testy one into the bargain.

'I'm apparently lost, madame. I'm terribly sorry.' She made her way back through the passage to the street and rejoined her companions.

She hurriedly consulted Georges, and they devised a plan. It was about four thirty. To return to Versailles by eight, Marthe must leave Paris no later than six and would have to leave Place de Grève about a half hour earlier. She might be inside for as long as an hour. Anne assigned her companions to hiding places, choosing for herself an empty stall sixty paces or so from the front of the building.

On this typical Sunday afternoon, the markets were closed. The large open space was given over to families with children, idlers, musicians and other entertainers taking advantage of the fair weather. With nothing urgent to occupy her mind, Anne's thoughts wandered back a year to the last time she stood near this spot, then filled with a raucous crowd. They had gathered to watch a young peasant woman, probably demented, being burned for the atrocious murder of her infant. Denise de Villers might meet a similar fate in the same place.

With a fierce effort of will, Anne turned her mind back to the present. At five thirty Marthe peeked around the corner of the passageway, then walked rapidly from Place de Grève in the direction of the coach stop on Place Vendôme.

When she was out of sight, Anne drew her companions together on benches in front of the Hôtel de Ville. 'Something strange is going on. Marthe left without the roses. What did she do with them? Why so secretive about it?'

'She could be having an affair,' Georges suggested. 'We need to learn more about that building. I might ask Quidor.'

Michou nudged Anne. The deaf woman had been trying in vain to read Georges's lips. Anne signed his remarks to her. 'I can help you,' she signed eagerly. 'I grew up here on Place de Grève.' She pointed to the building next to the Hôtel de Ville.

'That's the Hospital of the Holy Spirit, a foundling home where Michou lived for many years,' Anne explained. 'I was there once last year, looking for her.'

Michou took Georges by the arm and pointed to the building that Marthe had just left.

'The notary Monsieur Griffon owns it,' she signed, Anne translating. 'That's his office on the ground floor. He and his wife and their children have the first and second floors for themselves. Servants and renters live on the floors above them.' She explained that the notary guarded his building carefully because bold thieves infested the area. 'It would be very difficult for a stranger to enter.'

Georges grimaced.

Michou winked at him. 'But I'm not a stranger.' The nuns at the foundling home did business with the notary and had often sent Michou to him with messages. His housekeeper had also given her sewing to do. She signed to Sylvie. 'Come with me. We'll stay with the nuns for a few days, help them with the children. Maybe we can find out Madame Bourdon's secrets.'

Georges winked back. 'And how to get past that dragon at the rear door.'

CHAPTER TWENTY-FIVE

Cruel Questions

Sunday, June 10

A candelabrum and several sconces poured a soft golden light into Duchesse Aimée's gracious private dining room. Comtesse Marie and Colonel Paul de Saint-Martin had come together at a highly polished brown mahogany table for an exquisite supper. With little fanfare Robinette had decided to display her culinary talent with a *soupe aux marrons*, followed by *médaillon de veau avec légumes*, and finally *crème brûlée*. A new young maid was serving the meal, since Marthe had not yet returned. Anne was expected later. Georges would remain in the city.

'Our cook's a strange, secretive person, but an artist in the kitchen.' Paul tasted the chestnut soup, then cleared his palate with a glass of white wine from the duke's collection.

Marie agreed. 'Perhaps that's why Marthe puts up with her.

By the way, I persuaded the nuns at the convent to care for Blanche Moreau until the child is born. They will receive some of the money Duc Henri owes to Jules Blondel.'

'How was she when you left her?' asked Paul.

'Relieved, I think. Her relationship with the man has been difficult, for him as well as for her. It began nine months ago with a passion that blinded both of them to their pitiful lack of resources and their foolish expectations. When their passions cooled, her pregnancy locked them together. They began quarreling, which led to fights, she getting the worst of them.'

'Did she say anything that would implicate Blondel in the duchess's death?'

'I probed but didn't receive a yes or a no. He apparently never confessed to her. She's suspicious but won't accuse him.'

Over the veal and vegetables, Paul described interrogating Blondel that afternoon in the prison. 'He repeated the story he gave us Wednesday afternoon about going to the duchess's room early in the morning, admitting her accusations against him, then leaving by the servants' hallway. I tried to trick him. "No," I said, "You mean the private stairway." But he insisted he had used the hallway. It *must* have been Beauregard whom the maid Catherine saw.'

While the maid served the caramel custard dessert, conversation turned to lighter matters. 'Paul, for this evening I suggest a concert in the Princesse de Lamballe's salon. A string quartet will play chamber music by Joseph Haydn. And . . .' She paused, as if about to announce an unusual event. 'The princesse invited the Comte Honoré de Savarin. To her surprise he accepted. It seems he likes Austrian composers.'

Paul looked at her quizzically. 'Savarin? Should I know him?'

'Probably not. He's a reclusive man, widowed a few years ago, harder to meet socially than the King. For many years the palace archivist and librarian, Savarin investigates the record of everyone who seeks the King's favor. He could help me read Duchesse Aimée's journal. Names are abbreviated, many passages are in shorthand. Savarin's an expert at deciphering coded messages. The government occasionally uses him.'

When the maid had gone and they were enjoying the dessert, Paul asked his aunt, 'What have you discovered thus far?'

'From Lamballe I've learned that Aimée's father was Denis Louis Pasquier, a wealthy noble of the robe, who inherited a seat in the Parlement of Paris thirty years ago. During his judicial career he must have made many enemies.'

Paul raised an eyebrow.

'Within ten years,' she explained, 'he became a leading magistrate and passionate defender of traditional conservative principles. He claimed that moral laxity and godless philosophy were undermining the law. France was at war. Voltaire and his disciples were the enemy. In this crisis a magistrate's chief duty was to strictly enforce the criminal code and burn the blasphemers.'

'I see your point, Marie. Such a harsh bigot could easily have injured persons who might seek revenge even after he was dead.' Paul lowered his voice, though the maid had left. 'One of them might have killed his daughter or hired someone like Jules Blondel to do it.'

Marie entered the salon on Paul's arm. A shiver of delight ran through her body. The room was spacious—and splendid. Shining mahogany furniture, parquet floor, patterned cream *papier peint* on the walls, soft green drapes over the windows. Marie had chosen a rose silk gown and a diamond tiara. Paul wore a dark-green silk suit with gold embroidery. She had insisted they dress well for the occasion. The company would be brilliant.

The Princesse de Lamballe had gathered some twenty aristocratic men and women who shared a taste for Haydn's music. The Austrian composer had become fashionable in Paris. Three years earlier, the Loge Olympique orchestra had played several of his symphonies to large, enthusiastic audiences. Marie's favorite was the B-flat Symphony, called '*La Reine*' after Marie Antoinette.

This evening's entertainment featured the Quartet in D Major, the fourth in Haydn's Opus 20, known as the '*Sun*

Quartets' for their radiance. Her skin tingled with anticipation. For a moment, she found herself almost believing that she had misjudged palace society. It *could* offer pleasures worthy of civilized men and women.

The Comte de Savarin sat opposite Marie and Paul in the first row of a semicircle around the musicians. Marie hadn't seen him up close before. A slender, elegant man, her age, she guessed. His features spoke of mind over matter. His hair was brushed back from a high forehead, powdered and curled at the temples. His nose was aquiline, his mouth wide, his lips thin.

He had arrived alone shortly before the concert and sat by himself, his head inclined at a skeptical angle, studying the company with bright brown eyes alive with intelligence. When the musicians began to play, he became totally absorbed, especially in the cello passages. He was known to play the instrument himself.

At the intermission, Marie turned to Paul. 'Quick, engage him in conversation before anyone else does.' The count had hardly risen from his chair when Paul introduced himself and his aunt.

A veil of suspicion fell over Savarin's eyes. Marie was neither surprised nor offended. Upstart or spurious nobles must have often annoyed him with requests for genealogical information or certification of their claims. 'Monsieur,' she began. 'Have you enjoyed this evening's performance?'

'Why, yes,' he replied, lowering his guard a fraction. 'Lovely melodies, well played. In the slow movement the cello solo was glorious.' He went on to comment knowledgeably on the Austrian composer's works for chamber orchestras.

Marie was impressed and said so. 'Have you been to Vienna?'

'Yes, on several occasions. It's the musical capital of Europe, though I may be the only Frenchman who would admit it.'

'No, monsieur.' She pointed to Paul and herself. 'Here are two more who share your opinion.' Marie knew Vienna from trips there with her late husband. 'I have met Herr Haydn, or 'Papa Josef', as he is affectionately called. My nephew

Paul especially enjoys Haydn's younger friend, Mozart.'

By the end of the intermission, Savarin was smiling.

'May I visit your office tomorrow,' Marie asked. 'I have something concerning Duchesse Aimée to show you.'

'Really?' He studied her for a brief moment, his interest aroused. 'I would like to see it.' He smiled and bowed politely to her, nodded to Paul, and took his seat.

As she returned to her place, she felt exhilarated. She was certain that Savarin would dig out the journal's secrets. *But to what good?* warned a small, inner voice. Marie had to force herself to rein in her hopes. At this point, no one could say whether the journal would offer a solution to the murder.

Anne reached the palace shortly after eight in the evening, tired and hungry after a long day in Paris. The apartment appeared empty. Not a sound could be heard. The temporary servants who worked during the day had left. In the kitchen, only Bijou rose to greet her.

A few moments later, Robinette came out of her room. 'Madame,' she began. 'Comtesse Marie and Colonel Saint-Martin said they were going to a concert at Princesse Lamballe's salon. They might return late, so don't wait up for them.'

'Has Madame Bourdon returned?' Anne asked. The housekeeper's strange behavior in Paris had somehow made her movements seem unpredictable.

'Yes, a few minutes ago. She's resting in her room.'

Anne was about to ask for food when there was a knock on the door. The cook didn't move, seemed fixed to the spot, so Anne went herself. At the door a watchman handed her a folded slip of paper.

'A boy from the town gave it to me. Said it was for you from the prison. Urgent.'

Anne sent the man off with a coin. Her fingers trembled as she opened the message, crudely scrawled in pencil, barely legible. From Moses the friendly guard, she assumed.

the maid is bad. come.

201

Had Denise attempted to kill herself? Anne felt a frisson of anxiety. She returned to the kitchen.

Robinette was now sitting at the table, eyes wide with curiosity. Anne took a hurried moment to reflect on what to do. Should she go to the prison so late at night? Alone? She sat down opposite the cook.

Skirts rustled behind her. Marthe Bourdon came out of her room with a teapot. She stopped abruptly and glanced at the two women. 'What's the matter?'

'A message from the prison,' Anne replied. 'Something has happened to Mademoiselle de Villers.'

At first, Marthe's face registered only slight curiosity. But then her eyes widened with a look as of dread mixed with fear.

'Could she have . . . ?' she stammered, unlike her usual unruffled self.

'The message doesn't say what she's done,' Anne replied, frightened by the housekeeper's reaction. Did she also think that Denise had attempted suicide? 'I'll go to the prison right away.'

Robinette and Marthe objected in unison. 'It's dangerous.'

'I'll take a watchman with me.'

Moses had left word with the porter at the prison door to call him when Madame Cartier arrived. Anne and her escort from the palace were shown into a waiting room. Within minutes, Moses appeared.

'Come with me, madame,' he said. The palace watchman started to protest, but Moses waved him back.

Anne gave him a reassuring smile. 'I'll be safe. I know him.' She followed Moses from the room.

In a dark hallway out of hearing range, he stopped, glanced cautiously over his shoulder. 'Tell no one or I'll be punished. I trust you. We'll go now to the maid.'

He led Anne down a narrow, winding staircase to the basement. The stone walls were damp, the air fetid. His oil lamp struggled to pierce the gloom. He stopped at what seemed to be a cage. Peering through the bars, Anne saw a figure curled up on the floor.

'Denise!' Anne waved her hand.

The figure stirred, uttered a low moan.

Moses gave Anne the lamp and locked her in the cell. 'I'll come back in half an hour.' He disappeared into the dark.

The place became deathly silent. This was an isolated part of the prison. The darkness, like a soundless wave, threatened to overwhelm the cell's little island of light.

'What if the guard doesn't return?' Anne murmured to herself. Panic began to grip her. She fought back by turning her mind to Denise, who was whimpering.

Anne crouched down beside her, patted her head, then started with horror. Denise was nearly bald. They had cut off her hair. Gradually, the young woman responded to Anne's caresses. She sat up, her back resting against the bars.

'What happened, Denise?'

'This morning, even though it was Sunday, they took me out for questioning.' Two mean-looking men in leather jackets and caps had dragged her to a basement room. Sully was there with written questions. Denise was supposed to nod for yes and shake her head for no.

'He pointed to the question, "Did you kill Duchesse Aimée and steal her coins and brooch?" I shook my head. He looked very angry.'

The men stripped her, hung her by her arms from the ceiling, and cut off her hair. The count accused her again.

'I shook my head.'

He wrote that if she confessed, he would ask the judges to grant her a quick and merciful death. If she refused, he would demand the full rigor of the law.

'"And here's a taste of it," he wrote.'

One of the men held a walnut up to her face, applied a screw to the nut and crushed it, then pointed to her thumb and sneered at her.

The other man flexed a whip in her face and hit a tall, thick wooden pole again and again. Little pieces of wood flew into the air.

'Like the flesh he'd rip off my back,' she signed.

They made her look at hot irons and pinchers, a rack, and other dreadful things, then shoved the questions in her face.

'I could hardly think. I just kept shaking my head. Finally, Sully wrote, "You will be sorry." They went away and left me hanging.'

Anne could barely contain her anger. She would have clawed Sully's face bloody. But he was safe and comfortable in his palace apartment. She felt helpless. Not long ago, English justice had treated her with similar cruelty. The memory still smarted.

Denise was staring at her with concern. Anne drew herself out of the past, recalling that the maid hadn't eaten all day. Anne had had the foresight to bring along bread and cheese and offered it now.

'Thank you,' Denise signed. 'When Moses came on duty, he brought me back here and gave me something to eat and drink.' She stopped. Her hands seemed to fail her. She chewed on her lip, then resumed signing. 'He said the provost will put me on trial tomorrow morning.'

'We'll do all we can for you.' Anne caressed the maid's cheek.

The guard returned and opened the cell. 'Time to go, madame.'

Anne embraced Denise and left the cell. At the stairs she looked back over her shoulder. The maid was lost in darkness.

CHAPTER TWENTY-SIX

The Trial

Monday, June 11

Early the next morning, Saint-Martin sat at the writing table across from Baron Breteuil. An urgent message had summoned him, one that Saint-Martin fully expected. Today, the provost was going to arraign the maid for the duchess's murder. Even thinking of Sully made the colonel seethe inside.

Anne had just informed him of yesterday's cruel interrogation of the maid.

The baron leaned forward, resting his arms on the table. 'Last night, Paul, the Queen called me and the Marquis de Sully to her study. The provost presented your report on the investigation thus far. You had found other suspects but no firm evidence against them, nor proof of any accomplices. He declared that the maid had beyond a doubt committed the crime.'

'The provost sees only what he chooses.' Saint-Martin could barely contain his contempt for Sully. Its futility compounded his distress. 'My report also pointed out that the maid might be a scapegoat. Beauregard, Blondel, and perhaps other suspects could have hidden the brooch in her mattress.' Saint-Martin hesitated. 'Did the Queen read my entire report?'

'She glanced at it.'

'And, her reaction?'

'She ignored the part about a scapegoat. It complicated her understanding of the case, confusing her. She preferred the provost's version and saw no reason for further delay. Since the maid is obstinate, the matter must be concluded swiftly with full rigor of the law. The Queen ordered the provost to charge the maid with the crime this morning. He asked for a full trial in his court. I insisted that he should merely indict the maid and bring the case directly to the Parlement of Paris. But the Queen disagreed. Parlement might draw the process out to no useful purpose. Sully had his way.'

'The devil must have his hand in this,' Saint-Martin remarked bitterly. 'Sully's trial will be a mockery of justice. And Parlement will routinely confirm the conviction. The maid will be brutally executed within a week.' He shook his head. 'On the other hand, a full trial before Parlement wouldn't be much more reasonable or humane. Our criminal code is barbaric and weighted against the accused.'

'True, Paul, but the magistrates would at least be obliged to examine the evidence and would do so with less prejudice than Sully. Parlement also works slowly and so we would have gained time. Unfortunately, the Queen won't change her mind.'

Saint-Martin hesitated, then asked softly, 'Why is she deciding these matters of life and death? Where's the King?'

Breteuil's expression was grim. 'He's in deep depression. Spends rainy days in his workshop tinkering with locks and clocks. In fair weather he goes out hunting. Defers to the Queen more often than not.'

'Then we have no choice but to continue trying to clear the maid's reputation.' He showed the baron a sealed message. 'It just came from Lieutenant-General DeCrosne with instructions to present it to the provost as part of my formal report during the trial.' He handed a copy to the baron. The baron read aloud:

Provost de Sully, This is to inform you that a certain Mademoiselle Cécile Fortier has given you false testimony against Denise de Villers. I caution you not to use said testimony in your charges against Mademoiselle de Villers. If you persist, I shall instruct the Parlement to disregard said testimony and bring your error to the attention of the Chancellor.
Lieutenant-General DeCrosne.

'My word!' exclaimed the baron, staring at the page. 'This will bring color to Sully's cheeks.'

Late in the morning in the provost's office the furniture had been rearranged for the trial. At one end of the room the provost sat behind a large writing table, together with an older and a younger magistrate. All three men were robed in black, their aspect solemn and remote.

'Who are they?' whispered Saint-Martin, pointing discreetly to Sully's two colleagues.

'The older one is Leduc.' The baron spoke softly out of the corner of his mouth. 'He's competent, fair-minded. The younger one is Moineau. He's lazy and ambitious, seeks to please Sully.'

Seated in front of them on a low wooden stool was Denise de Villers in a shapeless gray gown, a bonnet covering her cropped head. She glanced left and right, an apprehensive look on her face. At the baron's insistence, Anne stood beside her to interpret. The deaf woman could in fact read lips quite well, especially Sully's, for he spoke slowly and clearly. But Anne had advised her to feign incomprehension. Hearing and speaking through an interpreter would make it more difficult for Sully to browbeat her.

To Saint-Martin's surprise a few spectators had gathered in the room. Trials were usually conducted in secret. Baron Breteuil leaned over and whispered in his ear that the visitors came from the Queen's entourage. He nodded toward one of them. 'That's Madame Campan, an intelligent and well-informed woman. She will give the Queen an account of the proceedings.'

The provost declared the court in session and summoned Saint-Martin to report on his investigation. Sully himself paid scant attention, his eyes cast down, apparently indifferent to what was being said. When Saint-Martin had finished, the older magistrate asked whether there was any evidence of previous wrongdoing by the maid.

Sully glanced sharply at his colleague, a frown creasing his forehead. He raised a hand to protest.

Ignoring him, Saint-Martin seized the opportunity. 'I have indeed investigated her past behavior. By all accounts, she has an excellent reputation.'

Sully's eyebrows shot up. 'I have investigated her reputation myself and find it far from excellent. She's been a thief before. That point is settled.'

Clearly irritated, the older magistrate persisted. 'Colonel, will you clarify your statement?' Sully's color began to rise.

Saint-Martin explained the duchess's gift of the silk ribbons, summarized the report from the abbé and his students, then held up DeCrosne's message. 'The lieutenant-general has sent this to the court attesting to Cécile Fortier's slander of Mademoiselle de Villers.'

The magistrate glanced sourly at the provost. 'The Marquis de Sully has not shared the message with me.' He pulled at his robe, brushed a fleck off his sleeve. 'Please read it, Colonel.'

Saint-Martin read the message aloud, then handed it to the magistrate.

Sully was now obliged to deal with the matter. 'The lieutenant-general has been misled,' he snorted. 'My agent Jacques Bart has determined that a cabal of the accused woman's partisans is attempting to undermine Mademoiselle Fortier's credibility.' He waved dismissively at the message, as if it were a nuisance. The older magistrate sat back silent but unconvinced. Sully ignored him and proceeded to the interrogation of Denise.

He glared at her under bristling brows. With Anne's help, she had overcome her initial distress and now met his eyes with remarkable composure, considering the circumstances. Reading off a document, he charged her with stealing the duchess's coins, being surprised by her in the act, and killing her.

At each charge, Denise looked to Anne, who signed her its meaning. To each charge the deaf woman professed her innocence, and Anne said, 'Not guilty.'

The hearing ended quickly. The magistrates retired to another room. In a few minutes they returned.

Sully read their verdict. 'We find her guilty.' He paused for a moment, giving a hint of a smile to his compliant younger companion. The other magistrate's face remained impassive but his eyes betrayed his displeasure.

'The decision was two to one,' the baron whispered to Saint-Martin. There was a buzz of comment among the Queen's friends.

Sully went on to read the rest of the indictment. He would request the Parlement of Paris to confirm his finding and to punish the accused according to provisions of the Criminal Code. In the meantime she would be held in the Conciergerie, the Parlement's ancient prison on the Ile de la Cité, the island in the River Seine. 'The investigation is closed,' he declared, staring pointedly at Saint-Martin.

'The coins, sir,' the colonel shot back. 'I shall continue to search for them.'

'Save yourself the trouble, Colonel. We shall soon learn their whereabouts. After Parlement renders its judgment against Mademoiselle de Villers, we shall put her to the Question. She will reveal everything.'

Saint-Martin shuddered. The condemned maid would be tortured prior to execution. He glanced at Denise. The young woman sat rigid with horror. She had understood.

As they were leaving the room, the baron leaned toward Saint-Martin. 'Sully's witness, Mademoiselle Fortier, what's to become of her? He will try to ensure that she doesn't change her testimony.'

The colonel whispered in reply, 'He may be too late. This morning, Quidor brought her to the Hôtel de Police for questioning. Anne and I shall join him there. We hope to persuade or force her to retract.'

Anne and Paul reached Paris early in the afternoon and made their way to Quidor's office. He was his usual gruff self, seated behind a writing table cluttered with file boxes and loose papers. For a few minutes, while they sat off to one side, he dispatched agents to pawn shops, cafés, hotels, and brothels in his district.

The inspector beckoned his visitors closer. 'Now, we shall deal with Mademoiselle Fortier, a stubborn young woman, I must say. She has written furious notes, threatening me with the Marquis de Sully's wrath. I have written back saying that she's in my district, not his. So that's where we stand at the moment.'

'Perhaps I should meet her alone,' Anne suggested, 'and explain her options. I'll ask her to sign a retraction to be sent to the provost with signed copies to Lieutenant-General DeCrosne, to Abbé de l'Épée, and to the president of the Parlement of Paris.'

'And I'll put it in the hands of the city's hack journalists,' added Quidor. 'They'll build a fire of outrage against those who would cause the judicial murder of a beautiful young woman.'

A few minutes later, Anne met Cécile in a small interrogation room. She was smartly dressed. Shortly after breakfast, Quidor's agents had come to her garret room high above the milliner's shop. She had insisted on wearing a fine silk gown with pale pink and green stripes. On her head was a wide-brimmed feather-bedecked hat.

'I see that the Marquis de Sully has treated you very well,' Anne began gently. 'Would you tell me about your work at the shop?'

This mild manner seemed to surprise Cécile, and she became wary. Anne gave her an encouraging smile. She was soon signing enthusiastically about the fashionable customers she served, the expensive materials she worked with, the generous wages she received. She was better paid than any of the other milliners. And Madame Bouffant, her mistress, was so kind.

As the young woman related her good fortune, Anne studied her plain features, uneven teeth, short, stubby fingers. Her fine clothes failed to disguise a thick body and awkward bearing. Nonetheless, she seemed utterly convinced she was worthy of the good things Sully had provided and believed that they would be hers for as long as she wished.

'Cécile,' Anne signed at a break in her story, 'I must explain your situation.' She described her investigation into the lace-collar scandal and the written statement from the abbé and the students vindicating Denise. 'You see, Cécile,' said Anne, handing the statement over to her, 'there's no doubt where the truth lies.'

Then she laid out clearly and firmly Cécile's choices. If she continued to slander Denise, she would be arrested, charged with malicious slander, and condemned to the pillory on Place de Grève. 'Can you really imagine that the provost would continue to support you, once you were no longer useful to him, your credibility gone, your reputation ruined by public humiliation? Would Madame Bouffant continue to employ you?'

Cécile stirred restlessly, her hands clenched in her lap, and didn't reply.

'If you retract your accusations, it's true, you would lose these good things.' Anne gestured to the young woman's dress and hat. 'But you would also avoid the pillory and regain the favor of Abbé de l'Épée and the community of deaf people in Paris. He would find lodging and honest work for you.'

As Anne related these choices, Cécile grew still, her hands clasped tightly, a frown gathering on her forehead. Finally, she stared at Anne and signed, 'I told the truth to the Marquis de Sully. He will protect me. You're just trying to scare me.'

For a moment Anne felt sorry for the young woman who was clinging desperately to the recognition and prosperity she must have yearned for since childhood. But, unfortunately, she was putting in jeopardy the life of an innocent woman.

Anne's signing took on a sterner character. 'Cécile, even though you've slandered Denise, she continues to excuse you. Does it matter to you that she may soon be horribly tortured and then burned on Place de Grève?'

The young woman replied with a petulant sneer.

'Her death will be on your conscience for the rest of your life.'

A grotesque grin twisted the plain round face. 'She's going to die and I'm glad. She was mean to me.' Cécile sat back and crossed her arms in childish defiance.

Anne felt emptied of pity. 'I'm sorry, Cécile, but you leave me no choice. I'll turn you over to Inspecteur Quidor.'

Anne rejoined the inspector and Paul and described her unsuccessful appeal to Cécile.

'For the criminal charge,' said Quidor, 'I'll need a complaint from Mademoiselle de Villers.' He looked expectantly to Anne and Paul.

'We'll visit her in the Conciergerie as soon as we leave you,' Paul said, Anne nodding in agreement. 'At the least, we shall have exposed Cécile's lies to public scrutiny and brought them to the attention of the Parlement.'

Anne and Paul reached the Conciergerie just as the silver bell in its tall clock tower chimed five in the afternoon. The large rambling ancient building cast a chilling shadow over their path. The thick gray stone walls, scarce small windows, and round towers reminded Anne of a forbidding fortress. One of the towers was called *Tour Bonbec*, the babbler, where prisoners were tortured until they confessed. Anne shivered. The justice dispensed in this place was grim and heartless.

At the entrance, Paul identified himself and Anne to the turnkey. A guard led them through the building to the gallery where female prisoners were kept. They found Denise in a damp, windowless, straw-strewn cell with three other women, all of them hard-faced, menacing creatures. She sat on a pallet in a corner looking despondent.

'This won't do,' Anne whispered to Paul. 'These harpies will eat Denise alive.'

'You're right, Anne.' He pressed a coin into the guard's hand, spoke to him softly. The man shrugged his shoulders, then beckoned Denise to pick up the small bag of her possessions. The three of them followed the guard to another cell with a small, high, barred window. Two pallets rested on wooden frames a foot off the floor. He explained this was the best cell in the women's gallery. The other prisoner was also a well-mannered young lady. A court in Amiens had convicted her of killing her husband. She was kept here while appealing to the Parlement. At the moment, she was outside, walking in the women's tiny prison yard.

Paul left the cell to negotiate with the turnkey the cost of decent food and lodging for Denise. The guard locked Anne and Denise in the cell. They sat at a small table. Anne tried to raise the young woman's spirits with an account of how Françoise Arnaud had rallied the students at the institute to Denise's cause.

'They discovered that Cécile had deliberately hidden the lace collar and then maliciously accused you of stealing it.'

Denise's head snapped back as if struck. Her mouth opened in shock. 'I never suspected her,' she signed. 'Why would she do such a thing?'

'Envy,' Anne replied. 'It has consumed her like a cancer. She's plain-looking and awkward. Every time she looks into a mirror, she resents your beauty. When she walks in the presence of others, she resents your grace.' Anne paused. Denise was struggling with these hard truths. 'I wish I could say that she has changed for the better, but I can't.' She met the young woman's eye, then signed with brutal emphasis, 'Cécile hates you, Denise, and wants to see you destroyed.'

Denise closed her eyes, fell silent for several moments. 'The Devil must be loose in her.' She gazed at Anne with a desperate look. 'What can be done?'

At that point, Paul joined them. Anne gave him a quick glance, then turned back to Denise.

212

'For the sake of your reputation, we must change Cécile's mind, regardless of the Devil. I couldn't persuade her. Only force will work.' Anne drove her fist hard into the palm of her hand. 'Denise, you *must* prosecute her.'

The young woman frowned. 'I don't understand.' She was signing guardedly. 'What happens if she's convicted?'

'She'll be placed in the pillory for a few days.'

'No! No! I can't have that.' Denise leaped to her feet, shook her head violently in protest. 'People would taunt her, throw rotten eggs and fruit at her. She would be crushed, scarred, ruined for life. What decent man would have her? She would need to sell herself or go begging.'

A sudden flash of anger nearly blinded Anne. Such misplaced concern for a dangerous enemy! She felt the urge to grab Denise and shake sense into her brain. But a few moments studying her impassioned face convinced Anne that the young woman's determination was deep and sincere. Further argument was pointless.

Anne's temper cooled. She rose, embraced Denise, calmed her. 'As you wish, Denise. We shall leave Cécile to her own devices and find other ways to defend you.'

CHAPTER TWENTY-SEVEN

A Room with a View

Monday, June 11

Back in the palace at Versailles Comtesse Marie approached the Comte de Savarin's office for a late-afternoon appointment. In passing, she glanced at herself in a full-length wall mirror and forced a smile. A conversation about murder called for less than formal dress or high fashion. She had chosen a soft patterned pink gown, touched her cheeks lightly with rouge, and dressed her hair in a chignon. Her heart beat a little faster as she reached his door. She stopped, chided herself. Silly woman! She drew a deep breath, then knocked.

A servant let her in. After a brief wait in an antechamber, she was shown into a spacious room, its high walls covered with shelves of the written and printed memory of the palace and its inhabitants for more than a hundred years. The count had much of it in his head, at least so people said.

He greeted her with a bow, then led her to an upholstered chair in front of a large writing table. On its shiny brown mahogany surface rested a single file box. The label read 'Saumur'. He took a seat opposite her. She had wondered if the skeptical slant of his intelligence might intimidate her, leaving her tongue-tied. But he smiled in a friendly questioning way and put her at ease.

In a corner of the room stood a cello and a music stand. 'When the tedium of this work threatens to crush my spirit,' he remarked, having followed her glance to the instrument, 'I play a few bars of Haydn or Mozart.'

'Tedium? From what?'

'False claims of nobility. In pursuit of offices or pensions, clever men counterfeit patents of nobility back to Charlemagne, alter records of birth, marriage and death, invent family histories. My clerks expose some of these lies, but much of the work falls upon me.'

He glanced up at a wall of file boxes. 'If competent work rather than noble birth were the principal qualification for offices and pensions, I could burn most of that paper.' He smiled, gave her a little bow of the head. 'I speak such heresy only to an enlightened woman. I trust you've come here on serious business.'

She smoothed her gown, working up courage to ask a busy man for what could prove to be a time-consuming favor. 'Yes, I would like your help in a matter of life or death.' Marie went on to describe her nephew's fruitless effort to discover the killer of the Duchesse Aimée de Saumur. 'He has identified at least two likely suspects, Jules Blondel, Duc Henri's valet, and the late Chevalier de Beauregard. But there could be a person not yet identified, someone in the duchess's past, or her parents', who has taken a hidden revenge against her.'

214

Savarin paid close attention while Marie spoke. Now he raised a hand. 'I have kept myself informed about the case and commend your efforts on behalf of the maid. The evidence of her guilt appears dubious to me.'

Marie struggled to conceal her relief. His opinion had surprised her. He usually held people at a distance, giving the impression that he lacked interest and compassion. His deeply ingrained skepticism had also prevented him from joining the majority in palace society who believed in the maid's guilt.

Savarin leaned forward, hands clasped, arms resting on the table. 'If an enemy from the past wished to strike the duchess, he would have to make use of someone within the household to kill the duchess, steal the brooch, and put it in the maid's mattress, in other words, one of the suspects whom you have already investigated.'

Jules Blondel, thought Marie. Through his father, who practiced law at the Parlement of Paris, he might have known enemies of Duchesse Aimée's family.

Savarin took a deep breath. 'I sense here an intelligent, twisted mind who may have devised this deadly scheme, overseen its execution, and escaped notice. Ingenious. I'm intrigued.'

'What do you propose we should do?'

'We need to search in Aimée's history for an enemy with a connection to someone in her household. What do you know of her family?'

'A little.' Marie spoke of Monsieur Pasquier's notoriety as an intolerant, bigoted magistrate. 'For twenty years he pursued blasphemers, sodomites, heretics, and similar malefactors without mercy.'

'And,' Savarin added, 'with little regard for extenuating circumstances or sufficient evidence. Twenty years ago, his was one of the most strident voices raised against the Chevalier de La Barre when the case came before Parlement.'

Marie readily grasped his allusion to the La Barre case, arguably the most notorious judicial murder in recent French history. The youthful chevalier had insulted a magistrate in Abbeville who had retaliated with a trumped-up charge of blasphemy and had condemned him to death. Parlement had upheld the magistrate's sentence and gave him the perverse satisfaction of witnessing the young man's execution.

This atrocity prompted Marie to wonder, could Sully hold a similar antipathy toward the maid? He was pursuing her so obstinately. True, he had grounds to hate her. A mere servant, she had rebuffed his advances, knocked the porcelain teeth from his mouth, and laughed at him. But was there more? Had her father also offended him somehow? Marie voiced her concern to Savarin.

'That's plausible,' he replied. 'We should also look into the maid's family history.' He breathed out a sigh. 'We begin to see how vast the field of investigation becomes the farther back we go.'

In the course of this discussion, Marie grew confident that Savarin could be trusted. She handed him Duchesse Aimée's journal, explaining how she had found it hidden in the bedroom. 'It might answer some of our questions.'

'This is indeed interesting,' he said, flipping the journal's pages, dipping at random into its contents.

'And difficult,' Marie cautioned. Leaning over the table, she pointed out several passages in code or shorthand.

He reached for a magnifying glass—the handwriting was often minuscule—and peered at the text. 'I should be able to help you—my mind's true love is cryptology, the science of hidden meaning. The Ministry of Foreign Affairs sends me documents in code much more sophisticated than this. Leave the journal with me. I'll read it together with the Saumur file in a few days, depending on how much other work is brought to my desk.'

Marie thanked him, gathered her skirts, and rose to leave.

He walked with her to the door. 'I'm pleased that you came. I hope to help the maid.' He bowed and kissed her hand gallantly.

As the door closed behind her, she recalled a gleam of interest in his eye. She was surprised by the pleasure it gave her.

At the Hospital of the Holy Spirit Michou and Sylvie were in a small parlor overlooking Place de Grève, questioning nuns who might be acquainted with the notary's building.

216

They had to be cautious to whom they spoke. Some nuns were known to gossip.

Finally, Michou found a nun she had known earlier, who managed the hospital's money and appeared discreet. She also did business with the notary. Michou introduced Sylvie as a friend who would translate for her.

'I'm pleased to see how well you look,' the nun began. 'The abbé's institute has been good for you. And you are fortunate to have found such a generous friend.' She smiled at Sylvie.

Michou had liked this nun and had kept her informed of her recent progress in reading and writing with Sylvie's help.

'What can I do for you?' the nun asked kindly.

'Please tell me what you know about the notary's house,' Michou signed, Sylvie assisting. 'A friend of mine wants to rent a room on the square. He likes the location and the looks of the building. That the owner lives there means it would be safe and clean.'

From the start Michou realized she must conceal her plan to discover if Madame Bourdon was in that building and what she was doing. A way had to be found for Anne and Georges to investigate.

'There isn't a safer room on Place de Grève,' the nun replied. 'The notary Monsieur Griffon is a man of good character, wealthy and influential in the city. He gives money to this hospital.' She added that he was also a stern master of his clerks and his servants. They guarded the building as if their lives depended on it.

Last year, unfortunately, thieves succeeded in stealing a large quantity of silverware, a gold watch, and other valuable objects. The notary installed expensive new locks designed to thwart even the most experienced thief. He also placed a new, tough, sharp-eyed concierge at the rear door and threatened the servants with severe punishment if they allowed a thief to enter. Finally, he personally examined new servants and renters.

'But,' the nun concluded, 'the notary might not be able to rent to your friend. I haven't heard that any rooms are available.'

*   *   *

Michou placed herself and Sylvie among the stalls of used clothing near the notary's building to watch his servants and clients come and go. Michou hoped to recognize someone with whom she could strike up a conversation. At one point, the notary himself walked out the front door and crossed the square. A short, thin, dour man, he was quick as a sparrow and soon out of sight. A few minutes later, his housekeeper emerged from the passageway. Michou knew her well and considered approaching her. But the woman wore a grim expression on her face and walked with an angry step. Michou let her pass by.

Then a middle-aged man sauntered from the passageway, stopped to survey the square, and walked in their direction.

'That's the downstairs footman,' Michou signed to Sylvie. 'With the notary and the housekeeper away, he may feel free to enjoy himself.' Michou winked to Sylvie. 'He likes wine and frolicking ladies.'

'Oh,' mouthed Sylvie, swiftly grasping Michou's plan.

'Michou!' exclaimed the surprised footman, as he came upon the two women. 'How you've changed! You've put meat on your bones.' His eyes shifted to Sylvie. 'Your friend?'

Sylvie introduced herself. The man was an old rake but still had charm. At mid-afternoon he was also well mannered. She felt his interest grow as his eyes swiftly scanned her. She explained that they had been visiting the hospital across the square and were hungry. 'Would you care to join us in a café for a drink and a bite to eat? Michou has interesting stories to share.'

This forthright invitation from a beautiful young woman took him aback, but he quickly rallied. 'Drink, in fact, was on my mind.' He assessed the two women again. 'I can suggest a café that's fit for ladies.'

He was true to his word. La Jolie Veuve was plain but clean, and half-empty. A few men and women from the nearby central markets chatted quietly over glasses of wine.

'We'll pay our own,' said Sylvie with a smile and ordered wine and bread and cheese.

The footman nodded readily in agreement and ordered wine as well. 'I'm pleased to see that Michou has found such a lovely friend. She used to seem lonely. Most people couldn't understand her. But I know a few signs.' He turned to Michou and signed, 'How have you been?'

'Very happy,' Michou signed in reply. She nodded to Sylvie, who went on to describe Michou's good life at the institute and her success as a painter of miniature portraits.

The footman listened politely, his eyes feasting on Sylvie.

'Now tell us something about yourself, Monsieur Footman, and the fine house you live in.'

With Sylvie skillfully guiding him, and the wine loosening his tongue, the footman explained that the house was fine indeed. He had a small room of his own and ate well. Unfortunately, the master harried the servants mercilessly. 'Work, work, work. He's never satisfied. Nearly brought the housekeeper to tears this afternoon.'

'It's a tall building. Any renters?'

'He lets out rooms in the top floors.'

'To whom?'

'Bourgeois men with good manners and money, mostly merchants doing business in the markets.'

'Any women?'

He chuckled. 'I know what you're getting at, young lady. No, none of that kind. The master's wife is strict with him.' He waved a qualifying hand. 'But we do have a respectable lady, a handsome one for good measure, who rents the garret room overlooking the square.'

Sylvie led him on with a look of interest.

'She moved in a month ago. For the time being, she uses the room only on Sundays.' He hesitated. 'Are you thinking of a room for yourself and Michou?' He stared at her for a moment with a mixture of lust and wry humor. 'There's one available,' he continued. 'I could put in a good word for you.'

'I'd like a room for myself,' she replied, meeting his eye, 'sometime in the future. But now I'm inquiring for a friend. He needs a clean, safe room when he occasionally visits Paris.'

'It's clean and safe enough,' he remarked without any apparent disappointment. 'Your friend should speak to the notary. He'll return to his office in an hour.' The footman finished his glass of wine, rose from the table, and bowed politely to Michou and Sylvie. As he left, he turned to them with an afterthought. 'You might warn your friend, the empty room is in the garret facing the courtyard. Its door is opposite the handsome lady's.'

Shadows slowly crept across Place de Grève as the sun sank in the west. Georges studied the notary's building. Its façade darkened. Flecks of light began to appear in its windows. Georges had heard from Sylvie. A room was available across the hall from Marthe Bourdon's. He should apply to Monsieur Griffon in person.

At first Georges had thought he should approach the notary as a police agent and claim the vacant room for his investigation of Marthe. On second thought, however, he decided to dissimulate. The notary had connections to the judiciary. For whatever reason, he could ask a magistrate to intervene, oversee the investigation, become troublesome. Moreover, the notary's relationship to Marthe was unclear. If alarmed, he might alert her. It seemed best to keep the household in ignorance of the investigation. Who could know what it might uncover?

So, Georges approached the notary's office as a merchant from Rouen with business at the central markets. He looked the part—he wore his plain brown suit and a wig. And the Norman accent of his youth came back easily to him. He took the name of his cousin, Roger, a merchant in Rouen, whose identity he sometimes used—with permission after the fact.

The footman showed him into the office. The notary looked up from a document he had just sealed and waved Georges to a chair facing him. 'So, you would like to rent a room here?' He studied the stranger with a swift, critical eye, glanced at Georges's false identification papers. 'How did you know I had one?'

'The nuns across the square thought you might. They said it would be clean and safe.' Prudence ruled out mentioning that two women in a café had also enticed the information out of the notary's own footman.

'Your papers appear to be in order. The only room available

is in the garret. Leave a deposit of eighty *livres* with me now, returnable when you vacate. The rent is seventeen a month, payable in advance. The room will be ready for you Wednesday afternoon.'

'Isn't that a bit high for a garret room?'

'Take it or leave it.' His jaw set firmly.

Georges sighed audibly. 'I'll take it.'

The notary reached into a drawer and pulled out a printed sheet of paper. 'Here are the rules of the house.'

Georges glanced at the sheet. No visitors. 'Occasionally, I bring my nephew with me.'

The notary frowned. 'Add three *livres* to the rent. One key. He must come and go with you.'

The business was quickly concluded, the money paid. Georges signed for Roger Charpentier and left the office. He realized the notary would make some inquiries in the market but hopefully would not check everything his new renter had told him.

As darkness fell over Versailles, Jeanne Degere left Comte Fersen's apartment in the palace and made her way into town. Her older brother Benoit met her nearly every evening for a bite to eat. He was waiting as usual in the little café near the prison. They greeted each other, ordered soup, and exchanged small talk. Their table was off in a corner where they could not be overheard.

He leaned forward, spoke softly. 'They came for the maid, took her to the Conciergerie.'

Jeanne heard sadness in his voice. 'You liked her, didn't you?'

He nodded. 'She called me Moses. Looked kindly at me. Warmed my heart.' He met his sister's eye. 'She's innocent.'

'Yes, I know. I've been talking to the maids and guards at the palace. They say she crossed the provost once, smashed his teeth. He's out to kill her. Let that be a lesson to all of us.'

'Do you know who else is unhappy with the provost?'

'I could name several—and they keep it to themselves. Who do you have in mind?'

'The provost's agent! Could you believe it?'

'Jacques Bart? Not in a million years. How did you find out?'

'Had a drink with him and a couple of guards this afternoon, just after they took the maid away. "What a pity," he said. I was amazed. He wouldn't explain what he meant. Sully would cut out his tongue. But after a few more drinks he told me that the provost has turned cool towards him, speaks harshly. He's afraid something bad's going to happen. Sully's spies watch him closely. He said they watch me too.'

Benoit went back to his soup, his forehead creased with concern. 'I'm in trouble, Jeanne. Sully knows I helped the maid.'

She reached across the table and patted his hand. 'We'll work something out. I'll pass this information to Comte Fersen at the palace. In the meantime, try to find out why Sully has turned against his agent.'

They finished their supper and parted. She watched her brother trudge back to the prison, his shoulders squared, as if marching into battle.

CHAPTER TWENTY-EIGHT

Shared Guilt

Tuesday, June 12

In the garden of their residence on Rue Saint-Honoré, Anne and Paul sat at breakfast reviewing yesterday's trial and imprisonment of Denise. Their mood was somber. Dark thick clouds overhead muted the loveliness of the rose beds, the chirping of sparrows. The threat of rain was heavy in the air.

As they neared the end of the meal, Georges joined them. 'I have good news.' He pulled up a chair. Anne offered him coffee. He declined. 'Thanks to Michou and Sylvie, I've rented a room in the notary's building across the hall from

Marthe Bourdon's and will move in tomorrow afternoon.' He leaned toward Anne. 'I'd like my nephew to help me find out what my neighbor is up to.'

'Your nephew?' For a moment Anne stared at Georges, not grasping his point. 'Oh, am I supposed to come along?' Her pulse quickened at the prospect.

'I *could* borrow one of Quidor's agents. But he'd miss things you would notice, and he couldn't be trusted with secrets.'

'And I know the suspect.' She glanced at her husband. His brow had creased with concern, as it usually did when she was about to take a risk. 'What do you say, Paul?'

He nodded hesitantly. 'Bourdon is behaving oddly. We need to know why.' He paused, gazed at her, produced a thin smile. 'Your sharp eyes might find an answer.'

His halting approval, Anne realized, was rooted in a chivalrous, patronizing attitude toward women, which he had only recently overcome. His trust pleased her. She returned his smile, then assured Georges, 'Your nephew will join you.'

At mid-morning, the skies cleared after a brief downpour. Anne and Paul visited Denise again in the Conciergerie, this time to probe into her family's history for a hidden enemy. She was alone in the cell, curled up on her pallet, facing the wall. As they approached, she rolled over and greeted them with dull, dispirited eyes.

Anne knelt down beside her, caressed her forehead. 'Where's your companion? Out walking in the prison yard?'

'No, she's upstairs. Magistrates are questioning her. It's her last chance. They'll decide her fate this afternoon.'

'Has she spoken to you about her case?'

'No, when she saw I was deaf, she gave up trying to talk to me. A man came to visit her yesterday. I think they're lovers, the way they looked at each other. The magistrates probably think that's why she killed her husband, not because he beat her.'

Anne was astonished. 'Did they talk about this while you were present?'

'Yes, they spoke plainly, as if I weren't there. I could read their lips well enough to get the gist. She was married to a hateful brute, so she turned to a lover. Her husband found out and beat her. She killed him with a knife while defending herself.' Denise sat up on her pallet and searched Anne's eyes. 'Would the magistrates understand her situation?'

'I believe they wouldn't,' she replied with a gesture of regret, then motioned Paul to sit next to her, facing Denise. The conversation moved on to the purpose of their visit. 'We need to look deeper into the past for a reason why someone would want to kill the duchess and punish you. What can you tell us about your father?'

'Only a little,' she replied with a wistful expression. 'He died two years ago. For most of my life I've lived with my aunt Agnès, his younger sister. I remember him as an old man who used to visit us. She would call me to the parlor to greet him. I would sit off to one side while they spoke to each other. When they threw side glances in my direction, I guessed they were wondering what to do with me.' Her gaze began to turn inward.

Anne gave her a reassuring nod.

'My father looked like an unhappy man,' Denise continued. 'The corners of his mouth turned down, as if he had forgotten how to smile. He used to live in Abbeville, then moved to a town house in Paris. When I was older, I went there once for tea. That was when he and Aunt Agnès decided to send me to the abbé's institute.

'I asked my aunt, why didn't my father like me? She said that he had set his heart on a strong, healthy boy but got a deaf girl instead. I knew that my mother had died after giving birth to me. I guess he blamed me for that too.' Denise lowered her eyes. Thin lines of bitterness gathered on her face. 'He gave Aunt Agnès money for my upbringing, but didn't want any more to do with me.'

'During his last years in Paris, he became an invalid and lost much of his wealth in bad investments. He grew to like me then. Said I was a clever girl, a pretty one as well.' Her expression softened. A hint of a smile came to her lips.

'Tell us about your aunt,' asked Anne.

'She was like a mother to me.' Denise smiled fondly and

224

explained that her aunt had never married. Now nearly sixty years old, she lived in modest comfort on income from a trust fund. Very intelligent, with enlightened views on education, she had tutored Denise to read and write far better than most young women, hearing or deaf.

And taught her manners. They used to go to fashionable cafés and to marionette shows, walked in public gardens, visited exhibitions of art. In recent years, Aunt Agnès suffered from ill health, seldom ventured out of doors, had never been to Versailles while Denise worked there.

'Where can we find her?' asked Anne.

'On Place des Vosges in the Marais,' replied Denise. 'Give her my love.' The maid's lips quivered, her eyes began to tear. Anne embraced her and stepped back. The cell door creaked open. The young woman waved as they left.

Place des Vosges was a symmetrical, once-elegant square. But now its brick-and-stone buildings appeared rather dilapidated. Agnès de Villers lived in rooms lighted by dormer windows in a steeply pitched slate roof. A young maid met Anne and Paul at the door and led them into a small, shabby parlor.

A few minutes later, a thin, bent woman with dark, deep-set eyes shuffled into the room on the maid's arm. The old woman greeted them warmly. They reported on their recent conversation with Denise and their need to search for clues in the family's history.

Madame de Villers listened attentively. 'I am grateful for your kindness toward her. Shall we move into my study for tea? I'll tell you what I know.'

The study was also a small room, its walls lined with shelves of books. A writing table stood by the window, a tea table and chairs by the fireplace. A bed of glowing embers faintly hissed.

The maid served tea and sweet biscuits, then withdrew.

Anne opened the conversation. 'What could you tell us about your brother? Had he ever done anything that would have caused a person to take revenge on Mademoiselle de Villers?'

'I shall not speak ill of the dead. *De mortuis nihil nisi bonum*, as the Romans used to say. Like his father before him, he was a rich bourgeois, a counselor in the royal court at Abbeville. His intelligence and his learning were barely average, and he didn't try to improve. Comfort and peace of mind were his highest aspirations. He always tried to ingratiate himself with his judicial colleagues, followed their opinions rather than his own.'

'It's hard to imagine how such a man could anger anyone enough to seek revenge,' observed Anne.

Paul raised his hand to object. 'Unless through sloth and lack of courage he failed in his duty to seek the truth and serve justice. He would be like a watchman asleep or drunk on duty. Should the city burn down, the surviving citizens might hang him from the nearest lamp post. If Monsieur de Villers were to go along with colleagues bent on evil, he would be as guilty as they and draw anger as well as contempt to himself.'

Anne met her hostess's eye. 'Can you think of any instance in which your brother's faults caused him to injure someone?'

The drift of the conversation had begun to distress Madame de Villers. She stared into her teacup for almost a minute, then looked up with a pained expression. 'During the time he was a magistrate in Abbeville, I lived in Paris and didn't follow his affairs closely. And I'm not schooled in the law. It's so complicated, arcane, even absurd. I wouldn't know where truth and justice lie.' She breathed out a sigh of exasperation.

Anne could see that something was nagging at the woman's conscience, despite her protestations. 'Our common sense can often detect injustice even when hidden in legal wrapping.'

Madame de Villers nodded reluctantly. 'In the summer of 1766, the royal court in Abbeville convicted a young nobleman, Chevalier de La Barre, of blasphemy and sacrilege and sentenced him to death. He had failed to remove his hat when the Blessed Sacrament passed by in procession. He also owned a copy of Voltaire's impious *Dictionnaire Philosophique*, and he claimed Saint Mary Magdalene had once been a whore.'

She flinched at the last word, drank from her cup, then

continued. 'I thought the case was incredible. By that time, blasphemy had become commonplace in literary circles. Magistrates paid no attention. So, I wasn't deeply concerned about the young man's fate. Our Parlement in Paris had the last word and would surely do the sensible thing—reduce the offense to a misdemeanor. Instead, Parlement confirmed the Abbeville sentence. I was astonished.

'I learned that old personal grievances against La Barre and his family had moved Duval de Soicourt, the presiding judge in Abbeville, to puff up the young man's indiscretions into a capital offense. Like a craven coward, my brother concurred. Enlightened men and women loathed and shunned him. He sold his judicial office, moved to Paris, and lived a lonely life thereafter. He never recanted.'

'What a travesty of justice!' Anne exclaimed. 'Did La Barre have any friends or family who might hate your brother for what he did or didn't do?'

'La Barre was unmarried and had no children. His defenders never called for vengeance.' Her voice wavered. 'So far as I know.'

'After what happened to the young man,' Anne remarked, 'anyone bent on revenge would hide that resolve, lest he suffer a similar fate.'

'Yes,' granted the elderly woman with a sigh. 'Such a person would act in secret ways.'

'Madame,' said Paul, 'your brother was but one of many magistrates responsible for the young man's death. Could you recall the members of Parlement who reviewed La Barre's case?'

'They were a group of twenty-five, and their session was brief and secret. Later, Voltaire identified them but I can't remember their names.' She hesitated, then raised a finger. 'Except for Monsieur Pasquier, the one who took the lead in denouncing the young man. I saw Pasquier later and can't forget his wild, bulging blue eyes.'

Paul appeared thunderstruck. He turned to Anne. 'Duchesse Aimée's maiden name was Pasquier. And her father was a magistrate in the Parlement, a notorious enemy of blasphemers, heretics, and the like.'

'Then Duchesse Aimée and Denise de Villers had something dreadful in common.' Anne's voice threatened to tremble. 'Their fathers were both guilty of La Barre's judicial murder.'

Early that evening, Paul drove to Versailles, reluctantly leaving Anne behind at their home on Rue Saint-Honoré. She would prepare for tomorrow's search of Marthe Bourdon's rooms. He leaned back in the rumbling coach, closed his eyes, and savored the memory of his wife as a young girl in summer theater at Château Beaumont, and again as a grown woman investigating her stepfather's death. Tall, lithe, beautiful if not pretty. Above all, spirited. That's what he most liked about her and meant to cherish for as long as he lived.

She thrived on challenges, physical and mental. He wished he had seen her at Sadler's Wells in Islington, walking the high tightrope, fearless, focused on the task. Danger quickened her movements, brought a dazzling luster to her blue eyes. Even thinking about her, he felt invigorated, counted himself blessed.

These musings continued until he arrived at the palace. The housekeeper met him at the door, performing the footman's function. Like most of the duchess's servants, he had been dismissed over the weekend and had left the palace, facing an uncertain future.

'May I have a word with you, Colonel?' She was her usual cool, collected self. 'Alone.' She glanced in the direction of his parlor. 'This concerns the investigation.'

'Of course.' He followed her and closed the door.

When they were seated, Marthe began by clearing her throat. So, she was a little nervous after all, he thought.

'I understand, sir, that the provost has completed the investigation of Duchesse Aimée's death and the maid will be judged by Parlement.'

'That's correct.'

'Also, today, the baron's office has verified my inventory of this apartment's furnishings.' She paused, looked at him directly. 'May I assume, sir, that you no longer need me here, either as a suspect or as a housekeeper? Am I now free to leave?'

The questions caught him by surprise. He should have anticipated them. In the present financial crisis, she could not expect to find suitable employment in the palace. But this would not be an opportune moment for her to return to Paris. She might go to Place de Grève and surprise Anne and Georges searching her rooms.

'May I ask if you have already made arrangements for another situation?'

'The owner of the Normandie, a hotel near the Palais-Royal, has offered me the position of housekeeper. I intend to accept. If you were to release me with a letter of good conduct, I would give him my decision and leave tomorrow.' She hesitated. 'I wish to take the cook Robinette with me to work at the hotel. We've been together for many years. It would be difficult for her to find a situation elsewhere.'

'Madame, this is short notice. I understand your wish to leave, but I would like both of you to stay a few more days. Comtesse Marie and I have unfinished business in the palace that requires us to remain in this apartment. Your services and those of the cook will be necessary.' He paused. 'Also, I may wish to speak to you and her. The Marquis de Sully has completed his work on the maid's case, but I have not. You may send word of your acceptance to the hotel tomorrow with the promise of arriving on Monday.'

A frown gathered on her forehead. 'If that is your wish, sir.' She rose stiffly from the chair. With a curt nod and a rustle of skirts she left the room.

He remained seated for a few moments, listening to her fading steps, then the slamming of her door. Would she complain to the provost? He might agree to give her the recommendation she needed and send her off to Paris. He might even complain to the Queen that the colonel continued to investigate a matter that she thought was closed. In any case, Anne and Georges must be alerted.

CHAPTER TWENTY-NINE

Lost Love

Wednesday, June 13

A nne woke with a dull headache, missed Paul at her side. She had slept restlessly during the night. At bedtime, a messenger had brought word that Denise's companion had lost her case. Parlement had confirmed the local court's verdict that she had murdered her husband. In two weeks she would be tortured in the hope that she might implicate her lover. Shortly afterwards, she would be burned alive in Amiens's market place.

Anne threw aside the covers and sat stiffly on the edge of her bed. Fresh, horrifying images of the young woman's forthcoming death surged into Anne's mind. 'Good God!' she murmured. How has Denise reacted to this appalling news? She must have put herself in her companion's place and despaired. Her innocence seemed irrelevant, for the law was a heartless monster.

A distant clock struck seven, jolting Anne to her feet. She threw cold water on her face, dried herself with a towel, then leaned out the window. Scattered clouds scudded across the sky. Breathing deeply of the fragrant morning air, she gazed down at the garden. The porter's terrier was lapping water from the fountain. The rose bushes were in full bloom, a thick carpet of white and yellow, pink, and many shades of red.

She hurried her toilette, dressed, and went down to the garden. Her headache had vanished. In a few minutes she picked three large yellow roses, snipped away their thorns, and prepared a bouquet for Denise. There would be time during the morning to visit her.

At breakfast with Georges in the garden she reported an

incredible coincidence. Yesterday, while visiting Denise's aunt, she had learned that the young maid's father had acquiesced two decades ago in the notorious judicial murder of the Chevalier de La Barre.

'The Chevalier de La Barre? I remember the name.' Georges grimaced 'And the incident at Abbeville is still fresh in my mind.'

'There's more,' Anne continued. 'Duchesse Aimée's father, Monsieur Pasquier, was one of fifteen magistrates in the Parlement of Paris who confirmed the death sentence. Indeed, he was the most vicious of them all.'

'I didn't know that.' Georges's eyes blazed with anger. 'What struck me most at the time was Louis XV's hypocrisy. That high and mighty lecher refused to save the lad even though an archbishop asked him to commute the sentence to life in prison.' Georges shook his head. 'Sorry to go on ranting.'

Anne gave him a forgiving smile.

He had hardly finished speaking when a message arrived from Paul in Versailles. He warned that the housekeeper might come to Paris on that day or the next and visit her rooms in the notary's building.

Georges glanced at Anne. 'Could you go there immediately and alert Michou and Sylvie? I have work in my office for the Royal Highway Patrol. Later in the morning, I'll check with them.'

'I'll leave now.' Anne hurried into the house to pick up the roses for Denise and was on her way. A half-hour later, she found Michou and Sylvie in the square, glancing anxiously at clouds gathering in the sky, buying a few things in order to blend into the crowd. They tried to keep the notary's building in sight without attracting attention to themselves. Both were dressed like other women in the market, in well-worn gray woolen dresses decorated with bits of colored ribbons.

Sylvie had shed much of her aristocratic heritage of fine manners and cultivated language. The role of a market woman seemed to amuse her. But her pretty face was difficult to disguise. Even vulgar curses and obscenities coming from her mouth sounded refined. Wisely, she spoke only when necessary, letting Michou take the lead. They had watched all day

Tuesday, gathering impressions of household activity from servants they chanced to meet.

Anne warned them about Marthe's possible arrival and said that Georges would come by shortly. They agreed to watch through the morning.

From Place de Grève Anne hurried to Denise's prison. Though she lacked Paul's authority, the guards recognized her and let her in. She gave them the customary coins. One of them led her to Denise's cell and waited outside. The young woman was alone, sitting on her pallet with a book.

In response to Anne's quizzical glance Denise spelled out the title with her fingers. The *Imitatio Christi*.

That had to be *The Imitation of Christ*, Anne concluded, though she knew no Latin. She had heard of it in England. A devotional book.

'The abbé's copy,' Denise added. 'Françoise Arnaud brought it yesterday after you left.' She patted the book. 'I was reading it last night when they came for her.' She nodded to the empty pallet. 'She fought them like a wildcat, biting and scratching. They shackled her with chains and carried her out screaming.'

'Did you learn her story?'

'Yes, earlier in the day we exchanged notes. She had killed her husband with a kitchen knife while he was beating her. His family had influence in the local court and gained her conviction.' Denise opened her book, fanned its pages. 'I tried to show her passages that I liked. She was too upset to read anything, much less a book in Latin.' Denise managed a small, sad smile.

Anne was surprised by the serenity she found in Denise. True, the guards treated her much better than other prisoners, thanks to Paul's high rank and his money. Nonetheless, her cell was dark and damp, her food barely adequate and monotonous. Worst of all, her future prospects were bleak. She faced horrors enough to test even the strongest spirit.

'You need these as well as the book.' Anne offered her the yellow roses.

The young woman lifted them to her nose and inhaled their fragrant scent. 'Lovely. How thoughtful. Thank you.'

*　　*　　*

232

At noon Anne returned to her home on Rue Saint-Honoré. The clouds had darkened, and scattered raindrops had begun to fall in the courtyard. Georges was waiting for her inside, already dressed in his brown suit and wearing a powdered wig.

As he handed her a similar costume, he remarked, 'We should reach the notary's office at about one o'clock and pick up our key. That's when the servants sit down to dinner. According to Michou, the concierge eats with the rest of them and trusts her daughter to guard the door. She's less vigilant than her mother, who might follow us up to our room, or spy on us later. Michou and Sylvie will continue to watch out for Marthe Bourdon.'

Anne put on her suit, dulled her face with powder, and donned her wig. In the mirror she was a younger and much slimmer version of Georges's provincial businessman. She took a few steps back and forth like a man. Georges studied her carefully, then gave a nod of approval. They left by the rear way through the garden.

In Place de Grève they met Michou and Sylvie under a yellow awning at a used-clothes stall. It offered a clear view of the notary's building. Drops of rain fell by fits and starts.

'Since you last saw us, we've gone into business,' Michou signed. 'We've rented this stall. Bought a few pieces of clothing elsewhere in the market and we're selling them here. If Madame Bourdon comes while you're upstairs, I'll put on a red scarf. One of you must look out the dormer window.' For a moment, she paused, then gazed at them with tense eyes and signed, 'Good luck.'

In the anteroom to the notary's office Anne and Georges met a clerk sitting at a writing table. His master was about to go to dinner, he said. At that moment the notary appeared at the door, recognized Georges, glanced hurriedly at Anne, and beckoned them in.

'Your room is ready, Monsieur Charpentier. I consulted an acquaintance from Rouen. You are in good repute there.' He handed a key to Georges with the distracted air of a man whose mind was intent on his dinner. 'The concierge will let you in.'

After they had left the office, Georges whispered to Anne, 'I must compliment my cousin Roger on his reputation and thank him for lending it to me. Fortunately, we also look alike.'

They continued around the building to the rear entrance and knocked. A young woman peered out of an adjacent window.

'Roger Charpentier,' Georges said, holding up his key.

The door opened. A strong scent of lamb stew filled the entrance hall. The young woman searched them with a sharp eye as they passed her and ascended the stairs.

At the second landing, Georges leaned toward Anne and whispered, 'She may be following us or listening to our steps, so we'll go to our own room first and wait a few minutes until we're sure the way is clear.'

Their room faced the courtyard and was lighted by a single, dirty dormer window. The ceiling was low. The walls were covered with water-stained, cracked plaster. A table and a pair of wooden chairs stood in the middle of the room. Two straw pallets lay on the bare wooden floor.

They closed the door, then opened it softly and listened to sounds from the stairway. The creaking of old boards mixed with faint distant voices and the light patter of rain on the roof.

After several minutes, Georges pointed Anne to the head of the stairs. She was to stand guard while he picked Marthe's lock. Minutes crept by. Then a door slammed, a voice called out. Anne bent forward straining to hear steps. Instead, there was an ominous silence. She glanced impatiently over her shoulder. Georges leaned against the door, ears tuned to the lock's slightest sounds, fingers conjuring the mechanism with slender metal tools. Finally, he stood up, breathed a sigh of relief, and beckoned Anne.

'Let's see what we have here.' He pushed open the door, and they walked into a small entrance hall. An umbrella and a pair of boots stood in a corner, a cape hung on a wall peg. The inner door was also locked.

'She's making it difficult for us,' he complained. 'I'm intrigued.'

This lock was easier. In a minute, Georges opened the door

and they stepped inside. Anne gasped, astonished. The room was a shrine. Against the left wall was a small altar with a prayer stool in front. Two short, thick, half-burned candles stood on the altar. Wax had pooled around them. Anne imagined Marthe praying there.

Hanging on the wall between the candles, where one might expect a crucifix, was a miniature portrait of a handsome young man. His hair was black and wavy, his features delicate and refined, his eyes mischievous. He appeared to be about twenty years old. Beneath the portrait two wilting blooded roses lay in a low, dry dish.

Georges studied the back of the portrait. '*Jean-François, mon chevalier*. 1765. Abbeville.'

'Abbeville? Where's that?' asked Anne. 'Denise and her aunt mentioned the place yesterday.'

Georges hung the portrait back on the wall. 'In Picardy near the Channel coast two or three days journey north of Paris.'

Anne walked to the window and gazed across the large open space to the Hôtel de Ville, the city hall. Below, in the market stalls, men and women bustled about with their wares, seeking shelter from the rain. Anne focused her eyes on where Michou and Sylvie should be. There was the yellow awning. Good. Michou stood in front, a hood over her head. No red scarf yet.

As Anne continued to survey the square, the scene she had witnessed last summer took shape again in her mind, the burning of the young peasant girl who had killed her infant. The market people and their stalls faded into a noisy, gawking crowd straining to see the spectacle. She closed her eyes, still the scene tormented her.

'Look at this!' Georges exclaimed.

She swung around. He had pulled up a floorboard and was searching through a folder of clippings and notes. 'Marthe has a keen interest in the La Barre case and many of its magistrates.' He set aside the folder and reached into the dark hole again. 'What's this?' He pulled out a small packet of letters, neatly tied together with a faded red silk ribbon.

'I believe we should read them.' He glanced at her for confirmation, as if she were his full-fledged partner.

'Yes,' she replied, appreciating his respect. 'Marthe is a

suspect. Like other servants she had opportunities to kill Duchesse Aimée. Thus far, we've not found any reason for her to have done it, but we shouldn't stop looking. Nothing's sacred any longer. Denise might soon die out there.' She pointed down to where she would stand tied to a post, surrounded by faggots.

Georges held up the packet, stared at it from above and below, from each side. 'Marthe probably remembers exactly how these letters looked when she last tied them together.' He laid them on a small table and carefully removed the ribbon.

They began reading, Georges at the table, Anne standing by the window, often glancing down at the yellow awning. A half-hour later, they stopped and gazed at each other. Anne had tears in her eyes. Even Georges's were moist. These were love letters from twenty-two years ago. Tender and passionate, most of them could have been written by lovers anywhere. What set these letters apart was the last one.

Marthe, chérie. A kind guard will bring this message to you. Give him a coin. Tomorrow I shall die. All is not lost. Something of me will live on in our child. Raise her to think well of me. I am innocent of all charges. Those who have accused me will answer to a just God who is not deceived. With all my heart, your Jean-François.

'She must have lost the child, or given her up,' mused Georges. 'I understand her better now. Suffering has toughened her.'

'Sadly.' Anne gazed out the window again, imagining Marthe as a young woman reading the letter years ago and many times since. Last Sunday, perhaps, by the light of this window. The ink had faded, the paper was worn. Then, slowly, Anne began to feel light-headed. *Jean-François . . . a judicial murder . . . Abbeville . . . some twenty years ago.*

'Georges!' She swung around toward him. 'Can you remember the Christian name of the young man, the Chevalier de La Barre?'

Georges looked up from the letters on the table, puzzled at first. Then, the truth began to dawn on him. He pointed to the portrait hanging above the altar. 'It must have been him,

Jean-François, the chevalier. The time and place are right—1760s, Abbeville.'

Anne nodded. 'Denise's father was one of the three local magistrates who sentenced him to death. If Marthe Bourdon knew that, and why shouldn't she, then she would have a strong reason to hate Denise. And take revenge on her. That's not all. We also know that Duchesse Aimée's father argued for the death sentence in Parlement.'

'We're in luck,' Georges exclaimed. 'A prime suspect! Marthe Bourdon is beginning to look like a masterful schemer avenging her lover's death two decades ago. Now we have to find proof that she actually killed the duchess or had someone else, like Jules Blondel, do it.'

Anne reflected for a moment. 'Georges, we should take these letters with us. They reveal her motive for killing Duchesse Aimée and implicating Denise.'

Georges stared at the letters, silently read the last one again, sighed. 'As long as she doesn't suspect us, she won't move them. If she were to discover them missing, she would feel threatened. Might attempt to flee, become violent. I'd rather leave them here.'

Anne shook her head. 'Too great a risk. She could grow suspicious of us and fear the letters might be discovered. She'd destroy them. We'd better take them with us.'

Georges leaned back, tapping on the table. 'Perhaps you're right. We're going to confront her sooner rather than later.' He slipped the packet into his coat pocket, tucked the folder under his shirt.

Anne glanced out the window at Michou below, a solitary sentinel. Still no red scarf. Everyone else had sought cover. A further, hurried search of the room yielded nothing of interest. They left, locking doors behind them, and made their way back to Michou and Sylvie. As they approached the stall, Georges looked up through the rain to the dormer of Marthe's room. 'I have the crazed idea she's planning to watch Denise's execution from that window.'

Anne reached Versailles by coach in the evening. The rain had stopped, but the paving stones still glistened. Georges had

237

stayed behind at his office on Rue Saint-Honoré. With Quidor's help, he would investigate Marthe's background, beginning with her parents' hotel, which she used to manage. Michou and Sylvie would take turns watching the notary's building for another day or two.

Marthe answered the door to the apartment. Her manner seemed brusque, her voice colder than usual. Or, Anne wondered, was she now more aware of Marthe's 'toughness' under the impression of the visit to her secret room? The housekeeper retreated to the kitchen while Anne sought out Marie and Paul.

They were in Marie's room waiting for supper, each enjoying a small glass of port. Anne joined them. While pouring her glass, Paul reported having seen Comte Fersen off to his regiment in French Flanders. 'I spoke to him again about Denise's case. He listened sympathetically but said he could do nothing while he was away. He hoped to return to Versailles at the end of the summer. I said that would be too late.'

'Had the Queen shown any inclination to intervene on Denise's behalf?' asked Anne.

'Frankly, no.' Paul replied. 'Fersen tried to bring up the matter tactfully, but she wouldn't listen. Family problems preoccupy her. Her daughter Sophie is near death and her husband is depressed.'

'What exactly is his problem, Paul?' asked Marie with a hint of exasperation. 'Comte Fersen should know. He's the only one the Queen confides in.'

'The King lacks confidence in himself. Affairs of state worry him to distraction. He leaves them to his ministers and trudges upstairs to his workshop or goes out hunting all day. When he returns in the evening, he eats and drinks himself into a stupor.'

'How dreadful!' Marie exclaimed. 'The country will go to ruin. The Queen must *do* something.'

'Fersen insists the Queen is a kind, caring woman and wishes the country well. But she has neither the ability nor the training to conduct affairs of state. For her own sanity's sake, she must set limits to what she may be asked to do. She will not try to rule France from her husband's throne, despite what her critics say.'

'What of Denise?' Anne asked.

'It's the King's duty to oversee the administration of justice. Should Parlement uphold Denise's condemnation, the King could commute her sentence.'

'Would he muster the will to do it?' Anne persisted.

'I asked Fersen,' Paul replied. 'He thought the King's likely to do nothing, let "justice" take its course.'

At the tinkling sound of a bell, Anne, Paul, and Marie set aside their glasses and moved to the private dining room for supper. Robinette and Marthe stood ready to serve soup, *omelette aux fines herbes*, garden greens, cheese, and white wine. Though Anne hadn't eaten since breakfast, the food failed to entice her. She still felt deeply troubled by the culpable failure of the King and the Queen to ensure justice for Denise. Nonetheless, she cautioned herself not to complain in front of the servants.

Paul opened the conversation, inquiring about her visit to Denise that morning. Anne began her story, intending to be brief and circumspect. An hour in the Conciergerie, that dark pit of despair, offered little that seemed suitable for polite table conversation. But she noticed Robinette straining to overhear. That inspired Anne to go into greater detail, especially concerning the forthcoming torture and burning of Denise's condemned companion, a fate that the deaf maid herself faced in the near future.

Robinette became so engrossed that her hands trembled as she held a hot serving dish. Anne stopped speaking momentarily out of fear that the woman would drop it. Her anxious behavior had puzzled Anne before. She resolved to take Robinette aside and explore what troubled her. Perhaps tomorrow.

After supper, when they had returned to the privacy of the duchess's bedroom, Anne described searching Marthe's room in the notary's building. She also read from a copy she had made of La Barre's last letter to Marthe. When Anne finished, the room fell unusually silent.

'What can one say?' asked Marie. 'I have a feeling that Marthe witnessed his death and part of her died with him.'

Anne nodded. 'Leaving her perhaps with a twisted soul bent on avenging his death.'

'Let's not rush to judgment,' Paul warned. 'Neither the duchess nor Denise had offended Marthe. If she sought revenge, she should have killed their fathers, neither of whom acted alone. Many other magistrates were also guilty of the young man's death. Moreover, Marthe's religious devotion appears focused on what she's lost, her lover. I detect the scent of sorrow and regret more than the odor of hate.' He paused, glanced at his companions for agreement.

Anne shook her head. 'I grant that her grief appears genuine. And her religion moves her to honor the memory of her young man. But hatred and revenge may lie deep in her soul, hidden even from herself.'

'That may be true,' Paul conceded. 'In any case, on the basis of what I know now, I couldn't persuade a magistrate to arrest her.'

'But we must thoroughly investigate her,' Anne insisted.

'And,' observed Marie, 'I shall keep all this in mind when I meet Comte Savarin tomorrow morning and discuss Duchesse Aimée's journal. I'm curious about her reaction to her father's role in La Barre's tragedy.'

Jeanne Degere hurried through the dark, wet streets to the café, impelled by her brother's note. *Urgent*, he had written. Earlier in the day, she had reported to Comte Fersen before he set off for his regiment. For the present, he had warned her, he could do little in the maid's case. She should inform him by the courier of any new development requiring his attention. That responsibility made her anxious now.

As she neared the door, she heard her name whispered from a dark alley. Benoit beckoned her.

'Two of Sully's spies are in there.' He jerked his head toward the café. 'Follow me.' He led her deeper into the alley out of sight of the street. 'We'll talk here.'

By this time, her heart was pounding. 'Benoit, what has happened?'

'The provost's agent Jacques Bart says he has secret information that would save the deaf maid's life, but he doesn't know what to do with it. He can't bring it to Sully, who would silence him forever.'

'Why doesn't he go to Colonel Saint-Martin?'

'Bart's shy of him—a nobleman and an army officer. Bart also needs protection. The investigation is over. The colonel's no longer in charge.'

'Won't Bart tell you what he knows?'

'I asked him. He said that's too risky.'

'Keep in touch with him. I'll ask Comte Fersen what to do. The message will go by courier tonight.'

CHAPTER THIRTY

Hidden Lives

Thursday, June 14

A s Marie dressed for a mid-morning appointment with the Comte de Savarin, she rehearsed in her mind two questions from last night's supper conversation. Was Marthe acting out the part of an avenging angel, plotting retribution for her lover's brutal death? Were Denise and Aimée surrogates who bore their fathers' guilt?

A friendly pat on her shoulder recalled her to the present, less serious task. 'You look elegant, Marie.' Anne took a step back and studied the countess with a critical eye. 'The Comte de Savarin should be pleased.'

Marie looked in the mirror at her patterned green silk gown and simple gold necklace. She touched her cheeks with a little rouge. 'Is it obvious that I would dress to please him?'

'I think he will take it in the right way. He's a man of discriminating taste—and a gentleman.'

With Anne's words echoing in her mind, Marie walked briskly through busy hallways to his office. He rose from his writing table to greet her and showed her to a chair. A clerk was at a table off to one side, his pen scratching across a sheet of paper.

Marie noticed the count had also dressed for this occasion. His buff silk suit was delicately embroidered with silver. There was warmth in his welcome. Duchesse Aimée's journal lay on his table.

'Deciphering the text came easily,' he began. 'My clerk has copied out the most interesting passages.' He handed her several closely written sheets of paper. 'While you read, I'll work at this table. Interrupt me when you are ready and we shall have a discussion.'

Marie thanked him and settled back in the chair with the copied text. He turned to his work. The journal began in 1762, when Aimée's parents first discussed plans for her marriage. She was fifteen years old. For three years the young woman recorded encounters with prospective husbands at parties, balls, visits to friends and relatives. She must have appeared to the world as an amiable, pleasure-loving young woman.

But her journal revealed a different person, dark, ironic, melancholic. Over the years her entries became more and more perceptive—and caustic—toward the people nearest her. She described her mother as a bleating sheep, her father as a rutting boar. Aimée's closest confidant was her maid, a cultivated older woman, who gave her a taste for the authors found on her shelves—Molière, Pascal, and the others.

Her parents were wealthy but had only recently been ennobled. Their chief concern was to marry their daughter into an old noble family. She increasingly resented their indifference to her feelings, but she believed that resistance was futile. They chose Henri, Duc de Saumur, a dissipated, forty-seven-year-old widower in need of money. He gladly agreed to the match. Aimée was almost nineteen, a blooming beauty, and heiress to a large fortune.

So far, Aimée's story didn't seem unusual to Comtesse Marie, who knew well the marital conventions of the French aristocracy. Young women were often mere pawns in a social chess game. In this case, Monsieur Pasquier, shrewd in the law, made sure that Aimée's future spendthrift husband couldn't plunder her dowry. The marriage contract assured him only a modest annual sum. He would have to outlive his young wife to gain her money.

The next entry in the journal caused Marie to interrupt Savarin. 'I see here in the summer of 1766 that Aimée protested against her father's role in the La Barre case.' That wasn't a complete surprise. Though young and seemingly frivolous, Aimée kept herself well informed about the more notorious criminal matters that came before Parlement. She also deplored her father's frequently harsh opinions.

'Yes, indeed!' The count laid down his pen and rested his arms on the table. 'Her behavior was remarkable. I wouldn't have believed she had the courage to denounce him to his face.'

Aimée had in fact come to hate her father. Her journal recorded that he bullied her and his wife, often shouting at them and sometimes striking them. He also preyed upon the serving girls, dismissing them if they became pregnant. A vocal defender of the Church against Voltaire and other godless critics, he privately mocked the clergy and its teachings.

'Please read aloud the entry of July 1, 1766,' the count asked. 'Your voice will recall hers.'

Marie raised the page, cleared her throat, and began.

Father returned home early in the evening from Parlement and rushed into the parlor. Very agitated. Mother and I were having tea. He said fourteen of the twenty-five magistrates had followed his lead and had confirmed the Chevalier de La Barre's conviction for blasphemy. But, to his disgust, they had also lessened the young man's punishment. 'The blasphemer should be burned alive,' said father, 'not decapitated first.' He went on ranting about insolent youths who read Voltaire and other enemies of God rather than listen to their parents and to the Church. I was so angry I could hardly speak, but I didn't want to criticize father in front of mother and the servants. When he went into his study, I followed him and closed the door. 'Hypocrite!' I screamed at him. 'You condemned the young man for reading Voltaire's *Dictionnaire Philosophique*. It's in your own library.' I picked the book up from its shelf and shook it at him. 'I've seen you reading it. And you say the Chevalier de La Barre must die because he has insulted God. You, sir, break most of His commandments daily. And today you have committed murder!' I walked out before he could reply.

'End of the entry,' Marie remarked, laying the paper down on the table. She felt drained.

'Unfortunately,' said Savarin gently, 'Aimée paid a high price for that courage. Afterwards, her father beat her, locked her in her room, and within weeks married her off to Henri de Saumur, whom she had come to loathe. She never spoke to her father again. It was as if she had purged him from her life.'

Marie pointed to a passage. 'In 1782, the journal records simply, "M. Pasquier died today, I didn't cry. That part of me died years ago."'

'*Lacrimae rerum*,' Savarin murmured. 'Life's tears. Poor Aimée. One could weep for her.'

The room fell silent. Even the clerk had stopped writing, his pen held in mid-air.

For a long moment the count gazed at Marie, then said quietly, 'Shall we continue?'

She nodded, picked up a sheet, and began to read again. A year ago, the duchess decided to hire a new personal maid. Madame Bourdon proposed the young deaf woman Denise de Villers and presented her résumé. The duchess would have rejected a deaf woman out of hand, but she recognized Denise's father as one of the Abbeville magistrates who had condemned La Barre. Intrigued, the duchess interviewed Denise, found her eminently suitable, and hired her.

Marie laid the copy on the table. 'What do you think we've learned?'

'Until I read this journal,' he replied. 'I thought I knew Aimée. I now see how much I misunderstood her.'

'Was anyone aware of her attitude toward her father in the La Barre case?'

'I don't think so.' He paused briefly to recollect. 'To my knowledge the duchess never talked about the affair or anything else that was disagreeable. To the end, she wore that mask of carefree gaiety which won the Queen's affection.' He looked at her quizzically. 'Why do you ask? Should the La Barre case matter?'

Marie hesitated to answer. It didn't seem opportune yet to expose Madame Bourdon's affair with the unfortunate young chevalier or her motive for killing the duchess and incriminating the maid. But Marie felt she could trust Savarin to keep a secret. He was notoriously averse to gossip. By confiding in him, she might win his goodwill and sharp intellect for Denise's cause. Could his clerk be trusted? She glanced at the man. Savarin detected her concern. 'Have no fear. His discretion is complete.'

'Yes, then, the La Barre case might matter. Apparently unbeknownst to anyone, Madame Bourdon had secretly loved La Barre and bore his child. That gave her good reason to hate Messieurs de Villers and Pasquier and to seek revenge. But, if she knew their daughters had deplored La Barre's death—that Aimée had even suffered for denouncing her father—she would be less inclined to punish them.'

Savarin exhaled as if struck in the stomach. 'And, if she killed Aimée without knowing her story, what cruel irony!'

Anne waited near the kitchen, listening to the banging of pots and pans, then the sharpening of knives. Robinette was completing her morning tasks and would soon be free for a few hours. With such a small, undemanding household, she had more leisure than she was used to. She had taken to walking in the palace garden when weather permitted or simply disappearing for an hour or two.

This was a beautiful late-spring morning, the trees in full leaf under a clear blue sky. Robinette would very likely go out, perhaps offering Anne an opportunity to talk to her without fear of being overheard or interrupted.

She was a solitary person, dependent on her only companion, her half-sister Marthe. Other servants claimed that Robinette's father had repeatedly sexually abused her. Later, her husband had nearly beaten her to death. Marthe had befriended her, given her shelter and work. For years thereafter she clung to

Marthe. They became a complementary pair, Marthe taking the lead, Robinette following. Seldom far apart, they never seemed close or intimate.

This morning Marthe was working on bedlinen downstairs in the laundry. As Anne had hoped, Robinette went out alone. Anne followed her at a safe distance through the palace to the garden terrace. When she stopped to take the view over the fountains and the Grand Canal, Anne hurried up to her side, smiling.

'Madame Lapire, may I walk with you?'

The request startled the woman speechless. Before she could object, Anne took her under the arm and propelled her forward, chatting about the lovely spring weather and the beauty of the flower beds.

Privacy was hard to find. The paths and *bosquets* were alive with men and women enjoying the garden. Anne led Robinette on a long walk until they reached a grove where they were finally alone and could rest on a bench in the shade of ornamental plane trees.

To Anne's delight, Robinette began to inquire about Denise. How was the prison? Was she cold and lonely?

Anne explained the depressing conditions of Denise's imprisonment at the Conciergerie and the steps Colonel Saint-Martin had taken to alleviate them, then moved on to what seemed to concern Robinette, the maid's fate. 'Unfortunately, we've been unable to discover the person, or persons, who killed Duchesse Aimée. Denise will soon go before Parlement.'

Robinette's face grew taut.

Anne went on to describe a horrific scene—Parlement's black-robed, glowering magistrates perched on high benches, passing judgment on the helpless maid crouched on a stool below them. And then her punishments—torture, burning alive.

'But they won't condemn her, will they?'

'Denise is expecting the worst. I fear for her.'

Robinette looked down at the ground and wrung her hands.

Anne put an arm around the woman's shoulder. 'Tell me, dear, what's the matter?'

Robinette bent forward, covered her face. Sobs racked her thin body.

Anne held her, tried to soothe her. A minute or two passed. Finally, the woman sat up. Anne offered a clean handkerchief. Robinette wiped her tear-stained face.

'I don't know what to do,' she said in a choking voice.

'Who are you afraid of?'

'Marthe.'

'Why?'

'She would deny everything. No one would believe me.'

'I would believe you, Robinette.' Anne caught the woman's eye. 'I know about Marthe and the Chevalier de La Barre.'

'What?' The woman gaped at Anne.

'And I've discovered her hiding place on Place de Grève.' Anne took Robinette's hand. 'What happened to her child?'

Robinette stared at the ground for a moment, then looked up. 'After they executed Jean-François, Marthe and the baby came down with a fever. The baby died, Marthe almost did, too. It was awful. No one knew but me. Her family was still in Paris.'

'Marthe has done something bad, hasn't she?'

'She will never forgive me.' Robinette stared at Anne like a frightened child, then took a deep breath, mustering her courage. 'She stole the little plate.'

'The plate?' For an instant Anne was baffled, then she recalled that a silver plate had gone missing from the kitchen and had mysteriously returned.

'Tell me about it.' Anne's heart had begun to beat faster.

'Late at night, a few weeks ago, after a dinner with many guests, I had washed and wiped it. Marthe was putting it away. She turned her back to me and hid the plate in her apron.'

'How could you tell?'

'I knew how many we should have. While I washed and dried, I kept count, as I always did. Servants are often accused of stealing and are punished unfairly. We must be very careful. Marthe and I were alone at the time. When she left, I counted again. One small plate was missing.'

'Why didn't you accuse her?'

'Didn't dare. She'd be angry and accuse me of the theft. Who do you think the duchess would blame? At the time,

Marthe shielded me. Told the duchess someone else must have taken the plate. One of the guests.'

Anne frowned in disbelief.

'It's true. Even great lords and ladies filch things in the palace. One of them stole the King's gold watch.' She paused for a breath. 'I couldn't imagine what Marthe would do with the plate. So, for the next few days I watched her. Then, three days before the murder, I saw her sneak out of Denise's room when she was away. I became suspicious, searched the room, and found the plate hidden in the maid's mattress. I secretly returned it to the kitchen.

'Why did you think Marthe hid the plate in Denise's room?'

'At the time, I couldn't imagine why.'

Anne leaned toward Robinette and took her hand. 'Now you're beginning to understand, aren't you?'

'Yes, Marthe wants Denise to die. But why?'

'Because her father condemned Jean-François to death.'

'But *she* didn't do it.'

'Correct. Will you help save her?'

Robinette looked away, shoulders slumped.

Anne repeated urgently, 'The maid's innocent.'

With a painful effort, Robinette straightened up and gazed at Anne. 'If she's innocent, does that mean Marthe killed the duchess?'

'I can't say yet.' Nonetheless, a feeling of relief welled up in Anne. A credible witness had appeared. If she could be persuaded to testify, she might point to the true killer of the duchess. The two women rose from the bench. On an impulse, Anne threw a sidelong glance at Robinette, then turned away in shock. For the span of an instant, there was an unmistakable, self-congratulatory grin on the woman's face. Had her confession been a cunning betrayal of her half-sister?

CHAPTER THIRTY-ONE

A Chance Discovery

Thursday, June 14

A s they approached the palace, the noon sun beating down
on them, Anne cautioned Robinette to say nothing about
their conversation. They should enter the palace separately.
Marthe might sense her half-sister's betrayal, grow suspicious,
perhaps abuse her or worse. She agreed, anxiety beginning to
pinch her wrinkled face.

Anne reached the apartment first. Marthe opened the door,
greeted her without any apparent suspicion or concern, then
went off to the kitchen. Anne listened for a few minutes until
she heard the doors of the linen closet opening and closing.
Marthe was putting away the laundry and would also iron
collars and cuffs. That should keep her in the kitchen for a
while.

Anne found Paul and Marie sitting at a table in the latter's
room. She still wore the green silk gown and gold necklace
from her visit with Comte Savarin. Her eyes glittered with
exhilaration. She gripped Anne by the hands. 'The count has
deciphered Duchesse Aimée's journal. I was about to tell Paul
what I'd learned.' She went on to describe the murdered
woman's abusive relationship with her father and their
confrontation in his study. 'Read this page where she accuses
him of murdering the Chevalier de La Barre.'

Anne took the journal to the window, stared at the opened
page. Her imagination could hardly grasp the young Aimée
standing up to such an overbearing father.

'What rare courage!' She closed the journal and returned
it to Marie, who gazed at it thoughtfully for a moment, then
laid it on the table.

'I also have something to report.' Anne sat down, smoothed her dress, then gazed levelly at the others. 'Robinette has implicated Marthe in the duchess's murder.'

'What?' exclaimed Paul.

'You recall the missing silver plate, don't you? Marthe apparently stole it from the kitchen and hid it in Denise's room. Robinette retrieved the plate before it could cause harm to anyone.'

Paul leaned forward eagerly. 'Marthe must have wanted Denise to be accused of theft.' He hesitated for a moment, doubt beginning to line his brow. 'But, of murder as well?'

'Isn't murder the most logical conclusion?' Anne asked. 'After Marthe killed the duchess, she put the brooch in Denise's mattress to further implicate her.'

'Not so,' Paul replied. 'Either by arrangement with Marthe, or before she could carry out her plan, Blondel might have killed the duchess and shifted the blame to Denise.'

'That's far-fetched,' said Anne, irritated by her husband's habitual caution. 'More likely, Marthe did it by herself. She had both opportunity and strong motive.'

'Are you *sure* Robinette told you the truth?' Paul's tone had become testy.

'If she lied, she's a better actress than I'd give her credit for.' But in the next breath, after recalling Robinette's sly grin in the garden, Anne relented. 'Hatred of her half-sister probably moved her more than concern for the truth.'

'Another issue to investigate,' Paul conceded. 'We know little about her.'

Marie waved a conciliatory hand, then got up from the table to put the journal away. 'Supposing Marthe is now our chief suspect, how shall we prove that she actually murdered the duchess?'

'For a start, we could search her rooms for the missing coins,' Paul replied. 'The provost's agent Jacques Bart went through the entire apartment the day of the murder. But he might have overlooked a clever hiding place, and he didn't bodily search the servants. Marthe could have hidden the stolen items on her person and afterwards moved them elsewhere.'

250

'You two shall examine her rooms,' Marie proposed. 'I'll find a way to draw her out of the apartment.'

Paul agreed. 'I'll send word to Georges in Paris to investigate Robinette's background as well.'

As Anne and Paul rose to leave, Marie raised her hand to hold them for a second. 'I can't help wondering, had Marthe known that Aimée had condemned her father's injustice, would she have applauded the duchess or killed her anyway?'

Comtesse Marie engaged a light carriage for the afternoon. She and Marthe would visit Jules Blondel in the provost's prison and Blanche Moreau at the convent. The prisoners might need food and clothing. This would also be an opportunity to bring Marthe and Blondel together and detect possible signs of a secret pact between them.

As the two women rode from the palace, the countess tentatively inquired into Marthe's prospects for a position at the Normandie. She explained that she had accepted the proprietor's offer. He had promised that she could begin work on Monday.

'If Colonel Saint-Martin releases me with a good reference, I'll move from the palace early Monday morning.' Her voice hinted of uncertainty.

'We've been pleased with your service and wish you well.' Marie felt uncomfortable. In view of Robinette's accusations, Marthe's future had become problematic. She might not be a free woman on Monday.

Their first stop was the provost's prison. The women met Blondel in the same small room where Denise had received her visitors. He arrived in drab prison garb, manacled and shackled. The guard remained in the room.

A week in prison had left Blondel depressed, his voice a lifeless monotone. When Marie described Denise's plight in the Conciergerie, he shrugged his shoulders. 'It can't be worse than this place.' He appeared to quickly regret his self-pity. 'I'm sorry, she faces a painful death. That *is* worse.'

'How have you been treated here?'

Blondel glanced at the guard standing by. 'They haven't beaten me.'

A prudent answer, Marie thought. 'We've brought something to cheer you up.' Marthe gave him the basket of food and clothes.

'I hadn't expected you to do this,' he said. 'Thank you.' His voice gained some life and warmth. 'Have you had any word from Blanche?'

Marie shook her head. 'We'll visit her next.'

'Tell her I'm sorry I've treated her badly.'

'I shall, gladly.' Marie searched his eyes. He seemed to speak from the heart.

On the way to the convent, Marie gave Marthe a sidelong glance. The woman maintained a calm appearance, except for clasping her hands tightly. She had done the same during their conversation with Blondel. Marie had watched for veiled messages passing between them but had not noticed any.

'Monsieur Blondel's violence has got him into trouble,' Marie offered.

'He's not a bad sort of man,' Marthe observed sensibly. 'Weak but not evil. Duc Henri was unfair to him, provoked him to do foolish things.'

The convent was a graceful two-storey stone building on a quiet courtyard away from the street. The two visitors were led to a parlor with a view over a well-tended rear garden. Blanche was sitting peacefully on a shaded bench when a nun called her in. She greeted her visitors, looking well fed and contented. 'These things will come to good use,' she remarked, accepting the gifts of food and clothing. 'There are women here who are less well provided for than I.'

Marie passed along Blondel's words of regret.

Blanche received them with a grimace, then softened her expression. 'And how is he?'

'Ruing his mistakes,' Marie replied.

'As well he should!' Blanche exclaimed. 'Still, I hope fortune smiles on him. Our child will need a father.'

As Anne and Paul entered the housekeeper's parlor, Anne

wasn't hopeful. The likelihood of finding evidence was slim. The rooms had already been searched. She also felt like a thief stealing into another person's privacy, trying to uncover her dark secrets. How could Paul and Georges do this kind of work year after year without becoming hardened, losing part of their humanity?

The housekeeper's rooms were as neat as Anne remembered from her first visit almost two weeks ago. The search began in the parlor with the jade vase from the Chinese guest. Empty. They also searched other curious objects on the high shelf, looking for false bottoms or hidden compartments. Their efforts proved fruitless.

In the bedroom they inspected a writing table and found a copy of Marthe's letter to the hotel proprietor. Nothing remarkable about it except for its firm, clear script. They went through a shelf of her books, mostly devotional. A slip of paper in one of them, François de Sales's *Introduction to the Devout Life*, caught Anne's eye. She opened to a well-used page. Marthe had marked a passage.

> Even just anger, once welcomed, is with difficulty expelled. It enters small as a little twig, but soon grows into a hatred from which we can hardly free ourselves. Anger draws nourishment from a thousand false pretexts. Was there ever an angry man who thought his anger unjust?

Anne studied the passage, then shook her head. 'I feel as if I've just looked into Marthe's soul.' She handed the book to Paul. 'She's struggling with anger.'

'That's likely, Anne, given what we just learned about her dreadful experience in Abbeville.'

A Bible lay on a bedside table. Anne opened it at the Old Testament, flipped its pages, looking for notes and markings. Underlined passages in the Books of Exodus, 21:24, and Leviticus, 24:20, prescribed harsh punishment for evil-doers, an eye for an eye. That stern kind of justice might appeal to a rigidly devout woman like Marthe who felt grievously wronged.

In Deuteronomy 19:16–21 an underlined passage had also

been copied on to a scrap of paper. While reading it, Anne felt her chest tighten.

'Listen to this,' she said to Paul. 'Marthe must know it by heart.'

> If a false witness rise up against any man to testify against him that which is wrong . . . Then shall ye do unto him, as he had thought to have done unto his brother: so shalt thou put the evil away from among you . . . And thine eye shall not pity; but life shall go for life, eye for eye, tooth for tooth, hand for hand, foot for foot.

A passage followed from the Book of Numbers, 14:18.

> The Lord . . . by no means clears the guilty. He visits the iniquity of the fathers upon the children unto the third and fourth generation.

In the margin was written, *See also, Exodus, 34:7*, which repeated God's intention to punish generations of children for their fathers' evil deeds.

Anne recoiled at these passages. To punish the innocent seemed utterly unfair, unworthy of God, whose foremost quality was merciful love. 'What does Marthe's preoccupation with divine vengeance mean?' she asked. 'Has she merely wrestled with the idea like preachers do? Or, did she embrace it, become the instrument of God's wrath?'

'If we could answer those questions, we would probably solve the case,' Paul replied. 'From her character and experience I can understand why she might find divine vengeance attractive and think of God in a harsh light. It's a fact that many children and children's children suffer from their parents' folly. But I don't think that's God's work.' Paul gazed at the devotional books on the shelf, then at the Bible. His brow furrowed with concern. 'Is Marthe perhaps a bit crazy by religion?'

'Yes,' Anne replied, 'but she still knows what she's doing. Her religion may be a way to express grief and anger at the death of her lover. From these passages,' Anne pointed to the open Bible, 'it's a short step to killing Duchesse Aimée and Denise de Villers for wrongs their fathers committed.' Anne closed the Bible and returned it to the bedside table.

'But we shouldn't conclude that she took that step.' Paul looked around the room, then mused aloud, 'Have we overlooked anything?' He pointed to the bed.

'She wouldn't hide anything there,' objected Anne. 'That's the first place we'd look.'

'But it wasn't,' Paul replied with a grin. 'Besides, she might move evidence there after the room was searched.'

Anne studied how the bed was made up, hoping to remake it so Marthe wouldn't notice it had been disturbed. She found nothing in the bedding, then worked her way into the mattress. She felt through it slowly, until near the end her hand touched a sharp, hard object. She retrieved it carefully.

'What have you found?' Paul asked.

'Look!' Anne held up a long, shiny knife. 'Let's talk to Robinette.'

The cook was bent over the kitchen table rapidly slicing a carrot for supper. Her brow was knotted, her jaw stiff. An aggravating thought apparently troubled her mind. She attacked the vegetable with cold fury, scattering thin orange disks across the table.

Anne hesitated, then approached her with the knife from Marthe's bed. 'Is this yours, Robinette?'

The woman nearly leaped out of her chair, a feral expression on her face, her knife at the ready.

Anne took a step back. 'Sorry, I didn't mean to startle you. I think this belongs in the kitchen.'

The cook blinked, lowered her knife. A mixture of embarrassment and irritation flickered on her face. She thrust her head forward and peered at the knife in Anne's hand.

'It's the deaf maid's. Missing for weeks. Where did you find it?'

'I'd rather not say,' replied Anne. 'Tell me, how do you know it belongs to her?'

'By the look of it, one of the cast-offs that I let the maids use. They would ruin my knives.' She pointed to a V carved into the handle. 'That's her mark.' She explained that Jacques Bart had come to investigate but couldn't account for the knife's disappearance. 'He didn't really search thoroughly. Wasn't worth his time and trouble, he said.'

'I'll keep the knife for now,' said Anne, placing it carefully in a bag. She turned to Paul. 'We should talk about this in the garden.'

At mid-afternoon under a warm sun, the open floral terraces had heated up and were nearly deserted. High scattered clouds slowly drifted in from the west. A ten-minute walk from the palace brought Anne and Paul into a grassy amphitheater facing a cascade. Water tumbled down a semi-circle of rocky steps, casting cool mist into their faces. For a few minutes they stood arm in arm, savoring the water's rhythmic gurgling murmur, then moved away to a shaded bench.

'Why would the housekeeper steal Denise's knife?' asked Anne, inspecting its sharp but nicked and uneven blade.

'To kill the duchess, then leave the weapon at the scene. Denise would be accused of premeditated murder.'

'But the killer used a poker instead. Did Marthe change her mind?'

'Perhaps, for whatever reason, she decided to make the murder look as if it had been done on the spur of the moment. Or, her imagination balked at bright red, flowing blood.'

'Or,' Anne suggested, 'someone else killed the duchess before she could.' Anne replaced the knife in the bag.

Paul rose from the bench and extended his arm to Anne. 'I think it's time to take Marthe into custody.'

Anne took his arm, and they set off for the palace. 'But why did she keep it when it could no longer serve her purpose?'

'Seems odd, doesn't it?' Paul shrugged. 'She may be less rational than she appears, and more dangerous.'

Colonel Saint-Martin and Baron Breteuil waited patiently in an anteroom to the provost's chambers. The evidence that Saint-Martin brought against Marthe had convinced the baron to reopen the investigation. He had notified Sully of the need for a hearing.

After a few minutes, a bailiff appeared at the door and

called them in. Sully was seated at his writing table, a scowl on his face. He greeted them crossly. 'Why didn't you uncover the housekeeper's connection to the La Barre case earlier?'

'The cook feared Madame Bourdon and wouldn't come forward until she realized that an innocent person was about to be executed for the duchess's murder.' Saint-Martin hastened to explain how Anne and Georges had painstakingly unearthed Bourdon's secret love affair. 'In conclusion,' he allowed himself to say, 'the investigation simply couldn't be hurried.'

Baron Breteuil quickly added that the case against Mademoiselle de Villers had fallen apart. A preponderance of evidence showed that Cécile Fortier's accusations against Denise's character were false. Marthe stole a plate and hid it in Denise's room to further tarnish her reputation. Marthe could also have planted the stolen brooch. A knife was found in her bed. An accomplice like Jules Blondel might have the stolen coins. 'And,' the baron concluded, 'we now know that Marthe had motive as well as opportunity to kill the duchess and had taken certain preliminary steps to carry out her plan.'

The provost waved his hands as if clearing the air of nonsense. 'The maid still stands convicted of murder,' he sputtered. 'The rest is merely conjecture.' These dismissive words failed to conceal anxiety lurking in his eyes. He grudgingly agreed to a hearing the next afternoon. In the meantime, he would take both Robinette and Marthe into custody as material witnesses and would question them separately. In addition, he wanted to see a new report from Colonel Saint-Martin, together with copies of the duchess's journal and the packet of Marthe's love letters.

As they left Sully's office, Baron Breteuil turned to his companion. 'Paul, I sincerely hope this is the last twist in this case. We are beginning to look foolish.'

'I share your feeling, sir,' the colonel replied. 'But that's a risk we must take. Pursuing the truth can cause a mess. Old wounds open up, incriminating lies are exposed.'

Early in the evening, Robinette and Marthe were serving supper to Anne and Paul in the private dining room. Comte Savarin had invited Marie to a concert for a select group in his apartment. There was a loud knock at the entrance. Anne knew what it meant. Marthe put aside her tray and was about to go to the door. Anne raised a hand to stop her, then went herself.

As she expected, two provost's bailiffs were there. The older of them announced loudly that they had come for Robinette the cook and Marthe the housekeeper. His manner was rough, his speech rude. Both men carried manacles.

Anne blocked the door with her body and gained time by asking to see their papers. Meanwhile, Paul joined her. Anne nodded toward the manacles. Paul frowned, introduced himself. 'Your instructions are to escort the two women, not to arrest them. Put away the manacles. They won't be necessary. I'll vouch for my servants.'

Chastened by the authority in his voice, the bailiffs adopted a more civil demeanor. Paul invited them into the hallway, then asked Anne to inform Robinette and Marthe they were to go to Sully's office to answer questions. He would want them to stay overnight. They should take along what they would need.

When Anne returned to the dining room, the two women were standing by the table, glancing apprehensively at each other. They had heard the loud voices. As Anne told them of the provost's summons, they seemed surprised and looked at her with reproach.

'What's this all about?' Marthe demanded.

'New evidence has come to light in the case of the Duchesse de Saumur. The provost wants to speak to you about it. You are not under arrest or charged with a crime.'

'Bijou will miss me,' Robinette wailed.

'I'll take care of her,' Anne promised.

Lips tight, neck rigid, Marthe struggled to contain her anger. Still, she went to her room and gathered her things. Followed by the bailiffs, the two women left in icy silence.

258

CHAPTER THIRTY-TWO

Sibling Treachery

Friday, June 15

A dense cover of clouds parted at dawn over Versailles. A thin ray of sunlight stole into the kitchen. Anne had gone there earlier than usual to help the new young maid, who was struggling with unfamiliar surroundings. While they made breakfast, Bijou appeared out of nowhere, padded to his bowl by the stove and stared. Empty. Anne gave him milk, petted him.

She served Marie in her room, then brought the tray to Paul. He was at his desk finishing the report for Sully. A waiting servant took it from his hand and left for the provost's office. Anne poured coffee, they took bread and began to eat.

A knock on the door interrupted them. Anne opened for a servant with a message from Georges at the Châtelet.

'Give me the gist of it,' Paul said.

'Georges will remain in Paris to interrogate Hoche.'

'He had better cooperate or he will be hung.' Paul lowered his cup, threw her a skeptical glance. 'It remains to be seen how much truth he will tell.'

'There's more,' Anne went on. 'Georges's search of court records for early 1765, has revealed that Robinette, unmarried, was accused of killing her newborn son, its father unknown. Marthe saved her by swearing the death was an accident.'

Paul lowered his cup. 'The records contradict the tale Robinette told you about herself, a widow whose only child died in infancy. Her credibility is undermined.'

'That's true,' Anne agreed, handing the message to her husband. 'The incident also appears to have bound the women

259

to each other. For Robinette to testify against Marthe will be difficult. I fear she will change her mind when the provost questions her.'

Paul sighed. 'Then her testimony will be useless to us, leaving Denise in prison to face the magistrates in Parlement.'

At mid-morning, Anne saw Paul off to the provost's hearing. Marie had left earlier for an appointment with Comte Savarin. Since both Marthe and Robinette were away, Anne could freely search the cook's room and her clothes. There wasn't much to inspect. Anne examined the bed thoroughly, turned the table and the chairs upside down, went through the clothes hanging on a rack, tapped the walls. Nothing out of the ordinary. She got down on her knees and pried at the floorboards. None were loose.

Finally, she sat down on a chair, crossed her arms, and closed her eyes. What had she overlooked? Suddenly, she felt something land in her lap. Bijou. The cat crept around in a narrowing circle until he found a spot he liked and curled into a fuzzy orange ball. Soon he began to purr.

Anne raked her fingers through his thick fur, tickled him behind the ears, stroked him under the chin. His green eyes closed down to thin slits of sensual pleasure. A sense of peace came over Anne as she idly fondled the cat.

Then her fingers stumbled upon a ribbon around his neck, hidden deep in the fur. She traced the ribbon to a small, round, white tag hanging from a short thin wire. She lifted the tag and read on one side *Lapire*, on the other *Bijou*, both names in crudely printed semicircles. The tag seemed new, its color fresh and unscratched.

As she fingered the tag, she felt that its painted surface was uneven. She removed the tag, held it at an angle to light from the window, but still couldn't discern a design. With her penknife she scratched away a bit of the paint until she came to metal. It glittered. She feverishly scraped away more paint until a king's face appeared in profile on a bright golden surface. A *louis d'or*!

Meanwhile, the colonel and Baron Breteuil took seats in the provost's office. The furniture was arranged as it had been for Denise's trial. Sully had brought together the other two magistrates and sat between them at the table, staring straight ahead. His face seemed dark, inscrutable. Saint-Martin felt uneasy.

Finally, the provost gave a signal to the bailiff, who left the room. In a few minutes he returned, leading Robinette to the stool in front of the table. The magistrates gazed at her as if they knew every evil deed she had done, every lie she had told. Her eyes darted about the room like those of a trapped animal, then fixed anxiously upon her inquisitors. Paul understood her anxiety. Anyone but a hardened criminal would feel uneasy in the provost's courtroom.

Sully went immediately to the heart of the matter. 'Tell us about the missing silver plate that found its way into Mademoiselle de Villers's room.'

Robinette cleared her throat, spoke too softly at first. At a word from Sully, she raised her voice and haltingly described the scene in the kitchen after the party. 'Madame Bourdon turned her back to me as if to conceal what she was doing. I became suspicious, counted the plates when she left. One was missing. Later, I saw her coming out of Denise's room, glancing left and right like she was afraid someone might catch her. When she was gone, I sneaked into the room, found the plate, and put it back in its place. I didn't say anything. Didn't want any trouble.'

The magistrates leaned forward attentively while she spoke. After a few more questions, they asked about Marthe's love affair with the Chevalier de La Barre and its aftermath. Yes, she replied, Marthe had witnessed the execution. The shock nearly killed her. Subsequently, she had seemed obsessed with the magistrates who had judged the young man. She clipped newspaper articles about them, questioned their servants, and so on.

The baron leaned over to Saint-Martin and whispered in his ear. 'Watch their faces.' He nodded toward the magistrates. Their expressions were hardening. 'They must wonder if someone might take revenge on them for past unjust verdicts.'

When the interrogation was finished, Sully told Robinette that she was free to leave.

'Next witness,' he cried out.

Marthe Bourdon entered, as erect as ever, but with uncertainty etched in her face. When pointed to the stool, she balked at the indignity and sat down only as a bailiff advanced on her.

The magistrates began a series of questions, cleverly designed to anticipate her explanations, involve her in contradictions, insinuate more knowledge than the magistrates in fact possessed. Marthe calmly maintained she knew nothing about the murder of the duchess, had no reason to harm her.

'No reason, madame?' Sully scoffed. 'Monsieur Pasquier, father of Duchesse Aimée, voted for your lover's death. And Monsieur de Villers, father of Mademoiselle Denise de Villers, shared responsibility for that death. Is that not sufficient reason for a crime of revenge?' Sully then lifted up the small packet of love letters tied by the faded red ribbon. 'Can you still claim that you had no reason to harm her?'

While the provost was speaking, Marthe's back grew rigid. At the sight of the letters, her hands flew to her mouth. 'Oh, no!' she cried.

Saint-Martin detected a thin, gloating smile on Sully's face—the witness had revealed a guilty conscience. Instead, Saint-Martin sensed a feeling of outrage that her sacred place had been violated.

'And a witness has come forward,' Sully continued unperturbed, 'who will testify you stole a silver plate and hid it in Mademoiselle de Villers's mattress. Do you deny that?'

Marthe hesitated to reply, wondering who that witness might be. Then, suddenly, she realized it must be her half-sister Robinette. 'Treacherous ingrate!' she exclaimed, rising to her feet. 'She lies!'

The bailiff rushed to her side and forced her down on the stool.

'In the early hours of June first,' Sully went on, 'you entered the duchess's room and killed her, then . . .'

'I did not kill her,' Marthe protested.

'If not,' Sully resumed, 'then you tricked Mademoiselle de Villers into killing her.'

'I did not,' she shouted. 'I have been betrayed!' She clenched her fists. Her face was now florid with passion. The bailiff edged closer to her.

When she had calmed herself, the magistrates pressed her with more questions about the murder of the duchess. Had she done it herself or had she had an accomplice? If not Mademoiselle de Villers, then Monsieur Blondel? Where were the missing coins? Why did she keep a kitchen knife in her bed?

Marthe replied in a firm voice that she had nothing to do with the murder, didn't know where the coins were, and had no idea where the knife came from.

Throughout this interrogation, Paul found himself inclined to believe Marthe, especially about the knife. Why would she keep it, weeks after the murder? Clearly, she didn't know it was in her bed. Her half-sister might have hidden it there to implicate Marthe in the murder.

Sully glanced left and right to the other magistrates. 'Any more questions for the witnesses?' he asked.

They shook their heads. But, to judge from the expression on their faces, they had questions to discuss among themselves.

'Remove Madame Bourdon,' the provost told the bailiff.

She rose without protest before he could lay a hand on her and walked stiffly out of the room, the bailiff following closely behind.

The magistrates leaned back, fussed with their robes. Sully announced that he and his colleagues would meet again the following Monday, when they would hold a formal hearing and come to a decision on Madame Bourdon. Saint-Martin caught Sully's eye. It was confident and malevolent. He still believed the maid had killed the duchess. Would he find cause to condemn Marthe as well?

As Colonel Saint-Martin and Baron Breteuil left the room, they glanced quizzically at each other.

'Come to my office, Paul. I'll order lunch. We must discuss the cook's testimony.'

'Yes, I feel uneasy about it.'

Anne heard footsteps in the kitchen. Bijou leaped from her lap and dashed out of the room. Robinette appeared in the doorway, startled to see Anne.

Before she could utter a word, Anne held up the coin. 'Explain this. I discovered it on your cat.'

'I found it,' Robinette stammered, groping for an answer.

'Show me where,' Anne demanded.

The cook turned around hesitantly and led Anne to the front hall. 'Here.' She pointed to the floor. 'The duchess must have lost it that morning when I let her in.'

'You hid it, rather than return it to her. That brands you a thief.'

They retraced their steps and stood facing each other in the middle of the kitchen.

Anne met the woman's eye, spoke in a low, insistent voice. 'Your tale is incredible. The police will conclude that you killed the duchess and took the coins, then put one of them on Bijou and hid the rest. You also hid the brooch in the maid's room to shift the blame unto her.'

'That's not true,' Robinette whined pitifully. 'I didn't kill the duchess. . . . She was already dead. And I left the brooch in the jewelry cabinet.'

This indeed was a new twist. Anne stared at the cook. 'Sit down and explain what happened.' Her whining continued for a few moments while she settled into a chair and smoothed her dress. Finally, she grew calm enough to tell her story. In the early morning hours of June 1, she had fallen asleep in a kitchen chair. Suddenly, she awoke. An instant later, Bijou scampered into the room and hid under the table. Alarmed, drawn by loud, angry voices, then a crashing sound, Robinette hurried toward the duchess's apartment. A few moments later, she heard a distant door close. That had to be the private exit.

'Did you say, *voices*?' Anne thought of Denise who had no voice.

'Oh, yes, the duchess and someone else.'

'Male or female?'

'Can't say for sure.'

Robinette had waited a minute, thought of rousing the maid, found her fast asleep. She returned to the duchess's door, edged into the room, and saw her on the floor.

'She looked dead, her face covered with blood. I didn't know what to do. Then I thought of the jingling coins—they were ringing in my ear.' An hour earlier, on the way to her rooms, the duchess had shaken her wrists as she often did when the coins had brought her good luck at cards.

The idea seized Robinette. Those solid gold, good-luck coins, a small fortune for an old cook, were hers for the taking. No one would see her. The police would think the killer had stolen them. The killer! She had to move quickly. He might return.

'He?' Anne asked again. 'Was it a male voice you heard quarreling with the duchess?'

Robinette screwed up her face in an effort of concentration. 'I'm still not sure.' She had rushed to the jewelry cabinet in the dressing room and seized the two coin bracelets. The ruby brooch tempted her, but taking it seemed like challenging fate, too risky. She left it, fled back to the kitchen, and hid the bracelets in a secret drawer where she kept her savings. Later, she told the provost and his agent that she had slept through the entire incident, hadn't heard a thing.

Anne listened to the cook with a mixture of amazement and disbelief. At the end, she studied her closely, saw no obvious signs of deception. Her story was plausible and consistent with what Anne knew of the case. Yet, who could say that Robinette found the duchess dead? She could have killed her before taking the coins.

'Show me the secret drawer. I want to see the coins.'

Robinette had spoken rapidly, breathlessly, as if rushing through a story she had rehearsed. Now, she fell into a brooding silence, probably asking herself, had she done the wrong thing, been tricked? She would now lose the coins, her nest egg. Her eyes fixed Anne with a malevolent stare.

Anne felt a frisson of fear. They were alone in the apartment. The cook was an old, small woman, but now seemed to be drawing on an inner reserve of strength. Anne's breathing quickened, her jaw tensed.

For a long moment, they faced each other over the table like gladiators about to clash. Then Robinette sighed, shook her head in defeat. 'I've moved them. Follow me. I'll show you.'

*   *   *

The heat in the attic was oppressive. Anne patted perspiration from her face. Robinette seemed untouched. They had wended their way through the palace, climbed up servants' stairs, and entered a large storeroom of old, discarded furniture. Thin shafts of light came through small semicircular windows in the low slanting ceiling. The air was musty. Dust covered every surface.

Anne gestured for the cook to take the lead. At the far end of the room she pushed a screen aside, revealing a locked door. From the belt at her waist she produced a key.

How had she got hold of that? Anne wondered.

'The coins are in here.' These were the first words she had spoken since leaving the apartment. She opened the door and waited for Anne to go in.

'You first,' Anne said, straining to discern what lay ahead. A pair of small windows lighted the room. As her eyes adjusted, she made out the shape of trunks, large and small.

'Costumes, old clothes, kitchen and tableware from years ago,' said Robinette as she stepped into the room. 'No one comes up here any more. It's one of my favorite places.' She nodded toward the windows where an upholstered chair stood next to a fine mahogany tea table. A tray of glasses rested on top. 'I sit there with a bottle of the duke's brandy and fancy myself a great lady.'

'Amazing, Robinette! How clever you are!'

'Wait till you see this.' She led Anne to a tall armoire standing against a wall, opened it with another key, and reached in with both hands.

'Here are the coins,' she said, holding a small pouch in her left hand . . . and a long sharp kitchen knife in her right.

Anne jumped back a step, glanced toward the door. Too late.

Robinette leaped between Anne and the door and kicked it shut. There was a wild look on her face. She put the pouch in her bodice, adjusted her grip on the knife.

It seemed best to distract the woman with conversation. 'Why did you kill the duchess?' Anne spoke as calmly, as kindly, as she could under the circumstances. 'Had she mistreated you?'

Robinette stepped to within a pace, held the knife at Anne's throbbing heart. 'I despised her for years, a pathetic creature, a parasite, as useful as one of the cockroaches in my kitchen. Did nothing but primp herself, gamble, carry on with one young man after another. She never remembered my name, looked right through me when we happened to meet. Believe me, it felt good to kill her.'

'How did it happen?' Anne asked.

'Like I told you, I woke up, heard noises, and ran to see what was going on. When I went into her room, she was lying on the floor, her face all bloody. She had fallen, must have hit the edge of the bedside table. She wasn't moving, looked dead. I went into the dressing room, found the bracelets in the jewelry cabinet and started to leave. "Help," I heard from behind. She was up, wobbling on her feet and staring at me. I could hardly believe my eyes. When I didn't move, she staggered toward the bell rope to call the guard.

'I realized the coins would be missed, and I would be accused. The poker was close. I grabbed it with both hands and hit her. I've already told you the rest.'

'But I'll ask again. Did you take the brooch?'

'No, I left it in the box with the rest of the jewels.'

Then *who* took it? Anne wondered. Could Marthe have sneaked into the room and stolen the brooch? Anne plunged on. 'And Denise's knife. Why did you hide it in Marthe's bed?'

'I hate her. Full of religion. Hypocrite! Claims our mother ordered her to look after me. But she's always treated me like dirt.' She grinned at Anne. 'You believed my story about Marthe and the plate, didn't you? I made it up. Fooled the magistrates too.'

'You fooled us all, Robinette. You're very clever. Why didn't you leave Marthe years ago?'

'I shall one day,' she replied with feeling. 'In the past, if I wanted a new situation, I've always needed her recommendation. When I've asked for it, she's claimed I couldn't manage to live on my own, too ignorant and unstable. I know if I tried to leave, she would tell the world I had a bad character. Had once killed my baby. Could never be trusted.'

Her expression hardened. 'Now, it's time to deal with you.' She thrust the knife forward. The point pierced Anne's bodice.

'Over there.' Robinette gestured with her head to a large trunk a dozen paces away.

Anne realized that the cook planned to force her into the trunk, fasten the lid, and leave her to suffocate to death. No bloody mess left behind on the floor or on the killer's clothes.

'Help me lift the lid,' ordered Robinette.

The trunk wasn't locked. They loosened the clasps and heaved the lid up. Suddenly, Anne had an idea, a highly risky one.

'Climb in.' Robinette thrust the knife again. Anne felt a sharp pain in her chest. 'They'll never find you!'

Trembling, Anne leaned over the edge of the trunk, peered into the dark open space, then suddenly recoiled, screaming, 'My God! A dead baby's in there.'

For an instant, Robinette gaped at Anne with horror, then bent over the opening.

Anne jerked the raised lid. It came crashing down on the cook's neck. The knife fell to the floor. Her body hung motionless from the trunk, her head inside.

With shaking hands Anne lifted the lid. The cook's body slid down to the floor. Anne felt the woman's wrist for a pulse. None. The heavy lid had broken her neck. Anne had meant only to stun, then disarm her.

Time came to a halt. Anne stood by the trunk, shivering violently, breathing in short gasps. Finally, a wave of relief swept over her. And gratitude. Years of acting on London stages had given her quick wits and steady nerves.

Paul opened the door. His face blanched. 'Anne, look at you.' He took her by the arm and drew her into the apartment. 'I returned from the baron's office a few minutes ago and didn't find you or Marie here.'

'I'm well,' she assured him. With a gesture she dismissed the blood spots on her bodice. 'I'll change to clean clothes in a minute, but first I must tell you what happened.' They moved into the duchess's bedroom and sat by the window.

'Robinette is dead.'

'What?' Shock and incredulity spread across Paul's face. He studied Anne's disheveled appearance. 'Did she attack you?'

'She did indeed. Let me explain.' Anne went on to describe her discovery of the coin on Bijou, the confrontation with Robinette in the palace attic, her confession and violent death. 'And here are the missing coins.' Anne retrieved the pouch from her bodice, laid it on the table.

Paul seemed speechless for a moment, then exhaled. 'I'm happy you aren't hurt.' He held her in a warm embrace. 'And I'm proud of you,' he said. 'We finally know who killed Aimée.' He glanced at the spot where her body had been found.

Anne added, 'Mademoiselle de Villers should now go free.'

Paul nodded, then raised a hand of caution. 'We still have an unresolved issue. Up there in the attic, Robinette had no reason to lie to you. Yet she denied putting the brooch in Denise's bed. So who did? Who wanted to implicate the maid in a crime for which she would pay with her life?'

'Marthe,' Anne replied. 'She could have discovered the murdered duchess, stole the brooch, hid it in the bed when Denise left to prepare breakfast.'

'That's worth pursuing. But first–' he pointed in the direction of the attic–'we must tell the provost that he and Jacques Bart have work to do.'

Anne thought the heat in the attic had grown worse, if possible. An investigation was underway. The provost and his agent had responded quickly to Paul's message. Anne and Paul met them at the duchess's apartment and led them to the trunk room. The cook's body still lay crumpled alongside the trunk, like a worn rag that someone had tossed aside.

While going about his work, the provost showed no feelings, no signs of concern. His questions to Anne were routine, his manner cool and distant. Bart, on the other hand, seemed oddly preoccupied. When he was under the provost's eye, he was correct, even servile, and went about the investigation of the trunk room with a skilful, experienced hand. But, once out of his master's sight, he seemed ill at ease, and threw anxious sidelong glances at Anne.

His search of the room turned up a small treasure trove of stolen items: a couple of gold watches, assorted silverware, gold coins, fine pieces of lace. Robinette had robbed throughout the palace without arousing suspicion. Anne imagined the small, cat-like woman at night, moving about in darkened rooms, stealthily opening a door, feeling her way to a jewelry cabinet. Or lifting a watch off a drunken courtier.

When the investigation ended, the body was moved to the basement. Before leaving, Sully asked Anne for a written deposition and Paul for a report the following day. At Monday's meeting, the provost would add Robinette's death to the agenda.

Paul spoke up. 'Shouldn't the maid be released from prison, now that the duchess's killer has been determined?'

'Colonel, I intend to reflect on the matter over the weekend. We have received the cook's confession unwritten and at second hand.' He glanced at Anne. 'Of course, I don't mean to impugn Madame Cartier's veracity. It is, however, my rule to require two witnesses to an oral confession. The cook may have become delusional and imagined she murdered her mistress. She may have merely stolen the coins.'

'That's highly unlikely,' Anne exclaimed. 'I've lived with her for two weeks. Up to the end, she was a cunning and deceptive person, but as clear-headed as you or I. She knew exactly what she was doing when she confessed and attacked me.'

Sully countered with a skeptical smile, bowed, and left with his agent.

CHAPTER THIRTY-THREE

Crime in a High Place

Friday, June 15

In the duchess's private dining room a meager supper was coming to an end. Anne had shared news of the day with Marie over bread and soup. One of Lamballe's maids, a poor substitute for Robinette, had prepared and served the meal. Paul had eaten with the baron to discuss the new turn of events. Word had been sent to Marthe in prison of her half-sister's death. She sent no reply.

There was a knock on the door. Anne rose to answer it. Who could be calling at this late hour? Anne opened the door to a young woman in a commoner's clothes and bonnet, her cloak speckled with rain. Comely, sturdy, with tanned face and rough hands, she looked familiar. Anne couldn't place her, but must have seen her somewhere in the palace or its garden.

'Anne Cartier?'

'Yes.' Anne let her into the entrance hall.

'I have a message for you.' She handed over a folded scrap of paper. 'I wrote it for him.'

Meet me for the maid's sake. Come alone. My sister, Jeanne, will show you the way. Moses.

Anne was in a quandary. She knew Moses. He had proven himself trustworthy before. But Jeanne was a stranger, though her frank, level gaze was reassuring.

Anne led her into Marie's room and explained her mission.

'I should go with you,' Marie said. 'You don't know what to expect.'

The visitor objected. 'Madame Cartier is to come alone. My brother must be very careful. His message is only for her ears.'

'We can trust Moses,' said Anne, who felt she knew him better than the countess did. 'I'll be safe with his sister.'

Anne changed to street clothes and followed Jeanne into the town. Under the street lamps they stepped over pools of glistening water but the rain had stopped.

'What's your brother's name?' Anne asked. It surprised her that one could understand a man's character from a few meetings at the prison, but know so very little *about* him.

'His real name is Benoit,' his sister replied. 'Degere, like me.' He was a soldier at sixteen, she went on, fought in the Seven Years War, served in America with Comte Fersen, and retired from the army in 1783. Fersen helped him get the job at the prison.

Anne also learned that he was good company and drank with other guards from the prison and the palace. He despised the provost but had the good sense not to show it.

'Why has he concerned himself with the deaf maid?'

'He likes her, admires her courage and her beauty. She's kind to him. Early on, he realized she was innocent. He knew about the provost's shattered teeth and his grudge against her.'

At a nondescript café a few steps from the town market, Jeanne broke off their conversation, looked around to see if anyone was following them, then led Anne into the barroom and nodded toward a door.

Anne tentatively scratched on it. Nothing happened. She glanced back at Jeanne who mouthed, 'Go in.' She entered a dimly lighted storeroom. A moment later, Benoit stepped from behind a pair of drapes, locked the door, and gestured to chairs at the far end of the room.

Anne spoke first with a question that had nagged her. 'How did you know that Denise called you Moses? She can't speak.'

He beat his breast penitently. 'Guards must eavesdrop on the prisoners. That's why we allow visitors. I've heard you repeat the name to the countess. I like it.'

'Have you heard everything else, as well?'

He nodded. 'You helped convince me that the maid is innocent. But I couldn't tell anyone. The provost's spies are everywhere. Jeanne is the only person I really trust—besides you.'

'I see.' Anne gave him a nervous smile, encouraging him to carry on.

He drew closer, spoke in a low voice. 'This is what I must tell you . . . ' He glanced instinctively over his shoulder. 'The Marquis de Sully himself hid the ruby brooch in the maid's bed.'

'What can you possibly mean?' Anne was stunned.

'His own agent will explain.' Benoit turned toward the drapes.

Out came a man, dressed in a plain buff woolen suit, unremarkable in every way—except for the intelligence in his face. 'Madame Cartier, I'm Monsieur Jacques Bart, the provost's agent. We met each other a few hours ago in the palace attic.'

'You looked familiar then. Had I seen you before?'

'Yes, madame. The Marquis de Sully ordered me to investigate you. I may have ventured too close and you noticed me. I feel fortunate to have discovered in you, a person to whom I can entrust my secret.'

He drew up a chair and joined Anne and Benoit. 'From the moment we arrived at the scene of Duchesse Aimée's murder, the provost behaved strangely. During an investigation he's usually methodical, precise, cold-blooded. But, in this case, he seemed tense and careless. Something preoccupied him.

'He ordered me to search her desk. I sensed he wanted me out of his way. So, while pretending to read her papers, I watched him in a small mirror that I carry. He entered the dressing room, saying he would search it. He didn't realize that the large mirror there reflected his every move. Like a common thief, thinking he couldn't be seen, he slipped a brooch from the duchess's jewelry cabinet into his pocket and quickly left the bedroom. A little later, he returned, ordered me to search the deaf maid's room. Guess what I found in her bed? The brooch!'

'Incredible,' exclaimed Anne. 'Why haven't you come forward with this information earlier and exposed the provost?'

Bart lifted his hands palms up in a helpless gesture. 'He would deny the accusation, turn it against me, then crush me

273

like an insect. Since the day he stole the brooch, he has probably wondered if I saw him. He distrusts me, spies on me. He'll find a way to silence me.'

Anne studied the man. He seemed overwrought but fully lucid. She believed she was hearing the truth.

'The maid will soon be executed,' he continued. 'I cannot remain silent. But, if I'm to tell my story, I need powerful protection. That's why I've turned to you.'

He gave her a wry smile. For he must have realized how absurd his remark sounded. What could she do?

'Baron Breteuil trusts your husband and the countess. They trust you. *Voilà*.'

For a long moment, Bart gazed at Anne, as if reassuring himself that he *could* trust her. 'This is what I propose.' He drew a deep breath. 'Listen carefully and tell your husband.'

CHAPTER THIRTY-FOUR

Liberation

Monday, June 18

Anne entered Baron Breteuil's office with an uneasy feeling in her stomach. Even a balmy spring morning had failed to calm her spirits. So much was at stake. Paul caught her eye, mouthed encouragement. He was seated at one end of the baron's writing table, Lieutenant-General DeCrosne at the other. Between them sat Breteuil, stern-faced, his formidable powers ready for confrontation. Off to one side, Georges beckoned her to a chair next to him. The room was deathly quiet. No one smiled. She could sense tension rising.

It had been a weekend of feverish activity. The baron had arranged this meeting in complete secrecy, nearly a miracle in the royal palace. Several high-ranking personages needed to be persuaded that it was a good idea. It had been equally difficult to bring together the low-ranking actors. They had much to lose if the meeting failed.

'Good,' declared Breteuil, mustering a thin smile for Anne. An empty chair faced him. 'We're all here, except for the provost. He should arrive any minute.' Anne detected a flash of anger in the baron's eyes. He hated Sully. But by the time the provost sat down, the baron would have controlled his feelings.

Minutes later, a servant opened the door. Sully took a few steps into the room, surveyed the persons gathered there, and froze.

'What's this?' He scowled grimly. 'The King's message led me to expect a conversation with Baron Breteuil. This looks like a court martial.' For a moment he appeared undecided, nervously gripping the hilt of his sword. He took a step backward as if about to leave.

Breteuil raised a warning hand. 'His Majesty has determined this meeting's agenda, sir, and who should attend. Please be seated.' The baron motioned to the chair.

The provost's face turned livid with indignation, his head cocked in a demand for an explanation.

The baron continued. 'We now have convincing proof that the deaf maid Denise de Villers is innocent and that you, sir, are guilty of a serious miscarriage of justice. Do you wish to hear this, and other charges, within the privacy of these walls? Your alternative is public disgrace and incarceration in a royal fortress.'

Sully hesitated for a moment of calculation, then sat down, crossed his legs, leaned back defiantly. 'Show me your proof.'

The baron signaled to Paul.

He rose from the table, met Sully's eye. 'You have insisted on the guilt of Mademoiselle de Villers, deduced from the brooch in her bed and a pattern of petty theft. We will deal with the brooch soon. As for her reputation, I'll call on Madame Cartier, who has questioned deaf witnesses.'

Gathering her courage, Anne walked to the table, laid a file in front of Sully, and addressed him evenly. 'In these papers, verified by Inspecteur Quidor, the students, teachers, and the director of the Institute for the Deaf testify to Mademoiselle

275

de Villers's excellent character. They also refute Mademoiselle Fortier's charges against her.'

Anne held up another file. 'The Comte de Savarin has copied passages from Duchesse Aimée's journal expressing affection between the maid and her mistress and mentioning the ribbons that the maid was alleged to have stolen. They were gifts.' She laid the file on the table.

Sully skimmed through both files with studied indifference and tossed them on to the table.

Paul ignored the provost's contemptuous gestures. 'Sir, you claim that Robinette Lapire was subject to delusion and merely imagined she had killed the duchess. According to your theory, she took the coins after the maid had killed Duchesse Aimée. My adjutant Georges Charpentier has gathered evidence to the contrary.'

Georges rose and stepped forward a few paces. 'Over the weekend, I interviewed virtually everyone at Versailles who knew Robinette Lapire. Without exception, they agreed she was solitary and eccentric but perfectly clear in her head. Beyond a doubt, she knew what she was doing when she admitted killing the duchess.'

Georges brought a file to the table and laid it in front of Sully, who casually examined its contents. 'A waste of time,' he muttered.

Paul drew closer to Sully. 'Your case against the maid has always come down to the ruby brooch found in her bed. Who could have hidden it there? And when?' Paul turned to Anne. 'Madame Cartier.' He bowed slightly. 'The late Robinette Lapire told you that she stole the gold coins shortly before dawn on Friday, June 1. What else did she notice in the jewelry cabinet?'

'A ruby brooch, sir.' It felt odd to be questioned by one's husband. He remained straight-faced, except for a hint of pleasure in his eyes.

'Did she take it?'

'No, she left it there.'

'That's all, madame.' He put her written statement on the table.

At the baron's signal, the side door opened. Benoit Degere entered, accompanied by Jacques Bart.

276

'Do you recognize your agent, sir?' Sully was gaping at Bart. Paul didn't wait for a reply. He turned to the agent.

'Tell us what you saw that morning when you examined the murdered duchess's bedroom.'

Bart glanced at Benoit for support, avoided the eye of his master, and spoke in a low, halting voice. 'The provost told me to examine the duchess's desk while he searched the dressing room. He was acting oddly, unlike himself, so I watched him in the mirror. He put the brooch into his pocket and left the room. Afterwards, I found the brooch in the maid's room. The provost said to me, "Now we have solid proof that she killed her mistress."'

Sully sat up straight, his jaw stiff with anger. 'You've forced him to tell this tissue of lies,' he spluttered, shaking a finger at Paul.

'He has spoken willingly.' Paul beckoned Benoit Degere. The old soldier limped forward, gazed calmly at Sully and said, 'Friday evening, your agent Monsieur Bart told the same story to Madame Cartier and to me, freely, in the café by the prison.' From her seat off to the side, Anne agreed.

'Monsieur Degere is a credible witness, sir,' Paul reminded the provost. 'You hired him yourself on the recommendation of Comte Fersen. And Monsieur Bart, your agent, is known throughout the palace as an honest man.' He pulled a file from his portfolio and put it on the table in front of Sully. 'Each of these men has composed a written version of his testimony and signed it—as has Madame Cartier.'

The provost reached for the file, his hands trembling slightly. As he scanned its contents, he grew pale. The trembling of his hands increased until he couldn't read and had to lay the file on the table. He cast a venomous glance at Bart.

'There is my report.' Paul handed Sully two closely written sheets and said, 'The investigation is completed. You, sir, stole the ruby brooch from Duchesse Aimée's jewelry cabinet and hid it in the deaf maid's bed. She is proven innocent and you stand convicted of miscarriage of justice.'

During Paul's presentation of the evidence, Anne kept Baron Breteuil in the corner of her eye. He said nothing, hardly moved a muscle, his attention riveted on Sully.

At the conclusion of Paul's report, the baron leaned toward the provost and patted the files. 'Sir, over the past two days, His Majesty has studied this case.' Breteuil paused to allow the provost to grasp the gravity of his situation.

'His Majesty believes you have falsified critical evidence— the brooch—to the prejudice of a young deaf maid. He also knows your hidden motive for persecuting her. He therefore instructs you to turn the case over to your fellow magistrate, Monsieur Leduc.'

Breteuil shoved a royal document across the table to Sully. 'This contains the King's instructions. As of today, you shall also retire from the office of provost and spend the rest of your life at your country estate. A coach is waiting outside to take you there.'

Sully lifted the instructions with cautious hands, as if it were laced with poison, and carefully examined the seal, then the text. His lips tightened. Bitterness hardened his face. Anne could guess what he was thinking. The Crown had dismissed fifty years of loyal service without ceremony or gratitude. The blame fell to a feckless dolt of a King, so easily duped by Breteuil.

'Sign this, sir.' The baron handed over a letter of resignation, then pen and ink.

Sully held the letter, grimacing as if he had been stabbed, and began to read. His eyes weighed every word. Anne could almost hear the whirling wheels of his mind. After a minute or two, he evidently reached a conclusion that satisfied him. A calm, stony expression came over his face. He paused for a moment to draw a deep breath, then picked up the pen, dipped it into the ink and signed the letter.

Breteuil retrieved it, blotted it carefully, and put it in his portfolio, unable to suppress a smile of satisfaction. He patted the files of investigative reports again. 'Those files which incriminate you will be kept in a secret archive. Hopefully they will not be needed.'

'Do not attempt to retaliate against the witnesses,' added DeCrosne. 'I have taken steps to remove them from the reach of your allies in the palace and have placed them in other areas of royal service.'

Sully rose stiffly from his chair. His legs seemed unsteady. He pointed a finger at Breteuil. 'Baron, you have won this battle. Enjoy it while you can.' He quietly left the room.

The others exchanged glances, then guarded smiles of relief. Like Anne, they had all expected Sully to erupt, vent his anger at having been exposed as a felon and stripped of his power. But he must have realized that he could have fared much worse, been closely confined in a royal fortress. This private confrontation had left him with at least a small measure of freedom and self-respect. Later in the day, he might unload his frustration on to his coachman or valet. And, while exiled from the Court, he could pass his days plotting revenge against Breteuil and other enemies.

That afternoon, under a cloudy sky, Paul and Anne made their way to Paris in a private coach. They had left Comtesse Marie behind to oversee the packing of their things and the closing of the apartment. In the portfolio under his arm Paul was carrying papers for the release of Denise de Villers.

The coach suddenly lurched forward as it made its way through heavy traffic in Sèvres. Anne's mind turned to certain unresolved questions.

'What are you thinking, Anne?' asked Paul.

'Why did Marthe change her plan? She had plotted for so long and in such elaborate detail.'

'I asked her just before we left Versailles. She claimed that the horror of her scheme suddenly struck her and prevented her from carrying it out.'

'Do you believe her?' asked Anne.

'Not entirely,' he replied. 'I accept only that her conscience may have delayed her. In the meantime, someone else killed the duchess. At first, she suspected the Chevalier de Beauregard, then her half-sister. But she couldn't bring herself to betray her to the police. Claimed their mother had ordered her, years ago, to take care of Robinette. In any case, Marthe left Denise to her fate.'

'Marthe's anger has turned her into a moral monster.' Anne sighed. 'Still, I feel sympathy for her—in a sense, a victim of the law. Does she face prosecution?'

'According to strict justice, she probably deserves the fate she intended for Denise. But, royal magistrates may not punish her for what she intended but didn't carry out.'

For a few minutes, as the coach rolled on toward Paris, a heavy silence gripped its occupants. The conversation had depressed Anne's spirit. Next to her, Paul appeared equally unhappy.

Finally, Anne spoke up. 'Anger has ravaged Marthe for twenty years. What could be done to change her? If she remains bitter and vengeful, Denise will be greatly distressed.'

At the Conciergerie Anne and Paul followed the warden to the women's prison yard. Denise was walking there, reading a book.

Anne approached her, signing enthusiastically. 'Denise, we've good news for you.'

The young woman looked up, frowned with confusion. Slowly, a hesitant smile appeared on her face.

'You're free.' Anne embraced her, then led her to Paul at the entrance to the garden. 'We'll take you with us.'

Denise glanced doubtfully at the warden standing behind Paul.

Paul bowed and handed her the document releasing her.

She read it with wide, incredulous eyes, and returned it to him. 'It's like rising from the dead,' she signed slowly. 'An answer to my prayers.'

Anne nodded. 'And to the love and hard work of your friends.' With a kindly smile Anne waved in the general direction of the Abbé de l'Épée's institute.

On the way to the institute Anne studied Denise, who sat alert and expectant on the coach seat opposite. She had bathed, then dressed in a patterned rose silk gown delicately embroidered with silver thread. The maids at Rue Traversine had fitted her with an attractive wig. Apart from the pallor of her face, there was little about her appearance to show what she had been through.

Except her eyes. The horror of arrest and imprisonment for a dreadful crime, the prospect of torture and a public execution, had left their mark. Gone was the young woman's complaisant trust in a kindly world and her own talents. She was now keenly aware that life could be fickle and cruel.

The coach stopped at the institute and let them off. The porter gave Anne a conspiratorial glance as he showed the way to the parlor. The door opened to an ecstatic, if voiceless, welcome. Françoise Arnaud was there with many of the students. Off to one side, Michou, Sylvie, and André waited to meet the person for whose liberation they had worked. Anne noticed that Sylvie and André held hands. Michou glanced at them benevolently.

The crowd made way for Denise to approach the abbé seated at the far end of the room. He rose stiffly to embrace her. She bowed her head for his blessing.

During the party that followed, Françoise drew near to Anne and signed secretly so Denise wouldn't notice.

'Have you heard what's happened to Cécile Fortier?'

'No, we haven't been to the Palais-Royal.'

Françoise's eyes widened. 'An hour ago, one of our students was passing by the millinery shop as the mistress put Cécile out on the street. We've just learned that a relative has taken her in as a scullery maid.'

'She might learn a useful lesson in humility,' Anne remarked. 'If she does, the deaf community would reach out to her again.'

CHAPTER THIRTY-FIVE

Final Reckoning

Wednesday, June 20

The morning was cool and cloudy. An inauspicious omen? Anne wasn't sure. She and Denise stood waiting in the entrance hall of La Normandie, the *hôtel garni* on Rue de Valois. Yesterday, Marthe had taken up her new housekeeping position, shortly after being released from Sully's prison. Unaware of her vengeful plan, the public regarded her in a sympathetic light, another victim of the provost's brutal methods.

Denise had insisted on visiting Marthe. Last night, Anne's account of the housekeeper's scheme had deeply disturbed the maid. 'I've done her no harm,' she had signed tearfully. In this visit she would attempt a reconciliation.

Anne had also placed selections from Duchesse Aimée's journal in the maid's hands. 'Did anything you read upset or surprise you?'

Denise had taken a moment to reflect. 'Her story truly moved me. But I wasn't entirely surprised. She had shown me a little of that side of herself.'

As a servant showed them into the housekeeper's parlor, Anne watched Denise carefully for signs of distress. The young woman did in fact almost stumble but quickly recovered her balance. Her face was pale and drawn.

Marthe entered the room in a fine gray woolen gown. Her face was drawn, her shoulders bent. Sully's inquisition and Robinette's violent death had chastened her. When she saw her visitors, anger sparked in her eyes. She had evidently not been told whom to expect. Her head cocked with suspicion as they greeted her. She merely glanced at

282

the flowers they had brought, then made a polite gesture to be seated.

Anne explained frankly why they had come, signing to Denise as well. The deaf woman studied Marthe's face, searching for signs of regret. The housekeeper didn't alter her expression, seemed indifferent to Denise's wishes.

Denise grew increasingly frustrated. Finally, she touched Anne's arm and began to sign for herself, Anne translating. She declared that the execution of young La Barre was an atrocity and she honored Marthe's grief. Her own father's complicity in the crime was inexcusable. She was sure that later in life he regretted what he had done. Nonetheless, she understood why Marthe would find it difficult to forgive him. But why punish his child who wasn't even born when the incident occurred?

Marthe stared at the young woman, then spoke in a low monotone. 'The sins of the father shall be counted against his descendants even unto the fourth generation.' She lapsed back into an accusing silence.

Denise gave up, visibly shaken.

Anne opened her portfolio, drew out Duchesse Aimée's journal, and began to read a series of especially poignant passages. Marthe sat up straight, blinked with surprise. At Aimée's condemnation of her father for the judicial murder of La Barre, Marthe's brow creased in disbelief. When Anne came to Pasquier beating his daughter, Marthe breathed aloud, 'The bastard!'

For the next several minutes she bent forward, listening intently to the hidden life of the duchess that emerged from the journal. When the reading ended, there was a long pause. Marthe stared down at her hands, her lips pressed tightly together. Finally, she looked up, pointed to the journal. 'I wish I'd known earlier. I'm sorry for her. I judged her badly.' She turned to Denise, struck her breast, and murmured, 'Forgive me for hating you. I was wrong.'

Anne embraced Paul warmly. He had just come from Paris to the outdoor theater at Château Beaumont. She had arrived earlier with Comtesse Marie and Denise, who now waved to

283

him from the grassy stage below, framed by a boxwood hedge.

He waved back and called out a greeting to them. A few minutes later, they left for tea at the château.

'There's news, Anne.' They sat in the upper tier of benches, looking down at the empty stage. 'Yesterday, Hoche opened up. I offered him a few days in the pillory and several years in prison instead of a public hanging. And he agreed to remain silent about the Queen's affair with Fersen.' Hoche had then admitted his theft of money and jewels from the Duc d'Orléans. Gaillard had escaped, probably to England.

Anne's interest in Hoche, Gaillard, and criminals in general had diminished since Denise was freed. As Paul spoke, she watched the sun cast long shadows across the stage. For several minutes, they sat together silently drawing up memories. Anne thought of the summers here before the war, acting in Shakespeare's *A Midsummer Night's Dream*. Her favorite role was Puck.

Paul read her mind. 'I recall you dashing across the stage in a green costume, a bright red tassel whirling from your cap.' He took her hand, squeezed it gently.

A few moments later, his expression turned ironic. 'Thinking of country pleasures reminds me of Sully's good fortune. By now, he has reached his estate and settled into his comfortable exile.'

Anne made a sour face. She hadn't voiced her opinion before, but she resented the leniency shown to the deposed provost. 'The plain truth is that he tried to kill Denise. That's what the law calls "attempted murder."'

'You're right, Anne. I argued with the baron and the lieutenant-general that Sully's crime was serious and premeditated. He had also violated his official obligation to render justice impartially. His punishment should have been a life in chains at hard labor. Impossible, they replied and chose merely to remove him from power, avoid scandal, free the maid.'

Denise's hellish weeks in prison rushed to Anne's mind. 'As we speak, Sully is breathing pure country air. He will soon sit down to a delicious dinner, a fine bottle of wine within his reach. At the end of the day, he will recline in a clean soft bed. Where's the justice in that?'

'Imperfect,' Paul agreed. 'The alternative was a trial before Parlement. It might have acquitted Sully and shifted the blame for the brooch from him to his agent. The deaf maid would still be in Parlement's clutches. A majority of the magistrates might be as unfair to her as they were to La Barre. Fortunately, the baron and the lieutenant-general warned the King of a judicial scandal during this difficult time for the Crown. His Majesty knew Sully better than we realized, recognized the maid's innocence, and accepted the compromise.'

Anne shook her head. 'For weeks, the King has been irresolute. Why did he suddenly involve himself in this case and act decisively?'

'His change of mind also surprised the baron. Do you have a theory?'

'Yes, I do. I'm convinced Comte Fersen played a key role. Over the weekend, he must have decided that the deaf maid was guiltless and a judicial scandal was imminent. He warned the Queen. She persuaded the King to allow Breteuil and DeCrosne to work out the solution. Fersen and the Queen kept themselves from public view.'

Paul nodded. 'And perhaps Fersen felt disposed to do the right thing, at least in part, because we returned the stolen note and letters to him.'

It didn't much matter to Anne how Fersen felt. 'I think the future will not be kind to "Josephine" and her count. Their world is changing in uncertain ways. They had better seize happiness while they can.'

Author's Note

The fictional travail of Denise de Villers was inspired by the real *causes célèbres* of Marie Cléreaux, 1785, and Victoire Salmon, 1781–1786. In each case, malevolent prosecutors nearly brought innocent young housemaids to the scaffold. Cf. Sarah Maza, *Private Lives and Public Affairs: The Causes Célèbres of Prerevolutionary France*, Berkeley, 1993. For the less fortunate La Barre, see Marc Chassaigne, *Le Procès du chevalier de La Barre*, Paris, 1920.

In 1787, French criminal justice still allowed a form of interrogation under torture, which was called the Question. It was applied to persons condemned to death, in the hope that they would reveal accomplices. Seven years earlier, the royal government had abolished torture prior to conviction. In 1789 a royal ordinance abolished all forms of torture. The scene in which Sully tries to frighten Denise into a confession resembles a mitigated legal torture, 'presentment', in which the accused was bound upon the rack, as if about to be tortured, and there interrogated.

The Institute for the Deaf on Rue des Moulins was the creation of Abbé Charles-Michel de l'Épée (1712–1789). Ordained a priest in 1738, Épée was denied a license to officiate because he refused to take an oath against Jansenism, a reform movement within the Catholic Church. The hierarchy opposed his ministry throughout his lifetime.

While living in Paris on a small allowance from his parents, he is reported to have encountered a pair of deaf twin sisters who received no religious instruction. 'I am prohibited from leading the hearing to know God,' he said. 'I will lead the deaf to know Him.'

He harnessed this religious zeal to an enlightened passion for the practical application of science. He converted the sign language of the Parisian deaf community into manual French by inventing signs for French words and word endings and using French word order. His students displayed their achievements in science, philosophy and languages to large distinguished audiences. His institute evolved from its cramped quarters in his own home into the present French national school for the deaf.

He welcomed visitors and shared his expertise generously. His disciples founded schools in France, America, and Austria. Thomas Gallaudet brought his method to Connecticut. The fictional Anne Cartier resembles one of Épée's female students, Charlotte Blouin, who established a school in Anger that still functions.

No one doubts that Queen Marie Antoinette and Comte Fersen were close friends. The perennially intriguing question is how sexually intimate was their relationship. At the root of the problem is a lack of evidence. Their papers do not yield a definitive answer. The possibly relevant pieces, especially Fersen's, have been deliberately destroyed.

This vacuum offers a tempting opportunity for an historical mystery. Here, as elsewhere in *Noble Blood*, I try to tell the story within the bounds of historical fact and reasonable inference. That Fersen fathered Marie Antoinette's son, Louis-Charles, was physically possible. Was it likely?

The legion of biographers and historians who have thus far wrestled with this issue fall roughly into two camps. Those who believe that the Queen and the count were sexually intimate include Antonia Fraser, *Marie Antoinette: the Journey*, NY, 2001; Evelyne Lever, *Marie-Antoinette*, NY, [1991] 2000; Evelyn Farr, *Marie-Antoinette and Count Axel Fersen: the Untold Love Story*, London, 1995; Carolly Erickson, *To the Scaffold: the Life of Marie-Antoinette*, NY, 1991; Stanley Loomis, *The Fatal Friendship*, Garden City, NY, 1972; Alma Söderhjelm, *Fersen et Marie-Antoinette*, Paris, 1930.

In the opposing camp are those who argue that the friendship was more likely without sexual intimacy. Chief among

287

them is H. Arnold Barton. His *Count Hans Axel von Fersen*, Boston, 1975, a thorough, reliable study, deserves careful consideration. Other works include André Castelot, *Marie-Antoinette*, Paris, 1958; Henry Vallotton, *Marie-Antoinette et Fersen*, Paris, 1952; Charles Kunstler, *La Vie privée de Marie-Antoinette*, Paris, 1938.

For Marie-Antoinette's largely unwarranted scandalous reputation consult Chantal Thomas, *The Wicked Queen: The Origins of the Myth of Marie-Antoinette*, NY, [1989] 1999.